P

THE ABRUPT PHYSICS
OF DYING

ABOUT THE AUTHOR

Canadian by birth, Paul Hardisty has spent 25 years working all over the world as an engineer, hydrologist and environmental scientist. He has roughnecked on oil rigs in Texas, explored for gold in the Arctic, mapped geology in Eastern Turkey (where he was befriended by PKK rebels), and rehabilitated water wells in the wilds of Africa. In 1993 he survived a bomb blast in a café in Sana'a, and was one of the last Westerners out of Yemen before the outbreak of the 1994 civil war. Paul is a university professor and Director of Australia's national land, water, ecosystems and climate adaptation research programmes. He is a sailor, a private pilot, keen outdoorsman, ironman triathlete and conservation volunteer, and lives in Western Australia with his family.

The Abrupt Physics of Dying

PAUL E. HARDISTY

**ORENDA
BOOKS**

Orenda Books
16 Carson Road
West Dulwich
London SE21 8HU
www.orendabooks.co.uk

First published in ebook by Orenda Books 2014
This B-format edition published by Orenda Books 2015

ISBN 978-1-910633-05-2

Typeset in Garamond by MacGuru Ltd
Printed and bound by CPI Group (UK) Ltd, Croydon CR0 4YY

SALES & DISTRIBUTION

In the UK and elsewhere in Europe:
Turnaround Publisher Services
Unit 3, Olympia Trading Estate
Coburg Road
Wood Green
London
N22 6TZ
www.turnaround-uk.com

In Australia/New Zealand:
Australian Scholarly Publishing
7 Lt Lothian St North
North Melbourne
Victoria 3051
Australia
www.scholarly.info

For details of other territories, please contact *info@orendabooks.co.uk*

When the sky is torn
When the stars are shattered
When the seas are poured forth
When the tombs are bust open
Then a soul will know what it has given
And what it has held back

The Holy Qu'ran, Sura 82: 1–5

Part I

1

No Way Back from Here

20th April 1994. Lat 14° 53'N; Long 48° 27'E,
Masila Plateau, Southern Yemen

The Kalashnikov's barrel was surprisingly hot. He imagined the brand the flash suppressor would leave in the middle of his forehead, the desert sun heating the metal to burn skin, a neat round scar marking him forever as godless, or, if it were a hole, dead. It had been a long time since someone had pointed a gun at him.

Claymore Straker sat motionless in the passenger seat of the Land Cruiser, staring down the barrel at the dark, bloodshot eyes of the man whose finger was a mere twitch away from redistributing his brains, and waited for the panic to rise in his chest. Facing the end of his time, calculating a life's worth, weighing his heart against a feather – surely these things should be cause for terror, or at least reflection. But he felt neither fear, nor panic, nor the urge to run. What came was more a sense of a long journey gone wrong, the feeling of arriving at what should have been the destination, only to find the sun-burned skeleton of a home, the wood long since scorched the colour of bone, the parched hills beyond showing through open windows and fallen walls, the cloudless sky piercing the gaping holes in the roof. Thirteen years ago he'd taken a wrong turn. And somehow he'd ended up here, looking back along the length of a gun barrel at a kid not much older than he'd been, back then, when he'd killed for the first time.

A bead of sweat tracked down his temple and dripped from the hinge of his jaw to spatter on his shirt. The sound it made was that of an insect hitting a windscreen. Another followed, the same rupture. It had been only a few minutes since they had been forced to the roadside, and already the inside of the vehicle was like an incinerator. What had led this kid here? Clay wondered. Had he had a choice? Was he, as Clay had been back then, desperate to prove himself, terrified of screwing up, preferring death over the humiliation of failure? And now that he was here, in the temple, what would he learn about himself?

The kid was speaking to him now, yammering in high-pitched Arabic. He wore a charity drive jacket over a faded *thaub* that probably hadn't been washed since it was made. The cloth wrapped around his head – the traditional Yemeni headscarf, the *keffiyeh* – looked like a roadside mechanic's shop rag, torn and stained. Clay figured the kid for eighteen, no more, despite the weather in his face – much younger than the other gunman who now stood at the driver's side with weapon levelled at Abdulkader's neck.

The kid pushed the barrel harder into Clay's forehead, forcing his neck back into the headrest. Again, the same words, louder this time, more insistent. He seemed to be looking at the steering column, the keys.

'Look, I don't understand you,' Clay said. His voice was calm and even, someone else's. '*La'a atakalim arabee.*' I don't speak Arabic.

'He wants you to get down from the car,' said Abdulkader. 'Slow. Keep your hands where he can see.'

Clay heard the grating sound of the driver's side door swinging open. The other gunman barked out something in Arabic and the kid snapped his rifle back from Clay's head and stepped away from the open window, the weapon now set to drive rounds through the thin metal of the door, straight into his torso. Clay stepped out onto the pulverised dust of the road. By now Abdulkader was beside him at the roadside. They stood with their backs to the vehicle, hands clasped behind their heads. The two tribesmen stood facing them, the car keys dangling in the older man's hand. They seemed to be examining Abdulkader: he was clearly one of them, a Hadrami, perhaps not from this part of the Masila, but not an outsider. He spoke the same guttural dialect, carried his grandfather's curved, rhino-horn-handled dagger, the *jambiya*; he, too, could trace his lineage back to the Prophet.

The older man was speaking now, spitting out rusty-iron words, jerking the hoe of his beard towards the ground as if he were trying to cut a furrow in the sand. Abdulkader answered. A conversation ensued, the man questioning, Abdulkader's gravel-road voice rumbling in response. This continued for some time, the tone modulating between near fury and friendly chat. And then the older man laughed. The few teeth he had were stained a deep shade of brown, like weathered tar. He reached over and put his hand to the barrel of his kinsman's rifle and lowered the muzzle until it pointed to the ground at Clay's feet.

'We will go with them,' said Abdulkader. 'Sit in the back seat.'

Clay did not move. As long as they were still out here, on the road, talking, they had a chance. The moment they got back into the car, they would be prisoners.

'Tell them to go home, Abdulkader. This doesn't have to end badly for anyone.'

Abdulkader looked at him a moment, turned to the older man, translated. The older man listened, paused a moment as if reflecting on what he had heard, then fixed his gaze on Clay.

'*La*,' he said, jerking the barrel of his rifle towards the car. No. '*Emshee*.' Move.

'Please, Mister Clay, do as he says,' said Abdulkader, turning and climbing into the front passenger seat.

Clay planted his feet, stood facing the two gunmen, the older man frail, wizened, his beard tinted with henna, the kid taller, with deeply veined arms and a long sinewed neck that sprouted from narrow, slumped shoulders. He stood with the muzzle of his AK pointed down. Like him, it looked battered, poorly cared for. Fear swirled in his eyes.

Clay opened his palms, showed them to the gunmen, the universal sign of greeting, of supplication: I hold nothing that can hurt you.

'*La'awh samaht*,' he said. Please. 'Let us on our way, before someone gets hurt.' He looked back along the road towards the Kamar-1 well. '*Jeyesh'a*,' he said. Army. 'The Army is close by. Tell them, Abdulkader. If they go now they'll be safe.' They had no escort, but it was worth a try.

The kid blinked twice, a question forming on his face. The elder tribesman, clearly the leader, barked out something in Arabic. The boy levelled his weapon and jabbed it into Clay's ribs. The safety was off.

Abdulkader started translating, pointing back along the road, but the old tribesman cut him off, silenced him with a single word.

Clay could feel the AK's muzzle trembling, see the kid's hand shaking on the pistol grip. He looked into the young man's dark brown, almost featureless irises, the black retina, and locked them.

'No way back from here, *broer*,' he said in English, knowing the kid would not understand.

'Please, Mister Clay,' called Abdulkader from the car. 'Get in. He will shoot you if you do not.'

The kid flicked a glance towards his kinsman, gave his AK a jerk, digging the muzzle hard into Clay's chest.

Clay stepped back, put a half-step between them, hands still clasped behind his neck. He was a head taller than the kid, had a good twenty kilos on him, more. Clay reached slowly into the breast pocket of his shirt. 'I have money,' he said, pulling out a thick fold of Yemeni *rials* and holding it out towards the gunmen. '*Faddar*,' he said. 'Please, take it and go.'

The kid's eyes widened. The older man frowned, extended his stance, made to swipe Clay's fist away with the barrel of his weapon.

It was the mistake Clay had been waiting for. He opened his hand, caught the barrel in his palm, and tightened his fingers around the wooden forestock. The AK's muzzle pointed skyward. Yemeni banknotes fluttered to the ground. Time slowed. Clay started to rotate the ball of his right foot, the pivot that would swing him away from the kid's line of fire and bring his weight around into the old man taking shape – his knees starting to bend, centre of gravity lowering, left elbow drawing back for the strike. The calculations were already done in his head: twenty-five hundred Newtons of force delivered with an angular momentum of twenty-six joule-seconds. Enough to crack bone, shatter cartilage. In a heart-skip it would be done. The old man would be down, the AK would be pointing at the kid. Clay could feel rage fire its waking reactions – that fission improperly buried in his core, suspect and unstable. Soon it would start to cascade and then it would be too late. There could be only two outcomes, and in each the kid would die.

Clay opened his palm and let the rifle go. He raised his hands slowly back to his head. He'd held the barrel for a quarter of a second only, long enough that the old man would know what could have happened. The last banknotes settled to the ground like winter leaves.

The old man jerked his weapon away, stepped back. He glanced quickly at the kid as if embarrassed at being caught out, then glared at Clay. The kid still hadn't reacted, just stood there slack-mouthed, the killing end of his weapon still inches from Clay's chest, the fear in him palpable now, a stench that thickened the air around them.

Abdulkader said nothing, just sat in the Land Cruiser's passenger seat as if resigned to this fate, this direction that events were taking. Soon, its trajectory would harden and grow strong and send them all tumbling into a place he had spent the last decade trying to forget.

The older tribesman raised his weapon, aimed it at Abdulkader's chest. The safety was off. He spoke. The anger rose in his voice. The message was clear.

Clay took a deep breath, looked into his driver's eyes. Abdulkader had joined the company as a driver two years ago, just after first oil. The money he earned helped him to support his two wives and seven children. Although Clay hadn't known him long, a year perhaps, he'd grown fond of this man, his hundred-kilometre silences, his deep, considered logic, the gentle way he had with his children – balancing the littlest ones on his knee, laughing as he watched his sons kicking an old under-inflated football around the dusty paddock, the way he cared for his goats, pulling a stone from a kid's cloven hoof, feeding a sick doe with his calloused palm.

Clay raised his hands. '*Tammam*,' he said, turning slowly and opening the car door. OK. '*Ma'afi mushkilla.*' No problem. Easy. He stepped slowly to the car, climbed into the back seat.

The older tribesman lowered his weapon, walked around to the driver's side, got in behind the wheel, started the engine. The kid signalled Clay to move across the seat, got in, closed the door. After ten minutes on the trunk road, the older tribesman slowed the vehicle and turned it onto a narrow stone track that skirted the edge of a broad scarp. Clay could just make out the headworks of the new Kamar-3 well in the distance. Looking down from the scarp, the land fell away into a broad graben dissected by the root ends of dozens of smaller wadis. Eventually some of these coalesced to form one of the main tributaries of Wadi Idim, a deep canyon that ran down to the escarpment and burst out onto the coastal plain.

The vehicle lurched along the rocky track for what could have been half an hour, maybe more, the terrain a monotony of serried gullies and swales cut into the twisting contour of the scarp's edge. From the air, this landscape had the appearance of a slab of dried flesh, hooked and hung, the deep wadi dendrites like dark arteries in negative relief. But here, tethered to the ground, straight-line distances were meaningless, one mile of map progress won only with two miles of relentless contouring around mesa and wadi, a journey of seemingly endless wanderings.

At the apex of one of the gullies, indistinguishable from any of the others, the old tribesman stopped the car. He opened his door, stepped to the ground and crouched to lock the hubs. Then he got back behind the steering wheel, put the Land Cruiser into four-wheel drive, and started the vehicle lurching down the slope.

From the back seat, Clay could make out only the faintest indication of some sort of track, a few stones piled here and there, a shelf of wheel-crushed slate, occasional tyre marks in softer sand. Through the heat haze, away in the distance, the dark clefts of a series of steep-sided wadis cut deep into the limestone bedrock. The cliffs of each facing wall shone white in the distance like the teeth of some Triassic carnivore reborn from the rock of its deathbed. The satellite imagery had shown no settlements anywhere near here. From memory, that whole series of wadis, still perhaps ten or more kilometres away, petered out somewhere west of Idim, and had appeared to be inaccessible by vehicle. Not a bad place to be if you were trying to hide, or if you didn't want witnesses.

Clay reached across the seat back and touched Abdulkader's shoulder. 'What do they want?' It wasn't money, and it wasn't Abdulkader's battered old Land Cruiser. Were they to be hostages, pawns in the increasingly bitter feud between the tribes, the government, and the oil companies, or just examples, their bullet-holed bodies a warning to those who might think the tribes irresolute and fractious?

The old man turned and glowered at him. Abdulkader said nothing.

Clay assessed options. He had pushed as hard as he dared back at the roadside. By the way the old guy was driving, it was clear he was determined to get away from the road and out of sight as quickly as possible. The kid was nervous, twitchy, obviously inexperienced. His finger was on the AK's trigger, not on the guard, and the safety was off. The muzzle was pointed at Clay's ribs. Side on, Clay had little chance of disarming him before he got off a shot. And with Abdulkader in the passenger seat directly in front, the risk of trying was too great. He would have to wait.

Clay sat back and watched the dry benchland rattle past, limestone rubble and shale plates strewn over the flat ground with not a living thing to grace any of it.

Soon they were descending a narrow defile in the rock, in places barely wide enough for the vehicle. As they cut down-wadi, the air became cooler and they fell into shadow. Battlements of rock towered above them, vertical blocks of massive dolomite the colour of scored hide, sheer and featureless. Ahead, the canyon narrowed to nothing more than a crevasse, the width of a man's shoulders. The elder tribesman stopped the vehicle in the lee of a huge limestone boulder, turned off the engine, and motioned with his head to get out. If they were going to do it, this was as good a place as any.

The gunmen herded Clay and Abdulkader towards the rock face, weapons levelled. Abdulkader was talking to them, pleading, but the men stood impassive, checking their magazines. Clay felt his stomach go cold. The elder tribesman shouted a command, levelled his weapon, flicked the AK to auto, and widened his stance. The kid, to his right and a few paces back, raised his weapon to his shoulder, sighted down the barrel at Abdulkader.

'No,' Clay shouted. 'Stop.' He stepped forward, put himself between Abdulkader and the gunmen.

The old guy narrowed his eyes, yelled out something.

Clay raised the palm of his right hand to his chest. *'Ana,'* he said in Arabic. Me. 'Leave him. It's me you want.'

It wasn't so bad, dying.

٢

The Sun

The old tribesman was about ten paces away. He looked at Clay for a moment, then past him to Abdulkader. The kid stood staring down the sight of his weapon. Clay met his gaze, stared back. At this range, he knew his body would provide only minimal shielding for Abdulkader. He tensed, ready to charge. If he was going to be killed, he would die fighting, perhaps giving Abdulkader a chance. That's how he'd been trained. Even though it was long ago, it was all there, so close to the surface, so readily exhumed and brought back to haunt.

The old man barked out a command. The kid blinked, stood unmoving, seemed not to understand. The old man shouted again, louder this time, and turned to his understudy. The kid lowered his weapon, stood staring at the old man, a look of confusion spreading over his face.

Clay coiled his muscles tight. This was the opportunity. 'He can't get us both,' Clay whispered. 'As soon as I move, go.' He judged the distance, readied himself. The old guy was a second and a half away, maybe less, the kid just beyond him, close. Clay burst forward, a sprinter from the blocks.

But Abdulkader was already moving, cutting obliquely to position himself between Clay and the old man. He stopped and turned, faced Clay, opened his arms wide as if to catch him.

Clay pulled up, stood staring at his friend. 'Get out of the way,' he said.

Abdulkader did not move. 'Do not fight them.'

Clay glared. 'I know what you're trying to do. Don't.' Clay moved right, then left, but Abdulkader followed, keeping himself between Clay and the gunmen.

'There is no need, Mister Clay.'

'*Yallah,*' the old tribesman shouted, jerking his AK in the direction of the crevasse.

The kid started to move, backing away, weapon raised. His sandalled feet shuffled through the dust. He reached the canyon wall, pushed his back against the wall of rock, and stood there looking back at Clay and Abdulkader, that same perplexed look on his face. The old tribesman shouted at him again. He peered into the crevasse for a long moment, looked back at his kinsman, and disappeared into the wall of rock.

'Now's the time, Abdulkader,' said Clay, grabbing his friend by the arm. 'He's alone.'

Abdulkader gripped Clay's forearms, holding him fast. His eyes were wide, sky clear, insistent. 'Please, Mister Clay. You must trust Allah.'

Clay looked down, back up at his friend. 'Only about two people in this world I trust, Abdulkader. Allah isn't one of them.'

Abdulkader frowned.

'*Ah'ituts beyah'lahu,*' shouted the old tribesman, now distinctly agitated. He had moved back, put more distance between them, and now stood poised with AK on hip, motioning towards the crevasse.

'He wants us to follow the boy.' Abdulkader pointed to the narrow opening in the rock, a black fault in the featureless grey dolomite. 'In there. *Inshallah,* we must go in there.'

Inshallah. God willing. Of course. It could only be thus. Here, Allah endured, clung still to an ancient and fearsome power in the minds of men. Clay bowed his head. 'And what, my brother, if God wills it, will we find?'

Abdulkader dropped his hands to his sides, stood staring into Clay's eyes for a long time. Then he turned and started towards the gap in the rock and followed the kid into the fault.

Clay looked over at the old gunman, at the AK47 aimed at his chest. 'Nothing to it, is there?' he said to the old guy.

The tribesman's eyes flickered, hardened.

'Trust.'

The old guy raised his weapon, wedged the stock into his shoulder. Clay knew that look. Last chance.

Clay shrugged, smiled at him and followed Abdulkader into the Earth.

☾

After twenty minutes of walking they reached an impasse. The canyon had widened slightly, but the way was blocked by an ancient rockslide. Boulders the size of freight cars tilted on end formed a wall of rock thirty or more metres high. There was no way over. They moved closer and hugged the north wall of the canyon. The kid turned to face them, slung his weapon, and crouched facing a small opening at the base of the slide. Then he lay flat on his stomach and, with a quick flick of his legs, disappeared into the hole. The older tribesman stood a few paces back, weapon ready.

'Go,' said Abdulkader.

Clay crouched down and peered into the hole. A twisting labyrinth illuminated by a thousand dusty beams led away into the geometric chaos of the slide. He looked back over his shoulder at his friend.

'*Allah akhbar*,' said Clay.

It took the better part of half an hour to navigate the rock maze. He was much bigger than the Yemenis, and by the time he emerged down-wadi his clothes were torn and he was bleeding from cuts to his shoulders, forearms and knees. It was like arriving late and underdressed in paradise.

The softer layers of rock at the base of the cliffs had been cut away, leaving a series of broad overhangs. Beneath, gnarled acacias, ancient ironwood and camelthorn reached their branches out towards the light in every shade of green. The sound of running water echoed from the canyon walls. The air swirled with the smells of charcoal, fresh dung, cardamom, chlorophyll. A thin column of wood smoke spun up towards the overhang and dispersed in the cool current of air that flowed towards the lowlands.

Clay looked up at the narrow rail of blue high above. The opening in the plateau was a few metres across at most. No wonder the satellite images had not revealed vegetation.

'It is a good place, no?'

Clay snapped his head down in the direction of the voice. A small man dressed in a tan *thaub* and clean black-and-white *keffiyeh* stood before them. The left side of his face was over-sized and misshapen, almost pre-human, with a dark, heavily lidded eye buried in a deep well of bone, black as a moonless night in the Empty Quarter. He was unarmed. The two gunmen had disappeared.

Abdulkader bowed and greeted the man in Arabic, touching the tips of his fingers to his forehead and chest. The man responded in the same way.

'Come,' said the man. He led them through the trees and up a rock ledge into a small open cave cut into the side of the canyon wall. The oasis spread still and green beneath them. He crouched beside a hearth of stone and bid them sit. 'You are with the oil company?' he said in English.

Clay nodded. 'My name is Clay Straker.'

'Clay,' said the man. 'This is an unusual name. It is not from your Bible.'

'It's short for Claymore.'

The man narrowed his good eye. The other floated there, unresponsive. 'You are named for a weapon. A sword.'

When he was young, he'd liked his name, liked its meaning. Now he hated it.

'Not my choice.'

'It is an honourable name.'

Clay said nothing.

The man shifted back on his heels, brought his knees up close to his chest, narrowed his good eye. 'Do you know why you are here, Mister Claymore?'

Clay looked over at Abdulkader and back at the man. 'Not for a *brai* and a beer, I'm guessing.'

A hint of a smile twitched in the Arab's mouth, disappeared. 'No.'

'We have done you no harm, nor you us,' said Clay. Not yet. 'Please. Let us go. This can still be retrieved.'

'Retrieved, Mister Claymore?'

'Sent in another direction.'

The right side of the man's face twisted into a smile. He picked up a stick and poked the embers. Without looking up he began to speak. His voice was soft, like the sound of the water bubbling from the spring below, his Arabic an ancient chanting melody. After some minutes he fell silent and sat staring into the coals.

Clay had followed as best he could, gathering an occasional word, the fragment of a phrase. The language dripped violence; the mutant face was serene. He looked to Abdulkader.

'This man is from an old and important Hadrami family,' said Abdulkader. 'Three years ago he went to Sana'a with his father to ask the President for a share of the oil that was discovered here. Promises were made, he says. We have all heard these stories. Instead, President Saleh sent his secret police, the PSO. They killed his father. Now they want him.'

Abdulkader looked at the man a moment, paused, then turned to face Clay. 'He is called *Al Shams*. The Sun.'

Clay felt a cold spine of ice shiver through him, the coldest desert night. He knew that name. 'Jesus Christ,' he whispered under his breath. Clay stared into the deep well of the man's dead eye. And in that darkness he could see it all so clearly. It was a Friday, he remembered. He had decided to take the afternoon off to look around old Aden. Thierry Champard, one of the engineers who ran the oil-processing facility, had offered him a ride into town, had been on his way home after an eight-week stint. He was off to the airport, happy, he told Clay, because he missed his two young daughters, happy because his wife would be waiting for him at the airport in Paris. He was planning on spending Christmas at the family's country cottage in Brittany. He'd shown Clay photos: a beautiful blonde in a bikini posing holiday-style in a summer rose garden, one hand behind her head, the other on an out-thrust hip, her mouth partially open, as if caught in mid-sentence, mid-sigh, at the start of a whispered kiss; two smiling children on the beach, their doll-like faces peering out from under nests of thick sun-bleached curls, the sky-blue eyes, the pouty red-plum lips, the dimpled high-boned cheeks, girlish copies of the woman in the roses. Champard dropped Clay in the centre of town, near the *qat* market. The streets were packed after morning prayers. They shook hands, agreed to meet up for a beer the next time they were both in country. Clay closed the car door, walked about twenty steps, turned, made eye contact, and smiled. Thierry waved. Clay was halfway through mouthing the words thanks and good luck when the silver Land Rover disappeared in a nova of orange flame.

That was six months ago.

The day after Thierry's death, Clay had been ordered home, as had many other contractors and non-essential personnel. The rest was a story he had heard only in fragments, mostly as rumour, third and fourth hand, since he'd returned to Yemen. The Yemen government had quickly blamed the murder on a group of suspected militants led by a shadowy figure calling himself 'The Sun'. A manhunt was launched by the Army and the PSO, but Al Shams and his men had vanished. Not hard, in this part of the world. As time went by, things calmed down, and soon Clay was back in the country helping Petro-Tex with environmental permitting for the new Kamar oilfield, one of the biggest discoveries ever made in Southern Yemen.

The Arab continued speaking, the tone harder now. Again he paused, allowing Abdulkader to translate. 'He says this oil is a curse. The people of Hadramawt see nothing. There is no money, no jobs, only soldiers, deep wounds in the land, and death.' Abdulkader scooped up a handful of sand from the ground and let it fall away between his fingers. 'Did you hear of the ambush at Katima last year? That was this man. They killed six government soldiers and took many weapons.'

He remembered reading about it. They had caught the soldiers in a pass in the mountains. They wouldn't have had a chance. Thierry Champard hadn't either. It was only luck – whatever luck was, the random collision of events, the probabilities of place and time and a thousand other variables – that had spared Clay that day.

'He says they will kill more, until the government gives them what they want, or they close the oilfields.'

'Retrieved, Mister Claymore?' said Al Shams in English. 'That time has long since passed. Too many have died. Still more, I am afraid, are destined to perish.'

Clay looked down into the cold pitch of Al Shams' dead eye. He could feel the turbulence close by, that incipient buffeting at the margin of chaos, a fall coming. He stood, tried to push away from the edge. 'I cannot answer for the government,' he said. 'I am a hydrologist, an engineer. My job is to talk to the people and to listen to them. I study the land and the water. I report my findings to the company so that it can protect the people and the environment. The company wants to help the people, even if the government does not.'

Before Abdulkader could start to translate, the man spoke in rapid terse English, looking straight at Clay. 'If this is so,' he said, 'why does the company need the protection of soldiers?'

Clay opened his hands and held them palms up. 'We have no protection,' he said, 'as you can see.'

'Ah, but you are an oddity, my friend,' Al Shams replied. 'The Army is everywhere. Your Petro-Tex has been here for almost three years, and things only become worse.'

'I can assure you that the company is committed to complying fully with all appropriate regulations ...' said Clay, reciting from the company's public engagement handbook. It was what he was paid to do.

'Do not patronise me, Mister Claymore. You know as well as I do that the regulations in Yemen are weak, ineffective and readily by-passed.'

Clay continued: '… and to comply with best industry practice wherever possible. Petro-Tex is committed to minimising the environmental and social impacts of its operations on the people of the Hadramawt.'

Al Shams blinked. The good eye flashed. The other disappeared behind a veil of wrinkled skin, its opaque depth reappearing only slowly as the mangled tissue drew back. Then he smiled. 'You do not believe what you say, Mister Claymore. I can see this.'

Clay said nothing, sat listening to the empty echo of his own words.

'The company,' spat Al Shams. 'Petro-Tex. You speak as if this thing were human, one of Allah's creations. It is not. It is inanimate, soulless, not of this world. It exists for one purpose only, as we both know.' He stamped the ground with his foot. 'To get the oil that lies beneath this land. Our land. It will do anything to get it. It will pay people like you whatever it must to placate the villagers, to assuage the regulators. It will bribe, and kill. It exists only to enrich its shareholders. Such a thing as this is incapable of caring.'

'I can assure you …' Clay began, '… that the company …'

Al Shams raised his hand. Clay fell silent.

The Arab was quiet for a long time. Then he looked up and brought his good eye to bear on Clay. 'My people are dying. Your oil is killing them. What you must ask yourself, Mister Claymore, is if you care.'

And in those few moments, as he looked around at the riot of trees shot from naked rock, he asked himself just this question, and determined that yes, he should care – and even vaguely remembered doing so once – but that, in fact, right now, and for a long time now, he felt nothing at all.

Clay shivered and closed his eyes. Then he pulled himself back and looked into the Arab's eyes and said: 'I don't make the decisions.'

'Ah yes, only following orders. So much of your history is like this, is it not? Your people have lost their way, my friend. They worship things other than God.' Al Shams looked away for a moment as if contemplating some deeper meaning. 'But my question was not about power, Mister Claymore. I asked if you cared.'

Clay looked up. 'What I think doesn't matter,' he said. That illusion had been dead a long time, buried somewhere in the Angolan bush.

Al Shams narrowed his good eye. The other remained fixed, staring out at some distant point beyond the canyon wall. 'That is where you are wrong, Mister Claymore,' he said. 'And you are too young to be so wrong.'

Clay Straker took a deep breath. He didn't feel young. 'Look, Al Shams,' he began, his voice tight. He cleared his throat, sought a deeper octave. 'I may well be wrong. I've been wrong about a lot of things. But I can't help you. You've got the wrong people.'

Al Shams pointed the stick at Clay's chest, moved its charred tip slowly towards him, pushed it into the place where his heart was. 'No, Mister Claymore, we have exactly the right people. And with you, both of you, we are going to send a message to Petro-Tex. One they cannot ignore.' By now the gunmen had reappeared at the end of the ledge. Al Shams waved and they moved closer, levelling their weapons.

Clay pushed the stick away with his hand. 'Whatever your issue with Petro-Tex, it's got nothing to do with my driver. He has a family, sons. Let him go.'

Al Shams looked up at the thin blade of sky. He seemed to be searching the length of the precipice. 'War is coming,' he said. 'Much will change, *inshallah*. The sky will tear, the tombs will bust open. Then you will know yourself. These are the words of God.'

Clay considered this for a moment. 'I've seen those tombs, *broer*.' He glanced up at ramparts of broken rock, back at the deformed face. 'It's not knowledge you find.'

Al Shams rose, wiped his hands one upon the other. 'Without Allah's wisdom, Mister Claymore, there is no knowledge. Now you will excuse me. Do not attempt to leave.' Then he turned and strode towards the path that led down to the wadi floor.

The two gunmen moved aside to let Al Shams pass.

Clay scrambled to his feet. 'You asked me if I cared,' he called out. 'Do you?'

Al Shams stopped.

'Do you?' Clay repeated, louder this time.

Al Shams turned and faced him.

'What do you think, Mister Claymore?'

'I think you speak well.'

The muscles on one side of Al Shams' face contracted, forcing up one corner of his mouth, narrowing the good eye, brightening the skin of one cheek. But the mirror was flawed. Whether by birth or some horrible accident, the flesh of the other side remained slack and grey, unaffected by the brief spasm. The effect was hideous, destabilising. Al Shams looked down, up again. 'I speak, Mister Claymore, for the innocent.'

'Words.'

'More than words, Mister Claymore. Truth.'

'Truth, then: Abdulkader is innocent. Free him.'

Al Shams looked up to the sky. 'It is in the hands of Allah,' he said. And then he turned and disappeared into the green depths of the chasm.

٣

You Should Pray

Night fell hard in the Empty Quarter. Clay shivered in his T-shirt and moved closer to the fire, trying not to think about the fleece jacket rolled up in his pack in the back of the Land Cruiser, and the bottle of whisky stashed under the front seat. It wasn't that far away, beyond the rockslide, perhaps a kilometre up the canyon. He peered into the darkness. There was no sign of Al Shams' men, just the first stars flickering in the deep blue trench of sky above.

Clay leaned in close to his friend, kept his voice to a whisper. 'This is the man who killed Thierry Champard.'

Abdulkader shifted in his crouch, poked the fire, said nothing.

Clay knew better than to rush the Arab to words. He waited. The stars turned. After a while Clay said: 'He's not going to let us go.'

'*Inshallah,* he will.'

'God willing? No, Abdulkader. If we're going to get out of here alive, we've got to do it ourselves.'

Abdulkader threw another log on the fire. It flared and caught. 'Only Allah gives life. Only He takes it. *Allah akhbar.*'

'*Allah akhbar,*' Clay repeated, a habit now after so many days in the desert with this man. God is great, the words engraved on the silver ring Abdulkader wore on his right index finger, his only adornment, his father's prized possession.

Yes, perhaps God is. But Clay doubted it. He glanced over at Abdulkader, but his driver's expression remained as immutable as the rock of the plateau, the dark andesite skin fissured by sun and thirst, head and jaw hidden behind the green-and-black *keffiyeh* of the Hadramawt, his eyes shielded beneath shocks of wiry grey hair.

'The Land Cruiser isn't far,' he whispered.

Abdulkader rocked back on his heels, squat on his haunches, and poked the fire.

The rockslide was no more than twenty or thirty metres away, a few seconds at a sprint. Once inside its labyrinth they would be undetectable. They could pick the right moment, get to the car, and be gone before anyone had time to react. It was dark. There was no moon. He had seen only the two gunmen, the two who had hijacked them. There could be more farther down-wadi, but the darkness would give them a chance.

'Al Shams has the key,' said Abdulkader.

'I can start it. I'd rather take my chances than wait here for Allah to decide.' A violent surge of adrenaline shot through him, jerking him to his feet. 'Let's go.'

Abdulkader stretched out by the fire and cradled his head in his arm. 'No. If we run, they will kill us. Sleep. Trust Allah.'

The old ghosts were here now. He drew out the plan in his head, assigned roles. 'Get up, Abdulkader. It's time to *ontrek*.'

But Abdulkader did not move. He stayed as he was, curled up by the fire; he looked up at Clay through narrowed eyes and did not look away for a long time. 'You should pray,' he said.

'You've told me before.' They had all done it back then, good Christian boys, in their holes with SWAPO raining down *kak*, believed with every part of themselves that they would be heard, spared. And the emptiness of it had been revealed in each shattered corpse he had pulled from the ground. Prayer was for the weak, the unscientific, the deluded. You had to believe in something. But not that.

He stood there for a long time watching the firelight dance on the overhanging rock. Like Africa, the rocks here, the sky, the rolling expanses, these green intrusions forced up through cracks in the Earth's concrete. Thirteen years wound back and Eben was there, swimming in the river, smiling and waving from the deepest part where the water was dark and cold, his limbs pale, moving ghostly in the tannin-brown Cunene water, Clay on the bankside watching for crocodiles, R4 assault rifle at the ready. So long ago now, only days before that last mission into Angola, Operation Protea the generals had called it, after which everything changed and nothing was ever the same again.

Clay forced a laugh, coughed, looked across the fire at Abdulkader. The man's stoic fatalism – that granitic belief in a higher power – was something he had never understood. Empirically, it made no sense. Observation denied it. And yet envy flooded through him now, raw, thirsty, an insatiable dark negative that seemed to pull in everything around him, leaving him standing alone and naked, the last torn strips of his logic hanging like rags from his frame.

'The accident,' said Clay, throwing his voice out into the void. 'Who pulled me out?'

Abdulkader looked up at him a moment, his face painted orange by the firelight, then lowered his eyes.

'You did, Abdulkader.'

The Arab looked up again, said nothing.

'It wasn't God.'

'It was his hand.'

'No, Abdulkader. It was you. You decided. You saved my life. This is exactly the same.'

'No man decides, Mister Clay. Only Allah. You must give yourself.'

Clay turned and walked towards the ledge. Away from the fire the cold came quickly. He looked over the precipice, down to the darkness of the wadi floor. The rockslide was there, its patchwork of jumbled surfaces just visible in the starlight. The gunmen were gone. There didn't appear to be anyone between them and the slide. He turned and faced Abdulkader, ready to try one more time. But his friend's body rose and fell in untroubled sleep – he had prayed with the sunset, and now he was ready for whatever would come.

Clay moved closer to the dying fire, sat. Loneliness came. He tried to recall the vestiges of the Lord's Prayer, dredging deep harbours of memory, but the words that came made him shudder, a hypocrite calling to the heavens. It was Allah, apparently, and not JC, who would decide.

He closed his eyes.

Soon, the dreams came. Thirst always made them worse.

Later, how much later he did not know, he woke with a start. The fire had died. His shirt was soaked. His heart hammered in his chest. Axe blades of pain slammed into his head. He pushed himself up, shivered in the cold. Abdulkader was there, cocooned in sleep, his breathing lapping the rockface like water. Clay looked at his watch, up to the sky, dawn still a few hours off. He opened his eyes wide, breathed the cold air, felt it flow deep into his lungs. He held it there as the doctor had shown him, exhaled, breathed in again, tried to fight back the remnant shards of his sleeping hallucinations. But this was their time, and they were determined. Faces came, hovered there in the darkness before him, sounds, the burnt edges of landscapes, gaping wounds pulsing, though his eyes were open, voices and smiles of those long dead breaking the banks of his consciousness, flooding his senses. He opened his eyes wide, focussed on his breathing, reached for the woodpile. His hand closed around a gnarled bone of camelthorn. He raked the stick through the ash, uncovered a few remaining coals, beacons in the darkness. He got to his knees, bent his head to the ash as if in prayer, blowing up a lonely flame. It flickered and died, was reborn in a rush of oxygen. He cupped his hands around it, felt its far-off warmth, urged it to life. He peeled a strip of bark from the twig, touched it to the flame. It flared and caught. Another. Soon the fire was going and the dreams were gone.

Clay sat close, tried to warm himself. He gazed into the flames, watched the chain reaction build, gases mixing and igniting, impurities bleeding in colour. He fed the fire and watched the sky lighten.

Stars vanished.

A hint of colour refracted along the dark edge of the canyon wall, day finally coming.

Soon, the heat would come, crushing everything.

☾

Clay rose to his feet, joints stiff, ran his tongue over the dry skull of his mouth.

Abdulkader looked up at him. 'Again, you did not sleep,' he said.

'I was praying,' Clay said.

Abdulkader frowned.

'*Sabah al khaeer,*' came a voice from the darkness. Al Shams stood in the gloom at the far end of the cave, hands clasped before him. 'Good morning,' he said. He was alone.

Abdulkader rose and inclined his head.

Al Shams moved closer, emerged from the shadows. 'I sense you are an intelligent and honourable man, Mister Claymore. So I ask for your help.'

Clay stepped forward. He was within four paces of Al Shams now, towered over him. He could take him down in one surge, push him over the ledge. You've got it wrong, he thought. I'm neither. That was what war had taught him, made of him. He said nothing.

'This you will do for us, Mister Claymore. Go to Um'alat, speak with the *mashayikh,* the sheikh there. Go also to Al Urush and Al Bawazir. There is evil being done in these places. Desecrations I do not comprehend, corruptions of nature. Perhaps you can understand them, with your science. See for yourself what your oil company is doing. And then deliver this message to your infidel masters: all that is within this land is a gift from God to those that have lived here since before the Prophet. It is twice blasphemy: to deny them a share in this wealth, and to harm them in its taking. When you have done this and learned the truth, find me. Without this knowledge, our people cannot protect themselves. Now go in peace, Mister Claymore.'

Clay reached out for the cavern wall, steadied himself. The sandstone was cool and damp, like sandpaper, the silica studs hard, reassuring.

Al Shams stepped forward and put his hand on Clay's forearm. 'I am giving you an opportunity, my friend, to find what you have lost.'

His gaze cut into Clay's eyes. The asymmetry was painful. He had lost a lot of things, was pissed that it was so obvious to this man.

'Remember always that God is great.'

Clay looked away, down at the dust of centuries. Evidence for this would be good. Again, he said nothing.

Al Shams removed his hand. 'And no, we are not responsible for the unfortunate death of your Monsieur Champard.'

Clay took a step back, glanced over at Abdulkader.

'Be serene, Mister Claymore, in the knowledge that there will be a *yawm'idin*, a day of reckoning, for us all.' Al Shams raised his hand and the two gunmen appeared from the far end of the ledge – the same two gunmen from the day before. The older man, the one with the hennaed beard, placed something in Al Shams' hand. 'You may go,' said Al Shams, dropping the Toyota's keys into Clay's outstretched palm. 'But your friend will remain as our guest.'

Who You Might Have Been

Clay dropped his hand to his side, flicked the ignition key with his thumb so that the blade protruded between the index and middle fingers of his right hand, closed his fist around the bow. Al Shams was close, within striking distance. The kid was a couple of paces behind and to Al Shams' right; he was left-handed, which meant he would have to swing the AK through almost ninety degrees to get a shot at Clay, and, even then, would risk hitting Al Shams. The older gunman was to Al Shams' left, but right-handed. Same problem. OK for escorting someone when the danger was external, but no good when the threat was close in, front on. They had it backwards. Neither had slung their weapons. The closer Clay got to Al Shams, the harder it would be for them. Abdulkader was the only problem. He hadn't moved, stood back by the fire, five paces away from the elder gunman, a clear straight-line shot.

Clay looked Al Shams in the good eye. 'I'll do what you ask. I'll go to Al Urush. I'll talk to the villagers, see what I can find. But I need Abdulkader. He knows the country, the people, the roads. We're a team. I can't do it without him.'

'Do not be disingenuous, Mister Claymore. You can, and you will. And if you do not, your friend will die.'

'Please, Mister Clay,' rumbled Abdulkader's voice from behind. 'Do as he says.'

'I'm not leaving without him.'

'Then neither of you will leave.'

Clay was silent, stood his ground.

Al Shams spread his arms slightly, opened out his palms. 'Please, Mister Claymore. Be reasonable. Go now. Do this great service for my people. If you do, your friend will be freed. You have my word.'

Clay took a step forward, tightened the angles. 'He's no good to you as a hostage. Petro-Tex is not going to bargain for a driver, a local. If you want leverage, you need me.'

'No, Mister Claymore. The leverage I want is not with the company. It is with you.'

A cold tumour of realisation lumped in Clay's chest. He had always hated irony.

The older gunman chambered a round.

'Please believe me,' said Al Shams. 'I do not wish to kill you, or your friend. But I will if I must.'

Clay hesitated. 'You think I'm lying. You think that if you let us go, I won't help you.'

The edge of a smile formed at the corner of Al Shams' mouth and was gone. 'I *know* you will not help us, Mister Claymore. You do not want to be involved. I can see this in you very plainly. Well, now you are involved.'

Clay looked back at Abdulkader, but his friend stood mute, expressionless. And in that fragment of time compressed between his last utterance and the attack he was about to initiate, Clay wondered again at the power of events to obliterate the dim recollection of 'who you might have been', at how completely he'd been bludgeoned into the man he now was.

Clay bowed his head, opened his arms as if resigning himself to his fate. He could sense the men facing him relax as they anticipated his capitulation. He took a slow step towards Al Shams, paused a moment.

Half a second, no more.

Enough to hear the morning breeze hush across the lip of the canyon.

Enough to feel the new sun on his neck, watch it cast shadows across the ruins of Al Shams' tortured face.

Clay burst to his right, pivoting towards the old man and putting Al Shams between himself and the kid. Before the old man could react, Clay brought his left knee up hard, smashing the old guy's pelvis. The Arab's mouth opened, the first note of a groan hanging in space, truncated an instant later as Clay's right fist smashed into his face. Clay felt the key go in, the give as a membrane flexed, heard the slight pop as it broke, then the sucking sound as he pulled back his fist, the key with it. The old man fell back screaming, reaching instinctively for his face. Clay grabbed the AK as the old man let go, jerking the stock back hard. There was a crack as the rifle's butt plate caught the old man in the jaw. He crashed to the ground, blood pouring from his mouth and left eye. As before, out on the road, the kid was slow to react. He stood blinking in the morning sun, a look of puzzlement spreading across his young-old face. But Al Shams was quick. He'd already shifted left, clearing the kid for a shot, and was moving towards the cave entrance. Clay found the AK's pistol grip with his right hand, flicked the safety, already down and off, bringing the rifle up for a shot. The kid had recovered now, was swinging his weapon around. As he did, he fumbled momentarily, looked down. He'd forgotten to disengage the safety. The AK's safety switch was on the weapon's right side, forward of the trigger guard. Left-handed, the kid had to reach over the top of the gas block with his right hand to get at the lever. It was a clumsy manoeuvre and it took time. By the time the kid looked up, Clay had closed the distance. Side on, he let go a kick that caught the kid in the chest, just below the neck. The kid grunted with the impact, toppled backwards, and disappeared over the ledge, the AK clattering down over the rock after him.

Clay swung around and took aim at Al Shams. The kid's body thudded into the wadi floor. The sound echoed from the canyon wall.

'Stop,' Clay said.

Al Shams froze.

'Turn around.'

Al Shams turned, reached out his hands, palms upraised, a preacher appealing to his congregation. He looked disappointed. 'This changes nothing, Mister Claymore.'

'Like I said before, this can still be retrieved.'

Al Shams glanced at the old man.

'I think not.'

The old guy was on his knees now, his hand covering his left eye. Blood flowed out between his fingers, dripped to the ground.

'I can get him to a doctor, if you help me.'

'*Inshallah,*' said Al Shams.

Clay called back over his shoulder. 'Let's go, my friend. Help the old guy. Our host is going to walk the three of us out of here.'

'You do not understand, Mister Claymore. This is not for me to decide.'

Anger, at bay until now, rose inside him. 'Just like Aden? Was that Allah's will, too? Thierry Champard blown to pieces?'

'As I told you, this was not our doing.'

'You claimed responsibility.'

'We did not.'

'It was in the papers.'

'And you believe this propaganda? Do not be so naïve.'

Clay took a breath, pulled back the AK's bolt, checked the 7.62 millimetre round in the breech. *This* was death, this projectile nestled in its chamber, the firing pin millimetres away, ready. At 715 metres per second, the 7.9 gram bullet would cover the four metres and reach Al Shams in 0.0056 seconds, entering and exiting his body before he had a chance to blink. And it was men who decided this, not God. 'Here we go,' said Clay, wiping the unwanted calculation from his head. 'You are going to lead us down to the rock slide. Go slow.'

Al Shams stood unmoving. His expression was serene, beatific, his one good eye piercing, alive, the other a black stone plucked from the sun-baked plateau. He looked up for a moment and then smoothed his robe with his hands. 'No, Mister Claymore. You will do as I have asked. It is God's will. This you cannot deny. You cannot see it now, but you will. I pity you your emptiness, Mister Claymore.'

Clay heard a rush of air, like the sound of a bird swooping close, and then the crack as the back of his skull ruptured in a blinding flash. He was unconscious before he hit the ground.

Not Yet a Commodity

He awoke face down in the sand where they had left him. A river of heat shimmered on an empty vertical horizon, land and sky indistinguishable. It was as if he were looking through one of those thick, almost-liquid Cairo smogs that would descend in the hottest days of summer, locking the city in a coffin of car exhaust and smoke from the burning landfills and airborne lead from the smelters along the Nile. Sand crusted the corners of his mouth, frosted his eyelashes. He spat and turned his head. A dark shape loomed close. He raised his head and propped himself on one elbow. His skull felt as if it were about to implode. He lifted his hand to the back of his head, ran his fingers along the swollen matting of hair and blood. A thick warm liquid trickled over his top lip and into his mouth and out over his chin and neck. The taste was vaguely metallic, aluminium or stainless steel, like licking a knife.

He struggled to his knees, rubbed his eyes, looked around. Abdulkader's Land Cruiser was there, a few metres away, ticking in the heat. Clay pushed himself to his feet, swayed on unsteady legs, took a few steps, slumped against the car's side, and looked inside. He knew that it was empty, that his friend was back there, a prisoner, a hostage. He shuffled around to the driver's side door, opened it, climbed out of the sun. The key was in the ignition, dried blood set into its grooves. The dashboard's digital thermometer read fifty-one degrees. Clay looked out across the sameness of the plateau, the limitless empty blue of the sky. There were no landmarks, no roads. Overhead, the sun was near its zenith. He had no idea where he was.

Clay took stock. He had plenty of fuel, half a tank and two extra jerry cans in the back. They'd left him half a litre of water, his compass and notebook. They hadn't touched the whisky. But Abdulkader's Kalashnikov was gone, as was the handgun he kept in the glove box. It was nearly midday. That put him a maximum of 250 kilometres cross-country from the Kamar-1 well and the pipeline trunk road. By the look of the land, he guessed they'd taken him north, further towards Wadi Hadramawt, probably east, too. There was a second set of tyre tracks nearby that disappeared to the south-east. If he struck south, eventually he'd hit the trunk road that paralleled the escarpment and the coast. There was no question now of trying to go back for Abdulkader. Unarmed, alone, he had little chance of finding him, let alone getting him safely away. Destiny crystallised around him, inescapable, just as Al Shams had said it would.

Clay found the medical kit under the seat, took three painkillers, swilled them down with whisky, and cleaned out the wound on the back of his head as best he could. He pushed a compress bandage down hard onto it to stop the bleeding, secured it with his head-cloth, and set out overland.

An hour later he was still heading south, not a road or track in sight. He leaned forward in the seat, let the superheated air whipping through the open window vaporise the sweat from his shirt back, and looked out across the dead-flat loneliness to the shimmering heat of the horizon. This was the hottest place on Earth, and soon it would be summer. Even the Bedouin rued these months. It should have been a good place for forgetting. That's why he'd come.

Now he knew that for him there would only ever be remembering.

He reached the Kamar-2 pipeline road just over three hours later. It took what remained of the day to reach Wadi Idim and the pass down the escarpment. As if rebelling against the loss of its owner, the old Land Cruiser blew out its right front tyre shortly after. Only one spare remained and the whisky was gone by the time he emerged onto the coastal plain. Al Shams' men had taken what little food he had stashed in the vehicle, and the last of the water was long since gone.

He stopped by the roadside and unrolled his blanket under shuddering stars, but despite the codeine and the whisky, he could not sleep. The last moments at the canyon played themselves out again in his mind. He'd screwed up. The kid must have survived the fall – it wasn't far, four metres at most – climbed back up to the ledge, got behind him. He'd been distracted by Al Shams, had allowed himself to be drawn in, to lose focus. Had Abdulkader tried to warn him? He hadn't heard a thing.

After four restless hours he continued on his way, dread marshalling within. Al Shams had made it clear: go to the villages, deliver the message to Petro-Tex, or Abdulkader would die. Bring the Army, and Abdulkader would die. That Al Shams could track his movements, verify his actions, Clay had no doubt.

By mid-morning he was approaching the village of Um'alat along the broad flat wadi of the same name. Goats scattered as he passed, dust rising in puffs from their hooves. A lone camel, its front legs hobbled, foraged among the stunted acacia that snaked along the grey cobbles of the main channel. Here the wadi narrowed and turned north toward the escarpment. The village, a tight cluster of tall, mud-brick buildings set on the wadi bank, rose through the dust and heat like some pre-Islamic apparition. He rolled Abdulkader's Land Cruiser to a stop just outside the main gate, turned off the engine and stepped to the ground.

Within seconds he was surrounded by children – miniatures of the men who'd taken his friend, dark-haired, dressed in rags. They laughed and smiled, followed him as he walked toward the main gate, tugged at his sleeves. An older boy approached, dressed like a man in a *thaub* and a tweed jacket, sandals fashioned from car-tyres and goat leather, a Kalashnikov slung over his right shoulder. The boy raised his hand to his forehead and said in English: 'Follow.'

They were expecting him.

The boy led Clay to a low, whitewashed building on high ground overlooking the village. Inside, the single room was packed with tribesmen, all standing, all talking – the Bani Matar, Sunni Muslims of the Shafa'i sect. This ancient clan had dominated this part of the Masila since the time of Persian rule and the dawn of Islam. They had endured the Caliphate, seen off the Ottoman occupation, fought the British, survived Egyptian chemical weapon attacks in the 1960s, and outlasted the Soviets. Tough didn't even begin to describe them.

The boy led him through the maze of bodies to a small stool at the far end of the room. Opposite, waiting, sat the *mashayikh,* the sheikh. The room went quiet. Clay sat, opened his notebook to a blank page, glanced up at the tribesmen packed like judge, jury and mob into every corner of the mud-brick room, and listened.

The *mashayikh* reached for the Kalashnikov leaning against the wall, swung it level and balanced it across his knees. The trigger pointed out like an accusing finger, the whole of it beautiful, hateful, a work of calculated, merciless perfection. Clay stared at it, entranced, unable to break away.

'Mister Straker,' the *mashayikh*'s voice broke through, heavily accented, frayed.

Clay looked up, breathing hard.

The *mashayikh* fixed him with a long stare. 'My people are worried,' he said after a time. 'The children are ill.' Grumbled translations rippled out across the room. 'It has begun in Al Urush, six months ago. A sickness. The children bring up food, their skin breaks open. Now it is worse.'

Of course it could have been anything, despite Al Shams' assertions: gastrointestinal infection, an outbreak of measles, flu, who knew. There were always complaints manufactured to claw money from the operators: goats run down by pipe trucks, camels poisoned by fictitious gas clouds, crops ruined by oil-tainted water that sprung mysteriously from the ground. He had heard it all before, in villages and settlements just like this all over the region, with no claim too spurious.

And so, as the Arab spoke of the inadequate compensation, of the lack of jobs for the young men, of the corrupting influence of the oil workers, Clay Straker's thoughts were elsewhere. He watched the *mashayikh's* mouth move behind the short-cropped grey beard, heard the words arch out over the dozens of armed tribesmen, registered the murmurs of translation and the spreading echoes of agreement. He could even pick out the occasional word or phrase: *khawga*, foreigner; *molhed*, godless one; even once a hissed *shatan* – hard to miss, the origin of the English word of the same enunciation. Would this Al Shams, who seemed to believe so fervently in the power of God, actually murder Abdulkader, one of his own, one of the very people he purported to be fighting for? The events of the last day began to dissolve away and lose substance as fatigue and pain and hunger took hold, and he knew that no matter what he said back at the office in Aden, all that would remain would be another paragraph in a report, another message for the bosses to ignore. *Naafi*, as they used to say in the Battalion. No ambition and fuck-all interest. Enough for Al Shams? He doubted it.

'Mister Straker?' The *mashayikh* was leaning close, looking into his eyes. 'You bleed.'

Clay ran his hand across the back of his neck, closed his eyes a moment. His hand came away wet with blood. He looked up, wiped his hand on his trouser leg. 'It's nothing.' He took a sip of tea and put the glass on the small wooden table between them. 'Please continue, Excellency.'

The *mashayikh* closed his eyes a moment, opened them. 'We see many trucks, many men coming. What is the plan of your company, Mister Straker?'

'I am a contractor, Excellency. Petro-Tex is not my company.'

'But you are here. You speak for them.' More murmurs from the crowd.

'I am doing community consultation and environmental impact studies only. I listen and report back.'

The *mashayikh* motioned with his head towards the notebook spread open on Clay's knee. 'Now you can report.'

'The illness. Yes.' He started to scribble in his notebook, but the pencil lead gritted over the silt that dusted the empty page, fracturing the words. He wiped the paper with the side of his hand and started again.

'It is said that Petro-Tex is making the oil factory on the *jol* bigger. They do this to take more oil from our land. Is this true, Mister Straker?'

The room erupted again, everyone speaking at once. Some were shouting now, spitting out their accusations in the harsh Arabic dialect that he was only just beginning to understand. The *mashayikh* raised his hand to restore a degree of calm.

Clay wiped the sweat from his eyes. The back of his hand came away streaked with mud. 'The oil-processing facility on the plateau is being expanded. As part of the expansion programme, the company will build a school for your children, and they will drill a new water well for you.' The standard line. By now he could recite it without thinking.

The *mashayikh* wrapped both hands around the barrel of his rifle. 'We have no need of your well. The *ghayls* – our springs – have provided for our people for all time, thanks God.' Another chorus of murmured agreement: *Al hamdillulah* – thanks be to Allah.

The *mashayikh* smoothed out the folds of his crisply laundered *thaub*, pulled a handkerchief from his jacket pocket and wiped the dust from his polished leather brogues. 'Your company will take no more oil until the sickness is stopped, Mister Straker.'

'Respectfully, Excellency, it is not possible that our operations could cause the type of illness you have described.'

Again the plaintive murmurs, accompanied by the sounds of feet shuffling on sand and the metallic clink of sling-strap buckles on curved magazines and folding stocks. Above the din, a voice rose from the back of the room. Heads twisted to listen; the men quietened. A young man dressed Saudi-style in a flowing white robe stood against the back wall, one hand resting on a young boy's shoulder. He was tall, clean-shaven, light-skinned, almost European-looking. He was Clay's age, maybe younger. He spoke slowly, his voice like wind sculpting rock, deep and resonant.

'The poison that afflicts our children comes from the facility. It comes in the air, down the wadi, when the cool winds blow from the plateau. We can smell it, foul like the vapours of hell. This is done by the government and the company to push us from our land. It is intentional.'

When the young man had finished speaking, the *mashayikh* inclined his head and turned towards Clay. 'This is my son, the chief of Al-Bawazir. Are his words true, Mister Straker?'

Clay shifted his weight on the handmade wood and woven reed stool. The thing was unsteady, too close to the ground, and he had to rest one knee on the packed earth floor just to stay upright. He wanted to stand. He wanted to straighten his aching legs and walk across the room to the door and out to the waiting vehicle. But here, he knew, convention must be honoured. He was expected to answer.

He looked around the room at the tribesmen, their sun-worn faces as open and uncompromising as the rocky ground of their birth. They seemed to be studying him, his curious flaxen hair, his pale eyes. No one spoke. He looked down at the ground, at the clay and silt covering his boots. Something trickled down his back, along the gutter of his spine, sweat or blood or both. Someone coughed. He glanced at his watch. Time had a different meaning here. Not yet a commodity, it was reckoned still by the rhythm of the seasons, the comings of the winds and rains, the movement of planets and stars. In this place there was no fear of silence, no need to fill time and space with meaningless words.

Moments passed. A minute? Maybe more.

Finally Clay said: 'This is a European company, operating to the best international standards.' Again, what the script demanded.

The *mashayikh* narrowed his eyes. 'You insult us, Mister Straker. We know this is a lie.' He looked down at the weapon lying across his knee, caressed the smooth walnut handguard with sinewed fingers, and then locked his gaze onto Clay's eyes. 'We can make things very difficult, Mister Straker, if we choose.' Then he leaned close and whispered in Clay's ear. 'Also, we can cooperate. It is your choice.' His breath reeked of *qat* and alcohol.

Then the *mashayikh* stood and swung the Kalashnikov over his shoulder. The audience was over. Clay got to his feet and clasped the man's right hand in his own, making sure to keep his left hand, the unclean one, behind his back. He felt the grit in the *mashayikh*'s skin, saw the stains of years cracked and stretched over the bones, and looked into the murky tannin eyes. '*Shukran*, Excellency. I will take the message back to my superiors in Aden.'

'I will expect you soon, then,' said the *mashayikh* with a flourish of his hand as he turned towards the door, the room emptying around him.

Soon Clay was alone. He slumped onto the stool and drained the last of the sweet dark tea. Was that what this was all about? Money? Al Urush was less than an hour away. He would see for himself.

٦

A Melody of Spokes

Fifteen minutes out on the deserted main road, Abdulkader's Land Cruiser continued its rebellion. Clay pulled over onto the rough gravel shoulder, and for the second time in less than a day set about changing a tyre. He had just mounted the last spare and was tightening the lug nuts when a vehicle appeared in the distance. It was travelling at high speed, heading towards him, floating on the heat. A hundred metres away, the car slowed, a Land Rover, white, new. As it approached, Clay could make out a single occupant, thick black hair streaming from the driver's side window. Clay stood, tyre iron in one hand, and was about to wave when the driver gunned the engine. As the Land Rover flashed past in a hurl of dust and flying pebbles, the driver turned for an instant and looked at Clay through a tornado of whirling hair. For a fraction of a second their eyes met. Then she was gone. Clay stood gaping as the vehicle's wake disappeared in the shimmering heat haze. A woman driving alone out here was unusual enough. Even more startling was that she had been unveiled, and uncommonly beautiful.

Clay arrived in the village at the height of day, when the sun had reached its zenith and the ground baked in the heat. At a distance, Al Urush looked like any other hamlet on the coastal plain, a cluster of earthen-brick huts nestled within a shock of green palms at the base of the cliffs. The mouth of a steep canyon yawned above the settlement as if ready to swallow it complete.

He stared up at the escarpment, a massive wall of Palaeocene limestone that ran parallel to the coast for hundreds of kilometres in both directions and rose up to the barren tablelands of the Masila. The rock here was riven with long deep faults, veins carrying life to the ancient spring that wept from the base of the canyon walls. *Aflaj*, ancient hand-laid stone canals the width and depth of a man's hand, carried the water to the fields, houses and palm groves of the village below. And somewhere up there, high on the plateau, five kilometres up-wadi, the Petro-Tex central processing facility, the CPF, gathered in the oil produced from two major fields and dozens of wells.

The dirt track ended in a small clearing at the base of a massive dolomite boulder calved from the cliff face. Clay stopped the vehicle at the edge of the clearing. Nearby, two veiled women in black *burqas* and conical reed hats toiled in a stone field. Bent double at the waist, they worked the ground with medieval hands, pulling up sheaves of a meagre crop.

He sniffed the hot dry air – burnished stone and ripening dates, a trace of wood smoke. Nothing unusual or even vaguely industrial. At the far side of the clearing a small boy sat in the shade of a trio of date palms, cradling an old bicycle wheel between his knees as if it were a harp. Head bent to the instrument, the boy flicked a short stick down across the spokes, one after the other, *click, click, click*, with slow deliberation until the lower clunk of the rim sent him back to the hub to begin again. The boy looked up as Clay approached but did not stop playing, only watched and clicked out the one-note melody in time with Clay's footsteps through the dust.

Clay greeted the boy in Arabic. He could not have been more than five or six, the same age as Abdulkader's youngest son. The boy's face was sullen and grey, but his eyes were bright. There were open sores on his neck and arms. His name was Mohamed. Clay asked the boy to show him the *ghayl*, the spring.

The boy looked at him for a moment and then frowned. 'Why you are angry?' he asked in high-pitched Arabic.

Clay stood for a moment looking out across the plain, this part of the country so different from the veldt of his childhood and yet so reminiscent in its heat and unforgiving dry. He crouched down to the boy's level and tried to smile. 'I am not angry with you.' It was always easier speaking with children. His Arabic was almost at a six-year-old's level.

The boy's eyes widened and he smiled. His gums were red and inflamed. The boy pushed himself to his feet and stood clutching the bicycle wheel in both hands, turning it right and left, leaning into the turns, chattering in a shrill cracked boy voice.

Clay could not make out all the words.

'Toyota,' the boy said, pointing at Abdulkader's dust-covered vehicle.

'You want a ride?' he replied in English. The boy was making engine noises now from deep in his throat, changing gears, accelerating. Clay reached into his pocket and offered the boy a sweet. The boy took it and smiled again.

'*Ya'llah,*' said Clay, reaching down and swinging the boy up onto his shoulders. The boy squealed in delight, still holding his wheel. 'Let's take a look at the *ghayl*,' said Clay. 'Maybe we'll find something further up.'

Clay buckled Mohamed into the passenger's seat and jumped behind the wheel. The boy was chattering excitedly, pulling at his sleeve.

'*Aysh?*' asked Clay. What?

The boy put aside his bicycle wheel and pointed at the steering column.

Clay ruffled the boy's thin black hair. 'Cheeky monkey,' he said, something his father used to say.

Soon they were trundling down the narrow track away from the hamlet, Mohamed perched on Clay's lap, bony hands clutching the Land Cruiser's steering wheel. The boy steered with him, matching his movements. After a while, the boy directed him onto a rough stone track. The vehicle creaked and lurched past terraced flats of stubble wedged between rocky outcrops towards the cleft in the cliffs. The pitch of the track steepened. After a while Clay stopped, jumped out to lock the hubs, kept going. He thought again about the woman in the Land Rover, the surprise he'd felt seeing her, the perfect symmetry of her features, her big dark eyes.

Soon they had penetrated the opening in the cliffs where the wadi met the line of the escarpment. So blinding was the light reflected from the sheer wall of limestone that he had to look away, over to the darkness of the facing formations sheltered from the full fury of the sun. They descended into the bleached cauldron of the wadi bed and then climbed again towards the afternoon shade of the far cliffs. The track became rougher and less distinct. Clay felt his way up the hill, the tyres slipping on the loose stone.

'Stop,' said the boy. 'Now walk.'

They started up the slope towards the patch of green that marked the spring. After a few moments Clay stopped and looked back. Mohamed was already far behind. The boy struggled and stumbled on the loose scree, breathing heavily, his face covered in sweat. He stopped and looked up at Clay, swaying on bony legs. He opened his mouth as if he were about to call out, but then his face twisted in pain and he doubled over, his back and shoulders shaking as he spewed vomit to the ground in a series of wrenching contractions.

Clay ran down the slope, skidding along the loose scree to where the boy stood. He put his hand on Mohamed's back, feeling the last spasm shudder through his thin frame. The boy looked up and smiled. Vomit covered his chin and the front of his shirt. Clay crouched down and unwrapped his *keffiyeh* and wiped the boy's face and his shirt and ran his hand through the boy's dark hair.

'*Tammam?*' Clay asked, giving the thumbs up. 'OK?'

The boy nodded, managing a weak smile.

Then Clay hoisted him onto his shoulders and carried him up the hill, skin and bones, of no weight at all. At the top of the scree slope they came to a sharp vertical bluff as high as a camel's back. The bluff's frayed, fractured lip ran some hundred metres or more across the wadi to meet the cliff face, as if it had been tossed carelessly from the plateau to fall draped over the edge. A footpath ran along its base in both directions. Clay turned away from the cliff and started down the path towards the wadi bed, the bluff on his right, Mohamed's wet hands clasped across his forehead. He could feel the boy's pulse against his own skull, rapid, tripping, excited.

After a few steps the boy shook his legs and tugged at Clay's ears. '*La*,' said the little voice from above.

'What is it?'

The boy pointed back to the cliffs. 'I show you,' he said in English. '*Faddar*.' Please.

'OK, little brother.' Clay spun on his feet and started back along the bluff footpath towards the cliff, the little hamlet spread below them on the right. Soon he was threading his way through a maze of boulders, the path narrowing so that in places he had to turn side on – Mohamed still on his shoulders, urging him forward with little kicks, as though Clay was some mountain donkey and he a travelling Mullah. The rock dwarfed them on all sides, and it was as if they had been swallowed up by the lifeless, uncaring age of the place.

Mohammed squeezed Clay's head. 'Stop,' he said in English, pointing to the bluff. At first Clay did not see what the boy was showing him, such was its unity with the surrounding rock. It seemed impossible, but there it was – a scale of steps hewn into the limestone, a passageway disappearing into the rock. '*Aiwa, aiwa*,' said Mohamed. Yes.

The stairway, ancient surely, twisted up into the core of the bluff, the sides handtool-etched so that he could almost hear the men chipping away at the rock through the centuries. He climbed steadily, heart working harder now, cooler here in the bowels of the earth, his shoulders scraping the sides in places, until they emerged into sunlight so bright he had to shut his eyes.

The oasis was a series of five spring-fed rock pools set in the barren footings of the canyon's towering rock face, shaded by palms and acacia. The spring pulsed from the ground as if pumped from a heart, the clear water cascading over the grooved limestone from one pool to the next and the one after that. The place teemed with life: small green fish with silver bellies darted in the deep cool water, frogs croaked in the fringing reed banks, insects buzzed in dense shifting clouds of colour. It was one of the most beautiful places he had ever seen.

A group of children splashed in the deepest of the pools. They smiled as he approached. Their gums, too, were red and inflamed, their skin dappled with sores. At the water's edge, two women, clearly blessed by Allah, heavy with child, laid out their washing on the smooth rocks to dry in the sun. They whispered to each other as he approached. Clay looked towards them. One of the women raised her hands to her face and looked away. But the other met his gaze, and for a short moment she stared at him with dark, brazen eyes. Then she smiled and her teenage face vanished behind a drawn veil.

Clay swung the boy down to the ground and crouched before him. He took the boy's face in his hands and turned it to one side and the other. '*Tammam?* OK?'

'I am tired,' the boy replied in a thin, high-pitched voice.

Clay pulled a sweet from his pocket, offered it to the boy.

Mohamed held out his hand. It was covered in blood from Clay's head. 'You are hurt,' he said.

Clay reached for the boy's other hand, dropped the sweet into his palm, patted him on the head. 'I am fine, *al hamdillulah*.'

The boy muttered the same words, thanks be to God, closed his fingers around the candy, held it a moment, pulled off the wrapper, then popped it in his mouth.

Clay knelt and put his lips to the water. The first touch was cool, the water sweet. The boy crouched beside him and did the same.

Clay stood and sniffed the air. Iodine, salt, empty miles of hazy blue. The wind was from the sea. He reached into his pack and fished out an empty plastic water bottle, opened the cap. He was not prepared, but this would have to do. He crouched by the edge and dipped the bottle in the pool until the mouth was half submerged and held it there as it filled. Clay stood, stashed the bottle in his pack, and looked up at the women busy with their laundry. 'Stay here, Mohamed,' he said.

'I want to come.'

'I will come back. I have work.'

The boy bent the twig of an arm around Clay's leg. 'You are my friend,' he said.

Clay smiled. He crouched and put his hands on the boy's shoulders. 'You are my friend, too,' he said in Arabic. He reached into his pocket and poured a handful of sweets into the boy's outstretched hands.

He left Mohamed at the pools and set off along the gradually constricting wadi bed. After half an hour of hard walking he came to a place where the canyon narrowed into a steep defile. Vertical dolomite cliffs embraced a sheer fault line that blocked the way. He stopped and looked up. There was not a whisper of air, nor any angle in the sun to throw shadows. He turned and wiped the back of his hand across his brow and down his temple and looked back towards the green of the oasis no more than a kilometre below, little Mohamed just a speck now, still waiting by the water. Whatever Al Shams thought was happening here, there was no sign of it. Was the truth being spoken?

Is a woman beautiful or ugly? A glance is not enough. To know, you must marry her. That's what Abdulkader would have said.

V

Getting the Tone Just Right

He made the long journey back to Aden on autopilot, hundreds of kilometres of dusty, potholed road vanishing without a trace, mountains and bluffs, the black cinder cones of the Aden plain no more than a blur in the side window, the changeless sky as empty as a non-believer's soul, as blank.

It was early evening when Clay arrived in the waiting room of Petro-Tex's main Yemen operations office. He smiled at the busty blonde secretary. It came out more like a scowl. 'Howzit, Greta?'

She looked up at him, eyes narrowing. 'OK, Clay?' she said in a distinct Scandinavian accent. 'What happened to your face?'

Clay raised his hand to his jaw, the scrapes from when he'd hit the ground after being knocked unconscious. 'I was run over by a beautiful woman in Land Rover.'

She smiled, waved this away. She had lovely blue-green eyes. 'I never thanked you for the Kahlua.' Clay brought her a duty-free bottle every time he came into Yemen. You couldn't get it locally. 'Go right in,' she said.

Nils Karila sat behind a large desk strewn with papers, a shard of Indian Ocean blue just visible through the wood-framed window behind him. Production charts, reservoir maps, petro-physical logs and impenetrable seismic tracings covered the dingy walls. A rectangular picture frame hung on the bookcase, Karila and three blond children in red and blue winter jackets peering out from a polar snowscape. Slumped in his chair, he tapped with two fingers on a yellowing keyboard, the computer monitor looming above him like a stern and remote superior. His thin white hair was combed back over his scalp, barely covering the pink, sunburned skin.

'What do you want, Mister Straker?' Karila said without looking up from the keyboard.

'I ...' Clay stumbled, stopped, stared out the window. On the long drive back he'd rehearsed the message over and again, a hundred variants, playing out Karila's response in his head. And each time he had reached the same conclusion: there was no way to deliver Al Shams' message without endangering Abdulkader.

'Your report, Straker?'

'You'll have it in two weeks.'

'One week. You know the situation.'

If he told Nils now, they'd send in the Army. 'My invoice for the Kamar project hasn't been paid yet,' he said. 'It's been three months, Nils. I'm *swak*. Dead broke.'

Karila stopped typing and looked up from the keyboard. Albino eyes blinked behind a pair of wire-framed glasses; a burning Gitane hung from his mouth. He looked like he had worked through the night. 'Accounts assure me it will be paid this week.'

If he didn't tell Karila, he'd have no reply for Al Shams. 'That's what you said last month.'

'We are all very busy here, Mister Straker.'

Clay looked around the room. Would Petro-Tex try to get Abdulkader back? They'd never had a hostage situation before. 'Someone's getting paid, then.'

Karila glanced up at him, disapproval etched into every crease of his pursed pink lips. 'I'll speak to Dunkley today.' Dunkley was the operation's chief accountant.

Clay nodded, shuffled his feet. 'Ever think it's a curse, Nils?'

Karila hit the enter key, flicked his gaze across the screen for a moment, then looked up again. 'Curse? What are you talking about, Straker?'

'Oil.' Clay pointed to the wintertime photo. 'The cost.'

Karila glanced down at the picture frame, seemed to ponder this a moment, directed a stream of blue smoke at the ceiling with a long sigh. 'I've got a lot to do, Straker. Do you have something to report or not?'

Clay stood looking down at Karila, unsure where to start. 'Are you hearing anything unusual from the Oil Ministry?'

Karila waved at the air with his burning cigarette. 'I was in Sana'a the day before yesterday. The Minister mentioned nothing out of the ordinary. Why?'

He edged towards it. He had to try. 'It's getting tense out there, Nils. Rumours, threats.'

'If you are concerned you should take an Army escort, as I have repeatedly advised. That's what we pay them for. I don't understand why you insist on going out there for weeks at a time, alone.'

'I have Abdulkader.' Had.

Karila scoffed. 'One day you are going to get yourself into real trouble, Straker.'

He'd heard the same advice a decade ago, hadn't taken it then. 'Do you know who makes up that Army, Nils? Northerners, Zaydis: highlanders from tribes loyal to President Saleh. They're Shi'a, Nils. The people here hate them. They've been blood enemies for centuries.'

That same pucker of distaste. 'I have no interest in the local politics. My job is to get oil out of the ground. And you have been hired to assist in that goal, Mister Straker.'

'And to do it, I need the people's confidence. That is not going to happen with the Army shadowing me. Do you want your approvals, or have you decided to skip that technicality?'

Karila peered at him over smudged glasses. 'Not funny, Straker. Getting those permits as quickly as possible is a serious matter.'

'Then let me do my job.'

'As you like, Straker. I take no responsibility.'

'No, you don't.'

Karila frowned and stubbed out his cigarette in the ashtray on his desk. 'Now is there anything else, Straker?' He turned his wrist, exposed the white veinless skin of his forearm, glanced at his watch. 'If I don't have this production report on Parnell's desk within the hour, he is going to crucify me.'

Clay planted his feet. 'The villagers are concerned.'

Karila dismissed this with a swipe of his Gitane.

'I'm serious, Nils.'

Karila looked up. 'The usual complaints about jobs and money?'

'Always. But something's changed. They're talking about a sickness. They say it's coming from the CPF. We should check it out.'

'We are not in the social services business, Straker.'

'They're angry, Nils. They could make things difficult for us.'

'We cannot afford needless distractions. I need not remind you that we have a drop-dead date that is rapidly approaching. Focus on that.'

Clay thrust his hand deep into his trouser pocket, jangled worthless Yemeni coins through his fingers. 'OK, Nils. Understood.' He said it out of habit. He said it so that his client would know that he was part of the team, dependable. If you wanted to survive as a contractor, you had to espouse the common objective. He was pretty good now at getting the tone just right.

'Pay who you need to pay, Straker. We need the approvals in place within the next four weeks or we start cutting into the schedule. Every day we delay costs money. Did you tell them about the school we are going to build them?'

'*Ja*, the school,' Clay said under his breath.

'What did you say?'

'That you would build them a school.'

'Good, Straker. Good.'

The warmth of client praise flowed through him. It felt a lot like the dull burn of cheap vodka.

A determinedly overweight man in a pink golf shirt and pleated khaki trousers staggered wheezing into the office and collapsed into one of the leather armchairs across from Karila's desk. He was breathing heavily. Sweat glistened on his forehead, tracked across the cratered folds and overhangs of his strangely pallid, humid face. He looked like a burn victim stripped of his face bandages for the first time, pale, hairless, scarred, oiled and balmed. The man fumbled with his pockets, withdrew a plastic inhaler, put it to his mouth and thumbed the trigger. He sat a moment, chest heaving, eyes closed. After a while his breathing eased and he opened his eyes, blinked twice, glared at Clay.

'Fuck me, I do so hate this place,' he said in a constricted wheeze. He spoke exceedingly slowly, hovering on each word, drawling it into the next like a Baptist preacher gone rogue. 'Nothin' but dust here. Goddamn place is from dust *made*.'

'Hello Vance,' said Karila, brightening. 'You know Clay Straker, our environmental and community contractor.'

Clay nodded. They'd met once, in Parnell's office a year ago when Clay had first been contracted. Since then, he'd heard the rumours, of course. It was hard not to. But he'd ignored them, gone about his work, kept quiet. Time in the Battalion had taught him the percentage of bullshit that rumour usually contained.

Parnell stuffed his inhaler back into his trouser pocket and stared at Karila, dark-marble eyes twitching in shallow sockets. For a moment he looked as if he was going to speak, but then he just closed his eyes and slowly shook his head, left to right, back again, muttering something that Clay could not make out. Then he opened his eyes and ran his glare over Clay. 'My friend Karila, on the other hand, he loves it here,' Parnell said in his thick Southern accent. 'Ain't that right, Nils?'

Karila started to mumble a reply but Parnell cut him off, stared at Clay. 'What the hell happened to *you*?'

Clay glanced at Karila, back at Parnell. 'I've been halfway converted, if that's what you mean. Still an infidel though.'

Disdain flashed in Parnell's eyes. 'No, that ain't what I mean, Straker. I don't give a goddamn about your journey spiritual.' He shook his head, jowls swaying. 'Stone-age religion for fucking Neanderthals, in my opinion.' He pointed at Clay's neck. 'You're bleeding. *That's* what I mean.'

Clay reached up and touched his neck. His fingers came away wet with blood. He looked at Parnell. 'Cut my head.'

'I can see that.'

'With a flint hand tool.'

Parnell glanced at Karila and raised his eyebrows. Or rather he raised the hairless flesh on the ridge above his eye sockets, where two arched brows, pencil thin, had been clumsily drawn in with some kind of makeup, like something a young girl might do using her mother's compact. 'I don't really give a shit how you did it, Straker,' he said. 'I don't want it showing up on our health and safety figures. You *got* me?'

Clay said nothing, just stood staring at Parnell, thinking about Abdulkader.

'Mister Straker has been visiting the villages in the expansion area,' said Karila, quickly interjecting, the peacemaker.

Parnell ran his index finger along the edge of Karila's desk, streaked a line in the thin layer of brown silt that covered the wood, examined his fingertip, sniffed at it like a cur. 'Well? Whatcha gotta report, Straker?'

Clay swallowed and looked out at the ocean. 'The villagers in Al Urush are complaining that their kids are getting sick.'

'That's all we goddamn need,' Parnell said to Karila. He turned to Clay. 'Well?'

'There's nothing obvious. But I did see a young boy …' Clay trailed off, realising his error.

'Go on,' said Karila.

'He looked bad. Ill, I mean. Ulcerous mouth, pallid face. He threw up.'

The American laughed out loud, a deep, belly-shaking chortle that seemed to go on and on. He laughed until tears were streaming over his cheeks, finally erupting in a coughing wheeze that had to be doused with a shot from his inhaler. Parnell straightened in his chair, wiped his face on his sleeve, and took a deep breath. 'Now *that's* good, Straker,' he said. 'Fucking hilarious. Have you ever seen a Yemeni who wasn't sick? Good one.'

Clay ignored the American and reached into his backpack. 'I took a water sample. It may tell us something.' He put the bottle on Karila's desk, imagining Parnell with a broken nose and a couple of missing teeth, then realising it might actually improve his appearance. 'I'm going to have the lab run an ICP metals scan, PAH's, total organic carbon, volatiles and main ions. It won't cost you more than two hundred dollars.'

Karila looked over at his boss and frowned.

'Oh, and I met someone,' said Clay, trying to keep his voice flat. He had no choice. He had to deliver the message. 'Calls himself Al Shams, "The Sun".'

Both men looked as if they were going to fall out of their chairs.

Clay continued. 'He said Allah is going to sweep us away if we don't give the people a fair share. He said war is coming.' The hideous face was there now, the good eye raking its gaze over him. Clay blinked hard, tried to push it away, kill the words that had been swirling around inside his skull for the last two days. An opportunity, Al Shams had said. *I am giving you an opportunity.*

Karila was staring at him. 'Are you alright, Mister Straker?'

'Sorry?'

'I asked you a question.' Karila looked over at Parnell, back at Clay.

He hadn't heard a thing. His tune-outs had become more frequent lately, more vivid, just like the dreams. A split skull wasn't helping.

'Say again?'

Karila took in a lungful of smoke, rolled his eyes. 'I said ...' he paused, smoke pouring from his nostrils, '... where did you see him?'

'That son of a bitch,' barked Parnell. 'Vandalising wellheads, torching gen sets, siphoning oil from gathering lines.' Parnell frowned, stared into Clay's eyes. 'He's costing us a lot of money.'

'And people have been hurt,' said Karila.

Parnell closed his eyes a moment, caught his breath, looked at Karila. 'Get that lunatic Todorov in here,' he said. 'He needs to hear this. Get the Army on to this prick Mohammedan. Fry his Koran for breakfast.'

Karila spoke into the intercom and then looked up at Clay. 'Well, where was he?'

Clay stood, faced Parnell. Clearly he wasn't the only person in the room with mental-health problems. 'Don't you want to know what he had to say?'

Parnell looked up at him through narrowed eyes, if they could get any narrower. 'Answer him, Straker. Where was the fucker?'

A flood tide of pain was inching its way from the back of his head towards his eyes. He blinked, tried to focus on the map spread across Karila's desk. 'About two hours out of Idim,' he said. If he had a satellite image he could probably pinpoint the hidden oasis to within less than a hundred metres.

A man walked into the room. He was short and powerfully built, his neck a tangle of sinew that spread like rootwork down into a broad substrate of muscle rippling beneath a tight black T-shirt. A shoulder holster was strapped across his chest. Clay had seen him around the office a couple of times, once back before Christmas on his first stint in the country.

'This is Mister Todorov, our head of security,' said Karila.

'People calling me Zdravko,' he replied in a heavy Slavic accent. He had strong, even white teeth, pale eyes, fair brush-cut hair, and what looked like a still-healing scar showing just above the neckline of his T-shirt.

'Mister Straker has some information that may be of interest,' said Karila. 'About Al Shams.'

Zdravko arched his eyebrows, creasing deep furrows in his forehead. He closed the door and stood with feet planted shoulderwidth apart, arms folded across his chest, one hand on the butt of the automatic pistol at his ribs.

Clay fixed his gaze on Parnell. 'He said to tell you that you are a blasphemer.'

Parnell glanced at Karila, smirked.

'You are stealing from them, and poisoning them. They want their fair share, or they will make trouble. That's what he said.'

'Where you see him?' said Zdravko.

'Up on the *jol*.'

'Speak English for fuck's sake, Straker,' said Parnell.

Clay held a breath, let it go, the pain worse now. 'On the plateau.'

Zdravko's face opened up in a smile as expansive as his biceps. 'Plateau is big like my girlfriend's back end, Straker. Al Shams just one small asshole.'

Parnell smirked.

Clay turned to face Karila. 'They stopped us near the Kamar-I well, commandeered the vehicle. We drove for an hour, maybe more. It's hard to tell.'

'Where did they take you?' barked Parnell. 'Which direction?' He looked up at the security man and grinned. 'We've got the bastard, goddammit.'

Clay took a deep breath, remembering that piercing black eye, the intelligence cutting through the veil of fervour. He had a decision to make. 'Problem is,' he said, 'I'm not sure.'

The room fell quiet. The call to prayer rose in the distance and echoed across the city, drifting in on the breeze.

Parnell stood and slammed the window shut, muffling the muezzin's cries. 'Whaddaya mean, not sure?'

Clay swallowed. 'They blindfolded me.'

The room went quiet. Karila, Parnell and Zdravko stared at him. 'What did you say?' hissed Parnell.

Clay looked down at his hands. 'I didn't see a thing. I was blindfolded the whole time.'

Parnell stared at him for a moment and then pushed past towards the door. 'Cocksucker,' he muttered.

'This man Islamic terrorist.' Zdravko's smile was gone.

'Al Qaeda,' said Parnell.

Clay's stomach felt as if he had just jumped out into the void. Parnell nodded.

'The bastard uses religion to camouflage his greed. Same fucking hypocrites tried to blow up the World Trade Center last year.'

'We're not certain of that, Vance,' said Karila meekly.

Parnell turned and glared at his lieutenant, eyes bulging, cheeks reddening. 'The authorities have confirmed it,' he spat. 'This is the prick who blew Thierry Champard to pieces, goddammit.' Parnell took a couple of steps backwards as if suddenly deflated. He reached back for the arm of the chair, and sank into the worn leather. He stared at the floor for a long time. Then he crossed himself, pinned the points of his elbows onto his knees and cradled his head in his hands. 'Hardest thing I had to do ever, call Thierry's wife and tell her he was dead,' he said without looking up.

Karila looked down at his keyboard, tapped desultorily. Zdravko smirked, hid it with a cough.

'Why did he kill Champard?' asked Clay.

Parnell jerked his head up from his hands. His eyes looked like they were about to burst from their sockets. 'What kind of a bullshit question is that?'

'Why Thierry? Why there, in the middle of Aden?'

'How the hell should I know, Straker? Maybe you should have asked him yourself. You're the one who's been having tea with him.'

'Soft target,' said Zdravko. 'In Aden no protection.'

'What the hell is wrong with you, Straker?' said Parnell. 'We've got a chance to nail this guy. Whose side are you on, for Chrissakes?'

'I'm on Thierry's side.'

Zdravko glanced at Parnell, back at Clay. He spat on the floor. 'You lucky, Straker,' he said. 'Very lucky. Could have been you, very easy.'

Clay said nothing.

Parnell coughed, took a shallow breath, looked at Clay. 'What about your driver? Did he get a glimpse?'

'Abdulkader,' said Clay. 'His name is Abdulkader.'

'Did your driver see anything?'

'I don't think so. Maybe.'

'Well, get him in here so we can talk to him.'

Clay shuffled his feet. 'Can't do that,' he said.

'The hell you can't,' said Parnell, face reddening. 'Get him in here, most pronto.'

'I'm sure he'd be happy to,' said Clay, boring a hole through the American's forehead. 'But he's still there. They let me go, kept him.'

Parnell took a sharp breath.

Zdravko stretched an asylum grin. 'This good. Very good.'

Karila stood and looked at the map spread across his desk. 'Think about it, Vance. A hostage. This is a serious escalation, kidnapping Petro-Tex staff. We can push the government to act.' He smiled at his boss and jabbed the map with his index finger. 'Here,' he said. 'Kamar-1. It's a start.'

'Get the Army on it,' said Parnell, turning to Zdravko. 'Tell 'em everything we know. They want this fucker as much as we do.'

Clay's stomach lurched, sank.

'More,' said Zdravko. 'Much more.'

'What about Abdulkader?' said Clay. 'We need to get him back.'

Parnell twisted partially in his chair to face Karila. 'What's our policy on local casual labour, Nils?'

'Cash only. No contract. No obligation.'

Parnell crossed his arms across his chest and glared at Clay.

'I have an obligation,' said Clay, struggling to contain his voice.

Karila glanced over at Parnell. 'The car wreck in Lawdar, last month. Clay's driver pulled him clear.'

Parnell lowered his voice: 'This has nothing to do with what happened month last.'

'So you're just going to leave him there?' said Clay.

'No, we ain't,' said Parnell. 'We're going to get the Army and the PSO to go and take this fucker out, like I already said. Your driver can fend for himself, Straker. He's one of *them*, after all.'

'Then I'm going back out there to get him myself.'

Parnell jerked to his feet, sucked in his breath with a rasp. He looked like he was going to go into cardiac arrest.

'You stay put, Straker, goddammit.'

'Please, Straker,' said Karila. 'Go and see the doctor. He's in the building now.'

'Yeah,' smirked Parnell, 'go and get your head examined, Straker.' He grinned at Karila.

'Then I want you back here in an hour,' said Karila. 'We have an important visitor.'

'And don't leave Aden, Straker,' said Parnell, lumbering towards the door. 'The PSO is gonna want to talk to you.' He stopped short of the doorway, turned to face Zdravko and jabbed his index finger into Zdravko's chest. 'And you, Todorov, you make damn sure he talks to them.'

∧

Bulgarian Gangbang

An hour later, Clay stood in the office courtyard with the other employees, about forty in all, under a sky writ in drought. They had already been waiting half an hour and people were getting restless, shuffling about, shielding their eyes against the low-angled sun, chatting in half a dozen languages. Parnell had arranged the group with expats at the front – Parnell, Karila, Clay and a few of the engineers – the overseas nationals, Egyptians mostly, behind, and the Yemenis at the back near the compound's west wall: teaboys, cleaners, drivers, guards – all men. Now he paced nervously, wiping sweat from his forehead and neck with a greying handkerchief, checking his watch. Zdravko was standing at the main gate speaking into a radio handset. He clipped the handset to his belt, looked up at Parnell and nodded, barked a command at one of the Yemeni guards.

'Ready everyone,' shouted Parnell, clapping his hands twice, taking his place beside Karila and Clay. 'He's here.'

The steel gates rolled open. A black Mercedes sedan with tinted glass pulled to a stop in the courtyard. The gates closed with a clang. An expectant hush fell over the group.

Parnell pushed his hair back across his head. 'Let me do the talking, Nils. And keep your mouth shut, Straker.'

Clay speared out a ragged salute.

Parnell's jaw twitched.

A tall man in a perfectly tailored cappuccino wool suit and open-collared white shirt emerged from the Mercedes, looked briefly around the compound, nodded to Zdravko, and strode toward the waiting crowd. Clay recognised him from the photos in the newspapers. Rex Medved, President and major shareholder of Petro-Tex, made directly for Parnell, hugged him as if he were his best friend, and pumped his hand.

'Wonderful to be here,' said Medved, flashing an American dental-work smile. He was very good-looking, in a magazine kind of way: square-jawed, mid-forties, Clay guessed, salon-perfect skin, Caribbean tan. A diamond solitaire stud winked in his left earlobe.

'Thanks for coming,' said Parnell, a smile plastered over his face.

'On our way to Zimbabwe for a meeting,' said Medved, waving his hand as if to say it was nothing. 'Thought we would divert and see how you lot were doing.' His accent was upper-crust English, public-school intonation laced with arrogance. 'What's the point in having a jet if one can't take a little side trip now and again, eh?' He flashed teeth. 'I only have an hour.'

Parnell introduced Karila, then Clay.

Medved shook Clay's hand. They stood eye to eye, the same six foot three. 'Ah yes, Claymore Straker. I understand you have done good work for us.' Medved looked across at Karila. 'I want to do the right thing here in Yemen, Straker, look after the people and the environment. Keep it up.'

'Do the right thing. Look after the people. You can count on us,' said Clay. It was almost like being back in the Battalion. Parnell glared at him over Medved's shoulder. Clay shot back a plastic smile and, still clasping Medved's hand, leaned forward and spoke into his ear.

'My driver, one of your employees, has been taken hostage, Mister Medved, by locals who say we are poisoning their kids. We need to get him back, and we need to look into their grievance.'

Medved released Clay's hand, took a step back, stared him in the eyes. For a moment it looked as if he was going to say something. Then he looked away, smoothed his lapels, faced the crowd, and opened his arms wide. Behind him, Zdravko stood impassive, eyes shielded by reflective Raybans, watching, coiled.

'Thank you so much, Mister Parnell, everyone, for such a warm welcome, and for your great efforts over the past year.' Medved lowered his arms, smiled and nodded at Karila. 'Our operations are bringing badly needed revenue, jobs and prosperity to Yemen. We are doing good things here. The next few months will be exciting for all of us, and I need not remind any of you of how important our new expansion plans are. Get it done, and we will all share in the benefits.'

The crowd broke into applause. Medved took a step forward, bowed his head quickly, and stood clapping with the staff. Then he raised his hands. 'Thank you all. Now, please return to your good work.'

The crowd began to disperse.

Medved moved forward, grabbed Parnell's upper arm. His smile was gone. 'And now, gentlemen, if I could have a word with the General Manager, please, alone.' The two men disappeared through the front entrance, a schoolmaster hurrying a naughty pupil to the detention room.

Karila tapped Clay on the shoulder. 'What on earth were you doing, Straker? You were supposed to keep quiet. What did you say to him?'

'I told him I wasn't getting paid.'

Karila frowned. 'I'm starting not to like you very much, Straker,' he said, and strode away after his bosses.

❨

Clay returned to the company guesthouse late, fresh stitches throbbing in his scalp, his already shortened attention span fractioned by thoughts of Abdulkader. He showered, ate, and went down to the common lounge.

An F14 Tomcat shot across the television screen, twisting in a dogfight. Missiles fired, jerking heat-seekers trailing white spume. Clay sank into the couch as an enemy plane disintegrated in an orange ball of fire.

'*Top Gun*,' said an American contractor Clay had seen around in the guesthouse from time to time: Jim, one of the facility engineers. Tall man, lanky, strong Southern accent, a lost-and-found Florida Gators baseball cap permanently grafted to his head, tobacco chewer, pretty much kept to himself.

Clay nodded to him and put his feet up on the coffee table. Tom Cruise as a fighter pilot. Questionable. Something to help kill the hours, dull the frustration of having to stay put in Aden, deaden the guilt he was feeling. The man who had pulled him unconscious and bleeding from the burning car wreck on the road down from Lawdar only six weeks ago was a prisoner of terrorists, and now he had triggered the one thing Al Shams had warned him against: bringing in the Army. Perhaps Medved would push Parnell to take action. If it was really about money, as Clay was beginning to suspect, they could ransom Abdulkader back.

A third enemy aircraft plummeted ground-ward in flames.

Clay tore a tin of Budweiser from the plastic noose and handed it to the American.

'Thanks,' said Jim.

Clay pulled the tab on a beer and took a long draught. 'You heading up to the CPF soon?'

'Tomorrow.'

'What's with the lockdown out there?'

'They're worried about terrorists.'

'You mean the locals.'

'I guess.' Jim took another gulp of beer.

Clay put down his beer and leaned forward, forearms across his knees. 'Did you know Thierry Champard?'

Jim turned away from the screen and fixed his gaze on Clay. 'Yeah, I knew him. He was my back-to-back.'

'What was he like?'

'French.'

'I heard.'

'Great guy. The best.'

Clay looked over his shoulder. There was no one else in the room, the corridor was quiet. 'Do you know why Al Qaeda would have wanted him dead?'

'What's it to you?'

'The same guys have my driver, Abdulkader.'

Jim drained his beer, set the tin on the floor, tugged at the worn peak of his cap. 'He'd been in country for a while before I started here. Who knows what people get up to?'

'He never said anything to you?'

'Nope.'

'Nothing to suggest conflict with the locals?'

'Nothing.'

'A woman perhaps?'

'Ever meet his wife?'

Clay recalled the pang that had lodged in his throat that day on the way to the airport, looking at the photos of Champard's family. A family of his own. Funny how something you'd always taken for granted would just happen, could turn to an irrelevancy, an *impossibility*, so quickly. Without ever really thinking about it. Just there one day, and not there after. There had been a girl, once. They'd dated in high school but lost touch when he went into the Army. He'd come back on leave, a few months into his second tour, and she'd been waiting for him in the crowd at the airport. She'd been wearing a sexy, strapless, cotton summer dress and he remembered how her skin had felt when he'd held her, standing there in the arrivals hall with people streaming past them and the smell of shampoo in her hair and the way she was everything that the war wasn't, clean and soft and safe. He remembered the surprise at seeing her there, the way she'd thrown her arms around him, the way she'd run her fingers through his freshly cut hair. She'd tracked him down through his uncle, she'd said through the tears, after hearing about his parents' death. The next day he'd borrowed a mate's bakkie and they'd driven south to the ocean and along the coast to Port Shepstone, and taken a hotel room on the beach. She'd been warm and sympathetic and they'd made love as if it were their last days on Earth. He thought she might ask him about the war but she hadn't, and he'd realised he had no way of telling her anyway. A day later he asked her to marry him and she said yes. He was twenty and she was nineteen. They picked out a ring for her – a tiny flawed diamond set in fourteen-carat gold, all he could afford – in a shop in Durban the day he went back to the war. He'd written her for almost a year, whenever he could, until he was wounded again. She'd come to see him in the military hospital in Johannesburg, but by then he was someone else. He'd been distant and hurtful, his anger spilling out uncontrollably. She'd left the ring in an envelope with one of the nurses.

'Money trouble?' asked Clay.

'I said no, Straker. Drop it, OK?'

Clay swirled the beer in his tin and eased back into the couch. 'Dropped.'

Zdravko Todorov appeared at the common room doorway, a black duffel bag slung over his shoulder. He smiled, sat on the couch next to Clay, stared at the TV. Tomcat fighters catapulted from a carrier deck, afterburners roaring. Clay ignored him.

After a while Zdravko leaned over from the other end of the couch and said to Clay: 'American shit weapons.' He pronounced it *sheet*, weapons with a *v*.

'I heard that, asshole,' said Jim from the lounge chair.

'I am Zdravko,' said the man, winking at Clay, 'not asshole.' *Assxole*.

'With a name like that, you should be called asshole.'

'Does not change anything, my American friend. American weapons shit.' Zdravko laughed as if this was the funniest thing he had ever heard and clapped Clay on the back. 'Too complicated, breaking down, needs too much training to use,' he said to Clay behind a raised hand, sharing a secret. 'Russian weapons good. Bulgarian weapons good.' Zdravko palmed a small black pistol, examined it in an open palm. 'Makarov,' he said. 'Shoots good.'

'You and your fuckin' weapons.' Jim stood up and stormed out, cursing under his breath.

Zdravko pocketed the pistol and smiled at Clay. He stood and walked to the TV and ejected the DVD. 'Now we watch some real action,' he said, inserting another disc. He smiled, sat down on the couch, and banged a bottle of vodka on the table. Smirnoff Export overproof.

'My new friend,' said Zdravko. 'Drink with me.' The new DVD loaded, Zdravko hit play, thrust out his hand. Clay took it. Zdravko's handshake was a vice. Hours of gym time. Zdravko unscrewed the cap, held it on end between index finger and thumb as if inspecting for defects, took aim and flicked it out of the window. 'With friends, no need for this,' he said, landing a frying-pan hand on Clay's shoulder.

Clay stared at Zdravko's hand, into his eyes. 'Checking up on me?' he said.

'You hear Parnell. Go to PSO, everything OK.' Zdravko took a swig from the bottle, passed it to Clay.

Clay swallowed a mouthful of vodka, then another, passed the bottle back, and stared at the TV screen. Zdravko's movie had started out conventionally, pretty young things in risqué PVC, pink and hairless, sucking as if their lives depended on it. Now it was becoming noticeably harder. A lithesome brunette with silicone tits and perfect skin was being fucked by three men. When her mouth wasn't full, she cried out in dubbed English. The men were built like Zdravko, heavily muscled, with impossibly large penises and no pubic hair. Clay wished Zdravko would turn the sound down.

Zdravko beamed and passed the bottle, half-empty now. 'You like? Look, dual completion,' he laughed, an old oilfield joke. 'Good Bulgarian girls. You come with me to Bulgaria, I introduce you to girls like this, yes? Good girls. Not American pussy-whippers.'

It had been a long time since he had been with a woman, but the skin-mag marionettes on the screen weren't doing anything for him. 'I'll look you up next time I'm in Sofia,' he said, raising the bottle to his lips.

'This place is shit hole, yes? No women, no nothing. Just desert.' Zdravko refilled his glass. 'Only good thing is shooting. Everyone here is shooting.' He reached to the floor and unzipped a small duffel bag at his feet. 'This good weapon,' he said, handing Clay a short-barrelled sub-machine gun with a huge curved banana-clip.

Clay put the bottle on the table, hefted the weapon in his hands. It was surprisingly light, compact. 'AK74U,' said Clay.

Zdravko raised his eyebrows. 'You know.'

'I've ...' Clay stopped, took a deep breath. 'I've been on the receiving end.'

Another stare, longer this time. 'We call her *Ksyuka*, Russian girl name. Small – 5.45 millimetre. She hot. Shoots hot.' Zdravko looked over his shoulder and took back the weapon.

Weapons were ubiquitous in Yemen, but it was the first time he had seen a Petro-Tex contractor carrying anything quite so lethal here in Aden. Clay swallowed another mouthful of vodka, feeling it now, that familiar distance, like low cloud settling.

'Close range, cuts man in two pieces.' Zdravko drew his hand across his belly, left to right. 'Even idiot Parnell can do.'

Clay said nothing, stared at the screen, the girl's face dripping.

Zdravko tipped the bottle to his mouth, 'Tonight I go shooting. Come.'

'Sorry,' Clay said, his insides lurching. 'I have work tomorrow.'

'Tomorrow Friday, Straker. Day off.'

'Maybe next time.'

Zdravko shrugged as if to say that it was his loss. 'Not good, fucking terrorist assholes taking your driver.'

'Not good at all.' Terrorists. That's what they had called SWAPO, too, back then: *fokken terrs*.

'You lucky,' said Zdravko, pointing the *Ksyuka* at his own chest, then Clay's. 'I find them.'

Clay pushed the barrel away. He was pretty sure he wanted this guy nowhere near Abdulkader.

'What you do here, my friend?' said Zdravko.

'I spend most of my time trying to get paid.'

Zdravko laughed. It was a big laugh, big like him. 'Getting money from Petro-Tex is like getting blow job from Yemeni woman.' He roared again, eyes dancing, slugged more vodka and drew the back of his hand across his mouth. He tapped the *Ksyuka*'s magazine. It sounded full. 'Don't worry, my friend. We find assholes who take your driver. I cut them in two.' Zdravko pushed the bottle into Clay's hands.

Clay tightened his jaw, took a gulp, another. 'How much time have you spent in Yemen?' Not a lot, he guessed.

'Too much.' Zdravko slid his business card across the table: Z. Todorov, BRS Supply, Sofia.

Clay flipped his own card onto the table. Capricorn Consulting, an impressive name for a struggling one-man enterprise. He had set up in Cyprus almost three years ago, as much for the favourable tax regime as for the obscurity, a place to disappear to for a while. But clients had been hard to come by, rates low, his expenses far too high. He'd landed a few small jobs in Egypt and Jordan, but Petro-Tex had been his first big break, on paper at least.

Clay twisted Zdravko's card in his fingers, feeling the alcohol swim in his head. 'What kind of supply?' he slurred.

Zdravko grinned and poured out the last of the vodka. 'Usual stuff. Good business here in Yemen. Very, very good. This trip, I make enough money, I never work again. Go home, get girlfriend like that. Two.' He pointed at the pulsing screen.

Clay raised his eyes, finished the vodka. 'Clearly I'm in the wrong line of work.'

The Bulgarian smiled. 'You drink good, Aussie.'

If Zdravko wanted to think he was an Aussie, that was fine with him. For all he knew this guy could have been on the other side. There had been enough Cubans and Russians crawling around Angola in '79 and '80. Why not Bulgarians, too? He looked the right age – swallowed into the vortex with so many others, young, with ideals perhaps, dreams, thrown into the maelstrom and then excreted like so much waste, dead and maimed together in one stinking turd. He had that look: the ranging stare, the furtive flicking hyper-awareness, the fuck-you sneer.

'Not like these American pussies,' said Zdravko.

'With their crap weapons,' said Clay.

Zdravko boomed out a laugh, lifted the bottle, guzzled.

Clay looked at his watch. It was gone midnight and the movie was finished. He stood to leave, unsteady.

Zdravko grabbed his arm and pulled him back. 'You fight, Aussie? You like to fight?'

Clay laughed, but a spike of adrenaline pierced the vodka haze. His fingertips tingled with the surge. His mind cleared. He squared up to the Bulgarian. 'Depends.'

Zdravko smiled, put down the vodka bottle, and flicked out a quick left jab. The strike was hard, but aimed low, just under Clay's collarbone. Clay caught it easily with his left forearm, down and across, sending Zdravko's fist glancing harmlessly away. He shifted back, ready to counterpunch, stared the Bulgarian in the eyes.

Zdravko laughed, opened his right hand and clapped Clay on the shoulder. Clay let it land.

'Good,' said Zdravko.

'No,' said Clay. 'Not very good.'

'Shotokan?'

Johannesburg streets, he thought. Parachute Regiment training school, Bloemfontein. South African border war. But what he said was: 'Renbukai. *Ikkyu*. Brown belt.'

Zdravko laughed. 'Good enough.' He reached into his bag, produced another bottle, slammed it down on the table. 'Now, we start real drinking.'

Twisting by the Pool

He opened the fridge, pulled out a near-empty bottle of Smirnoff and a chilled glass tumbler and clunked them down on the papers scattered across his desk. His ears were still ringing from the shooting and the back of his skull felt like it was going to peel open and spill out his brains. Outside the second-floor room, the bank of air conditioners groaned at full power. Friday morning, and the streets were deserted, the faithful thronging the mosques and then off to chew the afternoon away. A holy day, a day of rest. He rolled the cold bottle over his forehead, poured a full glass and downed it in one go. The cold liquid burned his throat. He walked to the window and wound down the shutters against the sun, catching a glimpse of his face in the glass, his father's nose, his mother's eyes and teeth.

He had stayed for the second bottle. Halfway through, Zdravko had led him stumbling downstairs to his car, a big new black Land Rover, and driven him, lights spinning, to the outskirts of the city, talking non-stop, laughing that big laugh, until they reached an open piece of ground abutting the mountains. Zdravko had opened the back, lifted a panel, pulled out a *Ksyuka* and a couple of bandoliers of magazines and handed them to Clay. There must have been at least a dozen other weapons stashed in the hidden compartment, familiar-looking AK47s, a Russian-made Dragunov sniper rifle with an attached bipod and scope, at least two Uzis. Zdravko hauled out a muslin sack and threw it over his shoulder, grabbed two steel stakes and a sledgehammer, slammed the trunk closed. 'Could only get goat,' he muttered. 'We pretend is small Yemeni fucker, yes?' In a few minutes he had pounded the stakes into the ground about twenty metres from the car and trussed up the goat's carcass so it hung splayed and racked, white in the Mercedes' headlights. Then he stepped back and handed Clay the bottle.

'Watch this, Aussie.' Zdravko stood, checked the *Ksyuka*'s magazine, chambered a round, and banged off the whole mag in one go. The almost bisected halves of the carcass hung ragged from the ropes. Zdravko boomed and slapped Clay on the back. He was jumping up and down like a kid at Christmas, yelling, 'You see that Aussie? You see that? Like I say, yes? So fucking hot. You see that?' He changed mags and then set about ripping off a couple hundred rounds, emptying clip after clip, spraying wildly, the tracers ricocheting like fireworks in the night. Then it was Clay's turn. He picked a target, a cluster of stones at the limit of the Merc's lights and squeezed off a short controlled burst, then another, feeling the hideous, wonderful power of the thing. By this time Zdravko was weaving dangerously, the empty vodka bottle still hanging from his hand, talking wildly in Bulgarian, waving at him, yelling, 'Shoot, motherfucker, shoot', exploding in laughter each time Clay let off a burst. It was gone four in the morning when they stumbled back to the guesthouse.

It had been two days since he'd left Abdulkader in the desert. He tried to focus on the computer screen, on the work, this report that he would soon deliver to the hapless Yemeni regulators, another box to be ticked in the meaningless dance that passed for an environmental approvals process. His fingers moved over the keyboard. 'State of the art environmental controls applied to all stages of the production cycle.' The pixels glowed in the shuttered gloom. The cursor blinked away the minutes at the full stop.

He poured another vodka and picked up the letter from Eben's parents. The usual stuff: widespread damage, coma. Worse now, it sounded, than when he had last seen him, lying in bed, all the muscle gone, pale skin stretched over cheekbones, the eyes staring out at him, damning him. He had stayed half an hour, sitting next to his friend's bed under fluorescent light, staring at the puke-green linoleum floor tiles, watching the occasional passing of an orderly under the drawn dividing curtain, the flowers he had bought from the corner vendor on the street outside the hospital hanging in his hands, wondering why he had even bothered coming. He had taken a last look, pushed himself to his feet, crammed the flowers into the bin by the door, and walked out. That was twelve years ago.

Please, they wrote, could he send more money. They had moved Eben from the military hospital four years ago, horrified at the level of care, at the way everyone just wanted to forget. They found him a place in a private clinic they couldn't afford. Twelve years now he'd been like that. It didn't seem possible. Some days Clay wished they would just pull the plug. He had actually written them a letter a couple of months ago pleading with them to do just that, but had binned it. He should never have brought him out. He should have let him die there, staring up into the blue Ovamboland sky. If he had been stronger, a better friend, he would have.

Clay pushed back his chair and picked up the phone. 'Nils, it's Clay Straker.' He knew Karila would be there, even on a Friday. 'I left that tender on your desk yesterday. Did you get a chance to look at it?'

Clay looked down at his copy of the estimate. The margins were scribbled with red, numbers crossed out and recalculated two, three times. He had even lowered his rate slightly over the current phase.

The line was open, static only.

'Nils? Are you there?'

'That will not be acceptable, I am afraid,' came the voice on the line. 'We would like to extend your contract, Straker – the quality of your work has been good – but we have a lower bidder. I am sure you can understand our position.'

'Look, I can come down to seventy-five thousand. I can't go any lower, considering all that needs to be done.'

'Is that the best price you can give us, Straker?'

He was pretty sure that none of his competitors, the larger consulting firms, could go that low. He clenched his jaw. 'Bargain of the year, Nils.'

'And you guarantee we'll get our approval from the agency?'

'You'll have your permit. Just like last time.'

'Please send me a letter confirming your new offer, and we'll get back to you with our decision.'

'You'll have it today,' he said.

'There is one more thing, Straker,' came Karila's voice. 'There has been another attack. Two gathering stations were hit last night, generators destroyed, production off-line for twenty-four hours.'

'Jesus. Was anyone hurt?'

'Only a couple of Yemeni labourers. Cuts and bruises. They are in hospital now. It could have been much worse.'

'You really think this guy is Al Qaeda?'

'It is not my concern, Mister Straker. Vance Parnell is dealing with the government on this matter. Speaking of which, the PSO called this morning.'

Clay waited, let the line burn.

'They are expecting you this afternoon. They want to "confirm some details", as they put it.'

Clay's stomach contracted. Why hadn't Al Shams protected his location? His flunkeys, the two gunmen who had stopped them by the side of the road, had screwed up. It was pretty clear. Al Shams had had two choices that day – let him go, or kill him.

'I don't have time to loiter around in Aden all day, Nils. Not if you want those permits quickly.' He needed to get back out there, find Al Shams, and get Abdulkader back.

The line was quiet as Karila mulled it over.

'Today, Straker. PSO. Be at the Interior Ministry building in town, near the docks, at two o'clock, without fail. You can leave for the field tomorrow. Then get out there and get these people under control, Straker. Do what you have to do.'

'Jesus,' he breathed, palm clasped over the handset's pickup. 'OK, Nils. OK. By the way, still no cheque.' He waited for a reply, but the line had gone dead. He put the phone back in its cradle, and poured himself another vodka.

Two hours later he pulled into the palm-lined parking lot of the Mövenpick, the only half-decent modern hotel in Southern Arabia. He locked Abdulkader's Land Cruiser and walked across sun-softened tarmac to the front entrance, a noon buzz on. The pool was small, but it was filled with water, clean, and surrounded by towering eucalypts – imports, like him.

He spread his towel on one of a dozen or so vacant reclining chairs, pulled off his T-shirt, and ordered a large vodka and soda on the rocks from a uniformed attendant. A couple of hairy, burly, tattooed oilies were the only other poolside patrons. They wallowed on sunbeds in shorts and baseball caps, drinking imported beer.

The sun was hot. He laid back, closed his eyes, felt the sweat bead in his pores, track across his skin. He had done what Al Shams had asked. And in a few hours he had to face the PSO, the Political Security Organisation, Saleh's shadowy personal paramilitary security apparatus, partial, from what he had heard, to extrajudicial detention, harassment of political opponents, infiltration, beatings and torture. Surely Al Shams would have known that his message would have triggered Army and PSO interest. He was not stupid. Just the way he spoke suggested education and intelligence. And those flashes of violence, like a veil drawing back. Jesus Christ.

His drink came. He cracked open his book and tried to read. He ordered another drink. The two oilies finished beers and had just called for more when they went quiet and turned their heads in unison towards the patio entrance.

The bikini she was wearing would have turned heads on Bondi beach, but here, it was positively, wonderfully scandalous. She was petite, sculpted, a gymnast, thought Clay, or a runner, but for the considerable swell of chest that the string top struggled to contain as she walked. It was the woman in the Land Rover on the road to Al Urush.

The oilies were sitting up now and they called out to her to join them, beaming from behind reflective Oakleys. She smiled and moved to the opposite side of the pool, his side, dropping her towel, bag, and a couple of newspapers onto the chair next to his. He looked up at her, but she turned away, twitched to the pool's edge and dove in. The oilies glared at him. He shrugged his shoulders, grinned, raised his glass to them and went back to his novel: at night, when the other nurses were asleep, Catherine came to the wounded soldier and made love to him, straddling his shrapnelled legs. It was summer, the war raged, millions were dead, and the world was changing forever around them. They were in love.

'I have never believed he was a misogynist.'

Clay looked up from the pages. She was perched at the edge of the pool, looking up at him, elbows hooked on the tiled rim. Water dripped from her dark shoulder-length hair onto her bunched shoulders and beaded on her cheeks and nose.

He flicked his wrist, looked at the book's cover. *A Farewell to Arms*, an old Scribner's edition, one of his father's, one of the few of his things he'd kept. 'Hello,' he said. 'Again.'

She smiled. 'It's only people who have never read him who say that. They get it in their criticism courses and treat it as fact. Hemingway loved women. Achingly. He was awed by them, but he didn't hate them. He married four times, after all.' The accent was European, French, Italian perhaps.

'I can relate.' He tried a smile, was pretty sure it came out stupid-looking.

'Marriages?'

'Awe.'

She smiled, pulled herself up and sat side-saddle at the pool's edge, one knee up, foot on the tile, the other leg dangling in the water. It was quite a pretty pose.

'Fancy a drink?' he managed.

'A fresh lime, please.' She stood and walked to her sunbed, adjusted the parasol. The oilies gaped. She sat down and ran her hands through her hair. As she did, her bag fell to the tile between them. A few things spilled out: a book, Rimbaud, a hairbrush, a French driver's licence. Clay reached to help but she scooped everything up before he got a chance.

She smiled at him. 'My name is Rania.'

'Clay.'

'*Enchantée*.' They shook hands. She wore no rings.

'You work for Petro-Tex,' she said. It was a statement.

'Around here that's a pretty good guess.'

'I suppose it is.' She smiled, ran her hand through her hair.

'And I suppose you aren't a petroleum engineer's bored expatriate wife.'

She laughed and opened up one of her papers, the *International Herald Tribune*. 'Here,' she said, handing him the paper. She pointed to a short piece on page five: 'Islamic Terrorism on Rise in Yemen'. 'That's me.'

He scanned the article. Radical Islamist militants, planned attacks on American military personnel, the failed bombing at this very hotel two years ago, an emerging and as yet little-known group called Ansar Al-Sharia, an Al Qaeda off-shoot with links to Saudi Arabia and Afghanistan. Her name was Rania LaTour, Agence France Presse. He couldn't help being impressed. He handed back the paper and took a long drink.

'I am doing a story on unrest in the South, the emergence of a new rebellion.' Her voice was oddly childlike, a boy's.

'War?'

'It is a distinct possibility.' She sipped her drink. 'Have you not heard? Jets from the South knocked out Sana'a's two power stations yesterday. It is a serious escalation.'

'Jesus, no. I've been in the field.'

'Yes, I saw you.' She smiled.

'And you didn't even wave,' he said, signalling the waiter for another round. He remembered seeing other articles by this same Rania LaTour, now that he thought about it. She seemed very young to be doing this job in such a harshly male part of the world. She was very pretty.

'It's this character Al Shams I'm interested in,' she continued without a pause. 'I understand you know him.'

He sat back, suddenly feeling exposed. He could see how she had become a reporter. 'You tell me.' He was completely sober.

'You met him two days ago in the Empty Quarter,' she said, all business.

Clay took a deep breath, alarms going. He looked at his watch, stood and pulled on his T-shirt. He slid his sunnies into position and dropped a ten-thousand-rial note onto the table. 'I'm not allowed to talk to the press. Strict company policy. But I guess you know that already.'

She frowned. Even that was pretty.

'So,' he paused, thought about it, 'how about dinner tonight?'

The frown vanished. Her eyes sparkled yes.

'*Befok*,' he said without thinking.

'Pardon?'

'Sorry. Afrikaans. It means good. Really, really good.'

She beamed. 'I'm staying here at the hotel.'

A shiver spliced his spine. 'I have an appointment to get to now. How about I pick you up at five?'

She smiled yes.

He turned to go, smirked at the oilies. The fat one gave him the finger. He waved to them, grinned, took a couple of steps, stopped, turned around. 'Oh, and Rania.'

She looked up.

'Wear walking shoes.'

That Stuff Will Kill You

An hour later he walked into the Interior Ministry building and identified himself. The morning vodka was wearing off and he felt like *kak*. His head ached. He was pretty sure that Al Shams' men had fractured his skull. Sleep had become increasingly rare. The nightmares were back, worse than ever, a nightly forced march across the same bombed-out landscape that left him drained, exhausted. No amount of booze seemed to dull them. He had been too worried about Abdulkader and the PSO, too nervous about meeting Rania, to eat. Seeing Zdravko tailing him in his big black Land Rover on the way here hadn't helped.

He was shown to an airless, windowless concrete room, ushered inside, bid to sit in a chair facing a simple wooden table. The heavy steel door clanged shut behind him. He was alone. He sat, waited.

Much later, the door opened and two men entered. One walked past him and sat in the empty chair facing him across the table. He was short, with a light wiry build. The other man stood by the door and lit up a cigarette. Its acrid pall filled the room.

The man opposite looked a lot like Heinrich Himmler. Maybe it was just the little round glasses and rodent-like features, or the way he hunched over the table, scribbling notes in his dossier as if he had modelled himself after the man in the war documentaries. They had kept him waiting for over an hour, and now Himmler sat there flicking through the pages of Clay's passport, studying each stamp and visa with exaggerated interest. The other man pulled the door closed and leaned against the wall, cigarette burning between thumb and forefinger. He was fairer skinned than Himmler, handsome almost, with a black moustache and thick bristles of greying hair. In jeans and a black leather jacket over a Yale T-shirt, he looked very un-Yemeni.

Finally Himmler looked up and blinked. 'Claymore Straker from Great Britain,' he said in a thick Arab accent, crushing his vowels.

Clay sat and said nothing.

'Why do you not answer?'

'It was not a question.'

The man's lips stretched over his teeth in what might have been a smile. He looked down at the passport again, and back up at Clay. 'Are you Claymore Straker, British subject?'

'My friends call me Clay.'

'Then I will call you Straker.'

'And I'll call you Heinrich,' said Clay.

'Pardon me?'

Clay held his hand out palm up, tried a grin. He was pretty sure it came out like the scowl it was.

'You were born in South Africa.'

'My father was British.'

'You are South African.'

'Was.' He hadn't been back since the war, since they stripped him of his passport, sent him into exile.

Himmler narrowed his eyes. 'You have seen Al Shams, in Hadramawt, two days ago.'

'No.'

Himmler placed the passport down on the desk and made a steeple with his fingers – or was it a minaret? 'We have been told that you have seen Al Shams.'

'You were told wrong.'

'We have interviewed your colleagues, Mister Straker.'

'Then you know what happened.' He was being a hard arse. It was a dangerous line, he knew. But everything about the place, the man facing him, the situation, the totalitarian attitude, rankled him. He breathed deep, tried to settle himself.

Himmler's mouth distorted and his eyes narrowed. 'This man is an enemy of the state, Mister Straker. Do you understand?'

'And how, exactly, am I supposed to know that?'

'I have just told you.'

'A trusted source.'

Himmler slammed his fist down onto Clay's passport. 'Enough, Straker. Stop this now. If you do not cooperate, the consequences will be severe.'

Clay leaned forward and gave Himmler his best fuck-you stare. 'Don't threaten me, *jou bliksem*. I have rights.'

Himmler gave him that same incipient, stillborn half-smile. He seemed genuinely amused. Obviously he had no knowledge of Afrikaans. Clay smiled back.

'Rights, Mister Straker? You with your Apartheid? A white South African speaking of rights?'

'Haven't you heard? It's over.' Growing up, he hadn't given it a thought. It was only after he'd been wounded, been shipped home, that he'd started to see, started to fight against it. And now everyone just wanted to forget the whole disgraceful mess.

Himmler fixed him with a flat gaze. Malice flowed from his eyes. 'This is a matter of national security, Mister Straker. You have no rights here.' Himmler placed a pair of needle nose pliers on the desk. 'Tell me what happened.'

Clay glanced down at the pliers. 'Planning some DIY?'

Himmler smiled and placed what looked like a small white pebble on the desk, spinning it with his thumb. Clay watched the pebble spin to a stop. It was jagged, with a long twinned end and a flat crown. A tooth.

The other man, the one by the door, lit the second cigarette in his chain, inhaled deeply, and exhaled slowly through his nostrils. His eyes were dark, alive. For a moment their eyes met. Clay looked away, took a deep breath and leaned back in his chair, beating back the urge to jump across the table and choke the bastard facing him. There was no point pushing any further. He recited the speech he had been practising over the last day: they were stopped by the side of the road, forced from the vehicle at gunpoint, blindfolded and driven away. He spoke briefly with a man who called himself Al Shams. The message was simple: give the people of Hadramawt a fair share of the oil wealth, or the trouble would intensify. He had remained blindfolded the whole time. That was all he could say. 'He didn't seem much like a jihadist to me.'

Himmler took off his spectacles and cleaned them with a tissue. 'Is that so, Mister Straker? And you have had experience of these people before?'

'He seemed pretty apolitical. Just concerned for his people.' It hadn't come out right.

'This man is a terrorist, a murderer.'

'You killed his father,' Clay blurted out, not thinking. The man near the door coughed, lit another cigarette with the dying tip of the last.

'So you sympathise with this man, do you?' Himmler scribbled furiously on his notepad.

'He had me at gunpoint. What do you think?'

Himmler sat stone-faced.

Clay pushed back his chair and stood gripping the edge of the desk. 'Now can I go?'

'Sit down, Mister Straker.'

For the next forty-five minutes, Himmler questioned Clay about every detail: the exact point at which they were stopped, descriptions of the two hijackers, estimated time and distance of travel (an hour, maybe two, no idea), elevation gains or losses, smells (desert, diesel), sounds (did you hear running water? no), Al Shams' exact words (war is coming).

'You seem not to remember well,' said Himmler.

'Look,' Clay said after a long pause. 'I had a gun to my head. I wasn't playing detective. I've told you all I know.'

Himmler closed his folder, took off his glasses and stood up. 'You may go, Mister Straker. But please remember that you are a guest here in Yemen.'

Clay stood. 'Never leaves my mind.'

Himmler frowned, stacked and levelled out his papers, tapping them on end. 'Be sure to contact us immediately, Mister Straker, should you see him or hear from him again.'

Clay tapped his front teeth with his index finger, winked at Himmler, turned away and walked to the door, his insides tumbling.

The other man, the smoker, rose and held open the door. He was tall for a Yemeni, almost as tall as Clay.

'And Mister Straker,' Himmler called. 'I am sure you already know. We will be watching you.'

As Clay walked past the other man at the doorway he said: 'You'd better lay off those smokes, *broer*. That stuff'll kill you.' From the corner of his eye he swore he saw the man crack a smile.

☾

Out in the street, Clay breathed deep, steadied himself, and looked back over his shoulder. How long would it be until Al Shams learned of his trip to the Interior Ministry building, of this little interview with PSO? He knew he had just pushed Abdulkader closer to the edge. He walked to the Land Cruiser, unlocked the door, and sat holding the key in the ignition, looking out over the harbour, replaying the interrogation in his head. He was being pulled in, he could feel it – a malicious gravity. He had promised himself long ago – no more. No more war, no more killing. This wasn't his fight. He'd already almost certainly blinded one man. It had already gone too far. The airport wasn't far away, twenty minutes. He had just enough cash left for a one-way ticket to Cairo. There were daily flights. In less than twelve hours he could be waving goodbye to the whole mess from the jet's window: goodbye Abdulkader, any possibility of getting to know Rania gone, a farewell to the forty-two grand they owed him. Safe. Clear.

He sat looking out over the murky green water of the harbour, once the busiest in the world after New York and London, now a forgotten backwater, foul and stinking. Heat rose from the pavement, pulsed from the tin roofs clustered around the wharf. Workers trudged past him on their way to the docks, Somalis with coffee-coloured skin and piled turbans, barefoot Sudanese in rags carrying plastic bags, rope-thin Filipinos shading themselves with rubbish-tip umbrellas. Had he really fallen so low? That he could contemplate abandoning a friend, running from a fight? He shivered, shocked, disgusted with himself. The doctor had told him that it would be like this. That it would take time, a long time probably. That he should understand that he might never feel right, like himself again, that in all probability he would simply have to learn to accept who he had become.

No.

He started the engine and jammed the Cruiser in gear. In a few minutes he was speeding along the Corniche towards the industrial district, the saltpans shimmering like a patchwork mirage across the bay, the refinery and the buildings of Little Aden bathed in an uncertain afternoon light. He needed answers.

The laboratory was housed in one of five identical Soviet-built barracks, part of a military base now converted into an industrial estate at the edge of town. He clambered up the crumbling concrete steps to the second-floor veranda. An afternoon sea breeze had come up; the palms lining the parade ground swayed like drunken soldiers, trunks groaning. The beach, brilliant white in the late afternoon sunshine, shimmered against the deep-blue, white-capped ocean and a pure sky. Perhaps the lab results would tell him something about what was going on in Al Urush.

Clay pushed open the door. The front office was cool and dark, the shutters pulled down against the mid-afternoon glare. A dark-skinned Yemeni slouched behind a steel desk. The man looked up at Clay through narrowed eyes.

'*Merhaba*,' said Clay, using the secular greeting more common in this part of the South. 'I'm here for results on a water sample.'

The clerk searched through a bound ledger, flipping pages with dark fingers.

'Petro-Tex,' said Clay, showing his contractor's badge. 'It was two days ago. One bottle, a water bottle. Rush. I brought it in myself.'

'Yes, sir. It is here.' The clerk put his finger to a line on the list, glanced towards the laboratory area and back down at the ledger. 'Sir, there is a problem with this sample.'

'What kind of problem?'

The clerk pointed to the far column. 'Here. Sample insufficient.'

'It was a full one-litre bottle. There should have been plenty.' The tests he had requested would normally require less than half that amount.

'I am sorry, sir. We do many samples for Petro-Tex. Very good business with Petro-Tex. Very sorry.'

'Is the technician here? The one who did the work?

'Yes, sir.'

'I would like to speak with him.'

The clerk disappeared through the double doors into the laboratory and reappeared a few minutes later with a short, balding, bespectacled man with a greying moustache and large bulging brown eyes. It looked as if he had a thyroid condition.

Clay asked the man about the sample, pointing it out in the ledger, describing the big, light-blue plastic drinking-water bottle. Normally he would have used the proper polyethylene, glass and Teflon sample phials that good Western labs provided. 'It was an emergency,' he said. 'I wasn't prepared.' The clerk translated his question into Arabic.

'Yes, I remember,' said the technician in Arabic.

'Insufficient sample,' said the clerk.

'There was a whole litre.'

The clerk translated.

The technician babbled away, fidgeting with his hands, clearly uncomfortable.

'Sorry, sir. It was spilled,' said the clerk. 'This man apologises.'

The technician stood, head bowed.

Clay walked back down to the waiting Land Cruiser. Bloody crap

Yemeni lab. Poorly maintained and calibrated equipment, untrained staff, poor record-keeping. Damn it. He would have to take another sample next time out, with or without Karila's approval.

۱۱

Locked in

He had just enough time to drive back to the guesthouse, shower and change, get the meal packed up, and arrive at the Mövenpick before five. He waited in the lobby, ordered a whisky soda to calm the shattered obsidian of his nerves, and tried not to think about Abdulkader, the PSO or any of it. At a quarter gone he ordered a second, thought about calling up to her room, reconsidered. By half past and the third whisky he was feeling a lot better, but started to worry that she was not going to show.

He was about to walk to the front desk when a woman in a long black *burqa* with a shimmering gold-embroidered half veil stepped from the elevator, followed by two oilies dressed in jeans and T-shirts – the idiots from the pool. The woman stopped a moment, looked around the lobby, and started moving towards the main entrance, floating over the tile, the two oilies close behind. Clay stood. One of the oilies, the shorter one, fatter, grabbed her arm and spun her around. Male laughter echoed from the lobby marble. The woman was facing them now, looking up at the two men. Clay could hear the woman's raised voice, the men's laughing replies. Clay started to move across the lobby towards the trio, adrenaline surging, pace quickening. The woman was backing away now. The fat one grabbed her wrist, held her. 'Come on now, darlin',' he said in a gruff Southern accent. Louisiana, Clay thought, Oklahoma. 'Show us what y'all got under that there sack.' Clay was almost to the tile floor, ten metres from the woman, when he saw her lash out with her right hand. A loud crack split the air. Fat let go of her, put his hand up to his face.

Clay pushed his way between the woman and her assailants, stood to his full height, a good head taller than either man.

Fat's friend, more muscular, leaner, stepped forward. His breath reeked of booze and cigarettes. 'You got a problem?'

Clay guessed this one fancied himself a bit of a fighter. 'Nothing that can't be settled outside.'

Fat blanched, backed away. His friend stood his ground.

The woman tugged at Clay's arm. 'Please,' she said. 'Do not.'

Clay spun around. Only the eyes gave her away. She had the most amazing eyes. It was Rania.

'I can look after myself, Clay.'

'You heard the bitch, fuck off.'

Clay turned in time to see Fat's friend flick out a switchblade. He held it straight-armed, like a pointer. Clay pushed Rania back, gave himself room. By now Fat had backed away towards the elevator doors.

'Come on, asshole,' hissed the guy with the switchblade.

'Leave him,' said Rania. 'Please, Clay. Let's go.'

By now some of the guests had become aware of what was going on, and stood gaping at a distance. Somebody called for security. Clay started to step away, but Switchblade lunged. He was clumsy and slow, came at Clay with arm straight and extended. Clay took a step to his left, turned side on, caught the man's arm at the wrist, rolled in and pulled the arm back with all his force. He felt the tendons go first, audible pops, then a bone, louder, a crack. The knife clattered to the floor. Switchblade howled in pain, slumped forward. Clay brought his knee up hard into Switchblade's face. He felt something give way. Blood drooled to the tile. Clay let go of the arm. Switchblade dropped to the floor in a heap.

Fat stood back against the wall between the two lifts, mouth agape. Clay was only just aware of people screaming, a couple of security guards moving through the crowd towards them. He turned and looked at Rania.

She stood a moment, lifted the hem of her floor-length *burqa* to reveal a pair of low-top hiking boots. 'Good?'

'Very.' She had nice ankles. The black material of her veil cinched up. She was smiling. 'Ready?' he said, offering his arm.

'*Allons-y*,' she said, taking it.

Clay led Rania through the lobby and out of the front doors into the sun, feeling better than he had in months, clear-headed, precise.

They drove in silence through the flats of Khormasar, past the Inner Harbour and the Ma'alla wharfs, the water of the bay, that shallow protected shade of green, and then through Tawahi with its rundown mansions of Empire, the gardens leafy and green still, overgrown. The road narrowed as they reached the point and the last settlements, and soon they were following a gravel track that skirted the coastal bluffs, the Gulf of Aden opening up azure blue and blasted with light, the outer bastions of the crater towering before them now, mafic and barren.

He slowed the vehicle, rolled to a stop, shut down the engine. They sat gazing at the sea and the mountains. Clay pointed along the coast. 'You see that point jutting into the sea, where the rock goes green?'

She nodded yes, veiled still.

'Reservation for two, right there.'

The trail wound its way along the contours of the bluff, first through craggy fractured boulders, and then, as they rose up over the sea, into columns of barren rhyolite, the rock hot from the day's sun. They passed a series of sawblade cliffs, the weathered basalt fractured and crumbling. The varnished gravel of the path popped like bubblewrap under their soles and the smells of the sea swirled in the breeze. By now her veil and *burqa* were gone, rolled up and stashed in his daypack.

He stopped and pulled a stainless-steel water bottle from his pack. They had gained enough altitude now to see back across the point to the harbour and the old town, its stone buildings the colour of the surrounding rock, the sun low now in the western sky. Beyond, the coast swept away in a long sunburned arc up towards the Red Sea. He offered her the bottle.

She took it and drank deeply. Her face glistened with sweat. '*Magnifique*,' she said, looking out to the sea.

He looked out over the water. 'I was questioned today, by the PSO.'

She turned to him, eyes wide.

'They wanted information about Al Shams.'

She sat on the benched side of the slope and retied her boot laces. She looked up at him. A strand of hair fell across her face. 'You must be careful, Clay.'

'That's what the PSO said.' He smiled. 'Sounds a lot better coming from you.'

She stood and took his hand, looked him in the eyes. 'Please, Claymore. Promise me. The PSO is a very unpredictable organisation. Stay out of their way.' She ran her fingers across his jaw and then went up on her toes and kissed him on the cheek. Before he could react, she turned and started up the hill again, leaving him standing open-mouthed, as he watched the sway of her hips under very small, very tight shorts.

They walked on and reached the point just as the sun was setting. They found the spur of green basalt and Clay threw down a blanket, unpacked dinner, lit a small hurricane lamp. A series of pebbly coves and rock promontories spread out before them, with not a road or building in sight. A soft breeze played in her hair. They sat on the lichen-rainbowed rock with their legs dangling over the edge of the sheer drop and watched the sun dissolve into the water. They ate in silence, looking out over that small piece of seemingly untouched world.

'I am impressed,' she said finally. 'Such culinary skill.'

'My friend Atef, the cook at the company guesthouse, he made everything.'

She smiled. The sun was gone below the water now and her face shone in the lamplight. 'Give him my compliments.'

He reached for her hand. She looked away, but let him take it. He moved closer, his hip touching hers. The air around her was thick with perfume, smouldering lichen, jasmine. He breathed deep. She was trembling. Or maybe it was him.

'I am sorry for what happened,' she said. 'Back at the hotel.'

'Don't be. They were idiots.' One of them wouldn't be pretending to be a tough guy for a long time.

'You could have been hurt.' She dropped her chin to her chest. 'They saw me at the pool. I tempted them.'

Clay sat for a moment, analysing this. 'It wasn't your fault, Rania. They knew exactly what they were doing.'

'You have no idea what it is to be a woman here,' she whispered. 'This is not your world, Clay.'

'It's not theirs, either.'

He'd seen so many like them, clueless oil-industry cattle, moving between Western hotel, oilfield camp and business-class flight home, with hardly a look out the window.

She looked out over the water. 'The first time I came to Yemen, I checked into a local hotel in Sana'a. I was alone. The desk clerk kept looking past me, as if he was expecting someone else to join me. They were flustered and confused, like they were dealing with a problem they had never confronted before. Finally I was given a room. Later that evening I went down to the restaurant for dinner. When I returned to my room, there was a cot next to my bed. It was all made up with a fresh sheet; there was even a plastic baby rattle hooked to the rail.' She looked away. 'I do not expect you to understand.'

There was a lot he didn't understand. Too much. Everything. 'Alfa foxtrot seven six six oh two eight four seven nine one,' he said.

She looked at him, a question forming on her face. 'What is this?'

'All I know about you.'

She smiled. Her teeth were strong and white. 'I do not understand.'

'Your driving licence number.'

The dark planets of her eyes gleamed out at him from perfect orbits. 'Don't worry, I haven't been spying on you.'

Her smile dissolved.

'I saw it when it fell out of your bag at the pool.'

She caught a wisp of hair on her tongue, pulled it into her mouth, sucked on it a moment. 'You were in the South African Border War,' she said. 'In Angola.'

He took a breath, his turn to be surprised. 'It was a long time ago.' She had done her homework.

'Tell me.'

'There's not much to tell.' He'd never spoken about any of it. No one had ever wanted to know, and he'd never wanted to tell. He looked out over the sea, said nothing.

After a while she ran her index finger along his cheek, traced the scar there through its camber to his jaw. 'Please,' she said.

He turned to her. She looked up at him, her face open, receptive.

'We were protecting South Africa against the communists – that's what we were told. I was very young. I had no idea what I was doing. I was scared shitless or bored stiff the whole time.'

'You did three tours, were wounded several times,' she said, running her finger now along his right forearm, tracing the angry old ridgeline of scar tissue from wrist to elbow. It was as though, in this touching, she believed she could transduce words into flesh, reconstruct events from consequences. 'You were decorated.'

Part of him was flattered, but only a small part. Mostly he felt ashamed. He said nothing.

'Then court martialled and dishonourably discharged.'

'It was a long time ago,' he croaked.

'What happened, Clay?'

'Let's just say I'd had enough.' She'd obviously seen his SADF service record. How she'd done that, he had no idea.

'Of the fighting?'

'Of everything.' He gripped her hand, looked into her eyes, stared hard. 'Why are you asking me this, Rania?'

She held his gaze for a moment, lowered her eyes. 'It's what I do, Clay,' she whispered. 'I research.'

Clay said nothing.

After a while she said: 'Did you …?' but then stopped, fell silent.

She was staring at him, her pupils wide, dark.

'Hope you'd keep our date? Definitely.'

She smiled, lowered her eyes again, those long dark lashes. 'And after? The war, I mean.'

He searched her face but it gave nothing away. 'I drifted for a while, went to university, tried to get myself together.'

'Science.'

He looked over at her. 'Engineering. I liked the math, the physics, the certainty of it. It calmed me. I was good at it. I wanted to do something worthwhile. Hasn't worked out so flash yet.'

Her hand was still in his. He could feel the warmth there, the softness of her slender fingers. His own hand felt clumsy and over-sized in comparison. His insides were churning. 'What were you doing out there in the Masila that day, Rania?'

'Interviewing some of the locals.'

'Alone?'

'I am used to it.'

And she's telling him to be careful. Jesus.

She looked away, her face flushed in the hues of night coming. He bent to kiss her, but she turned away, pulled back her hand.

'I …' he stopped. 'I'm sorry.' Stupid.

She said nothing for a long time, just sat with her hands in her lap, staring out across the water. Finally she stood, rubbed her arms. 'We should get back.'

It was dark by the time they reached the car. She had not said much on the walk back down, and he had left her alone with her thoughts. Abdulkader's Land Cruiser started with a cough and she climbed in next to him. They drove back to town the way they had come, the docks and the ships in the harbour lit up, the cool night air flowing over them. He wished the drive would go on all night, up along the coast all the way to Ta'izz and the mountains.

But it was only a matter of minutes to her hotel. He pulled into the parking lot and turned off the engine. Covered again in the *burqa* and veil, she was almost invisible in the darkness beside him.

'I'm going to the Hadramawt tomorrow morning,' he said. 'I'll be back in Aden in a week. I'd really like to see you again, Rania, get to know you.'

She reached over and touched his arm. 'Please, Clay. I do not want to give you the wrong impression. I cannot get involved with anyone right now.'

Clay felt the ground fall out beneath him. 'I thought maybe …' He shut up.

She put a card on the seat next to him. 'If you would like to talk, on a professional level, I am based in Sana'a.'

'A professional level, right.' He closed his eyes.

'Yes. If you have information for me, about Al Shams and the rebellion.'

'Information, sure,' he managed. 'No worries.'

He expected her to get out, walk away. But she just sat there in the darkness, so close, an arm's length away, silent and dark.

'Are you seeing someone?' he said.

'*Mon dieu*, no,' she snapped and fell silent. After a while she said: 'And you?'

'Not now.'

It hadn't lasted long. None of them did. He'd met her at an expat house party in Cyprus six months ago. She was English, bored, attractive in that confident mid-thirties way. Her husband travelled for work. Like teenagers they'd skulked off to an upstairs bedroom and he'd taken her on the floor. She told him that her husband knew, that he didn't mind, encouraged her even. They'd been together four or five times only, usually after he'd returned from overseas, a couple of hours each time, no more. It had been lonely, dispassionate, hotel-room sex that left him feeling hollow and dead inside.

He could smell Rania's tears now, sweet almost, enzymes on bare skin. He rocked forward and grabbed the steering wheel, looking straight ahead into the darkness.

She opened the door, hovered there a moment, half in the vehicle, half out. 'Do you ever feel as if you needed to go back and choose again, Clay?' she whispered. 'As if you were locked in, going the wrong direction, but could not get out?'

But before he had a chance to answer, to say that yes, he knew exactly what she meant, was living it even now, she stood, closed the door, turned and walked across the parking lot towards the hotel.

He waited, hoping that she would turn and wave but she rounded the corner without looking back and was gone.

١٢

A Way of Saying Thank You

Early the next morning he left Aden running north through Lawdar, up to the edge of the great sand river of Ramlat as Sab'atayn and then across into Wadi Hadramawt from the west. On the high plateau the miles slipped by like drifting sand. Other than the occasional drill rig lancing a mesa and the new roads and oil pipelines that scored the hardpan, it could have been the Seven Pillars: the quiet of the tablelands, the wadis riven like scars across the earth, the sky a torn blue shroud, the relentless sun above.

By the time he reached Marib his neck and shoulders ached from constant craning and swivelling. He had seen nothing that would indicate he was being followed, but he could feel the eyes of the PSO everywhere, checking off his progress through each village and hamlet. Karila and Parnell had probably already given them his itinerary.

And Al Shams' name was everywhere: whispered in streetside tea houses or around early-morning braziers, invoked in oaths and prayers, *God protect him*, imagined in small boy's games, the towering hero slaying all enemies. Anointed by Allah, he would deliver to the people what was rightly theirs. Change was coming, they said.

After the long descent towards Ash Shihir he turned west again and tracked along the base of the escarpment towards Um'alat. He was still shocked that Rania had delved so deeply into his past, his present, was shaken that his efforts at anonymity had been so easily pierced. Her parting words rattled through his head. The wrong direction, she'd said. Locked in. And in those dazzling eyes, those tears, he'd seen damage.

Alone, he waited in the dust under a platinum Arabian sky. The *mashayikh* was already an hour late. He looked up at the ancient skyscrapers that rose as if by some miracle of mud and clay from the valley floor, their alabaster window frames paned in rainbows of coloured glass, and beyond, the bluffs that towered over the town and dominated the landscape for hundreds of kilometres in every direction. Except for the dilapidated truck parked nearby and the heaps of rubbish lining the street – plastic bags and blue polyethylene water bottles, car tyres, tins, batteries and moulded plastic parts – a century or more might have been wound back.

A new silver Land Cruiser rolled to a stop in the town square. The *mashayikh* was alone, dressed in the same tweed jacket and *thaub,* a Kalashnikov slung over his left shoulder. He greeted Clay in the elaborate way of the region, touching fingertips to chest, lips and forehead, and extended his hand.

Clay followed the Arab into a tall, whitewashed building and up four flights of worn stone steps. They entered a deep narrow room with big wood-framed windows ranged all along one side, the *mardar*. From here he could see out across the dry expanse of the coastal plain to the demesne of green farmland and palm groves huddled along the contours of the depression, and beyond to the flat scrubland shrouded in heat and dust.

They sat on cushions at the far end of the room. An old man brought a bundle of *qat* branches and two bottles of drinking water. Following the *mashayikh*, Clay selected a branch, dropped it in his lap, and started to pluck the leaves from their stems between thumb and forefinger, choosing tender new shoots from the red stems as Abdulkader had taught him and wedging them between his lower gum and the wall of his cheek. The *mashayikh* nodded and chewed in silence, steadily adding to the ball of green mash that bulged inside his left cheek. It looked as if he was trying to swallow a fist.

After two hours the subtle amphetamine of the leaves was in control of his nervous system. Sweat ran from his temples and trickled down his chest. The room was hot; there was no air. His heart rate spiked and dropped and spiked again as the cathinone raced through his veins. The effect was like dexedrine: not as strong, but a definite open-eyed buzz.

Finally the *mashayikh* spoke. 'At your request, Mister Straker, I am listening.'

'Is the illness still with your people, Excellency?'

'The children, Mister Straker, only the children. It has become worse since we spoke. Much worse.'

He felt his thumb twitch once, then again, and then his index finger started to jump on its tendons, and the thumb again until his left hand was trembling visibly. He pushed the offending thing hard against his thigh, but the *mashayikh* had seen it.

'I have discussed this with the General Manager,' Clay said. 'We have examined the information. The facility cannot possibly be causing the illness you described.'

'Only in Al Urush are our people suffering in this way. It is closest to your processing plant. Does that not seem a strange coincidence?'

'Al Urush is far from the facility,' he said. 'I have been there.'

'The sickness travels in the air, as my son said. It can go far.'

They would deal with it in the usual way. Clay pulled a manila envelope from his breast pocket and placed it on the floor between them. 'My superiors understand your concern, and although this problem is not the result of our operations, we are committed to working with you and your people to maintain good relations as the project moves ahead.' It sounded like someone else. Now came the real reckoning, Excellency.

The *mashayikh* looked at him and down at the envelope. His eyes were moist; cataracts drifted there like clouds. 'What is this, *khawga*?'

'A way of saying thank you for your cooperation.'

The *mashayikh* picked up the envelope and peered inside and replaced it where it had been. 'Our concerns are significant, Mister Straker. I am sure you can understand.'

'Can you assure us also of your son's cooperation, Excellency?' Clay remembered the handsome young man dressed in white, the way every tribesman in the room had turned to face him that day, gone quiet, nodded as he spoke.

The *mashayikh* grunted, took a sip of water. 'He is young and naïve. But he will do as his father commands.'

Clay placed a second envelope on top of the first. The *mashayikh* considered the pile for a moment, stood, smoothed down his robe, and walked to the window to look out over his domain. 'You may go, Mister Straker,' he said, still looking out of the window. 'But be aware, my friend, that I may have need of your thanks again.'

Clay stood next to the *mashayikh* and looked out across the plain. 'Tell Al Shams that I have done what he asked.'

'I beg your pardon?'

'Tell him I want my friend released.'

'What leads you to believe that I have any connection with that man? He is a terrorist.'

'Spare me the bullshit, your Excellency. Tell him.' Clay strode to the far end of the room, turned to face the *mashayikh*. 'And warn him. The PSO are coming for him.'

☾

Soon he was speeding along the dirt track that led to the highway. This part of his job was done. That was how it went. One glance inside was enough to conjure up dreams and send hearts racing. It was like looking through the gates of paradise ephemeral. Part of him had wanted the *mashayikh* to reject the bribe, spit it back in his face. But of course it always worked. It was only a matter of how much. At first it had been exciting, it had made him feel somehow strengthened against the vicissitudes of the world. Learning that everyone was susceptible, that we were all whores, had changed him more than he could have realised, had made him harder, meaner, more resilient somehow. It was not a bad thing. Everyone had a price. You only had to dig down far enough, cut through enough layers to find it.

At the turnoff to Al Urush he stopped the car and turned off the engine. The dust settled like a poured Guinness around him. Should he go back for another sample? By taking the money, the *mashayikh* had revealed the truth. The claims of illness were a hoax, a way of prising money from the company. Petro-Tex had set the precedent a year ago, paying off local leaders rather than dealing with their concerns directly, and now they were stuck with it. And what did that say about Al Shams? Was all this concern for the people just a screen for his political agenda? Was Parnell right? And what did that mean for Abdulkader?

He turned the ignition, jammed the car into gear and trod on the accelerator. Soon he was on the outskirts of Al Urush. As soon as he arrived, he could sense that something was wrong. The place was deserted. A pall of acrid haze swirled amongst the palms. He walked to a small mud-brick hut no larger than a garden shed, one of a cluster of similar buildings stumped at the base of the escarpment and banged on the door. After a minute a woman pulled the door ajar and peered out from the darkness. She held a fold of her dress across her face and spoke in a girlish voice. He was ushered inside.

The place smelt of urine, stale sweat and kerosene, and something else he could not place, decay of some sort, sublimates, rot. His eyes adjusted to the gloom: a dirt floor, two wooden chairs, a small table set against the wall near the door, a gas burner propped on a stack of mud bricks.

The boy lay on a steel frame bed at the far end of the room, a bicycle wheel clutched to his chest. He played a few notes on his instrument and looked up as if searching for encouragement. He was barely recognisable.

Clay stood in the semi-darkness and stared down at the boy, and suddenly it was the face of the SWAPO soldier who had crawled off into the bush to die. Clay had come upon him just beyond the *chana*. The soldier had propped himself up against a mopane tree in the sun and sat there staring with that grey gone look in his eyes, hands clasped over his torn abdomen. Clay had given him one in the head just to be sure. It had only taken a moment. Raise the R4, the South African version of the famous Israeli Galil assault rifle, accurate and powerful, pull the trigger. Done. And ever since, that fraction of a second had replayed itself a thousand times, a million, looping over and over in his dreams until the very thought of sleep filled him with dread.

Clay approached the bed, clenched his jaw. He forced himself to smile, but it felt twisted, fake. 'Mohamed.' Tears welled up, unbidden, burning. He blinked, pushed them back.

Mohamed stretched his lips over swollen gums. 'My friend,' he whispered in Arabic. Clay put his hand on Mohamed's head. The boy was burning up. In halting Arabic he asked the woman how long the boy had been like this.

The woman spoke in shrill tones. She waved her henna-adorned hands above her head and pointed repeatedly to the escarpment, something about the smoke, sickness, other children, babies.

'Only children?' he asked. He measured a child's height with a flat palm.

Again the woman erupted in a flurry of shrieks.

Clay pulled his camera from the pack, attached the flash and checked the film. He looked at the woman and pointed to the camera. She nodded. He took several photos of Mohamed and slung the camera strap around his neck, feeling like a ghoul, a calamity tourist.

Clay reached in his pocket and handed the woman a hundred-dollar note. 'Hospital,' he said, pointing in the direction of Al Mukalla. 'Get him to hospital.'

Of course, she had no way of complying. She looked at the bill, President and Independence Hall, and handed it back.

Clay pushed her hand away and turned and stumbled out into the midday glare, gagging at the smell. Heat poured in liquid waves from the escarpment and flowed down and across the little hamlet like a plague. Beyond the trees a thread of dark smoke rose into the sky. Dogs barked in the distance.

He walked quickly across the clearing to the cistern. He grabbed one of the plastic buckets that the villagers used, threw it in, let it fill, and pulled it dripping to the surface. He scooped some water into his hand and tasted it. It was brackish, estuarine, nothing like the water he had tasted only a few days ago at the pools a few hundred metres up-wadi from here. He pulled the conductivity meter from his pack, dropped the probe into the bucket and switched on the device. The readings oscillated and then stabilised, the glowing red digits burned into his memory. The water was much saltier than it should be. He measured pH, pulled his yellow fieldbook from his pocket, scribbled down the readings, poured some of the water from the bucket into a sample bottle.

Clay shouldered his pack, clicked off photographs of the cistern and the boy's house and the escarpment, and set off through the trees towards the smoke. A wail cut the air. It sounded like a pack of dogs howling. He walked on. The noise grew louder. He passed through a series of small fields shaded by palms and crossed a low earthen dyke to descend into a dark hollow. The place was strewn with rubbish, the air electric with the buzz of insects. The odour of decay was overpowering. Clay retched and jammed the tail of his *keffiyeh* over his nose and mouth. A pack of rib-cage dogs snarled and ripped at a heap of tiny glutinous carcasses, the eyes opaque and filmed over.

'Jesus Christ,' he choked through his scarf, still moving through the trees towards the smoke. Twenty minutes later he emerged into a rocky clearing at the base of a dolomite cliff. A small crescent of mud huts was built into the slope. A group of women stood in a loose semi-circle, covered head to foot in black, facing a pillar of fire. The flames danced up through the stacked wood, caressing a clutch of doll-sized bundles nestled atop the pyre. Oily smoke poured into the flawless sky. Embers leapt and spun into the void to be extinguished in mid-flight. The women wailed and moaned, hiding their faces in their hands, rocking their heads forward and back in a rhythm of grief. One of the women glanced up at him through a veil of tears. Their eyes met across the smoke. It was the girl he had seen washing clothes at the upper pool that day, no more than a week ago. There was no mistaking those eyes, even now. He took a step forward, raised his hand, but she looked away. There was no pity here for any of them, pinned to the stony ground beneath scorched walls of rock.

۱۳

One Man Is Nothing

He set off from the village, still in shock, Mohamed's mother in the back seat, her son in her arms. Seared fields of stone ripped past the open window, superheated air buffeting the side of his face, tearing at his hair. She was rocking the boy, whispering to him, stroking his matted head, the boy's face pale beneath her long brown fingers, her thick cracked nails. Mohamed's head hung limp, jerking with each bump in the road, his mouth open so that Clay could see the top row of little white teeth shivering in the rear-view mirror. Jesus, was he dead? Clay pushed down on the accelerator, urging the speedometer on. The Land Cruiser rattled along the washboard, the diesel whining at full power, road dust billowing through the windows. Clay reached into his pack and pulled out his *keffiyeh* and passed it back to the woman. 'For the dust,' he yelled, turning his hand around his head. She took it and laid it over Mohamed's face. It looked like a shroud.

An hour later he strode into the main entrance of the public hospital in Al Mukalla, Mohamed covered in road dust, limp and unconscious in his arms, his frail chest rising and falling. The boy's mother followed close behind, face covered, the tourniquets of her fingers coiling about themselves, releasing, cinching. He doubted she had ever seen a hospital, let alone been inside one. A soldier in a camouflaged jacket lay slumped in a chair just inside the door, a huge wad of *qat* pushing out his cheek. He looked up at them with lost, bloodshot eyes and waved them in. Half a dozen people sat stern-faced on a bench set against one wall. At the far end of the room, a male attendant in a green smock sat behind what appeared to be an admitting counter.

Clay made for the counter and stood looking down at the top of the attendant's head. A newspaper was spread on the desk. '*Salam*,' said Clay. The attendant did not look up. Clay tried again, more formally. '*Salam aleikum*.'

'*Aleikum salam*,' muttered the attendant, still not looking up.

Clay used his best Arabic. 'This boy needs a doctor.'

The attendant reached under the desk and produced a green form and placed it on the desk, still not looking up. It was in Arabic, the script dense, impenetrable. Cradling Mohamed in one arm he pushed the papers over to the woman, took a pen from his shirt pocket and held it out for her. She looked at the pen and up at him. Tears flooded her eyes. He motioned to the paper with his head, pushed the pen towards her again.

'*La*,' she cried. No. She trailed off into a back-of-the mosque lament that he could not follow.

Clay turned back to the attendant, understanding. '*Lau samaht*,' he said. 'Please. She cannot read or write.'

The attendant looked up from his newspaper. He was a youngish man, gaunt-faced, his skin pockmarked and oily. He glanced at the woman and then at the boy, and pointed to the form, speaking in rapid Arabic. Clay understood enough to get the message. The form was mandatory. He picked up the sheets and stared at the blank spaces, the tick boxes. He could feel the frustration taking bites out of whatever patience still lived within him. With Abdulkader here this would have been easy, but, now, it was impossible. He slammed the form down onto the desk. The attendant jumped back, looked up, wide-eyed.

'Doctor,' said Clay, tuning his voice for loud and authoritative. 'Now.' He jammed his index finger onto the desktop. Universal language.

'No doctor,' said the attendant, pushing his chair back from the desk.

'Doctor,' said Clay, more emphatic now. Behind him, he could hear the scrape of a chair. The soldier had awoken from his stupor and was watching them. Clay smiled at him and turned back to the attendant, sliding a fifty-dollar bill onto the counter top. The attendant looked at the bill, hesitated a moment, and snatched it up. Then he stood, took the form and a pen and asked the woman a question. She answered and he began to fill in the first boxes. Clay stood and watched the play of question-and-answer unfold, the woman becoming visibly more disturbed as they crept down the form, right to left. After a quarter of an hour the woman was in tears, the form only half complete.

'*Mushkilla?*' asked Clay. What is the problem?

'No papers,' said the attendant.

Of course they had nothing. No address, no identity cards. They didn't even exist as far as the government was concerned. The woman was sobbing now, trying to pull her son from Clay's arms. She wanted to leave. Clay tried to calm her but every time he spoke, she only shrieked louder. Mohamed was awake now, just, moaning softly for his mother. Everyone was watching. The soldier was standing, moving towards them. Clay could feel the situation unravelling. He hefted the boy up onto his hip and slammed his right fist down hard on the desk. The attendant backed away, glanced past Clay at the approaching soldier, then put the pen on the desk, pushed the papers aside, flopped back into his chair and crossed his arms. The oily face creased open to reveal a mouthful of straight yellow teeth. The bastard was smiling.

Something deep inside Clay ruptured. He could feel it go, like a ligament tearing from bone. Clay hoisted the boy over his shoulder, grabbed the woman by the forearm and before she or the attendant could react he wheeled left and strode past the desk and led her through the double doors and into the bowels of the hospital.

The hallway was long and poorly lit, every third overhead light tube dead, half of the rest flickering and buzzing, the tile floor wet in places, as if it had just been randomly mopped. An orderly in a sick-green smock looked up as they passed, a burning cigarette dangling from his mouth. They were halfway down the main corridor, past a couple of sidelined gantries, when he heard the shouting. He glanced back over his shoulder. The attendant was standing at the end of the corridor, one hand bracing open the door, pointing. The orderly paid no attention, kept smoking. A moment later the soldier appeared and the pair started down the hallway. Clay quickened his pace, dragging the woman behind. The attendant and the soldier were running now, their footfall echoing along the tile, gaining ground, pushing past green-clad staff emerged from doorways, peering left and right.

Up ahead another set of double doors and on the right an alcove, a sign, someone's name. Clay turned into the alcove and flung open the door. It was a consultation room. Small. A window onto the courtyard. An elderly patient in a greying hospital gown was sitting on the edge of an examination table, bony legs and darkly tanned feet dangling free, a man in a white lab coat pushing a tongue depressor into his mouth. Both men looked up as Clay burst in, frozen in the act, open-mouthed.

Clay pulled the woman into the office, closed and locked the door, laid Mohamed on the examination table next to the old man. Mohamed's mother went immediately to her son's side and bent over him, wiping his brow, whispering to him. Neither man said a word, just stood there gaping at him as if he'd just shown up in the Masjid Al-Haram battle bloody and carrying an R4.

'Are you a doctor?' Clay asked the man in the white coat.

'I am,' replied the man in English, glancing at the boy. 'And this is my office. You have intruded on a private examination. You must leave immediately. Make an appointment at admissions.' He spoke fluently, with an accent that sounded Lebanese, Egyptian perhaps.

Clay knew he didn't have long. 'I'm sorry, doctor, but this is an emergency. This boy is very sick. These people are poor, they have no identification, no way of completing the paperwork. Please, have a look at him. I can …'

A sharp rap on the door cut him short, voices from the other side throwing agitated Arabic. The doctor looked at Clay through narrowed eyes. He had a dark moustache and brown heavily lidded eyes underscored by dark circles. He looked weary. 'There are many poor here, many who do not have papers. There are procedures. You must leave.'

Clay looked over at Mohamed, his mother weeping silently. The banging on the door was louder now, insistent flat-palmed hammering. He took a deep breath, then took the doctor by the elbow, guided him to the far side of the room, hemmed him into the corner. Clay leaned in close, towering over the man, and still holding his elbow, said into his ear: 'Look, any minute the Army is going to come in here and take me away. Please, I'm begging you, examine the boy.'

Clay reached into his trouser pocket and pressed three hundred-dollar bills into the man's hand, two week's wages, more. The doctor opened his hand, looked down at the money, up at Clay, blinked twice, then nodded.

'Thank you,' Clay said, releasing the doctor's elbow and backing away. 'His name is Mohamed, from Al Urush. Please make sure they get home safely afterwards.' Then he turned and walked to the door and unlocked the bolt and pulled it open. The attendant and two soldiers almost fell in on top of him. 'Hello gents,' he said.

☾

Two hours later he reached Idim and the pass up to the plateau. Still buzzing from the encounter at the hospital, he drove almost without thinking, without registering the road, the miles slipping away unnoticed, as if they had never existed. All it had taken was money. After a few tense minutes, marched out to the back of the hospital to stand under the sun in the dirt, squadrons of flies swarming around overflowing bins of medical waste, the attendant and the two soldiers had accepted a fifty each.

The events of the past days played like a dream before his eyes, a waking nightmare where nothing is resolved, where every fragment of clarity loops back on itself and is lost. It took him most of the rest of the day to reach the turnoff from the trunk road, and another hour to find the track that led off towards the hidden wadi. He stopped the car, turned off the engine, and stepped down onto the pulverised gravel. The engine tapped in the heat. Far to the west, a tendril of purple dust rose oblique into the sky, a vehicle tracking towards Marib. Otherwise the horizon was an empty, shimmering mirage. He waited, scanning the plateau for any sign he was being followed, the flat stone strewn uplands, the hogback mesas, the thermal blur of the edge of the world, but there was nothing, no one.

He climbed back into the Land Cruiser, kept to the trunk road, watching the odometer click over. Ten kilometres on, he pulled over, climbed up onto the roof rack and scanned the horizon through binoculars. Stone, heat, sand. He jumped down to the ground, turned the vehicle around and sped back towards the track.

By the time he came to the maw of the canyon, the cliff tops were glowing with the last of the day's light. He left the Land Cruiser and made his way through the narrowing defile, everything darkening quickly now, familiar. Adrenaline surged into his system. Every sense tingled. He was walking point again. At any moment he would hear the sonic tear of bullets, the crash of gunfire. He found the opening in the rockslide and started to thread his way through the labyrinth, moving by feel and memory in the gloom. Twice he dead-ended and had to backtrack, slithering along the rough sandstone surfaces, twisting around corners, finding the route again.

When he finally emerged, the first stars were shining in a moonless sky. He stood in the wadi floor, just below the ledge where he and Abdulkader had spent the night, where he had last seen him, and listened to the silence of the whispering cliffs. He was about to move down-wadi when a sound broke the quiet, a tap, a scratch. He froze, listened. There it was again, more like crunching, footfall, perhaps. He swivelled his head, tried to triangulate. Again, tap. It was coming from the ledge. Someone was up there.

Clay moved across the sand of the wadi floor towards the canyon wall, heel to toe, as quietly as he could. The noise had stopped. He waited for a long time at the base of the ledge, straining to hear over the surging blood in his veins. Nothing. Then he crept up to the ledge and peered over the lip.

The fire ring was gone, the ashes swept away. A desert pigeon pecked at the rock. He could just make out the noise it made, the little taps of its beak against the sandstone. Clay looked up at the concave overhang, the inside of a curling wave. Any sound made here on the ledge was gathered and projected back down into the wadi below. Al Shams had heard every word he and Abdulkader had exchanged that night. He had heard them plotting escape, heard Clay's accusations, his blaspheming. Clay shivered, so close to oblivion again.

Clay continued down wadi, knowing now that Al Shams was long gone. Fifty metres on he reached a clutch of ancient stunted trees, a spring welling from a fissure in the base of the cliff, traces of a camp nestled there. Flattened shoals of sand and a partially burnt tree limb stumped into a blackened fire pit were the only testaments to recent occupation.

It was gone nine when he reached the Land Cruiser. He opened the driver's side door and reached into the vehicle to retrieve his water bottle. Standing in the glow of the interior light, he took a long drink, wet a corner of his headcloth and dabbed at the scrapes and cuts on his arms and legs. He had just rinsed the cloth when something hard jabbed into his back.

'Do not turn around.'

Clay froze, heart hammering.

'You were followed.'

'No,' he said. 'I was careful.'

'The PSO followed you.' He knew the voice, the diction. 'I followed them.'

Jesus Christ.

'Why did you return?'

'To find my friend, ask for his release. He is a good man. He does not deserve this.'

The object jammed harder into his back. 'Only Allah decides what we deserve.'

'Please.'

'You delivered our message.'

'Yes.'

'And now you have seen the evil.'

'At Al Urush, yes.'

'The boy, Mohamed. You are his friend.'

'You know him?'

'Of course. What afflicts him?'

'It's some kind of disease. An illness.'

'Our people are being poisoned.'

'I think ...' Clay stopped himself, filled his lungs, exhaled long. 'You think it's from the CPF.'

'That is what you must determine.'

'I have done what you asked. Let Abdulkader go.'

'I must know the truth. You must help us.'

Clay pivoted on one foot but a firm hand grabbed his shoulder before he could turn and face his assailant. He steadied himself against the car door. Suddenly he felt very tired. 'We had an agreement.'

The pressure in his back was gone, the hand removed. He could hear footsteps in the sand moving away.

'Turn around.' Al Shams was alone, a carved walking stick at his side. 'You are trained, you are a scientist, so you told me the first time we met. You must find the truth. We cannot protect ourselves if we do not know what is happening.'

Clay looked up at the night sky and back at the misshapen face. 'It's going to take time. Dozens of air and water samples, chemical analysis. And money. Thousands of dollars in lab work alone.'

Al Shams stood unmoving. 'Then you must begin now. But do it quickly, Mister Claymore. You have until the moon is new.

Eight days, no more. When you have the answers we need, go to Al Bawazir, find the young chief there. He is my nephew. He will give you instructions. But I warn you, if you bring the Army or the PSO, it will end very badly for your friend.'

'You're not listening to me, god damn you. It can't be done. Not in a week. The company won't have it.'

Al Shams sighed and shook his head. 'We each have our concerns, our priorities. You have yours, I have mine. My duty is to the people of the Masila. You have seen with your own eyes the tragedy that befalls them. Without knowing the cause of this illness, we are powerless to protect ourselves. No one else can help us. I will do what I must, Mister Clay.'

'Like killing Thierry Champard.'

'I have only one eye, Mister Claymore, but you are blind.'

Clay baulked, stepped back. 'Abdulkader is one of your own people, for god's sake.'

'That makes his complicity worse.' Al Shams sighed and stepped back into star shadow.

'Do you know what I think?'

'Go on, Mister Claymore. Be frank.'

Clay was shaking now, the words coming on their own. 'I think you're a fucking hypocrite. You talk about caring, about justice. All I see is kidnapping, murder, and greed.'

Al Shams drew a dollar symbol in the sand with his stick. 'Greed.'

'You want the oil money. That's what this is about.'

Al Shams looked down at the ground, erased the symbol with his sandalled foot.

'Do you know Sharia law, Mister Claymore?'

Clay nodded.

'From those who take, something is taken.' Al Shams looked up to the sky. Then he reached into the satchel at his side, pulled out a small bundle of rough cloth and tossed it to Clay.

Clay caught it with both hands. 'What's this?'

Al Shams said nothing, just stood staring at him with that dark eye. Clay folded back the sack cloth, damp and tacky in his fingers. A stale odour flooded his nostrils. It was a human hand, withered and dark, crisped into a half-formed fist, severed at the wrist.

Clay let out a groan and dropped the hand into the sand. He looked down at Abdulkader's silver ring. For a moment he stood, unable to breathe, leaning against the side of the car, trying to process this information. Rage rose in his chest. He stood to his full height and moved towards Al Shams, fists closing. 'You bastard,' he shouted, closing on the Arab, crouching into an attack stance. He was within striking distance when Al Shams levelled a pistol at his abdomen.

'Please, Mister Claymore. You are no good to me, or to your friend, dead.'

Clay jerked to a stop and stood fists clenched, the straight right kick to the torso now just an imagined echo. 'You'd do it, wouldn't you, you heartless bastard. You'd kill him. Maybe you already have.'

Al Shams moved back further into shadow and lowered the weapon. He stood for a moment, there beneath the cliff tops, a grey shape in the darkness. 'One man's life is nothing. Not yours, nor mine. Eight days, Mister Claymore.' And then he was gone, vanished into the rock itself.

The Rest of Your Life

The next day, Clay stood at the edge of a cluster of brown mud huts huddled against the cliffs and looked down into the gaping sinkhole in the limestone caprock, the dark surface of the water ten metres below: the *ghayl* at Al Bawazir. Above, an empty sky stretched away to the edges of the universe. Looking up, he could almost *feel* eternity.

Beside him stood the chief of Al Bawazir, the same man who had spoken from the back of the room during the audience with the *mashayikh* two days ago, the *mashayikh's* son, Al Shams' nephew. He was dressed in the same flowing white robes as before. Close up he looked much younger than Clay remembered, late twenties perhaps, his face almost girlish, with razor cheekbones, dark eyes and thick black lashes. 'You have been speaking with my father,' he said in near-perfect English, his voice deep, almost musical.

Clay nodded.

The chief's eyes flashed. 'My father is a fool. Do not interpret his weakness as mine.'

Clay said nothing.

'*My allegiance is only to those who fill my hands with silver coins …*'

Clay looked at the chief, a question.

'An old Yemeni verse. My country will never progress so long as it sells itself to the highest bidder. We must stop fighting each other and turn our energies to the true path. Only then can we take back our country.'

'You speak like your uncle.'

'I have many uncles.'

Clay paused, looked into the man's eyes. 'I meant the one who is threatening to kill my friend.'

The chief looked up at the sky. 'I agree with his aims, not his methods.'

'Then help me,' said Clay. 'Ask him to release my friend.'

The chief turned and faced him. His dark eyes reflected the water below, ripples of sky. 'It seems we need each other. My village, my family, are also threatened with this poisoning. Help me to protect them, and I promise to do what I can for your friend.'

Clay didn't have many options, and he needed allies. He offered his hand.

The chief blinked twice, shook Clay's hand. His grip was strong, sure. '*Inshallah*,' he said.

Yes. God willing. It could be no other way. Like so much in this place, even trust was subject to divine approval, and, as so often happened, instant and random repudiation. What else could it be in a country that, until the year Clay was born, was known as the Mutawakkilite Kingdom of Yemen: the Kingdom that depends on God?

The chief extended a long finger towards the *ghayl* below. 'Look. The water in the *ghayl* has fallen. You can see from the lines on the rock. The old men say never has it been this low. It began falling after the new oil well was drilled.' He pointed up towards the escarpment and the plateau beyond. 'There, at the CPF, near to the wadi. We have seen it.'

Clay rubbed his thumb over the embossed calligraphy of the ring weighing on the baby finger of his right hand. 'Who has seen it?'

'My son.'

Clay hadn't heard about any oil discoveries at the CPF itself. The facility had been positioned midway between the two original fields, Kamar and Haya, over 150 kilometres apart. The new discovery, the one that was driving the expansion, was even further away. He doubted the man's son could have seen anything. The plant itself was locked down, heavily guarded, ringed by electric fences and barbed wire. Locals were strictly forbidden anywhere near. Even he, a contractor, had been allowed access only once, early in the development programme last year. 'Are you sure?'

'He has seen the drill.'

'It must have been an exploration well.'

'No,' said the chief. 'There is a pipeline to the well now, a generator.'

'How did he see this?'

'He is a small boy, but strong. He has found a way through the fence, near the Bedou well in Wadi Urush, close to the facility.' The chief motioned towards the *ghayl*. '*Fa'ddar*,' he said. Please. Clay thought now how much he looked like Al Shams, how Al Shams might have looked if God had been kinder.

Clay descended the steep, time-worn track down to the water, the steps hewn from the rock, worn concave smooth by the feet of generations. He reached a wide, flat ledge where the trail ended. The porous cave-ridden walls of the sinkhole were stained black from this point down to the water level more than a metre below, like exposed rock at low tide. He tied a length of rope to a bailer and dropped it into the water, retrieved it full.

Suddenly the air exploded above him. A MiG in desert camouflage flashed low overhead, wings heavy with finned cylinders: rockets and bombs. The black maws of the engine intakes gaped against its sky-grey underbelly. The jet pitched up as it passed over and clawed its way into the sky, afterburners searing the air with orange flame. A strong smell of kerosene blanketed him as the jet climbed off towards the plateau.

He worked quickly, calibrating the instruments, recording the data in his notebook. The salinity was higher than it should be, according to the long-term records, but nothing like the levels he had just measured at Al Urush. He scooped up a water sample and stashed it in his pack.

A voice echoed around the rock walls of the sinkhole. He looked up.

The chief stood at the lip, waving his arms. 'You must go.' His voice was deep and strong. 'Hurry.'

Clay stowed his equipment and raced up the track. It took just a few seconds to reach the top. Beyond a low ridge that ran from the escarpment towards the sea, a thick streak of dust cut obliquely into the blue sky. A column of vehicles was approaching at high speed. 'Soldiers,' said the chief, pointing towards the escarpment. 'Go. Hide in the rocks.'

'I'll stay.'

'No,' said the chief. 'It is not good for you to be here. Please, go.'

Clay stood for a moment watching the dust spiralling closer. The chief reached out and touched his arm. 'Please, my friend. It is better for us.'

Clay sprinted to the Land Cruiser and started the engine. The chief pointed to a gap between two buildings. Clay waved and trundled the vehicle between the mud-brick houses and along a raised dyke that ran between two fields of date palms. He looked back. The tyres were raising no dust.

Clay turned the vehicle in the direction of the escarpment onto a widened footpath. He followed the path into a dense field of towering boulders and stopped the Land Cruiser at the base of two massive blocks of limestone. The car was completely hidden from the village. He left the Land Cruiser and moved on foot along a goat track that ran parallel to the fault line and then up a steep shale slope until he came to a small promontory. He lay prone on the rock and looked out over the hamlet below. The convoy ploughed to a stop at the edge of the *ghayl* in a swirl of dust.

There were five vehicles: three Russian-made military transports and two smaller four-wheeled vehicles with mounted heavy machine guns. A group of villagers emerged from the buildings and walked towards the trucks, led by the chief. Green-uniformed troops jumped from the transports and fanned out among the fields and buildings. Half a dozen other men, taller and more heavily armed than the Yemeni soldiers, dismounted the jeeps. They were bearded and dressed in a variety of camouflage patterns; some wore sunglasses. A Yemeni Army officer with gold epaulettes, and another man, smaller, dressed in khaki trousers, a black T-shirt and cap, approached the villagers. The locals clustered around the officer, waving and pointing. The bearded fighters stood a few paces away, watching, weapons ready.

Clay pulled the telephoto lens from his bag and attached it to his camera. Then he flipped the bottom of his vest up and over his head so that it formed a shaded cover for the lens, and focussed on the man in the black shirt. His face was obscured beneath the peak of his cap. Clay focussed back on the villagers. The officer stood among the throng, waving a paper in the air, a document of some sort. The tribesmen were arguing with the officer. Raised voices echoed from the cliffs, intermittent on the breeze, Arabic, clearly, but something else, too, words and tones he had heard before, but not here.

The chief stepped forward, his white robe rippling in the breeze. He turned to face his comrades and spoke, his voice rising on the wind. There was more jostling and shouting, the officer surrounded now by angry villagers. The man in the black shirt disengaged himself from the throng and faced the chief, pulled off his cap and ran his hands through close-cropped hair. Clay's heart lurched. He clicked the shutter. It was Zdravko.

Clay shook his head. What the hell was Zdravko doing here? And the Army, these others, these irregulars? Were they searching for Al Shams? Was that why the chief had ushered him away, bid him hide?

Clay didn't get a chance to be surprised. A shout echoed through the rocks. A blade flashed in the sun. The officer slumped to the ground holding his abdomen and disappeared under a mob of shouting villagers.

Zdravko grabbed the chief by the arm, dragged him back, away from the mob. Behind, the fighters closed ranks, raised weapons. They were screaming at the villagers. Through the lens, Clay could see their jaws moving under the butts of their weapons, magazines full, fingers on triggers. He snapped off another picture.

The villagers turned to face the fighters, fists raised, matching them voice for voice. Zdravko and the chief stood in the no-man's land between the two groups. The chief turned to face his men, palms out, pleading with them. Zdravko drew a pistol, pointed it at the chief's head. Clay's heart stopped. Jesus, no.

Clay was about to jump up, scream at Zdravko to stop when a single shot ruptured the air. The chief's right knee exploded in a shower of pink mist. He crumpled to the ground, a red stain spreading over his robe. One of the tribesmen broke from the group, sprinted towards his chief. Zdravko raised his weapon and fired three times at point blank range. The tribesman toppled into the dust at Zdravko's feet. By now the fighters had closed around Zdravko, stood with weapons levelled, a mere ten metres from the villagers. Zdravko stood over the chief, screaming at the villagers in Arabic, waving his pistol in the air, pointing it at the chief, at the mob, at his own head. Clay could see Zdravko's mouth moving, the spittle flying from his lips, his neck muscles straining, the sweat pouring from his face.

The chief was shouting back. Another shot pierced the air. The chief screamed in agony, his other knee smashed. The villagers surged forward but the chief turned to them, head craned back, warned them away. Clay could hear his words on the breeze, the voice strong even now, no, go back, don't. The villagers stopped short, metres now from their chief, from the muzzles of the fighters' weapons.

Clay pulled his headscarf up over his face and jumped to his feet. 'Enough,' he cried out at the top of his voice, his arms raised over his head, camera still in one hand. His voice echoed through the rocks.

Though he was a good 200 metres away, every face in the group turned at once in his direction.

'Stop what you are doing and leave now,' he yelled out.

Zdravko looked up at him for a moment, dropped his shoulders, lowered his pistol, and then turned away as if he had lost interest. Clay's heart restarted. He stood where he was, exposed, covered in sweat as if waking from a nightmare. None of the fighters had yet trained a weapon on him. He took a deep breath. Enough, he whispered. Enough.

By now, other uniformed soldiers were hurrying back to the square, attracted by the sounds of conflict. For a moment it seemed as if the fighters, too, would turn away. Zdravko took a step towards the vehicles, another. It was over. Clay exhaled.

Then Zdravko stopped, turned, stood staring up at Clay. Their eyes met. Clay's face was covered, his cap pulled down low. Even so, there weren't many foreigners of Clay's build wandering around this part of the Yemen. He was sure that Zdravko had recognised him.

Moments passed, seconds slowed into drugged minutes as they stared at each other. No one moved. The chief was moaning, conscious still despite his shattered knees. Zdravko looked down at the ground, scuffed his boot through the blood-soaked sand, looked back up. He raised his arm and aimed his weapon at Clay.

At that range even an expert shot with the Makarov would have difficulty hitting a target. Clay knew that as long as he stood his ground, the chief had a chance. Clay aimed his camera at Zdravko, focussed on his face, the handgun big now, pointing right into Clay's lens, the muzzle an empty black hole in Zdravko's sunburnt hand. He clicked the shutter, watched Zdravko's finger squeeze down on the trigger. The bullet would take about a third of a second to reach him, the sound of the gunshot about double that. Clay opened his eyes wide.

'No,' shouted the chief.

In one movement, Zdravko swung his weapon down and around, pivoted on both feet, and shot the chief through the middle of the forehead.

The chief slumped to the ground, motionless.

The fighters stood, silent, weapons trained on the tribesmen, looking at each other as if unsure what to do next. Moments slipped by. Then Zdravko opened his mouth. Clay saw it before he heard it. The muzzles of six automatic weapons flashed. The tribesmen, a dozen in all, disappeared. At that range, it was not a scything down of bodies, but a disintegration, the projectiles tearing flesh and shattering bone, ripping away limbs and faces in a cloud of blood and flying debris. Then the sound, the sickening crack of exploding gunpowder and expanding gases, the metallic clatter of firing mechanisms, the groan of dying men, cried across the rocks and along the cliffs, lingered for a moment in the swirling breeze, and died. Fourteen men lay dead in the sand.

Clay stood frozen, transfixed, finger shaking on the shutter control, unable to breathe. Thirteen years vanished and he was there again, amidst the screams, the noise, the dirt, the rush. He was a witness. That's what he would be now, for the rest of his life. He had photographed it all.

He watched as the fighters took out empty magazines and snapped new ones into place, as if unaware of the carnage they had unleashed. Clay stood with the camera glued to his face, his hands shaking. Zdravko was looking right at him. Clay could see every detail of his face, the golden stubble around his mouth, the creases in his forehead shining with sweat, his mouth moving, the meaty hands changing out the Markarov's mag.

Clay caught a flash of movement to Zdravko's left. One of the irregulars raised his rifle. Clay dropped to the ground just as the first rounds clattered into the rock above him, followed a fraction of a second later by the killing chant of the AK. He lay against the ancient seabed, the air above him filled with flying metal and pulverised rock, his insides tumbling, that familiar hollow sickness he'd always felt under fire, had prayed he'd never have to feel again. He hugged the rock, tried to push himself into its nullity, to become like it was, inanimate, uncaring, whole somehow, without friends or brothers or children who needed you, that you needed. The firing stopped. Target lost. Shouts of command echoed and fragmented among the rocks, across the years. He needed to move. Now.

Clay stuffed his camera into his pack and backed away towards the cover of a ridge of larger boulders that lined the slope. He set off in a low running crouch, contouring the edge of the splay fan, the escarpment cliff to his right, the sounds of shouting falling behind. He looked back across the slope, saw no one. He had covered almost 200 metres, moving away from the Land Cruiser. He ducked behind a cross-banded block of sandstone the size of a bus and sank to the ground, sweat pouring from his temples, his shirt soaked. Somewhere back in the direction of the village, an engine started up, and then another. Vehicle doors slammed.

And now, in the background, rising like a desert storm, the wailing of women. A long shiver, the tiny feet of a black spider, crawled up his spine. He stood, all clarity now, the old habits kicking in, found a handhold and levered his way to the top of the block. Prone, he edged his way forward over the breakaway until he could see back down the wadi. The Yemeni troops who had fanned out into the village were streaming back to the trucks. Women moved like black ghosts among the bodies of the dead, ignored by the soldiers, crumpled to the ground beside loved ones, screaming their anguish to the sky. Zdravko stood in the open front of one of the vehicles, scanning the slope through binoculars, pointing, shouting.

Clay took a deep breath. What had he just witnessed? Vengeance dealt? Honour restored? Here, nothing could be judged by the action alone.

A flash of movement in the rock caught Clay's eye. Two fighters were making their way up the slope towards the promontory where Clay had stood. They were now between him and the Land Cruiser, but it was clear from the way they were moving directly upslope that they hadn't seen him. Clay eased his head down, pushed his way back to the edge of the block. Then he jumped to the ground, slung his pack, and set off at a sprint. Carried along on a cross-current of fear and anger, he darted between boulders, working with the terrain, his feet skimming over the stones, ricocheting off oblique slabs, knees bouncing like shocks, moving steadily up-wadi, contouring the slope where the boulders were thick and high. There was no road here. If they were going to follow him it would have to be on foot. They would have to chase him down.

But too soon the pain came, the indiscipline of the last years shooting like acid through his muscles, his heart fibrillating as his brain commanded the machine to do something for which it was no longer fit. He stopped, chest heaving, leant against a boulder, looked back. Still no one. He ran on, anger propelling him through the distress, stumbling rubber-legged over the rocks. After a while he fell into a rhythm, the sprint long since over, his body working into it now, breathing smoothing out, heart rate stabilising, muscles and tendons answering autonomous commands, and after a while as the endorphins raced through him and euphoria came he almost forgot the danger behind and even why he was running.

Moving the Ball

Clay ran until darkness fell, collapsed to the ground, hungry and exhausted. Convinced that he had not been followed, he crawled into a space between two boulders and curled up like a stray dog, the world incomprehensible, the universe swirling above him, pure chaos.

He awoke cold, the sky grey, dawn still a few hours off. The wadi here was narrow, the texture of the opposite slope distinct, the caprock frayed into blocks at the escarpment's edge and toppled down the slope. He set off in the gloom, stiff-legged and thirsty, back towards Al Bawazir.

He reached Abdulkader's Land Cruiser by late morning. The vehicle was as he had left it, indistinct, one of thousands in this part of the world, dented panels, scraped paint, smashed light housings, twice re-treaded tyres. Either the soldiers hadn't found it, or they hadn't connected it to him. He walked down to the village, to where the men had died. The bodies were gone, the sand swept clean of blood. Even the tyre tracks of the vehicles had been raked away, the spent cartridge cases collected. In his head, he could still hear the screams, the clatter of the machine guns. 'God is great,' he said aloud, no one there to hear him. It was always the best ones who died. And the flawed, the undeserving, lived.

The drive to Al Mukalla was a blur. It was as if the world was collapsing in on him. Never had he felt so utterly alone, so lost. He hammered the steering wheel, screamed into the void.

A few hours later Clay walked into the front entrance of the hospital at Al Mukalla. The same soldier, one of the men he had bribed before, slouched in the chair by the door, too strung out on *qat* to notice as he hurried past the admitting desk and through the double doors towards the doctor's office. A diagnosis of Mohamed's symptoms would answer some questions: were the illnesses he had seen caused by chemical poisoning as Al Shams and the villagers suspected? Or was it bacteriological, viral – a disease of some kind? Something else, perhaps. Was the whole thing really just about money and politics?

He came to the office, the same door on the left, the same frosted glass above the doorframe, the sign board. He knocked and turned the handle, pushed open the door. A grey-haired man in a white lab coat sat at a little desk piled with papers. He turned to look back over his shoulder at Clay through narrowed eyes. His face was thin, the skin sallow, almost jaundiced under a fallow grey beard.

'May I help you?' the man said in Arabic.

'I … I am looking for the doctor,' Clay stuttered. 'This is his office.'

'This is my office.'

Clay glanced at the window, the courtyard, the examination table where Mohamed had laid.

'There must be some mistake. I was here just two days ago. I met with a doctor – I don't know his name. He said this was his office. He examined a friend of mine.'

The man swivelled his chair, smoothed his coat, slid his pen into his breast pocket. 'Ah, yes,' the man said in English. 'I am his replacement.'

Clay baulked. Jesus Christ. 'Where did he go?'

'He was gone by the time I arrived.'

Clay laced his fingers behind his head, looked to the ceiling. 'Did he leave any records?'

The man raised his eyebrows. 'You must know that I cannot …'

'Look,' Clay interrupted him. 'My friend, the one he was examining, a little boy from one of the villages, was very ill. His mother is illiterate. I need to know the results of the examination.'

The man pulled the pen from his pocket, rolled it between his fingers, shook his head. 'Even if I could show you, I assure you that this office was empty when I arrived.'

Clay stood staring past the doctor out into the parched courtyard. 'Thank you,' he said finally, and walked away.

That night Clay walked up the front steps of the company guest-house in Aden and went straight to the dining room. Karila and Parnell were seated at the table, hunched over heaped dinner plates. They looked up at him as he entered.

'What are you doing here?' said Parnell, shucking the exoskeleton from a prawn. The skin of his face looked as if had just been salon peeled, moist and pale like wet glue.

'This is the dining room. I thought I might eat.'

Karila raised his eyes to where heaven was supposed to be.

Clay approached the table. The smell of food sent pangs through him. He hadn't eaten for more than a day. He pulled out a chair across from Karila, next to Parnell.

'Go get yourself cleaned up, Straker,' gobbed Parnell, mouth full of prawn meat. 'This ain't a sty.'

Clay looked down at his silt-covered shirt and trousers, his plaster dust hands, and sat. He poured himself a glass of water from the jug on the table, drank it down.

'Did you hear what I said, Straker?' said Parnell. If anything he looked more bloated than Clay remembered, softer, the eyes darker, smaller.

'I heard you,' said Clay, and turning to Karila: 'I need to talk to you, Nils.'

Karila put down his knife and fork, swallowed his food.

'It's about Al Urush.'

'What about it?'

'Something bad is happening. Some sort of epidemic. I think the sheikh was telling the truth.' Why else would Al Shams be pushing so hard for answers, be willing to maim his own country-man? The young chief, who Clay had immediately trusted, had been convinced that this was no ordinary bout of sickness. And now he was dead, murdered by Zdravko. Clay swallowed hard, a dry stone in his throat.

Parnell shifted his bulk and grunted something Clay could not make out.

'We have already spoken about this,' Karila said in his usual businesslike tone. 'Al Urush is not our concern. If there is an illness, as you say, then it is something for the authorities, the Health Department.'

'I took one of the kids to the hospital.'

Karila and Parnell sat open-mouthed.

'But when I went back today, the doctor had been replaced. There was no record of the examination. It was as if it had never happened.' After another fifty dollars spent bribing the administrative clerk and two fruitless hours poring over hospital records, the clerk translating dates and names, Clay had driven to Al Urush. Mohamed and his mother were back in their house, the little guy even worse, limp on the creaky cot, barely able to open his eyes.

She knew nothing, or hadn't understood what the doctor had told her, if indeed he had told her anything at all. He'd spent over an hour trying to convince her to let him take Mohamed to Aden, put him in a real hospital, but she'd resisted every attempt, each of his clumsy arguments. Finally, in tears, screaming, she'd pushed him out of her house, slammed the door behind him, left him standing in the dust, the target of a dozen suspicious gazes shot through cracked shutters and shifted veils.

Parnell leaned back in his chair, clasped his hands behind his head.

'I appreciate your sense of public duty, Mister Straker,' said Karila. 'But you represent Petro-Tex out there. I am sure our lawyers would tell you that such actions could be misconstrued by some as an admission of responsibility. Please do not do it again.'

'You have got to be joking.'

'I am quite serious. We have to keep our eyes on the ball here, Mister Straker. And the ball is getting this expansion underway as soon as possible.' Karila looked over at his boss like a child at a doting parent.

Clay could see the tightrope under his feet, the chasm of his friend's fate opening up beneath. He took a deep breath, steadied himself. 'The sheikh said that the illness started about six months ago. Is there anything, anything at all, that has changed up at the CPF? Leaks, spills, gas venting, anything that might trigger a problem?'

Parnell rocked forward in his chair. 'There ain't nothin' up there but a few oil-water separators and a tank farm, Straker. It's not like it's a fucking refinery or something. This is a basic operation.'

Clay ignored Parnell and addressed Karila directly. 'The water is a lot saltier,' said Clay. 'Nearly 4000 milligrams per litre. Normally it's less than 500.'

'You know as well as I do that water quality there is highly variable, especially in the wadis,' said Karila. 'It is perfectly natural.'

'Whatever it is, they think it's us. It's ugly: sick kids, miscarriages. The payments aren't going to keep them quiet for long.'

'Get real, Straker. Look at the way these people live,' said Parnell, forking a slice of beef into his mouth. 'Raw sewage and trash everywhere. Are you surprised that they're all getting sick? For fuck's sake, Straker, you're acting like a rookie. You've seen this stuff before. That's why we pay you.'

Atef leaned his belly over the table to put a plate of roast beef with all the trimmings in front of Clay.

'*Shukran*, Atef,' Clay said, his appetite suddenly gone.

The cook smiled. 'How is it, Mister Clay?'

'About as well as Zamalek, to tell you the truth.' Zamalek was Atef's beloved Cairo football team.

Atef smiled. 'Yes, they lose again this week. No midfield, no attack. But we never give up hope.'

Clay forced a smile.

'Thank you, Atef,' said Karila. 'You can go.' He waited until the cook had left the room, and then turned to Clay. 'Did you make the necessary payments, Mister Straker?'

Clay took a deep breath. 'All done,' he said, holding his tone neutral. 'But Abdulkader is still out there, still a prisoner. We should offer a payment for his return.'

'We don't pay ransom to terrorists,' said Parnell.

'But we're happy to bribe communities.'

Parnell's cheeks flushed. 'It's not the same thing, goddammit, Straker, and you know it.'

'They are facilitation payments,' said Karila. 'Not bribes.'

'This is not going to go away,' said Clay.

'Straker, you're here to keep these people sweet. Not stir 'em up. The expansion is top priority. We expect our contractors to help move the ball down the field.'

Clay looked at the American and then over at Karila. That was where he should have stopped. That was where he had stopped every other time, his client happy, with a bit of luck the money in his account, his conscience – what little of it he had managed to salvage over the last years – absolved. But the words came anyway. 'Is that what Todorov is doing? Keeping people sweet?'

Parnell and Karila looked at him with blank expressions.

'What are you talking about, Straker?' said Karila.

They didn't know.

'Nothing. Look, we need to figure out what is going on. Let me go to the CPF, have a look.'

The other two men sat chewing their food. Clay picked up his water glass, looked through its distorting meniscus at Parnell.

'I thought you had taken a water sample,' said Karila.

Clay tipped his glass and let a drop of water fall to his napkin. 'Bloody lab screwed up – spilled it.'

Parnell coughed and fidgeted in his chair.

'I could take some proper air and water samples,' Clay continued. 'That would tell us for sure. It won't take long. I can do it right away.'

'Thank you for the suggestion, Straker. But that is not in the programme or the budget at this time. We do not have time or money to waste.'

'We're talking about less than five thousand dollars, Nils. No impact on schedule.' Before coming back to the guesthouse he had lodged the new samples from Al Urush and Bawazir with the laboratory, under his own name this time. If necessary he would pay for the analysis himself. Not that he could afford it. He was rapidly burning through the last of his cash.

Karila wiped his lips with his napkin, draped it over his unfinished meal, and lit a cigarette. 'The CPF is locked down. You know that. And even if it wasn't, it would make no difference. We are not the cause.'

'OK. We're not the cause. Let's prove it. To ourselves, to everyone, . to Al Shams.'

Parnell spat. 'I don't have to prove nothin' to a goddamned murderer.'

'Don't be hysterical, Mister Straker,' said Karila, smoke pouring from his mouth and nostrils. 'It is ludicrous even to suggest that air pollution from our facility is causing this.'

'It's even more ludicrous not to protect yourself against the suggestion.'

Parnell pushed his chair back with a loud scrape of wood on tile and levered himself to his feet. 'Goddammit, Straker,' he barked, eyes bulging. 'I don't want to hear any more of your bullshit. You got me? This is over. Now get on side and do your fucking job, or I'll get someone who will.'

Parnell and Karila strode from the room leaving Clay alone at the table.

After dinner Clay showered and locked himself in his room. He pulled a bottle of CC from his bag and opened the big window and looked out over the lights of Little Aden blinking in the distance. A warm breeze blew through the room. The sea air smelt of iodine and faintly of sewage. He unscrewed the bottle and took two big gulps of the whisky. He was still not sure about the illnesses. A sick boy was not unusual. He had seen a lot worse – polio cripples walking bent double with wooden blocks strapped to their palms, diseased urchins picking through steaming landfills, their eyes thick with flies. He had not seen or smelt anything in the way of air pollution, and a bit of salt in the water was not going to make anyone sick. These kids were malnourished and open to all kinds of disease and infection. Their little bodies were just too weak to cope.

But what had Zdravko been doing with the Army at Bawazir? What had sparked the killing? Karila and Parnell hadn't even twitched an eyelid. Was Zdravko working behind the company's back? And if so, to what end? More immediately, had he recognized Clay as the man who stood up on the cliffside and tried to stop the killing? If so, he was in real danger. Clay took another swig of whisky. His head was spinning. He closed his eyes. All that blood soaking into the parched ground. The broken bodies twisted like pretzels, the young chief dead on the ground, his white robes splattered with gore, the women wailing as they moved among the corpses, long plumes of dust spiralling away behind the fleeing vehicles into a sky so blue it crushed your eyes. He opened his eyes, shook his head, but all he could see were the sores on little Mohamed's arms, open and weeping, and Abdulkader's grizzled hand, hacked off God knew how, withered, dead.

He reached for the bottle.

There was a knock at the door. He stood, steadied himself a moment, walked across the marble floor and unbolted the lock.

Karila held up a bottle of schnapps and two glasses. 'Do you have a minute?'

They sat outside on the balcony and looked at the lights flickering around the bay. Karila poured out two glasses and lit up a cigarette. 'Don't worry about Vance,' said the Finn. 'He's not as bad as he seems, really.'

Clay took a sip of the alcohol. It was aspartame sweet, oddly artificial. 'He's a pompous son of a bitch and you know it. All that crap about moving the ball, as if this were some kind of game. Abdulkader is a prisoner, if he isn't dead already. And Parnell won't do a thing about it.'

Karila sipped his drink. 'Leave it with me, Straker. I'll talk to him, see if we can do something.'

Clay looked at the Finn. His pale eyes were haloed red. 'Let me do the testing at the villages, Nils. If we do it quickly, Al Shams will let Abdulkader go.'

Karila waved his free hand. 'You heard Vance. It's out of the question.'

Clay filled his lungs, held the air, exhaled slowly. 'OK then. Five thousand dollars ransom would do it, Nils. It's the going rate.'

Karila put down his glass, pondered this for a moment. 'That's a lot of money, Clay.'

'22,500 barrels a day,' said Clay, not trying to disguise the anger in his voice. 'World price twenty-one dollars a barrel, give or take. Cost of production and royalties, what, seven dollars? That's a net profit of 315,000 a day, Nils. A day.'

Karila glanced up and to the right.

'I'd pay it myself if I had the money.' He glanced at Karila. 'But I haven't seen a cent for three months.'

Karila frowned. 'I'm sorry you've had to wait so long, Straker. We'll get that sorted out right away.'

'Maybe I should start charging Medved interest,' he said. Both his offshore accounts in Cyprus were overdrawn, and the banks were screaming. He hadn't sent anything to Eben's parents in months. 'I really need that money, Nils.'

'I will look after it personally.'

'And Abdulkader?'

'I'll do my best.'

'*Inshallah*,' Clay said.

'Things are going well, Straker. Let's keep it up and get this past the regulators and finished. Finish the report so we can review it and sign off. Work your magic with the authorities. They trust you. There's a bonus for you if you finish on schedule. And then there is another big piece of work I would like you to do for us – a baseline assessment for a new exploration block further North in the Empty

Quarter – sole source, no bidding. We'll extend your contract imme-diately at 900 a day. How does that sound?'

Clay emptied the glass and put it back down on the table, calcu-lated the money it would bring in. In a couple of months he might actually have his head above water, ever so slightly. 'Hundreds.'

Karila pursed his lips. 'What is that supposed to mean?'

'It means good. Just pay me what you owe me, OK?'

Karila fiddled with the bottle, twisting it in place on the table, grinding glass on stone. 'Go to accounts first thing next week and Dunkley will have a cheque for you. And Clay ...' He had never used his given name before. '... the PSO called me today, asking about you.'

Clay's stomach lurched over the apex.

Karila cast a sidelong glance and refilled his own glass. 'They say you've been talking to the Press.' Karila lit another of his French cigarettes and inhaled deeply. 'That's a bad idea, Clay, from every-one's perspective. You know the rules.'

Clay tried to avoid the plume of blue smoke. 'Jesus, all I did was have a drink with a girl by the pool.'

'Yes, that LaTour woman. I heard. Stay away from her, Clay.'

Clay sat a moment, quiet, thought about this. Then he said: 'Didn't tell her a thing, Nils.'

'Good. And stay clear of the Mövenpick. That's an order. The management called me about your little altercation in the lobby. They are very unhappy that our people are engaging in "unruly behaviour", as they call it.'

'It was nothing, Nils.'

'So you don't deny it.'

'Why should I? It was after hours. It's none of the company's business.'

'Nothing, you say, Straker? The man you assaulted worked for one of our contractors. He was flown to hospital in Europe this morning with a broken arm and a fractured jaw, for God's sake.'

Clay said nothing.

'You're lucky he's not pressing charges.'

'He's the lucky one,' said Clay.

Karila frowned. 'Why do you have to be so difficult?' He sighed.
'Just remember what I said. We're counting on you.'

Clay leaned forward and grabbed Karila's wrist. 'And Abdulkader
is counting on *you*.'

The Finn's cigarette butt fell to the floor. It glowed there, brown-
ing the tile. Karila looked at Clay's hand on his wrist, then back up
at Clay. 'I said I'd do what I could.'

Clay let go.

Karila stood, crushed the cigarette with a twist of his shoe, gathered up the bottle and the glasses, and stood up. 'Trust me on this,
Straker,' he said. Then he turned and disappeared into the hallway.

Clay closed the door, walked over to the window, opened the
whisky and swigged a mouthful, and then another, trying to wash
the cloying taste from his mouth. Trust. He put the bottle down and
walked down the hall to the communications room. It was empty.
He picked up the sat phone receiver and punched in a number.

'It's Clay Straker.' The satellite connection hissed and warbled
behind the echo of his voice. 'What are you doing this weekend?' he
said. 'I need to talk to you. It's important.'

١٦

In Paradise

Clay woke early the next morning, the city still shrouded in sea mist, the streets empty. He dressed, threw a water bottle into his pack, checked his wallet and passport, locked the door to his room, and walked down the guesthouse stairs. He was opening the front door when Atef called his name.

The big Egyptian was standing in the doorway to the kitchen, his hands covered in flour. 'Telephone, Mister Clay.'

Clay looked at his watch. Not yet six o'clock.

'Here, in my kitchen.'

Clay closed the door and followed Atef into the kitchen. The air was thick with the smell of yeast, dough, rising bread. Atef handed him a flour-patched receiver.

'Clay Straker here.'

'You wanted to know about Champard.' The line was bad, the voice hollow.

'Who is this?'

'Look, I don't have long.'

'I'm listening.'

'It wasn't Al Shams who killed Thierry.'

Clay said nothing, waited.

'November 30th. That's the day Thierry was killed.' As if he could forget. 'Check the personnel records, Straker, the accounts.'

He could hear the Southern accent. 'Jim, is that you?'

'Dig, Straker.'

'Who killed him?'

'I don't know. But it wasn't Al Shams. Figure it out, Straker. But do it fast. They're on to you.'

'Why was he killed?'

The line hissed. Clay could hear breathing at the other end. 'Don't let them do to you what they've done to me.'

'Do what? What are they doing?'

'Someone's coming. I've gotta go.' The line went dead.

Clay stood for a moment, receiver in hand. Atef was watching him, sleeves rolled up over thick forearms, kneading a big lump of dough. 'OK, Mister Clay?'

'*Tammam,*' he replied, unsteady. He replaced the handset in its cradle on the wall. 'Did you know Champard, Atef?'

'Oh yes, Mister Clay. A very nice man, a good man. Always polite. When he stayed with us here he always left money for the staff. Very sad what happened to him.' The cook thrust a freshly baked croissant and a steaming mug of coffee into his hands. 'Before you go,' he said.

By early morning Clay had left the wide sweeping Southern plains behind and came into the fertile uplands of Ta'izz. It was just outside of Ad Dimnah that he first noticed it: a white Pajero, newish, with a dented front quarter-panel, tracking behind. At first, he paid it no attention. But as other vehicles came and went, the Pajero followed like a faithful dog, falling back as the miles clicked by and then surging closer again, always behind. An hour later he was in the mountains, the country here green, terraced from valley to peak, the narrow road twisting through mountain passes with purple rivers and foam-white rapids threading through the dark volcanic rock far below, the Pajero still following.

A road block just outside Ibb slowed traffic to a walk for miles in both directions. Clay inched along behind a dilapidated Toyota Hi-Lux heaped with fresh vegetables and sacks of grain. The vehicles in front stopped. He waited. After a while he killed the engine and got out to have a look. Ahead, every vehicle was being pulled over and searched. Soldiers swarmed over big eighteen-wheelers, opening cargo containers, inspecting documents. Two tanks, an armoured personnel carrier and a dozen heavily armed soldiers watched over the scene, weapons ready.

He glanced back along the queue and caught sight of the Pajero six cars back. Glare on the windscreen obscured any view of the driver. Zdravko usually drove a new-model black Land Rover, but that meant nothing. He could readily have switched vehicles to disguise himself. If it was him back there, Clay could use the roadblock delay between them – five vehicles to be inspected, five drivers to be questioned – to get a head start and hide in the hinterland off the main road. He considered strolling back along the queue to get a clear view of the driver, but thought better of it, got back into Abdulkader's Land Cruiser.

After a while, the queue moved forward. Clay started the engine, moved a few more car-lengths towards the road block. Another halt, longer this time. Again, he shut down the engine, got out, leaned against the Land Cruiser's passenger door, and looked up along the line of vehicles towards the makeshift roadside village festering around the checkpoint. He glanced over his shoulder. The Pajero was still there, a lone figure behind the wheel, a dark shape through the glare. Clay looked at his watch. An hour wasted here already, an hour he didn't have.

He was about to get back in the car when a detonation split the air, loud and close. Clay's knees gave way autonomously, pure reflex. Before he had time to register the noise, he was on the ground. Adrenaline burst through his heart, pounded into his feet and hands. Up ahead, more gun shots, two quick pops, a shout, the death rattle of an AK, then silence.

Clay looked up. Soldiers emerged from huts, clambered down from the tank, and gathered around one of the vehicles. Clay stood, brushing the dirt from his clothes. He watched as the soldiers pulled two men from the vehicle. They were limp, their clothes covered in blood. The unfortunates were dragged through the dirt and deposited at the roadside to lie open-mouthed with the rest of the detritus, the plastic bags, the animal carcasses, the rotting scraps and peels, the hulks and husks. Another man was marched away at gunpoint by two soldiers. His hands were tied behind his back and he was bareheaded. He slowed, stopped. The soldiers were shouting, pushing him forward. The man stumbled, fell to the ground. Unable to break his fall he rolled side-on to take the impact on his shoulder. One of the soldiers grabbed him by the back of his shirt and hauled him to his feet, pushing him along with the butt of his weapon. Clay watched the man disappear into a sandbagged bunker. Soldiers pushed the bullet-riddled car to the side of the road.

Finally, almost two hours after joining the queue, he reached the barrier and was directed to the side of the road. He offered his papers to an officer in a camouflaged jumpsuit and black beret.

The officer leaned in through the open window and scanned the inside of the car with flicking, nervous eyes.

'What is your business here?' asked the officer in English, staring at Clay's passport, the smell of booze heavy on his breath.

'*Inshallah,* I am going to Sana'a to visit a friend.'

'Get out of the car.'

Clay drew breath, held the air in his lungs, then let it go. It took ten or eleven long seconds. Then he opened the door and stepped down onto the smashed rubble of the shoulder.

The officer's head tilted back as Clay stood to his full height. His eyes narrowed and he took two full steps back, his hand reaching for his holstered sidearm. 'What are you doing in Yemen?' he said.

'Petro-Tex,' said Clay. That was usually enough.

The officer nodded, waving two bare-headed conscripts forward. The youths started going through the Land Cruiser, flinging open doors, peering under seats.

'It is not a good time to travel,' said the officer. 'The border may close at any time.'

'Border?'

'*Inshallah*, not.' The officer flipped through Clay's passport, looked at the photo page. 'However, I suggest you turn back.'

'It is only for a short time.'

'Go back. And consider leaving Yemen soon.'

'Sir, may I ask a favour?'

The officer put his hands on his hips, mulled this over. It was probably the first time he had heard that one today.

'May I take something from the car?'

'Please,' said the officer. 'Slowly.'

Clay stepped to the car, reached under the seat, pulled out a plastic bag containing two bottles of Jack Daniels and handed it to the officer.

The officer took the bag, looked inside. He stood a moment examining the contents. Then he closed the bag, looked up along the road and back, put the bag at his feet. 'I hope the one you will visit in Sana'a is a good friend,' said the officer. 'There will be many checkpoints.'

Clay grinned. '*Inshallah*, she will become a very good friend.'

The officer looked up, smiled. 'If you wish to return South, do not stay more than one day in Sana'a.'

Clay jutted his chin towards the bullet-riddled car at the side of the road. 'What happened?'

'Southern extremists trying to come North. They killed one of my men.'

Clay frowned.

'He is in paradise.'

'*Al hamdillulah.*'

The officer flicked up an eyebrow, stood staring at Clay. Then he repeated the invocation, thanking God. 'Go,' he barked, handing Clay back his passport, waving to the guards to raise the barrier.

'*Shukran.*' Clay started the Land Cruiser, and put it in gear. 'The white Pajero, six back,' he called to the officer as the Land Cruiser started to roll forward. 'You may want to check it.' Before the officer had a chance to react, Clay was through the barrier and accelerating down the road towards Sana'a.

١٧

No Shortage of Bastards

It was almost dusk when he reached the hotel. It was one of the last old Yemeni establishments left in the city. Not far from the Bab Al Yemen gate – where only yesterday, according to one of the truck drivers he had met on the road from Ta'izz, a thief's hand had been amputated and hung from the stone arch – the four-storey white-washed *funduq* stood serene within its ten-acre walled garden, an oasis. The gate guard hinged the steel panel door aside and Clay steered Abdulkader's Land Cruiser into the compound. The tyres crunched and popped along the winding gravel drive. King palms towered overhead, ancient. Birds darted among the woody acacias. He parked in front of the main entrance and turned off the engine.

The hotel seemed to have been sculpted rather than built, the alabaster mortar smoothed and layered on by hand over soft mud, artisanal. There was not a corner or edge to be seen. Inside, the lobby was cool, the blue tile-work floor like a glacial pond under a carved roof of ice. A spiral stairway, the steps hewn and polished from the same compound, swirled away to the upper parts of the palace. A portrait of Crown Prince Muhammad al-Badr, the last Imam of Yemen, hung from the near wall. Defiance shone from the canvas.

'You're late.' She stood at the bottom of the stairway in a floor-length robe, black with embroidered edges, flowers red and yellow. Her hair was swept back under a diaphanous black headscarf. His pulse took a jump.

'Beautiful,' he said.

She smiled.

'You live here?'

'I know the owners, a very old Yemen family.'

He looked down at his dust-covered trousers and boots. 'Sorry it took me so long,' he said. 'You'd think there was a war on.'

'Soon there might be.' She stepped towards him and offered her hand. It was soft and cool, like a child's. 'Come,' she said, pulling him towards the stairs. 'I booked you a room. How long can you stay?'

'Just tonight. I can't risk getting stuck here if war does break out.'

Rania frowned. 'I wanted to show you Sana'a.'

'Maybe next time.'

'If there is a next time.' She smiled. Pale enamel flashed between glossed lips.

He washed and changed and met her on the third-floor balcony that overlooked the gardens. Beyond the ataxia of Sana'a's rooftops, barren olivine and iron oxide cliffs hulked in the late afternoon heat. A waiter brought tea and departed. They were alone.

'I was followed,' he said, unscrewing the cap of his hip flask. 'I think I lost him at the checkpoint near Ibb.'

'You are a popular man right now, it seems.'

He fortified his tea, offered her some.

'No, thank you,' she said. 'I don't drink.'

Of course she didn't. He slipped the flask back into his pocket. 'Look Rania, I know it was sudden, but I need to talk to you. You said you wanted information. Well, I've seen something, witnessed something.'

She was alert now, her reporter's antennae fully deployed.

He tried to describe it, stumbled. He reached into his pocket and placed an exposed roll of 35-millimetre film on the table. 'It's all there,' he whispered. He hadn't dared have the film developed.

She looked down at the yellow-and-black film canister but did not touch it. 'The government has already blamed it on Al Shams.'

'That's bullshit. Have a look for yourself. The Army was there.' He paused, considering what he would say next. 'So was the security guy from Petro-Tex. The men who did the shooting weren't Yemenis, Rania. They *looked* like Yemenis, but they were speaking another language; it sounded like Turkish, but it wasn't.'

'Pashtun,' she said.

Clay looked at her, a question.

'Afghans.'

'Here in Yemen?'

'Al Qaeda. The government is inviting them in, offering them safe haven. In return, Al Qaeda moonlights doing Saleh's dirty work.'

'I thought the PSO were the presidential dirt-baggers.'

'The PSO *runs* Al Qaeda in Yemen; Ansar Al-Sharia they call it.'

Clay leaned back and took a deep breath. 'But then why is the PSO questioning me about Al Shams, while accusing him of being Ansar Al-Sharia? It doesn't make sense.'

Rania looked over her shoulder and leaned in close. 'When the Soviets invaded Afghanistan, Al Shams was one of thousands of Yemenis who answered the call of jihad. In the early eighties he became a *mujahideen,* fighting the godless Marxist infidel. Ten years ago he was badly wounded. After a long convalescence in a Pakistani hospital, he returned to Yemen and became the head of Ansar Al-Sharia. That's what my sources tell me. But two years ago, he went rogue, and now the PSO wants him dead.'

Clay took a shallow breath, looked up at the newly risen crescent moon, its point plunged deep into the blackened ridge. He and Al Shams had been fighting the same enemy – the communists – at the same time, on different continents. 'He's threatening to kill my friend.'

'Just as he killed another Petro-Tex employee last year.'

'Champard.' Jim's warning echoed in his head.

'Yes. A French national.'

'I know. I was there.'

Rania gasped, breathed out between pursed lips. 'You.'

'They almost got me, too.'

'I reported the story. It was very big news in France. Yemenis who saw the explosion told me that there was another foreigner there, but no one I spoke to in Petro-Tex seemed to know anything about it. About you. You were, are, my missing witness.'

'I was sent home on the next flight out, told to keep quiet.'

Rania bit down on her lower lip. 'What happened that day, Clay?'

He told her.

'Was it a car bomb, an RPG?'

He'd asked himself that question a thousand times. 'I didn't see or hear any kind of projectile. It wasn't that.' He knew the sound too well. 'Thierry never turned the engine off, just kept it idling while I got out. So it couldn't have been ignition-activated.'

'Remote control detonation.'

She knew her stuff. 'That's my best guess,' he said. 'The bomb must have been planted in the vehicle before we left the office that day.'

'And they waited until you were out and safely away.'

Clay's heart stopped, restarted. He hadn't ever considered this.

'Why were you spared, Clay? Do you have any idea?'

'Jesus. No. None.' Not luck, after all. Determinism.

Rania sipped her tea, looked out over the city.

'How did they know it was Al Shams?' he said.

'He claimed responsibility. And, ever since, Petro-Tex has been putting pressure on governments here and abroad to act against the terrorists.' Rania sipped her tea, replaced the glass on the table, and smoothed down her robe.

'Al Shams told me himself that he didn't do it.'

Rania looked at him sidelong, surprise in her eyes. 'Do you trust him, after what he has done?'

He didn't know what to think. There was something about the man. Despite everything, there was honour in him, that was clear – a hopeless, outgunned, surrounded honour that resonated with Clay, defied his anger. He said nothing.

'If I were you I would be very careful, Clay. Don't mention what you have seen at Bawazir to anyone – not yet anyway – especially not to your Petro-Tex colleagues. These are very dangerous people.' She scooped up the film canister and put it into his hand. 'And hold on to this.'

There was a rap on the shutters and the waiter appeared at the veranda doorway. Rania stood and walked over to where he stood. A brief conversation ensued. She closed the louvered door and returned to the divan. 'I hope you're hungry. I've asked them to bring up some food.'

He told her about Al Urush, about the boy Mohamed and his harp of spokes, of the lost sample and his suspicion of a link between the oilfield operations and the illnesses. He told her about Al Shams' warnings, about his confrontation with Karila and Parnell's threats, Abdulkader's misfortune.

'If I were you, I would be very wary of Vance Parnell,' she said. 'He has, how should I say, a *history*.'

Clay looked into her eyes, waited for her to continue.

'Three years ago, he was dismissed from an American multinational's Thai operations. He had been caught bribing high-level Thai government officials using money from a special corporate account. When the story hit the Thai press, the company made Parnell the scapegoat. A few months later he showed up in Jakarta, this time with one of the European oil and gas majors, divorced and in debt. Within weeks he was the victim of a car bombing, supposedly in retaliation for previous indiscretions. He survived, but was badly burned and spent months in hospital. He went back to work, but within a year was fired for assaulting a local employee. Apparently he took a baseball bat to one of the houseboys, almost killing him. After that, none of the big multinational oil companies would touch him. He arrived in Yemen shortly afterwards as GM for Petro-Tex. There is more, of course. Trouble follows this man like the plague.'

'Or he follows it.' *That's why we pay you.* Clay breathed deep.

She was quiet for a long time, looking out over the city as the sky atomised.

After a while she said: 'How serious is the illness?'

'Serious enough: dozens of children suffering the same symptoms. I'm told there have been miscarriages.' He thought of the girl in the village, the despair in her eyes as she watched her baby burn.

'What is causing it, Clay?'

'The villagers say it's something in the air, but the more I think about it the more I figure it's the water. That would explain the kids getting sick and not the adults. With their lower body mass, and more frequent exposure, ingested toxins would have a greater and more immediate effect. But there is no obvious source, and higher salt content alone wouldn't cause the symptoms we're seeing.'

The increase in salinity could be natural, of course, a consequence of the drought that the region had been experiencing for over a decade. Others could be to blame: farmers over-pumping the shallow coastal aquifers for irrigation. There was no way to know for sure without extensive fieldwork – aquifer testing, sampling, lots more chemical analysis. Most of the time all you had were a few bits of scattered data, a coarse idea of the geology, and a gut feel. And at the moment, his guts were in turmoil. He leaned back into the cushions and combed his fingers through his hair.

'You could ask them to let you test the air and the water,' she said.

'I tried. They're not interested. They say they're too far away to have any effect.'

'In that case, they have no need to worry. The tests would come out negative.'

'They are afraid, Rania. They don't *want* to know.'

She leaned closer. He could smell the perfume in her hair. 'And Al Shams?'

'He wants me to find out what's causing the illness.' Clay looked up at the moon, clear now of the hills, angry Mars strobing retrograde in the twilight. 'I have five more days to do it. If I don't, he kills my friend. Does that sound like Al Qaeda to you?'

'Kidnapping and murder? Actually yes, it does.'

'I mean the motive, Rania. He just seems to want a fair shake for his people.'

She clenched her jaw and looked away. 'You sympathise with him?'

'I just want to get my friend out of there.' He took a deep breath. 'I'm going to the regulators, Rania. I'm going to ask the Environmental Affairs Ministry to look into it, officially.'

A cold front passed across her face. 'If you do, you are putting yourself at grave risk. The PSO will know that you are agitating. They will accuse you of working for Al Shams. Besides, the ministries are all controlled by Saleh.'

He stared out at the darkening city. 'My contact in the environment ministry is a good man. He's corrupt, he's venal, but underneath I know he cares. With the regulators involved, Petro-Tex will at least be forced to acknowledge the issue, and Al Shams will know that I'm trying. It might make the difference for Abdulkader.'

Rania bit her lip, said nothing.

'Someone's got to do something, Rania.'

She was quiet a long while, sat twirling a cord of her hair between slender fingers. 'What proof do you have?'

'Right now, not much. A few samples, nothing definitive.'

'You know what will happen if Petro-Tex finds out you're trying to implicate them, don't you?'

'I'll never work in the oil industry again.'

'Or worse.'

'I've had enough of the bullshit, Rania.'

'You could quit. Leave Yemen.'

'I could. They'd just get some other bastard to take my place. Nothing would change.'

'No shortage of bastards, then.'

'Definitely not.' Clay looked into her eyes, reached for her hands, took them in his. 'Look, Rania, I'm not going to walk away from Abulkader. I have to find out what's going on. The best chance I have is from inside Petro-Tex. I need your help.'

She looked away, across the rooftops.

'There's a story here, Rania. A good one.'

'Without proof, there is nothing.'

'What about the massacre? The photos?'

'Ten locals killed in a gun battle in Yemen is hardly news, Clay. You know that. Besides, how does it tie in with the sickness? Publishing those photos alone will just add weight to the government's stance, that it was Al Shams' doing. That is not going to change anything, assuming of course that he was not behind it.'

The food came: unleavened bread, baba ganoush, olives, grilled chicken. They ate in silence. The waiter returned and cleared the plates, then brought tea.

After a while, Clay said: 'I'm going to tell you something.'

She smiled. 'I have all night.'

'You asked me about the war.'

She reached for his hand, sat watching him, waiting.

'I ...' He stopped. He felt light-headed. He started to speak. It sounded like someone else, the voice somehow rough, unfamiliar, a recording of him. 'My *valk* – platoon – had just choppered into a *chana* north of the border. There was contact off at the far end of the clearing, AKs, RPGs. Two men were hit before SWAPO withdrew. My squad was sent in pursuit. We came to a clearing. There was movement in the far trees, someone running. We opened up, all of us blazing away. When we got to the other side we found a small boy, a civilian, lying in the low grass.' He choked on the words. 'Shot through the stomach. Alive. Still breathing.'

Rania gazed into his eyes. He looked away.

'The old guys said he was as good as dead, that we should leave him. SWAPO was still out there. I could hear the Puma coming in for the casevac, low over the trees. Someone called in contact on the radio. We heard AKs opening up. The old *okes* were saying we should move. The kid was lying there, conscious, muttering in Portuguese. I told Eben to take the squad forward.'

'Eben?' she said.

'Lance Corporal Eben Barstow, 1st Parachute Battalion. My friend.' Now a permanent resident of the Rosedale Long-term Care Clinic in Johannesburg. Clay took a shallow breath. 'I picked the kid up, ran him back to the *chana*. I got there just as the chopper was getting ready to leave. They had already loaded our wounded. We were taking fire. I put the kid on the deck. The crew looked at me as if I was crazy.' He tracked back across the years, looked into her eyes. 'The medic felt for a pulse, looked up at me. All he did was shake his head. I lifted the kid from the deck just as the Puma took off, stood there in the rotor wash, him in my arms. I laid him at the edge of the *chana* under a tree. He looked like a ghost lying there in the grass, covered in dust.'

She was looking at him intently now. He could see her recording, analysing.

He looked down at the floor, decided to continue. 'That night, they told us over the battalion net that the space shuttle had just gone up. I looked for it in the sky. I don't think I've ever felt so lonely.' He felt the back of his throat tighten into something vile and tumescent. He tried to push it back down from where it had come. And then he said: 'I so much wanted that little boy to live, Rania. But he didn't. He just stopped breathing and that was it.' He had never told that story to anyone.

She squeezed his hand. 'Why did you go?'

He looked into her eyes, searching. Her pupils were dilated, eclipsed planets spinning in coronae of gold. Just looking made him unsteady.

'I was eighteen, Rania.' He looked away. How could he tell her what no one understood, what no one wanted to know. That he had *wanted* to fight. That he couldn't wait to go, test himself, face death and dispense it. And since then, God help him, nothing had even come close, whatever the strength, whatever the dosage or frequency. Not sex, not drugs, not science or determinism, certainly not booze, nothing. It hadn't been for lack of trying.

'Some things are worth fighting for,' she whispered.

'Not that, it turned out.'

'You were young.'

'There will be a *yawm'idin* for us all,' he said.

'A day of reckoning.'

'He who is hard in wrong will turn away, he will be put to the fire, neither dying in it nor living, with us will be their accounting.'

'The Koran,' she said. 'You have been studying.'

'Abdulkader is trying to convert me.' He looked down at his hands and back up at her face. The terrace was dark now, the ancient city awakening to night. Lights flickered through the trees, the smells of wood smoke and spices drifted up from the garden. 'I'm going to find out what is hurting those people, Rania, and I'm going to prove it. And I'm going to get Abdulkader out of there. Petro-Tex can go screw themselves.'

She reached out and touched his hand.

'But I don't have long, and my contact with Al Shams is dead. Getting the truth about Al Urush into the papers is the quickest, surest way to tell Al Shams what he wants to know and save Abdulkader.'

'Get the proof, and I will write the story.'

He leaned close. He could feel her breath on his neck. She smelt of jasmine and honey, sweet black tea. He slid his arm around her waist and drew her to him. She didn't resist, looked up at him and closed her eyes. He kissed her. She responded, her mouth opening, warm, her tongue sweet. They kissed for a long time and she moved closer, running her hands through his Velcro-short hair. When he touched her leg just above the knee he found that the hem of her robe had been hiked up. She let out a sigh and pushed her mouth hard into his. He knew he should stop, that it was too soon. But her gravity was strong. He ran his hand up the silky distance of her thigh. She moaned and parted her legs. Under the robe she was naked. When he touched her she gasped and writhed against his hand. She was as slick as a tidal flat in a flood tide. Her chemicals were everywhere, deep in his throat, his nostrils, his head. He was lost.

'Come with me,' she whispered.

Part II

١٨

First Kill

26th April 1994: Lat 15° 21' N; Long 44° 12' E., Sana'a, Yemen

He left her standing outside the hotel entrance under a grey dawn
sky. She had said nothing, avoided his kiss, and now he watched
her in the rear-view mirror as she stood with her arms crossed over
her chest. He slowed as he reached the end of the gravel drive,
stuck his arm out of the window, waved, watched in the mirror for
some response, but she stood unmoving, shrouded. Clay guided
Abdulkader's Land Cruiser through the open gate and onto the road
and began the long drive back to Aden.

Twenty-six hours later he walked along the washed-down early-
morning street toward the row of crumbling Communist-era
government buildings that loomed over the port. Gulls twisted and
cried overhead. A thin sea haze hung like a greying negligee around
the point and barb of the Crater, the extinct volcano that guards
Aden's fishhook harbour from the Indian Ocean.

Three copies of the environmental and social impact report for
the Petro-Tex CPF expansion – approved and signed by Karila and
Parnell earlier that morning – lay heavy in his bag. With little new
data other than the recent community consultations, he had relied
heavily on the phase-one facility construction report completed
three years earlier. He shifted the strap to the other shoulder to
better conceal the obvious bulk of the envelope in his breast pocket,
climbed the front steps of the Ministry building, ran up the three

flights of stairs to the Environment Directorate, and followed the dusty tile corridor to Ali Al Jabr's office, thoughts of Rania haunting him still, Abdulkader's ring a dead weight on his finger.

'Doctor, welcome.' Ali grinned with broken yellow teeth and clapped for tea. Since their first meeting almost a year and a half ago, Ali had insisted on the honorific, despite Clay's protestations that, in fact, he did not have a PhD, only a Master's degree – and more importantly they were friends, and so Ali should use his given name, just Clay, no more. But Ali would just wave his hand in the general direction of his colleagues and say: 'They must respect.'

'Sit, please, Doctor. It has been some time, yes?'

He agreed it had. The customary pleasantries were exchanged, the same jokes.

'Still no Mrs Doctor, yet?' Ali laughed.

'Still no.'

'I have three wives. All very good, very obedient. I find you Yemeni woman, yes?'

'I'll let you know, Ali.'

'You need sons.'

Sons. A picture flashed in the space between them and was gone. Clay swallowed, pulled the reports from his bag and pushed them across the desk without replying.

Ali eyed the bulge in his jacket. 'You need approval fast, yes? Like before?'

'Like before.'

Ali riffled through a report and put it back on the desk. 'Like before,' he said. '*Mafi mushkilla*. No problem.'

'Yes, there is a problem.'

Ali looked up, surprised.

'There is something I need you to do for me, Ali.'

The Arab looked up at him, straight-faced for a moment, and then broke into another filed-tooth smile. 'Yes, yes,' he said. 'No problem, my friend. I understand. You need it fast. Approval next week, yes?'

'No, Ali. I mean there is a problem at one of the villages. I am not sure what is causing it. I want you to help me look into it.'

Ali picked up the report again and leafed through the pages. 'Yes,' he said. 'Good. No problem. No problem.'

Clay leaned forward, his hands on the edge of the desk. 'Ali, listen to me. I am telling you that this time, there *is* a problem. *Tammam?*'

Ali closed the report and replaced it on the desk. His expression was neutral. 'We go shooting now, yes? We celebrate more business together.'

Two hours later they arrived at Ali's farm, set around a broad steep wadi a hundred kilometres north of Aden. Clay stood with Ali in the fine hard-packed mud of the bankside. Behind them, rows of date palms trembled in the breeze. Ali tossed three empty Lucky Strike packets to his son and waved him off across the wadi. They watched the boy skip out over the smooth white cobbles towards the far bank.

Ali's son set the packets upright line abreast on a square-cut boulder and ran back to the near bank to stand beside his father. The eleven-year-old pulled the AK47 from his back, unfolded the stock and locked it in place. Fully deployed, the weapon was almost as long as he was tall. The boy pulled back the firing mechanism and levelled the rifle. At 150 metres the packets were no more than white specks.

'My son will shoot first,' said Ali.

The crack of a single shot echoed down the wadi. One of the packets leapt into the air and spun back across the stones. Ali laughed, clapped his son on the back and said something to him in Arabic that Clay couldn't catch. The boy folded the stock, shouldered his weapon, and sprinted across the sun-bleached wadi bed. A few moments later he returned and handed his father the cigarette pack. There was a perfect 7.62 millimetre hole drilled dead centre through the red of the Lucky Strike bullseye. He handed the pack to Clay.

'*Mumtaz,*' said Clay. Excellent.

The boy smiled.

'This is why no one has ever conquered Yemen,' Ali said.

Clay reached into his breast pocket and withdrew the envelope. Ali grinned.

'Look Ali, I was serious back at the office. I want to look into this issue in Al Urush. People are getting sick. It might be connected to the Petro-Tex processing facility. I have three water samples at the lab now that should be ready tomorrow morning. But I'll need more. Help me. I can get equipment, collect the samples, but I need you to look at the results, make a judgement. We need to move fast.'

Ali took the envelope, opened it up and eyed the thick stack of American fifty-dollar bills, very nearly the last of Clay's cash.

'The same amount as before, Ali,' Clay said. 'As we agreed.'

Ali looked up. 'This is not usual,' he said. 'The companies investigate. We approve.'

'There's more if you help me.'

The Arab looked at him for a moment, as if considering this.

'Read the report, Ali. It's all in there.'

Ali thrust the envelope into his pocket and unshouldered his own rifle. His son was by his side. He peered along the length of the barrel and handed Clay the rifle. 'Shoot,' he said.

Clay flicked off the safety, checked the magazine, chambered a round, raised the weapon and pushed the wooden stock back into the muscle of his right shoulder. He took a deep breath and aimed down the sight, exhaled. He breathed in again, and then out slowly, started to squeeze the trigger gently at the bottom of the exhalation.

And how easy it had become, back then, how without qualm or conscience. In the lawless asylum of war, civilising conventions stripped away, killing was *good*. He could still feel his platoon commander's hand on his shoulder after his first kill, a SWAPO *terr* who had broken cover about a hundred metres ahead of the patrol, turned and ran. Clay had been on point, seen him first. It was still so clear, after all this time. The way the early morning sun slanted long through the trees, the way the leaves danced in the breeze, haloed with gold, the long, dry grass bladed and dewed, the air sweet and prism clean. He'd knelt, steadied his R4, sighted, breathed, taken his time. The round passed through the man's neck at the base of his skull. He'd fallen face first, the bullet's momentum throwing him forward like a rag doll. There was a puff of dust as he hit the ground, Clay remembered, and then shouting along the line as Crowbar strode up and stood beside Clay, looking down with that big farmer's grin on his face. *Fokken,* excellent, Straker. *Excellent,* his platoon commander had said.

Clay's chest tightened. He gasped for air. The target blurred and dissolved away. He lowered the weapon, dropped to one knee, jammed the butt of the AK into the hardened mud to steady himself, willing himself to breathe. Slowly, it passed. He looked up.

'*Tammam,* Doctor?' said Ali, looking down at him with an expression of concern. OK?

Clay took a long breath, stood, brushed the sand from the stock, raised the weapon, sighted and squeezed the trigger. A puff of dust rose a metre above and to the left of the target. He adjusted his stance, compensated for the Kalashnikov's kick, and fired again. This time the bullet struck inches to left of the package, sending chips of stone whirring through the air.

Clay lowered the AK's barrel, stock still lodged in his shoulder, and glanced over at Ali and his son. '*Tammam,*' he said. OK. 'But the people of Al Urush are not. They need your help. What's happening out there, it's conquest too, Ali.'

Clay raised the AK, sighted, and fired. The cigarette package spun away.

'Good aim,' said Ali.

Clay lowered the weapon, handed it back to Ali. 'So, you'll help?'

'*Inshallah,* you will have your approvals, Doctor,' said Ali. 'More, I cannot do.'

Bang, You're Dead

Later that afternoon, Clay hurried down the hall towards Karila's office, half-expecting the Finn to call him in, stab at the back pages of the report with a nicotine-stained finger, demand to know what the hell he had signed just that morning – what had now gone to the authorities. Clay had seen no sign of Zdravko since returning to Aden. His Land Rover wasn't in the office parking area.

Through the open door Clay could see Karila and Parnell sitting at the meeting table with two other men he didn't recognise. They were smiling, laughing. Parnell clapped one of the men on the back and shook his hand. They paid no attention as Clay passed on his way to the accounting department at the end of the corridor.

A dark-skinned Arab in a white shirt and tie looked up as Clay entered. He was seated behind a small desk in one corner of the room, surrounded by filing cabinets. He looked young, desk soft. There were dark circles under his eyes. Clay smiled at him, but he quickly went back to his ledger. Dunkley, the operation's chief accountant, sat behind a huge desk planted in the middle of the room. He let a pair of smudged spectacles fall onto its tether around his neck and looked up at Clay from across a cordillera of paperwork, stacks of hinged computer printouts, mountains of invoices. 'Heard the news, Straker?'

Clay shrugged no.

'The well test results for Kamar-4 have just come through. Forty metres of pay, reserves in the millions of barrels, the engineers figure.'

'I guess you get to keep your job, then.'

The accountant frowned. 'What do you want, Straker?'

'Karila said you'd have a cheque for me.' If he had any hope of finding out what was going on at Al Urush, he needed money to pay for samples, lab work, equipment, and he needed it fast. He'd already burned four days since Al Shams' ultimatum, with little to show for it. Even if he paid for rush analysis at twice the normal price, the lab would still need at least a day to complete the work.

Dunkley ran a hand across his shiny pate, tapped at his keyboard, peered at the screen. 'The invoice is with Parnell. Until he signs off, no payment. Sorry, Straker.'

Clay looked down at the floor, back up at the accountant. 'It's been three months since I submitted the invoice to you, Dunkley.'

'It's on his desk, Straker. I put it there myself. That's all I can do.'

'When?'

The accountant looked up over the rim of his glasses. 'When what?'

'When did you put it on his desk?'

'The day after you submitted it.'

'Maybe it got lost.'

'He knows it's there. We review all outstanding payables regularly. He was looking at it just last week.' Dunkley wiped his glasses on his shirt tail, perched them on his nose. 'Ever think maybe he just doesn't like you, Straker?'

'Almost every day.' Clay turned to leave. He was at the door when he looked back over his shoulder. 'Say, Dunk. I'm trying to track some payments going back to November 1st last year. Any chance you could help me out?' He said it as casually as he could.

Dunkley narrowed his eyes. 'What kind of payments?'

'Lab work we did.'

'What's it for, Straker?'

'I'm using the data in my report,' he lied. 'I want to tally the cost of the laboratory analysis.'

'Tell me what you're after, specifically, and I can check when I get a moment.'

'Just let me have a quick look at the accounts, can you? I only need a minute.'

Dunkley leaned forward, planted his elbow on a pile of papers. 'You know I can't do that, Straker.'

Clay tore a sticky note off the pad on Dunkley's desk, jotted down the name of the Aden laboratory company. 'OK then, for a start, can you have a look for any lab payments made on or around April 22nd of this year? I'd appreciate it.'

Dunkley looked down at the paper. 'I'll get to it when I can,' he said.

Clay reached over and pasted the yellow tab to the top of the accountant's head. 'Thanks, Dunk.'

The accountant snatched the note from his head. 'Bloody smart arse.'

☾

By the time Clay got back to the guesthouse he had already missed dinner, so he grabbed a sandwich and a beer from the kitchen and sat at one of the tables set out on the veranda. Just outside the throw of the floodlights, two armed guards squatted by the main gate, working on big wads of *qat*. The lights of Little Aden glowed in the distance. A breath of air flowed through the compound, the scent of iodine and salt, an undertone of sewage.

Atef appeared, a plate of cut fruit in his hand. 'Something for after, Mister Clay?'

'Thanks Atef.'

'I should make your sandwich. Much better.'

'Next time, brother.'

Atef wiped his hands across the white expanse of his apron. 'I can help you.'

Clay put down his beer, looked both ways. Atef sat beside him, leaned in, lowered his voice. 'My brother-in-law works in accounts. Also Zamalek supporter. I got him job here.'

The young man he'd seen today in Dunkley's office. 'Go on.'

'You need information from accounts, he told me.'

'Yes.'

'Tell me what you want.'

Clay told him. Printouts of all payments made two months either side of 30th November, delegations of authority, personnel records for the same period. Clay reached into his pocket and peeled a fifty-dollar note from his depleted roll and squeezed it into Atef's hand. 'Can you do that?'

'Yes, Mister Clay.'

'Be careful, Atef. And do it quietly.'

'Of course, Mister Clay. Do you want both sets?'

Clay looked up. 'Both?'

'My brother-in-law says they are keeping two sets of accounts.'

He should have guessed. Clay stood, put his hand on Atef's shoulder. 'If you can, Atef, great. *Mumtaz*. But please, only if your brother can do it safely. I don't want him to put himself in danger.'

'No danger, Mister Clay. He is very clever.'

Atef returned to the kitchen, left Clay alone again on the veranda. He sipped his beer, warm now. Rania had been right. Ali had refused to help, slammed the door in his face. Neither he nor his team were equipped to carry out the testing required, and Ali was savvy enough to know that you didn't mess with the Ministry of Oil. Clay was pretty sure that Ali didn't even read the reports he submitted, just filed them away and ticked the box – complete. Of course the executive summary and the early chapters of the report Clay had just submitted had mentioned nothing of the problems, just glowing accounts of the benefits of the project to the community and the country, with any and all harmful impacts designed out.

But deep inside the report, in a section entitled 'Discussion', Clay had buried a detailed description of the health impacts he had seen at Al Urush, along with what little data he had collected, an analysis of various possible causes, and a statement to the effect that the company had decided not to investigate the issue further, or to put risk mitigation measures in place. He had taken a chance, bet on the fact that Karila and Parnell wouldn't read the detail. Now there was a formal record, a written indictment, signed by Karila and Parnell. It was only a matter of time until someone in the company actually read it, and then the blade would fall. That afternoon he'd faxed the relevant pages to Rania in Sana'a.

He drained the beer and searched his conscience for the relief that he had only half-expected, but had not come.

Fourteen hours, maybe a bit more. That's all he'd had with Rania, the walk on the crater, the sojourn in Sana'a. Daughter of a French father and Algerian mother, she had grown up a devout Muslim in Algiers, speaking French at home, Arabic at school and on the streets, a *pied noir*. Her father had died when she was young, but she wouldn't say any more about it. She had studied modern literature and language at the Sorbonne in Paris, and joined AFP after graduation to become a journalist. Camus and Sartre, not surprisingly, were her favourites, Rimbaud, too. After a year in Morocco, she had applied for and been posted to Sana'a. That's all he knew about her. That and the fact that he had never met anyone like her. He had never felt skin so soft. He searched the memory of his movie crushes, drunken bar pursuits, all the hopeless distant admirations destroyed by proximity, but could find no equal. Four times that night they'd made love. At first she had been timid and tense, he clumsy and over-eager. After, he'd fallen into a deep dreamless sleep, only to be woken by her insistent mouth, and she was everywhere, surrounding him, enveloping him, and each time it was better, closer, gentler. And lying there with the ceiling fan turning above them, the shutters bathing their naked bodies in laths of pale city night, he knew that it was more than the desperation, more than the loneliness and the fear and the heartache that was making him burn.

It had been her first time. She hadn't said it, but he knew. And when he woke that morning to go back to Aden, he'd tried to kiss her and it was as if something inside her had snapped. She turned away and got out of bed and locked herself in the bathroom and he knew everything had changed. He dressed and waited for her, bewildered, his arousal choking on ash. After a time, she emerged, and she walked downstairs with him, silent, robed, a black headscarf pulled down tight and severe about her face, stood in the hotel entranceway and watched him go without a word. Twice since returning to Aden he'd called her hotel and left messages. There had been no reply.

A metallic rap at the main gate broke his reverie. One of the guards rose and opened the side door. There was a brief discussion in Arabic and a man appeared in the courtyard. He was dressed in a leather jacket and jeans, a black-and-white *keffiyeh* wrapped around his head. A burning cigarette hung from his lips. The guard pointed up towards the veranda. The man walked across the courtyard and up the stairs onto the veranda and stood before him.

'Jesus,' said Clay. 'You.'

The man offered his hand. 'My name is Hussein.' It was the man from the PSO interrogation, Himmler's sidekick, the chain-smoker. 'May I speak with you?'

Clay gestured towards the empty chair.

'Not here. I have a vehicle waiting. Do you feel like a drink?'

'I guess I don't have much of a choice.'

Clay followed the man out to the street, across the rutted dirt to a white Pajero sitting in the moon shadow of a razor-wire-topped wall. Clay recognised the vehicle registration number immediately. The car that had tailed to him to Sana'a.

Fifteen minutes later they were sitting in a dark corner of the bar at the Mövenpick Hotel. The place was packed. On stage a tiny Filippina singer in a short green dress and massive platform shoes was destroying 'Imagine' in broken English. She was the only woman in the place.

Hussein waved to the waiter and leaned across the table. 'Are you aware of the current political situation here in Yemen?'

'I always remember I am a guest here,' he said. 'I don't get involved in politics.'

Hussein smiled. 'My colleague can be a bit, well, *nerdy*, at times.'

'I've got nothing to tell you.'

'Indeed. Well then let me tell you. Relations between North and South have between deteriorating for some time now. A group of powerful Southern politicians and military men are agitating for more autonomy and a greater share of oil revenues.' He spoke fluently with a refined American accent – Ivy League, Yale perhaps, based on the T-shirt he had been wearing at the interrogation. 'They are orchestrating public protests, violence. Day by day the government is losing control. People are taking sides, declaring loyalties. It is a dangerous time.'

Clay nodded, said nothing.

'You have seen how dangerous,' said Hussein.

Clay looked the man in the eyes, tried to keep his expression neutral.

The waiter placed a bottle of Jack Daniels and two tumblers on the table. Hussein took his time pouring out two large measures. 'I never said thank you, by the way.' He raised his glass, took a sip, smiled.

Clay raised his glass to his lips, swallowed a mouthful. 'Don't know what you mean,' he said.

'The very nice officer you bribed at the checkpoint outside Ibb. Poor guy, someone had suggested that he should take extra care searching my vehicle.'

Clay said nothing.

'When he found out who I was, he was so worried that he offered me a bottle of Jack Daniels.'

'And who exactly are you?' said Clay. At least it hadn't been Zdravko tailing him. Maybe that meant he hadn't recognised him that day on the slope, although Clay doubted it.

'You were at Al Bawazir four days ago,' said Hussein, ignoring his question.

'I was …' Clay looked down, up again. 'I was taking water samples.'

'Three samples. Yes, I know.'

Clay took a deep breath, decided to keep quiet.

Hussein pulled out a cigarette, made a whole production of lighting it, dragging out a deep lungful, blowing the smoke towards the ceiling. 'Ansar Al-Sharia killed twelve villagers,' he said.

Clay swallowed a mouthful of bourbon. 'They may have done the shooting, but the Army set it up.'

For a moment he thought he saw a look of surprise flicker across Hussein's face, but then it was gone. 'Are you sure?'

'They just stood by and watched. What kind of place is this where the Army goes around slaughtering its own people?' As soon as he'd said it he realised the irony, wished he could take it back.

Hussein's mouth twisted into a wry smile. 'The question is, whose Army? Petro-Tex has been very clever.'

'Explain.'

Hussein tilted his chin up in the direction of the entrance. 'Do you see that man over there, the big Yemeni in the dark suit at the main table?'

Clay went to turn but Hussein reached for his arm and held him fast. 'Slowly,' he said.

A grey-haired Arab in a dark double-breasted jacket and tie sat at the head of the table, surrounded by Western businessmen. On his immediate left sat Rex Medved.

Clay bit the inside of his cheek, turned back to face Hussein.

'That is the Minister of Petroleum of the national government, one of the leaders of the Southern rebel cabal. The man with him is the President of Petro-Tex. He is here negotiating new exploration leases in the Southern oilfields.'

Clay sipped his drink. 'Look,' he said to the stranger across the table, 'if there is a point to all of this, get to it. I'm sure that you didn't bring me all this way to talk politics.' Clay drained his glass and wiped his mouth with the back of his forearm.

Hussein slid an envelope across the table towards him. He tapped the paper with the tips of two long fingers. 'I believe these are yours.'

There was a burst of laughter from the Minister's table. Clay looked over. The Minister stood and embraced a heavyset crew-cut man in a black suit. The two men touched cheeks on one side and then the other and stood shaking hands. The man beamed at the Minister, pumping his hand, booming a laugh across the room.

'Jesus Christ,' said Clay. It was Zdravko.

Hussein looked at him and back at the Minister's table. 'Do you know him?'

Clay swallowed a mouthful of whisky and then another, but did not answer.

He flipped open the envelope. There were three pages, the lab reports from the Al Urush and Bawazir samples, dated. He scanned the columns of figures, cross-checking the pages, annoyed that they could so easily end up in this man's hands. He was about to ask just how this had been accomplished when he saw Zdravko striding towards him, a big smile on his face, his double-breasted dark suit moving like reptile skin over his lithe bulk.

Zdravko was almost at the table now. Clay nodded to him, made to stand. All he could do was play it out, greet him as if nothing had happened, as if he hadn't seen what he'd seen. Zdravko smiled that big smile of his. Clay relaxed, offered his hand.

But then Zdravko's expression changed. His mouth set hard, a flat line. He glanced at Hussein, eyes narrowed, and then fixed his pale gaze back on Clay, accelerating towards them. Five metres from the table he changed course towards the exit. Ignoring Clay's out-stretched palm, he raised his hand in the shape of a pistol, aimed at Clay's head, and cracked off a round. Bang, he mouthed, you're dead. He winked and was gone.

Clay sat a moment blinking, unsure of what had just happened. Then he leaned back in his chair, finished his drink, folded the papers and slid them into his jacket pocket, trying not to look shaken.

'Friend?' said Hussein.

'I wouldn't say that, no.'

Hussein pushed back his chair and stood. 'And now,' he said, butting out his cigarette in the ashtray, 'we are going to take a little journey together.'

٢٠

Why You Do Nothing

.

It was the grey hour before dawn. Overnight, the city had been turned into a bastion. They passed through three Army road blocks in as many miles, the guards waving Hussein through by sight. Free of the city now, the Land Cruiser rattled along the crumbling two-lane coast road into the ancient heart of Arabia Felix. Pastel beaches and Aeolian dunes sprinkled with burnt scrub stretched away before them.

Clay pulled the envelope from his pocket and unfolded the three lab reports. He scanned the columns of figures, concentrations in milligrams per litre. The Al Urush sample showed elevated salinity, as he had measured before at the cistern, but there were more dangerous signs: significant concentrations of heavy metals, cadmium and lead, elevated organics, traces of barium. The numbers burned themselves into his brain. None of these things belonged. This water should be as pure as Evian. The Bawazir sample, taken just before the massacre, showed the same effects but at lower concentrations.

Hussein pulled over to the shoulder and switched off the engine. They walked to the top of a dune and looked out across the ocean. The water here was blue and clear, the beach alive with thousands of crabs that scuttled back and forth as the waves surged and retreated across the white sand. Sea birds wheeled and flicked in the breeze.

Hussein lit a cigarette, fuelled its embers and exhaled into the wind. 'Have you been up to the CPF before?' he asked.

'Only once. Last year, working on another project, I bunked in the camp for a few nights. Since then it's been locked down.'

'How many people work there, at any given time?'

'A hundred, maybe less. I'm not sure.' He looked at Hussein. 'What is it that you do, exactly?' He tried to sound casual.

'I am with the government.'

'What do you do for the government, other than take foreigners sightseeing?'

Hussein flicked the cigarette end into the dune. 'We should go, hit the road as the Americans say.' He turned away and walked back to the car.

Fifty kilometres west of Al Mukalla they stopped at a roadside teahouse. They left the vehicle and climbed the steps to a covered terrace overlooking the sea. A dozen wood plank tables were arranged under a wire-mesh and palm-frond roof that fluttered and crackled in the sea breeze. In one corner a group of tribesmen sat on a straw mat drinking tea. They looked up as Clay and Hussein entered. A loud conversation ensued. Clay and Hussein installed themselves at a table in the far corner. Hussein called for tea. After a while three of the men stood and wiped their hands across their sleeves, reached for their weapons and walked across the terrace to where Hussein and Clay sat.

Hussein greeted the men and offered them each a cigarette. They declined. Clay recognised one of the men from the first meeting with the sheikh. His face was like pitted andesite, weathered by who knew how many years of sun and labour. But it was his eyes that were unforgettable: blue as the sea, they glared out at Clay as the man spoke in rapid-fire Arabic, his tone rising, his hands tightening around the pistol grip of the rifle slung about his neck. Never once did his gaze waver – he was addressing Clay personally. Hussein listened, finishing one cigarette and lighting another, cool as a High-veldt winter's night. The man was shouting now, spitting out hard consonants. Clay stared back into the depth of his eyes, not daring to break contact. Finally the man slammed the butt of his Kalashnikov down on the tabletop and was silent. The other tribesmen murmured in agreement. Hussein stood and gestured to the men to please sit. They hesitated, looked back at their comrades at the other table, and sat. Hussein called for food and more tea.

Soon the men were helping themselves from a steaming platter of rice and goat meat. Hussein leaned towards Clay and said: 'They know you are from the company. He asks why you do nothing while their children and old people become sick. He says you gave money to the *mashayikh*. Is this true?'

Clay tried to push down the bile rising in his chest.

'He says the *mashayikh* should not have taken your unclean money.'

Clay said nothing.

'We must be careful,' said Hussein.

The meal finished, the tribesmen stood and left. Clay followed Hussein back to the car. Any vestige of control he might have had was slipping away.

They arrived in the hamlet just before noon, rolled into the clearing and stopped by the cistern. Dust thrown up by the tyres enveloped the vehicles. For a moment they sat blind as the dust settled. Then the picture was revealed: crops bent withered and brown in the fields, ancient trees hanging lifeless, stripped of green. By the side of the road a donkey lay dead and bloated beneath a writhing blanket of flies. The churning smell of death filled the air.

The little hut in the shadow of the big rock was unchanged: the wooden footstool tilted up against the wall, the varnish on the door long since peeled away, the wood cracked and grey, the bit of frayed cord knotted to a stake in the trampled ground in front of the window, once the dumb circular prison of a dog perhaps, or a donkey. He rapped on the door. It was then that he saw the boy's bicycle wheel lying in the dust at the base of a dead palm, propped up against a small mound of soil.

The door of the hut was ajar. They pushed it open and penetrated the gloom. Clay called out in Arabic: '*Merhaba, salaam aleikum.*' Hello.

A foul sulphurous odour overwhelmed him and he had to swallow back the urge to gag. As his eyes adjusted to the darkness he could see the makeshift kitchen with the gas burner, the dirt floor and the little chair, the steel-framed bed on the far wall. The woman stood before him speaking rapidly in high-pitched Arabic that he couldn't even begin to follow.

'*Whayn el walid*?' he asked. Where is the boy? He pointed to the empty bed.

The woman's eyes widened and then crumpled shut. She wrapped her arms around herself and started to rock violently back and forth, wailing some prayer or invocation, tears streaming down her withered face.

After a while the woman looked up, stared at Hussein, and then jumped forward and clasped his hands in hers and pulled him inside. Hussein kicked the door closed with his heel and wrenched himself free. The woman was shrieking at him, waving her arms above her head, hysterical. He held her by the shoulders, looked her straight in the eyes and spoke to her in a slow baritone. Something he said had an almost immediate effect. The woman stopped screaming and crumpled into a heap on the floor. She sobbed quietly in the dirt.

'Her son Mohamed died two days ago,' Hussein said.

Clay stood unmoving, transported back to another time, to another dead boy he had been powerless to save, life looping back on him, iterating, the tribesman's question now an explanatory proposition: why you do nothing. You do nothing because you are scared, because you are wilfully ignorant, because in the end you have less to lose by standing by and letting it happen. Or in Clay's case, helping it happen.

They left the woman curled there in the dirt and walked back to the vehicle. Hussein sat in the Pajero's driver's seat, the door open, lit a cigarette.

Clay stood in the dust of the square and tried to catch his breath. After a while he said: 'Are there others?'

'Many.'

Clay looked up into the monotonous depths of the sky. 'Why are you doing this?'

Hussein reached behind his back and withdrew a black automatic pistol, a nine-millimetre Beretta. He weighed it in his hand, examined it carefully as if looking for defects, and placed it on the dashboard. It gleamed in the sun. 'Let's just say I am interested in the truth.'

Clay looked back at the mound of earth under the dead palm, the harp.

'Is it the water?' said Hussein. 'Can the things on those laboratory reports do this?'

Clay looked at the gun and around the ruined village. 'It will kill crops and trees, but people, no. Not directly anyway. It's undrinkable.'

'Is it the facility?'

Clay stepped back, putting the Land Cruiser's open door between him and Hussein.

Hussein tossed his unfinished cigarette to the ground, picked up the handgun, got out of the vehicle, closed the door. 'Tell me.'

'I don't know.' Clay took a step towards Hussein. 'Look, maybe. The chemical signature suggests deep brine, a leak perhaps up at the facility. But it could be a lot of things, saline intrusion from the ocean.'

'Best guess.'

'Yes.'

'Then you are a murderer.' Hussein stood looking down at his feet, the handgun hanging loose in one hand, as if he was unsure whether he wanted it or not.

Clay tensed, ready to fight. Hussein was only two hard steps away. 'Murderer?' he said. 'I'm trying to get someone to do something about it, for Christ's sake. But no one seems to gives a shit.'

'Is that so? Since when, Straker, this newfound caring?'

Clay looked at the ground, did not answer. Hussein was right. Every step he'd taken over the last year, every bribe, every twisted interpretation, every carefully crafted report, had dragged him deeper. This newfound caring: it could be Al Shams talking. He choked back the urge to gag.

Hussein lit another cigarette, blinked the smoke from his eyes. Then he raised the handgun and tucked it into his waistband. 'Get in the car.'

٢١

Cathinone Sprint

During the five-hour drive back to Aden they chewed steadily from a large sheaf of *qat* that lay on the seat between them. Leaf by leaf, Clay built a tumour of green mash that stretched the skin of his cheek tight. Neither man spoke, Hussein hunched over the steering wheel of the Land Cruiser as the desert distances unravelled.

Surely here, where Allah was the sole arbiter of fate, cause and effect were now evident. And as the longshore dunes and the blue of the ocean flashed past and disappeared along the black ribbon of asphalt in the rear-view mirror, he was sure that Hussein was calling upon God to exact retribution. The instrument of justice was there, its square black butt wedged between Hussein's back and the seat cushion. All that was required was an agent to wield it. Out here, a body dumped face down in a scraped roadside hole would remain unknown to all except God.

And if justice was inherent, if it was *real*, if its existence were somehow twinned with a sentient, all-seeing deity capable of perfect knowledge and judgement, then surely he *was* guilty, and if anyone deserved to die it was him. How many times over the last ten years had he visualised his own end, put a gun to his head in the solitary depths of a black sleepless morning, determined to redress the balance, do what God had failed to do? But each time he'd desisted, stopped short of pulling the trigger, dragged himself out of the pit. And each time he'd wondered why.

By the time they drove through the gates and pulled into the office compound in Aden it was late, past eleven o'clock, and the cathinone was in control of his nervous system. His heart hammered at his ribs. Sweat poured from the backs of his knees and the top of his scalp and from every pore until his body was covered in a film of slime.

The nightguard waved them in. Only a couple of big Toyota Land Cruisers and a Mercedes diesel remained in the parking bays. The lights were still on in Karila's office. Hussein pulled the vehicle up at the front steps. 'Don't leave Aden,' he said.

Clay jumped out, ran up the big marble staircase three steps at a time to the first floor, and pushed on the door to Karila's office. It was locked. He rapped hard on the wood planking. Nothing. He tried again, shouting out the Finn's name, pummelling the door with his fist. There was no one. He spun away and lurched down the corridor towards the accounting offices. He searched the floor, but the lights were off, office doors closed and locked.

Parnell's office was at the top of the stairway, beyond the bureaucratic defences of the secretarial station, occupying the view corner of the building. Moon shadow cut the floor and walls into wedges of silver and black. The door was bathed in grey light from the secretary's computer screen. He pushed down on the handle. It was locked. He turned and looked back to the landing and the stairway and stood very still and listened, but all he could hear was the throbbing of his heart. The fluorescent dial of his watch showed 23:27. He pulled his knife from its pouch, flipped open the long probing blade and threaded it into the keyhole with a trembling hand. It didn't take long to tumble the bevel on the crude, locally made lock. The handle clicked and the door swung open.

All the trappings of authority were here: the nameplate announcing position, the oversized mahogany desk and leather armchair, the expansive meeting table, the charts and maps plastering the walls, and outside the big bank of windows, Aden's harbour shot across with the slimmest scar of moonlight. Almost out of time. He crossed the threshold and closed the door behind him. Reports and papers covered the desk: a geotechnical investigation for the expansion area, completion details for the new Haya-4 well, reserve estimates for the Haya field, an order for drilling in the new Block 57 exploration leases, stacks of bills and invoices.

Then something caught his eye. A plain manila folder set dead centre on the desk. A handwritten tab said: Production Data. Clay picked up the file, stepped into the moonlight, flipped open the cover. Inside was a stapled sheaf of A4 papers. He turned the file on end, squinted in the semi-darkness. The top sheet was a graph – a broad cross, like the blades on a pair of shears; a solid line showing steadily declining oil production over the past year, and, starting in October of last year, a dashed line indicating a rapid increase in water production. He integrated under the curve, mentally tallying the slices. Just over 21 million barrels of formation water – the ancient brine locked away with the oil deep in the reservoir – had been pumped out of the ground in just the last few months. It was a hell of a lot of water. And oil production was way down. It must be costing them a fortune. No wonder they were pushing this expansion so hard. It was a losing game: the more formation water they pulled out, the more reservoir pressure declined, and the less oil they produced.

Voices from outside shattered his concentration. He replaced the file, crouched down and stole across to the window, pulse racing. One of the guards was standing next to the Land Cruiser, talking to Hussein. Clay looked at his watch. He had been inside too long. He walked to the door and stepped back out over the threshold, jumpy from the *qat* and a dawning realisation that he had just crossed another barrier. He was about to close the door, when something he had seen made him stop.

He stepped back inside, strode quickly back to the desk and scanned the piles of documents. The corner of a staple-bound sheaf of paper hung from midway down one of the stacks. It was dated 22 April. He peeled off the top two inches of the pile and peered down at the document. It was a laboratory report. He picked it up and angled it towards the moonlight. He scanned the columns of chemical compound names and concentrations, memorised each figure. Everything he had specified. It was the original sample he had taken at Al Urush, the one the lab technician had said he'd spilled. He felt his stomach hollow out.

Twenty minutes later Clay was back at the guesthouse. He went straight to the communications room, punched Rania's number into the sat phone. After ten rings, the line went dead. He tried again, let the phone ring. He'd let it ring all night if he had to. Finally, minutes later, a desk clerk answered, clearly annoyed. Clay asked for Rania's room, waited as the line gurgled and hissed like antique plumbing.

'*Allo, oui*?' Her dream-interrupted voice, faint, a thousand miles away.

'It's Clay.'

Silence. And then: 'Claymore, *mon dieu*. It is the middle of the night.'

'Couldn't sleep.'

'What do you want, Clay?'

'I need to talk to you.' There was so much he wanted to say. An avalanche.

'I am listening.'

'Not over the phone. When can I see you?'

She sighed, was quiet a moment. 'It was a mistake, Clay.'

Clay stood staring down at the digital glow of the sat phone console, said nothing.

'Clay, are you there?'

'I'm here.'

'I am sorry, Clay. It was my fault. It was wicked of me. I should never have …' she trailed off.

'I know mistakes, Rania. And that wasn't one. Not by a long way.'

'I am not blaming you.'

'For Christ's sake, Rania. There's no blame here.'

'I am defiled.' Guilt dripped from her voice.

'You can't mean that, Rania.'

'I do not expect you to understand.'

'No, I don't.' He fought to control the anger welling up inside him.

She was crying now, sniffling. 'Please, Clay. It is over. It never began. I need you to respect my wishes.'

'Rania, please,' he began, trying to soften his voice. 'I promise you …'

She didn't let him finish. 'Go to bed, Claymore.' The line went dead.

He dialled the number again. It rang twice, connected, and went dead. He tried three more times. Same result. He walked to his room, jittery, hands trembling, stripped off his clothes and threw himself onto the bed. His heart raged in an amphetamine-fuelled sprint. Could a heart rip itself apart? He closed his eyes, breathed deeply, tried to calm himself and push away a growing sense of dread. Then the boy was there – Mohamed – staring out at him from the deep black sockets of a misshapen skull. The skin was white, covered in dust. The boy's mouth opened and closed, as if he were trying to speak. But there was no sound save the pounding in his head. He forced his eyes open. The harbour lights trembled across the walls. He swung his feet to the floor and pushed himself up. He stumbled to the armoire and fumbled in the dark for the bottle, collapsed back onto the bed and propped himself up against the wooden head-board. The vodka was warm but it went down like water until it was gone and soon oblivion overcame him.

٢٢

Liberal Shit

A searing red light tore him awake. Pain engulfed him, shooting from deep within his skull out through burning eyes. He looked at his watch: 10:30. Morning. Jesus. He pushed himself up from the bed and tried to stand, but a wave of nausea buckled his legs and he slipped on the tile. His jaw met the floor with a sickening crunch. He lay where he had fallen and waited for the room to stop spinning.

The side of his face was bathed in a cold slick. He opened his mouth and licked his lips. The acid taste of vomit and the smell of it turned his stomach inside out and jerked him awake. He pushed himself up onto all fours but a stab of pain tore through his palm – a shard of glass had driven deep into the meat of his thumb's abductor muscle. The floor was flecked with the shattered remains of the vodka bottle. He didn't remember having dropped it, but he was pretty sure that it must have been empty when it hit the floor. Blood dripped from his face and his hand, swirling red and fractal in the puke. For a long time he watched it, fascinated by the mingling of the two semi-miscible liquids. It was almost beautiful.

A loud knock at the door broke him free. He sat up, leaned against the side of the bed. 'It's open,' he croaked.

Atef stood in the doorway looking down at him. 'Mister Clay …' He closed the door, helped Clay up, sat him on the edge of the bed.

Clay pulled the shard of glass from his thumb. Blood welled thick and red from the wound. He leaned forward, jammed the wound down hard against his chest, let the chemicals spin through him.

'I will call the doctor,' said Atef.

'No. It's nothing. Thanks, Atef.' Clay pushed himself to his feet, walked to the bathroom, turned on the shower, stood under the steaming water. The tub ran thin red. He could hear Atef scurrying around in the room, the plop of a mop in a bucket, and then the door closing.

When Clay emerged from the bathroom, the mess had disappeared, the room sparkled. A steaming mug of coffee stood on the bedside table, a plate of freshly buttered whole-wheat toast. On the bed was a roll of gauze, a bottle of iodine, a large manila envelope. Clay dressed, sat on the bed, sipped the coffee, bound his hand, and opened the envelope. Inside were two dot-matrix printouts of accounts payable, covering the period from 3rd November to 30th December. Clay looked at the first printout, scanned the figures, awake now, lucid. Catering services, vehicle repair, parts, lubricants, office supplies, customs duties on imported pipe, workovers, everything you would expect from a company operating an oilfield. He ran his finger down the rows, found 30th November. He moved ahead in time. On 5th December, a round number: a hundred thousand US dollars. The string of zeroes ballooned out at him, glowed among a litany of sevens and forty-twos and thirty-eights. One hundred grand even, paid to Mansour for Import, Aden. He had never heard of them. He checked against the second printout. Same date. Ninety thousand paid to a numbered account in Cyprus. Ten to Mansour. Clay scanned up the list. There it was again. Another hundred grand. On the parallel list, again, ninety thousand to the same Cyprus account, the difference to Mansour. There were two other identical payments to Mansour, on 24th and 28th November, mirrored by corresponding payments to Cyprus the same day. Clay looked up, took a deep breath. Mansour was providing fake invoices, at a price. And someone was making a lot of money.

Clay pulled the Petro-Tex payroll records from the envelope, flipped through the papers, scanned the names, some familiar, some not: Karila, surprisingly underpaid, Dunkley, Parnell on a big package, most of it offshore, Z. Todorov, start date 14th November. Clay folded the printouts back into the envelope, stood on uncertain legs. They're on to you, Jim had said.

Clay found Atef in the kitchen.

'Good, Mister Clay?'

Clay nodded. 'Tell your cousin thank you. Who knows about the second set of accounts, Atef?'

'My cousin is not supposed to know. They think he is stupid.'

'Dunkley?'

'My cousin thinks yes. And Mister Parnell.'

Clay showed Atef the accounts page, stabbed his finger onto the name Mansour for Import. 'Can you check these guys out, Atef? It's important.'

'Trouble, Mister Clay?'

'Just be careful, Atef. Please.'

☾

It was gone midday when Clay reached the Petro-Tex building. His head was still swimming, and the events of the last days now seemed confused and twisted. Any earlier clarity had vanished. Halfway up the stairs he stopped and sat on a step and rested his head in his hands. He had to think.

Two days left. Four samples analysed, a clear upward trend in concentrations. Eleven murdered villagers. Mohammed dead. Al Urush water fifty times more saline than it should be. Hundreds of thousands of dollars syphoned from Petro-Tex operations to offshore accounts in Cyprus. Two million barrels of formation brine brought to surface in seven months. Thierry Champard blown to pieces in a car bomb. Too many unknowns and not nearly enough equations to solve them.

One of the Yemeni office boys appeared at the bottom of the stairs and started up the steps, a tray of steaming tea glasses rattling in his hands, then stopped dead and stared at Clay with his mouth open.

Clay tried to speak, to reassure the boy, but all that emerged was a strangled croak. The boy dropped his head and hurried up the stairs without looking back.

'*Tammam*,' Clay managed, pushing himself to his feet. 'It's OK,' he said to the empty stairway. 'It's really OK.'

He climbed to the landing and walked past Karila's office, down the hall to accounting. Dunkley was at his desk, a harried expression on his face. He looked up when Clay stepped in, gave him the up and down a moment and then shook his head.

'Just no? Care to know the question first?'

Dunkley folded his arms. 'Not really.'

'That information about the 22nd April sample?'

Dunkley shook his head, went back to his papers.

'How about the cheque Karila promised me?'

'Like I said, Straker. No.'

Clay stood for a moment looking down at the top of the accountant's head, the veins bulging under the skull-tight skin. 'Be careful, Dunk. You're not as good at this as you think.'

Clay spun around and went straight to Karila's office. The door was open.

Karila was sitting behind his desk, face bathed in blue light from the computer monitor, the document mirrored digital in the lenses of his glasses. Parnell was slumped in a leather armchair facing the desk. Both men jerked their heads up as he entered, looked at him as if he had just emerged from an asylum.

'Straker, what are you …' blurted Karila.

Clay sat down and faced the two men. 'We've got a problem.' There was something different about Karila's office, but he couldn't place it.

'You look more like caveman shit than usual, Straker,' said Parnell. 'What the fuck happened?'

'A day of reckoning,' said Clay, dabbing blood from the cut on his jaw. He captured Parnell in his gaze, held him there. 'Look, no bullshit, OK? Al Urush is dying. I was there yesterday.'

Parnell blinked twice, lids darting over dark beads, and took a deep breath. He hadn't applied his eye makeup today, and the grafts on his forehead bulged hideously. It reminded Clay of Al Shams.

'The PSO told me you were being interrogated,' said Karila.

'I was. Listen, damn it. People are dying out there.'

Karila tore his gaze away from the screen, plucked a smouldering Gitane from the ashtray with a bony thumb and forefinger, and inhaled deeply on the cigarette. 'We have already discussed this. The matter is closed.'

'It's the water, Nils. But, of course, you know that already.'

Parnell and Karila exchanged glances but did not answer.

'Where is it going, Nils?'

Same harried expressions.

'All that formation water that started to come in a few months ago. Millions of barrels of brine. Where is it going, Nils? Tell me.'

Parnell leaned forward in his chair and shot him a prosecutor's stare. 'That's confidential, Straker. How in the hell do you ...'

Clay cut him off. 'What are you doing with it all? It has to go somewhere.'

'That is a production matter,' said Karila. 'It has nothing whatsoever to do with your task – which may I remind you is to secure those approvals as quickly as possible.'

Parnell wheeled on his adjutant. 'Goddammit, Karila.'

Karila fumbled with a dossier on his desk. 'I don't understand, Vance. I took the strictest precautions ...'

Clay locked his gaze on Karila. 'There's a connection, Nils, between what is happening at Al Urush and all that formation water. The chemistry is similar.'

Karila looked over at his boss, then back at Clay. 'I don't know what you heard, Mister Straker, or how. But the fact is that we have expanded and upgraded the evaporation ponds. The system is performing according to spec. The water is not going anywhere. It is evaporating. Al Urush is more than five kilometres from the facility. There is no possibility that we are affecting them.'

Clay traced his finger across the map on Karila's desk, from the facility down to a little green dot that marked the oasis. The colour of paradise. 'What if the ponds are leaking? The rocks there are highly fractured. Contaminants move fast in a system like that. There could be all kinds of stuff in that produced water. Have you done any chemical analysis?'

'Only the routine, just what our production engineers need for their designs.'

'And?'

'And nothing. Just plain old formation water.' Karila adjusted his glasses. 'The ponds are lined, new. They're not leaking.'

'It can't be coincidence,' said Clay. 'The water in the *ghayl* at Al Bawazir is also showing signs of impact. Salinity has increased.'

Karila's eyes widened. 'Bawazir? What were you doing there?'

Clay looked into the Finn's pale eyes. 'Taking samples. Something is happening, Nils.'

'The water is being *e-va-po-rated,* Straker,' said Parnell. 'Spelled like it sounds.'

Karila looked at his boss. 'Besides, a small increase in salinity is not going to make people sick. You know that. It is a disease of some kind.'

'How sure are you that it's all evaporating?' Calculations flashed in his head: daily flow rate, average temperatures, wind speed, pond dimensions. 'That's a lot of water. There isn't enough surface area. Some of it could be percolating into the ground, finding fractures in the rock, migrating down to the oasis.'

'You ain't listening, Straker,' said Parnell. 'You had better start, *now.*'

Clay ignored the remark. 'Why don't you deep well it? Put it back in the formation where it came from. That's best practice.'

'Don't fucking well tell me how to do my job, Straker,' barked Parnell. 'I've been pumping oil out of the ground longer than your mother's been whoring.'

Clay glared at the American. '*Fok jou*, Parnell.'

Parnell jerked to his feet with surprising speed, stood quivering, fists clenched. Veins long submerged rose up and bulged in his neck. He took a step towards Clay.

Clay swivelled and faced the American, started setting a coil in his legs, bending his knees through a couple of outwardly imperceptible degrees. 'Come on, *baas,*' he said, flat. 'Have a go. No bat this time.'

Parnell stopped dead, glaring up at Clay. For a long moment he stood locked to the tile floor, chest heaving, eyes darting back and forth between Clay and Karila and the open doorway as if he expected someone to come bursting into the room to back him up. Karila just sat there, smoke drifting up from the cigarette between his fingers. And then Parnell backed away. Just dropped his eyes, took three steps back, bumped into the arm of his chair, stumbled. He muttered something Clay couldn't make out and reached for his inhaler.

'Please, gentlemen,' said Karila, intervening. 'Mister Straker, we have approval from the Ministry of Oil. There is no other economic way to dispose of the produced water.' The Finn sat impassive on the other side of the desk, the computer screen's data flickering across the surface of his glasses, the smoke rising from the cigarette burning in the drill-pipe ashtray on his desk.

'There is real potential liability here for Petro-Tex,' said Clay, trying to calm the hurricane swirling in his chest. 'If for no other reason, we need to figure out what the hell is going on.' Something inside him, he could feel it there, still clung to the hope that he could reason with these men, that somehow he could emerge from this unscathed, get the money he needed, save his friend. But it was fading like an equatorial sunset – fast.

'Did you submit your report to the regulators?' Karila asked. Clay nodded. 'Approval?'

'Within the week.'

'Well then, let's move on,' said Karila. 'Please wrap up your work as planned.' Karila slid the keyboard back into position. 'Thank you, Mister Straker. I am afraid we have another meeting now. You may go. And no more unauthorised trips to the field.'

Parnell slumped back into his chair and wrapped his mouth around the inhaler's orifice, breathed in the atomised steroid. Karila blinked at him through the haze of cigarette smoke, his expression fixed, vacant.

Clay's head pounded out the final agonies of an amphetamine and vodka hangover. He needed a drink desperately. An image of Mohamed's face, skin like photo-degraded plastic, grey and losing cohesion, pushed into his head and would not be denied. 'Listen,' he said, unable to control the emotion in his voice. 'People are dying, because of us. They barely survive on what they grow. If we foul their water, we destroy everything they have, don't you understand? Do either of you actually have any idea of what is going on out there?'

Parnell stared at him wide-eyed, as if he were some kind of religious zealot come to proselytise. 'We is in the oil business, boy,' he said, breathless, clutching his inhaler. 'Ya'll is in the wrong place if you want to be a do-gooder. Fucking liberal shit,' he coughed. 'Go an' join those cunts at the Nations Un-united.'

Clay paused, reset. He ignored the American and addressed Karila directly, balancing on tottering stones of patience. 'Let me go out there and take some samples, Nils, do some proper analysis. Then we can know for sure what's going on. If you're right and it's not us, then we're in the clear and we don't need to worry. If not, we can protect these people, and ourselves.'

'Mister Straker, I am not going to repeat myself. Our position on this is clear and consistent. What you speak of has nothing to do with our operations. We are not going to do anything, do you understand? We are not spending any more money. This discussion is terminated.'

'At least get those kids to a hospital and have them diagnosed.'

Parnell looked as if he was going to have a seizure. 'As if you give a shit, asshole. We know how ya'll treat the niggers in South Africa.'

Clay wheeled on Parnell, set up for a straight right, stopped himself, stood quivering, frustration burning inside like a virous ulcer.

Karila looked back down at his computer screen. 'That will be all, Straker.'

Every other time he had backed down, played by the rules, collected his money and gone home, never around to see the effect. It had always been so easy to do. He had discharged his professional duty and alerted the higher-ups of the risks and possible consequences, performed a ritual of absolution so mechanical and commonplace that each time he felt cleansed and almost purified as he walked away. Everyone was satisfied, the truth concealed conveniently behind graphs and tables and statistics compiled in lengthy impressive reports, technical jargon camouflaging the reality of destroyed villages and murdered children. But each time he left something behind, and in this creeping hysteresis what could not be retrieved grew and grew.

And then he realised what had changed, and why. The framed picture of Karila with his fair-haired family huddled in the snow was gone from the desk. Clay scanned the shelves and the walls but could see it nowhere, and he imagined it locked away in one of Karila's desk drawers, face-down, covered over with a protective blanket of production forecasts and revenue reports. The coward didn't even have the guts to face his own kids.

He planted his fists on the desk and leaned over towards Karila. His arms trembled as he glared at the man. 'You callous bastard. You know exactly what's going on. Otherwise why would you have intercepted that sample I took? You know what it shows. You just don't give a damn, do you?' The words emerged from his throat as a groan. He imagined his fist shattering the man's jaw with a satisfying crunch, the bone flexing slightly before giving way under the force of the blow. 'If you don't do something about this, I'll take it to the authorities.'

Karila shifted in his seat. 'Mister Straker, I think you will find that the authorities have quite the same opinion we do.' Karila lit another cigarette and inhaled deeply, cool as ever. 'We have no further need for your services. Be on the first flight out of Yemen this afternoon.'

Clay looked down at the two men. Karila picked up the phone and pressed a button.

'Todorov, yes. This is Mister Karila. Report to my office immediately.'

Parnell heaved his bulk around to face Clay. 'Fuck you, Straker,' he growled. 'I'll make damn sure you *never* work in the oil patch again.' He pronounced it *ahl*.

Zdravko appeared at the door, pumped, holstered.

Karila jabbed his cigarette in the air. 'Make sure that Mister Straker is on the KLM flight to Amsterdam this afternoon. Attend to it personally, Todorov.' Then he turned back to his computer screen, his face bathed once more in Microsoft blue as he tapped a message into the keyboard.

Zdravko smiled, wedged his hand onto the butt of his sheathed pistol. 'My great pleasure,' he said.

Clay glared wildly at Parnell then spun around and marched towards the door. Zdravko moved to block his way. Clay took a shuffle step to compensate and shot out a straight right. His fist slammed into the Bulgarian's solar plexus. It wasn't planned. He didn't visualise it or think it through. The dam of his frustration simply burst and the Bulgarian had put himself in the way.

Zdravko doubled over, slumped gasping to the floor. Clay strode past him and out across the marble foyer.

'Stop,' came a voice from behind.

Clay spun around. Zdravko was crouching with his back against the doorframe, a Makarov drawn and aimed at Clay's guts.

Parnell appeared at the door, slapped down Zdravko's arm. 'Put that away, you fucking idiot,' he snapped. 'This has gone far enough. Make sure you're on that plane, Straker, or this will get a lot worse real fast.'

Clay turned and took the wide staircase three steps at a time down to the main floor, ran to the parking area. He drove to the guesthouse in silence, parked, and climbed the stairs to his room. Clay was pretty sure that Zdravko had no intention whatsoever of seeing him safely on a flight out of Yemen. He had to get out and away, and he had to do it fast. Within a few minutes he had packed his instruments, the last bottle of vodka and his camera in his duffel bag. He ran down the stairs, found Atef in the kitchen. The big Egyptian turned as Clay came in, stood in front of his chopping block, cleaver in hand, white apron smeared in blood.

Clay put an envelope on the counter, placed a fifty-dollar bill on top. 'Courier this for me, would you Atef? Go into town to do it. Don't tell anyone. The address is on the front.'

Atef nodded, slid the envelope under his apron. 'We are sorry you are leaving, Mister Clay.' News travelled fast.

'Maybe I'll see you one day at a Zamalek game.'

Atef smiled, took his hand. 'Perhaps we shall win.'

Clay shouldered his bag. 'Maybe we will.'

Atef touched Clay's forearm, smeared blood there. 'One more thing, Mister Clay. I found Mansour. I went to their office.' Atef wiped his hands across his apron.

Outside, the noise of a vehicle approaching at high speed, slowing. 'And?'

'They are doing import-export. Oil equipment.'

'Legitimate, then.'

Atef nodded. 'I saw Mister Todorov there, speaking to one of the owners.'

Clay's heart lurched. 'Are you sure?'

'Yes, Mister Clay.'

'Did he see you?'

'I think no. I was across the street, having tea.'

Clay shook the Egyptian's hand. 'Stay out of his way. And look after yourself, my *broer*.' And then he was gone, out the back fire door, across the compound, through the back gate and into the backstreet Aden noon.

Swimming in the Disorder

Clay made his way through the maze of alleyways to the Tihama Road, where he hailed a taxi. He arrived at the Ministry building just after noon, made his way to Ali's office, and was told to wait. He sat in the Environmental Directorate waiting room, the pain behind his eyes barely dulled by six extra-strength ibuprofen, his mouth dry as a summer wadi.

Over the next hour he worked steadily, mostly from memory, compiling all of the data he'd acquired, copying it carefully in duplicate onto four notebook pages, then prepared two signed statements describing what he'd seen at Bawazir, what he'd photographed. He tore the pages from the notebook, folded each set in half, addressed one to Ali, the other to Rania. He looked at his watch. It was already two. No one had come in or out of the office. Zdravko would be going apeshit by now, screaming around town in that new black Land Rover of his. The Amsterdam flight had gone half an hour ago, him not on it.

Clay stood and walked to the secretary's desk. A bone-thin man with a black moustache hunched over a yellowing 1980s keyboard.

'Please tell Ali that it's urgent.'

'Mister Jabr not to disturb,' said the man.

'Please. Very important.'

The man picked up the phone, turned a single number on the rotary dial, spoke into the receiver, paused to listen, and replaced the handset in the cradle.

'Wait,' he said.

Zdravko could show up at any time. Perhaps he was already here, climbing the stairs, walking down the yellowing corridor. He was surprised Zdravko hadn't figured it out already. Not too bright.

Clay turned and walked across the waiting room and opened the office door. Three men in business suits sat examining a chart spread across Ali's desk. They spun around in their chairs to face him.

Ali stood and stared, eyes red and bulging. The secretary yelled something in Arabic. Clay kicked the door closed behind him and marched to the desk. 'I need to speak with you, Ali. Now.'

'Excuse, gentlemen.' Ali walked over and took him by the arm, guiding him out of the office. 'Doctor, please,' he whispered. 'I have good business here.'

'I don't have much time.'

Ali closed the office door and waved the secretary from the waiting room. They were alone.

'The water at Al Urush is being poisoned Ali. It's ugly – dead and dying children, miscarriages.'

'What is the cause?'

'Produced water discharge at the CPF.'

'Salt does not make people ill.'

'What is causing the illness is coming with the salt.'

'Oil?'

'Look, I'm not sure. Could be heavy metals, carcinogenic organics like benzene, I'm not sure yet.'

Ali coughed and looked up at Clay. 'How can this be?'

'A whole range of compounds can exist naturally within oil reservoirs, deep in the ground. They come out with the oil and the produced water, concentrate by evaporation and other processes. You can see it in the data I've collected. I don't have time to go into the technical details.' Clay reached into the breast pocket of his jacket, pulled out the addressed sheaf of notebook pages. 'It's all in here, Ali. Read the report I gave you too, read it carefully.'

Ali pressed his palms together and raised his hands to his mouth. He looked like a Christian child saying his prayers. Ali glanced back at the office door. Sweat beaded on his forehead. A drop ran along one of the deep fissures that framed his mouth and fell to the floor. 'Please, Doctor. You must leave now.'

'Do you understand what I'm saying, Ali? People are dying.'

'Please Doctor, this is for the Health Department. There is a disease, a fever.'

Clay grabbed Ali by the shoulders. 'No, Ali. Not disease. Not fever.'

Ali shook his head. 'No. No. Please go. Do not come back. This is closed, finished.' Ali reached for the phone.

'What are you doing?'

'I'm sorry. I must.' Ali started dialling.

Clay put his hand over the phone, killed the line. 'Please, Ali.'

Ali stood with the receiver to his ear. A river of fear ran in his eyes, thick and deep. 'I must.'

'Give me five minutes at least.'

Ali nodded.

Clay shouldered his bag and walked to the door. 'These are your people, Ali. Don't forget that. They need your help.' And then he turned away and double paced down the corridor to the far wing of the building and down the back fire escape into the alleyway.

The back streets of Aden steamed under a tropic sun. He threaded his way through the turbulence of the *suq*, spices swirling in the thickened atmosphere, children's clothes flapping on hangers from overhead cables, a river of people, him separate, foreign, just one more particle swimming in the disorder.

The Air Egypt office was just off Nasser Avenue, not far from the 25th October roundabout. AC units hummed like dripping hives studded across the back of the building. The rear service door was ajar. Inside, it was dark and cold. He made his way through the back offices and emerged into the marble foyer. A uniformed agent sat behind the counter working at a computer terminal. The agent looked up and rocked back in his chair. Clay could feel the man's gaze tracing over the cuts on his face.

'We …' the agent began, and fell silent. 'We are closed.'

Clay looked at his watch and then walked to the front door, pulled it open, glanced deliberately at the opening hours sign on the front window, closed the door again and walked back to the counter. 'I fell, that's all.' Clay ran his hands across his face. Plasma smeared his fingertips, the colour and viscosity of mineral oil. He reached into his pocket and pulled out the last of his cash. 'I need a ticket to Cairo.'

The agent tapped on the keyboard. 'Next flight in six hours.'

'Fine.' Clay sat in one of the chairs provided for customers and watched the man flick the keys, scan the monitor. He hunched down, back to the windows, feeling the traffic flow past, the eyes looking in. He still couldn't quite believe that Ali had picked up the phone, dialled the number. Right until that moment he had been sure that Ali, in the end, would come through. He was naïve. What a joke, after all this time. And now they were out there, and they were looking for him – Zdravko, the Ministry of Oil, the PSO, any of them, *all* of them for Christ's sake.

He watched the agent type his name into the keyboard. In a few hours he could be out – he was pretty sure that Zdravko would be watching the airport, but the PSO would be glad to see him go. Even Zdravko wasn't stupid enough to try to take him out in the airport itself, with so many soldiers and security people around. All he had to do was get there. He had done what Al Shams had asked. He'd determined the source of the illness, if not the precise nature of the cause. All the data he'd managed to collect was included in the report he'd submitted to the authorities. It was their responsibility, not his. He'd call Rania from the airport, dictate the information to her. She'd get the piece published tomorrow, the day of the new moon. Al Shams would hear of it, he was sure of it, and Abdulkader would be released. There was nothing more he could do. He was done fighting.

The agent pulled a docket from a drawer and started to write out a ticket by hand. 'That will be 850 US dollars.'

Clay started to peel off the bills, lay them on the counter, so normal now, a hundred, automatic almost, two hundred, buy your way out, three, buy their acquiescence, four, their cooperation, four-fifty, their silence. He stopped, his fist tightening around the wad of cash. Their end. He stood. His whole body was shaking, from the *qat*, the booze, the fear, the recognition of what he was doing, what he had become. He looked down at the agent, at the ticket now complete and sitting on the counter next to the bills. Then he grabbed the cash, crumpled it in his hand, drove it down into his pocket, and walked through to the back of the office and out the way he had come.

Clay jumped in a taxi and sank down low in the seat, his *keffiyeh* wrapped around his face. He asked the driver to take him to an old corner of the city on the other side of the crater, where the buildings hung onto the side of the volcano with fingernail foundations, a slum of steaming alleyways and sagging cables. Within the warren of narrow streets he found one of the cheap local hotels, booked in, paid cash, gave a false name. He bolted and chained the door, flicked on the ceiling fan, threw his pack on the bed and pulled the last bottle of vodka from his duffel bag. He threw open the wood-frame window and stood looking out over the harbour.

Ali was a good man, but Clay had pushed him past his limit. People were creatures of physics, nothing more. Each man had his threshold, each woman her breaking point. The fundamental laws of cause and effect were absolute. Action and reaction. Pull the trigger, fire the gun. The SWAPO bullet that had torn through Eben's head had taken away part of his brain. '*Vrek, broer.* Leave him be,' the old parabats had said, the ones who had seen it before. 'He'd thank you.' But Eben had lived because Clay had helped stretcher him back to the *chana*, put him on the Puma. And now for Abdulkader to live, Clay had to act. It wouldn't help Mohamed, but perhaps if he could find the cause of this, Al Urush could recover to mourn its dead, and one day he might be welcomed back in Yemen to do good and real work like he had wanted to do before he had been swallowed up by the irreversibility that makes people what they are.

He picked up the phone and spoke with the operator. Were the lines to the North still open? He recited the number slowly in Arabic. The ancient Yemeni telephone line hissed and cracked.

'*Allo,*' she answered in the French way, as a question.

'Rania, it's me.'

'I told you, Claymore. Do not. Please. '

'Look Rania, I don't have much time. Mohamed, that little boy I told you about, he's ...' Clay steadied himself. 'He's dead. Others besides. I've gone to the regulators, but they don't want to know. I've been sacked. I need your help, Rania. Please.'

The line went quiet. After a while she said: 'I am so sorry, Claymore, about the boy.'

He didn't answer.

'The situation is very bad here,' she said. 'The government speaks of nothing but war. The whole country is about to explode.'

'My time's up, Rania. I need you to write that story. Tonight. If you don't, Abdulkader dies.'

Silence on the end of the line.

'I have all the data with me. It's the water, Rania, like I thought. It's being poisoned somehow. I'm not sure how, exactly, or by what, but the people need to know. All you have to do is write it. Say "investigations are ongoing" or something like that, so Al Shams knows I'm still working on it. He'll understand.'

'No, Clay. Even if there was time to get something out in tomorrow's run, which there is not, my editor in Paris would never accept the story. There is not enough in it.'

'Include the massacre, then.'

'We already discussed that, Clay. I cannot.'

Clay tried to breathe, concentrated hard. The old line hissed empty between them.

'There is one way,' she said finally.

Clay waited for her to continue, swallowed hard.

'I know the editor of the *Yemen Times*, here in Sana'a. He is a good friend. I might be able to get something in with him.'

'That would do it, Rania.'

'I will do my best, Clay. But I cannot promise. You understand?'

'I do.'

'Our best chance would be if you could meet him – the editor, I mean. You could explain the situation, tell him what you have seen.' Another pause. She was thinking it through. 'The border could close at any time.'

He didn't have a vehicle. Taxi would be his only option. He looked at his watch. Curfew was already down. 'Meet me at Dhamar, halfway. I'll be in the lobby of the al-Dhubay Hotel tomorrow morning. I should be there by ten.'

'Dhamar,' she said. '*Oui.*'

'I like it when you say that.'

Could he hear her smile, just for an instant?

'Oh and Clay,' she breathed down the line. 'Bring the photos.'

He put down the phone and stood by the window for a long time, looking out across the bay, watching the ships swing at anchor, their lights coming on one by one as night fell. A pair of jet fighters streaked low across the bay, east to west, navigation lights blinking. Clay watched as they climbed away into the distance, the moon almost gone now, the unlit side grey and cold, the faintest rim of light kissing its edge like the hope of day. He drank, thought about Rania, about Eben, about little Mohamed, about what a mess he'd made of his life. After a while he lay on his back on the single bed, fully dressed, and folded his hands across his chest and closed his eyes and listened to the sounds of the city.

She was running along the beach in that bikini he had first seen her in, breasts rising and falling like the waves. Someone was chasing her. He called out but she could not hear him. A small boat, wood, mast split and hanging in the water, sail canvas flying in strips, drifted close to the shore. Someone, an old man, crouched inside the hull. He raised a hammer, a blunt thing, iron, and brought it down. A sharp crack echoed across the water. Splinters flew. Planking split. Shouting. Crashing.

He awoke heart pounding. A bright light blinded him. Someone grabbed his wrist and wrenched him to the floor. He landed with a jolt. Carpet, the legs of a chair, a pair of boots, black trousers, black shirt. Another man behind, picking up his duffel bag and shaking his stuff out onto the bed. Jesus Christ. He made to get up but was driven back to the floor by a withering kick to the ribs. The other man was picking through the contents of his bag, clothes, field instruments, a couple of books.

'What the hell?' he yelled, pulling himself up onto all fours.

The man in black jammed his boot into Clay's back, pinning him face down to the ground. His spine twisted under the weight. He turned his neck to face his attacker and looked straight down the barrel of a handgun.

'Take whatever you want,' Clay breathed.

Black's boot smashed into his face, driving his upper lip back into his teeth. His mouth filled with the haemic taste of blood.

'*Mafi mushkilla*,' Clay spat. 'No problem.'

Another blow snapped his head back.

The other man continued to take the room apart, drawers, mattress, backpack. Black grabbed Clay by the hair and pulled him to his feet. '*Yallah*,' he barked.

Childhood Drawings

He was hustled down to a vehicle waiting in the lane behind the hotel, hands tied, something hard and mean jabbed into his back. One of the men got in beside him and pushed his head down between his knees, a vice grip around the back of his neck. For half an hour, maybe more, he watched an empty blue-plastic water bottle roll around on the floor of the truck. Then the sound of a jet taking off – they must be passing near the airport.

After what felt like hours but could not have been more than a few minutes, the vehicle stopped. Doors were flung open and he was pushed out into the night. He glimpsed a two-storey building, half-finished, the brickwork un-rendered between concrete pillars, rebar sprouting from the roof beams, another vehicle parked in the dirt. He was about to turn and face his attackers when everything switched off.

☾

There was no light. It was hot. The air was thick with the smells of the ocean, bunker oil, human waste, his own blood. He was still in Aden, at least it smelled like Aden. He swivelled the weight of his head, a troglodyte whose eyes had long-since skinned over, evolution eliminating what was no longer required. If the sun was on the far side of the planet, or shining down on the harbour, here it made no difference. He looked at his watch, but the fluorescent dials did not show. He tapped his wrist where his watch should be. Abdulkader's ring gone from his finger, too. He started to crawl across the stone floor, sweeping one hand before him, but a barbed spike of pain drove through his side and he collapsed to the floor.

Without the sun or the stars for reference, time seemed to eddy and curl and lose cohesion. He had no concept of how long he had been in this place. Only the coagulant sealing the gash on the back of his head provided some measure; time reduced to a wattle of hair and blood, or the click of a stick across the spokes of a wheel that did not turn.

He fell into a fractured sleep and awoke in a spasm of pain. He tried to swallow, but his mouth was dry, his throat swollen. Thirst gripped him like a panic. In stages, he managed to bring himself to his feet. He swayed in the darkness, hands fending the depths. He staggered forward, searching for some limit to his universe. Something hard now at his fingertips, vertical. A wall. With one palm flat on the surface and the other arm forward he paced to his right. One, two, three, another wall. Turn. One, two, and again. Turn and continue. And then a seam, a change of texture. A door. Around again. A cell, six square metres at most. He traced his fingers along the edge of the door. No light showed, no current of air pierced the gap.

Fuck this. He pounded the door with his fist and called out, but was driven to his knees by a lance of pain. With the tips of his fingers he explored the swelling under his left arm. Cracked ribs, two at least, maybe three. The gash in his head had reopened and he could feel his scalp peeling back, the upright nails of ruptured sutures edging a budding flower of blood. He turned and rested his back against the wall and filled the void around him with every curse he had ever learned.

Perhaps they had forgotten him. Surely Rania would have started looking for him after he failed to appear at the rendezvous in Dhamar. She had contacts; she could exert pressure. He imagined her headline: 'Foreign oil worker disappears amidst accusations of poisoning'. He hoped that was exactly what she'd written, a clear message to Al Shams that he had kept his side of the agreement, enough to keep Abdulkader alive. They could not keep him indefinitely. He had heard stories of kidnappings that had lasted months, in the North, up towards Sa'da. Those had been tribal, mostly, the hostages treated with kindness, some leaving as friends with apologies all around. But this was different. Those men had been professionals, military perhaps. And this was a prison cell – not some stone goat shed up in the hills.

There was no sound save that of the workings of his body and the scream of pain in his head that seemed to grow and grow. He could not remember ever being so thirsty. Surely they would bring him water.

After a while he rose to his feet and faced the door as if it was a sparring partner. With all the focus he could gather he brought the edge of his fist down hard on the metal. I am a British citizen, he screamed. I want to speak to someone from the British Consulate. But there was no sound in reply, no light. He waited, panting in the heat, forehead pressed against the steel. Again he pushed away and hammered as hard as he could, repeating the words like a mantra, again and again until all that came forth was a rasp and he collapsed to the floor.

In the distance, a clutch of trees in a barren landscape, a desert plain, Yemen perhaps, but these are mopane tress. Ovamboland? He is searching for a place to shelter the abandoned children who huddle around him, feed and clothe them. He has money, bills from half a dozen nations, paper coloured with childhood drawings. Enough to do something. The desert is littered with abandoned military equipment, rocket launchers with empty rails, the charred bodies of tanks. There is old oilfield equipment also, a water tanker on its side, sand flowing from a gaping wound in its steel vessel. The skin of the plain has been cut open, the material scraped into long rilles that frame a white track. Near the trees, at the side of the road, there is a vehicle. It lies on its back, wheels to the sky. He walks towards it. It is a Ratel, an armoured transport. He knows what he will find, has been here so many times before. He tries to turn away, but he is drawn in.

Now he can see the holed belly, the blown-out hatch. And there is the space in the twisted metal. He will never forget that opening, the bodies inside limp and torn and still, the blood everywhere, beading on the metal, so much of it, such a deep, vivid red, its earthy sweet smell, the driver unconscious but breathing still behind the wheel.

A flash of light, a hollow clang and then darkness again, the crumbling firewall of a nightmare. He lay on the concrete floor and listened, eyes straining, blinded by the sudden illumination. Water. He could smell it. He got to his knees and groped ahead until his hand touched something cool. A cup. He sniffed the contents and lifted it to his mouth. The liquid flowed across his tongue and down his throat, pure and sweet, the most perfect thing in creation. Three gulps and it was gone. He crawled to the edge of the cell and leaned back against the wall and raised his knees to his chest and stared out into the darkness. He had crossed a threshold. Here, it was disequilibrium that held sway. Everything was coming apart. It had happened quickly.

His body's natural functioning continued. Without a toilet, he was reduced to squatting in the corner of the cell. Time was measured now only by the seemingly random deliveries of water and foul, inedible food, and the accumulating puddle of piss and shit in the corner. The stench of his own body amazed him. He was soon driven to the far corner, from which he seldom ventured, save to scurry over and recover the precious cup of water that appeared at the door.

He could feel himself weakening. The gash in his head had opened further, and was probably infected. He hadn't eaten since before talking to Ali. The smell of his own faeces kept him in a permanent state of nausea. He began to lapse in and out of consciousness, until he could no longer tell where the dreams ended and the reality of his existence began.

Sometime later he awoke on the concrete floor. The dreams had gone. He sat up, took a deep breath, felt the pulse of his heart, even and strong. Four times light had come. If he replaced the empty bowls by the door, they were taken away and brought back full. If he did not put them in their initial positions, the door was closed as soon as it was opened. The pattern was regular, he could see it now, morning and night. Two days he had been here, then. His body had already started to adapt to the rhythm. The next delivery was coming soon. It would start with the distant rattle of keys on a chain, the turning of a lock. Then footsteps approaching, boots on concrete, two sets, one crisp and sharp, the other shuffling. A key would rattle in the door lock, then after a moment the bolt would slide, hang up for a second, and then grind into place. One guard, the sharp walker, would open the door – he was the key man – and swing it open about six inches on quiet hinges. A blinding wedge of light would shoot across the floor and onto the far wall. Now he knew that the ceiling was high, perhaps three metres. At first he had closed his eyes, but then he began to gather information about his cell. On the third visit he had noticed a vent or window of some sort near the top of the far wall. Four times now he had seen it, concentrated on it. And in those few seconds of illumination, Shuffler would step forward and retrieve the bowls, his small dark hand reaching into the cell to pluck up each bowl in turn. Then he would clang two metal bowls onto the floor and slide each forward in turn with his sandalled foot, spilling some of the water. Then back, three shuffled steps and the slam as darkness came again.

With this clarity came a realisation: these people, whoever they were, had no intention of communicating with him. They were not after information that he might have, they did not want money or political leverage. He was being removed, made to disappear in a place where vanishing was commonplace, left to rot.

The fifth delivery came, same pattern, same timing, the flash of light, a star exploding, and then darkness again. Clay sat in his corner and ate the paste from the bowl, pushing his face into the mould, reaching with his tongue. He dared not use his fingers, by now surely crawling with *E-coli* or worse. He drank, used the rest of the water to wash the back of his head, letting it drip from the bowl onto the wound, listening to the sound the droplets made as they ran from his matted hair and hit the floor.

After a while he stood and walked to the other side of the cell. He put his hands to the wall, moved them across its rough surface, feeling for any imperfection, imagining its construction. Rendered breeze block, he guessed. That meant seams. He worked across the surface with his fingertips like a blind man, found a horizontal furrow about chest high, traced it along, gauging its depth. He found the place where the furrow was deepest, pushed his thumbnail into the groove and scored the cement. With his fingertip he tested the spot, felt for some expression. Nothing. He stepped back to the far side of the room, found his water bowl, brought its edge to bear on the groove, worked away with short hard strokes. Soon he could feel powder on his fingers. His pulse took a jump. He worked the bowl harder, with both hands, like a carpenter over a plane. The noise it made filled his ears, echoing from every surface, but he kept on. After a while he felt something raining on his feet, reached down to touch it, a soft fine powder. Cement. He worked until his arms were burning, retreated to his corner, rested.

Four times he returned to the spot, worked the edge of the bowl into the deepening groove, felt the mortar coming away, falling to the floor. He worked his finger into the rough opening between two blocks. It was no more than half a centimetre deep and a couple long, but it was enough. He swung his foot up and dug his two middle toes into the groove, and wedging his left hand against the adjacent wall, levered himself up until he was standing face to the wall. He reached up with his right hand and found the lip of the vent, swung his other hand over, and pulled himself up until his head was level with its base, his feet dangling. It was actually a recess in the wall, an opening about the size of a small suitcase. He rotated a wing up onto the ledge and extended his arm. His hand flailed in the void – it was deeper than he could reach. He hung there for a moment, breathing hard, resting.

Something crawled over his hand, brushed the hairs on his forearm, the lightest touch. He stilled himself, held his breath. A current of cool air reached him, flowed over his arm. It was coming from the end of the vent. Even over the reek of shit and urine, he could smell the outside, clean and fresh, the scents of early morning coming on this small current. He pushed his head into the vent, breathed deep, tried to fill himself with it. Perhaps this was ground level, his cell a basement, this a window well of some sort. He tried to wriggle his way in, wedge himself into the space, but the opening was too small, his shoulders too wide.

For a moment he hung there, not wanting to leave the flow of fresh air, until finally he could hold on no longer and dropped exhausted to the floor. He huddled in his corner, breathing hard, covered in sweat, cursing the darkness. He would have to find another way.

The Chemicals of Violence

Twice more the light came, and with it water and food. He ate the paste quickly now, gobbling it down, his body's demand for calories overruling his senses' recoil. Each time was the same, the door opening inwards, Shuffler's hands reaching in, then his right foot sliding in the fresh bowls. Clay started to measure the placement of his empty bowls, moving them a couple of centimetres further from the wall with each successive delivery. And each time Shuffler reached in a little further.

Three days he had been here now, best guess. Not once had anyone spoken to him, or even entered his cell. The longer it went on, the weaker he got. He knew he had to act soon. He sat by the door and waited. They would come soon with water and food.

When he heard the footsteps, sometime later, he stood and positioned himself in the opposite corner of the cell so that he would be able to see Sharp and Shuffler as they opened the door and exchanged the bowls. He knew now that this corner would not be illuminated when the door opened, he would be in darkness. Clay crouched with his back to the corner, his hands over his eyes so that only a slit remained, and counted out the timing of the sounds, key, lock, close, ten steps sharp, twelve steps shuffle, stop, key, bolt. The door opened. Sharp was small, half Clay's size, with baggy trousers and a thick moustache. He held open the door. Shuffler was taller, heavier, but not by much. Shuffler crouched down, reached in for the bowls. For a fraction of a second his head hovered on the threshold next to the steel doorframe, and then he pulled back, laid down the bowls, scraped them across the floor.

Clay sat in the darkness, trying to recall every detail. Neither man wore a uniform. Who were they? He had seen no weapons, but he hadn't had a clear view. Either man could have been carrying a sidearm. It didn't matter. Time passed. Clay rehearsed, playing the scene over and over in his mind. He dozed, woke, emptied his bowels, washed his hands with the water he had saved for this purpose, paced. It was coming. He placed the empty bowls a centimetre further away from the door than before, moved to the far wall. Soon now. He limbered up, stretched, felt his muscles work, broke a sweat.

The far door clanged shut. Clay moved to the hinge side of the door and waited against the far wall, his heart racing. He breathed deep, tried to steady himself. Sharp and Shuffler approached, their daily routine. Clay counted the steps. The bolt slid back, light burst into the cell. Shuffler reached in and picked up the first bowl. Clay waited until Shuffler's hand disappeared, counted three, then charged. He hit the door at full pace, driving all his weight through into his shoulder. It was as if someone had driven a splintered stake between his ribs. The steel plate snapped forward on its hinges just as Shuffler reached in for the second bowl. Clay felt a hard bump as the door knocked Sharp aside and then a spongy thud as the edge smashed into Shuffler's arm, pinning it against the steel frame. Shuffler screamed in agony as Clay leaned into the door, crushing the bone. Then he wrenched the door open, and half-blinded by the light and the pain piercing his side, pivoted around and threw himself through the opening.

Sharp was crouching on one knee, trying to stand, when Clay hit him with a full body tackle. The impact snapped Sharp back at the waist, sending his head down hard onto the concrete with a crack. Clay felt the man's body go limp. Shuffler was lying on his back, holding his arm, screaming in pain, oblivious. Clay jumped to his feet, lined up Shuffler's head and let go a withering side kick to the jaw. A tooth skipped out across the floor. Shuffler groaned and fell quiet. It had all taken a matter of seconds.

Clay hunched over, heart pounding. He was trembling. That old exhilaration pumped through him, a rampant overdose, the exquisite chemicals of violence blurring the pain, burning away every disguise. This was who he was. What war had made him. He tried to steady himself. He filled his lungs, held it, exhaled. He surveyed the room, a corridor. At the far end another door. He fumbled with Sharp's jacket, found a set of keys in the pocket, walked to the door. With trembling hands he tried a key, two, three, the metal rattling against the housing. He looked back at the two men lying on the concrete under the harsh fluorescent light. He shuddered, tried another key. The lock turned. He pushed open the door and looked into a dimly lit stairway. Rough concrete flights, formwork imprints. He closed the door behind him, bolted the door and started up the stairs, naked but for a pair of shorts. Two flights and another door, a different key. Warm night air flooded over him as he stood staring out into a dark alleyway. He flung away the key and started to run.

He ran through the night, moving through empty streets and across stony fields, the cloudglow of the city in the distance his only compass. At first he moved well, fear taking over now, urging him on. But he was weak, he had lost blood, eaten little, and after a while he slowed to a walk, panting, the sweat coagulating cold and tacky on his skin.

He crossed a field of ploughed up stubble towards a stone wall. Beyond, a row of stunted trees, another field, the lights of Aden glowing on the horizon. Far off, a line of red tracers arced silently into the sky, and then seconds later the staccato sound of machine-gun fire came shifting on the breeze, and it was like belonging. He stumbled to the wall. It was waist-high, hand-laid, unmortared. He wiped his eyes. To his left, stones arranged in a small arc barbed out from the wall, a palm-leaf cover laid over, a shepherd's hide. He dropped to his knees, crawled into the space, curled up and closed his eyes and let the night erase him.

Part III

٢٦

This Will Hurt a Bit

21st May. Somewhere outside Aden, Southern Yemen

Someone was calling his name, somewhere in the distance. He tried to push it away, but each time the voice cycled back, again and again until he was mired in it, enmeshed. There was a vague sensation of being cradled, lifted from the ground. And then he was drinking, the water flowing down his throat and splashing cool over his face and neck, filling his cells. Again the voice calling his name. Open your eyes.

They are open.

'Clay, wake up. It's me, Hussein.'

It was a long time before he could stand. Hussein coaxed him up, bracing his shoulder under Clay's arm on the undamaged side, hobbling him to an opening in the stone wall. Hussein lowered him to the ground, propped him up against the stones, pulled out a small Maglite and examined his face, eyes and the back of his head.

'I'm sorry I didn't come sooner.' Hussein tapped a Marlboro from a half-crushed softpack and offered it. Clay raised his arm to wave no and dropped it again with a sharp breath.

'You missed all the fun,' Clay said.

Hussein stood, smiled. 'Wait here.'

Clay reached up, grabbed Hussein's arm. 'How long was I in there?'

'It took me six days to find out where they'd taken you.' Hussein exhaled a long curl of smoke. 'And when I got there, you were gone.'

Six days. He put his head in his hands.

'Well done, by the way, getting out.'

Clay looked up as if through a squall, tried to shift his weight, winced. The ember of a cigarette flared. Clay could smell tobacco smoke swirling about him. Vertigo loomed.

'Don't try to move,' said Hussein. 'Wait here. I'll be back.' And then he was gone.

After a while Clay wobbled to his feet, felt his soles raw against the coolness of the dirt. The sky was lightening, dawn a few hours off. The country here was flat, a tapestry of stone-walled fields pierced by the dark remnants of volcanic intrusions, dykes and sills, blood-red cinder cones. Stone watchtowers loomed over the fields like medieval sentinels. A vehicle approached, headlights searching across the landscape. Clay hid his eyes as the Pajero pulled up alongside him. Hussein wrapped a jacket around his shoulders and helped him into the passenger seat. Soon they were speeding along the highway, direction Aden.

'Who were they?' Clay finally managed.

Hussein frowned. 'They just follow orders.'

'Whose orders?'

'Someone at the Ministry of Oil, here in Aden. I don't know who.'

'Petro-Tex.'

'Whoever it is, they are not pleased with you,' said Hussein. 'Giving out information a little too freely.'

'Ali,' whispered Clay. 'You'd think he'd care a little more about his own bloody people.'

Hussein glanced over at him. He looked surprised. 'Would you?' He stressed the first word.

Clay leaned forward and cradled his head in his hands. 'No.' He closed his eyes and let a wave of pain warp through his skull. His head had started to bleed again; he could feel the blood running slick and warm down the back of his neck. Hussein handed him a rag, and he jammed it onto the wound, held it down hard with his head between his knees, wobbling on the edge of consciousness.

On the outskirts of the city Hussein stopped the car and led him into a crumbling Soviet-era concrete building and up three flights of grimy steps to a dimly lit corridor. Hussein rapped on a door. An old man answered, let them in. He was dressed in a cheap woollen suit and a tie that looked as if it had never been unknotted. The apartment was cramped, every space covered in books or boxes. Hussein spoke to the man in a language Clay could not identify – was it Farsi? The old man gestured towards the kitchen, pulled out a chair and guided Clay to it.

The old man stood before him, reached up and placed his hand on Clay's jaw, turned his head to one side, then the other. Without saying a word, he looked into Clay's eyes, opened his mouth and peered inside, and then tilted his head forward to examine the wound. Then the old man went to the kitchen and returned with a basin of tepid water and a towel. He washed Clay's head gently, wringing out the cloth in the basin, the water swirling red. He cut away the matted hair with scissors, continued cleaning the wound. The antiseptic burned like fire.

Clay could feel the suture thread tugging at his scalp as the old man worked. It took a long time. After, the old man bandaged his head with a compress and gauze, and sewed his lip. The pain was flawless, detailed.

'This will hurt a bit,' the old man said afterwards.

Clay laughed. The old man smiled.

The old man examined Clay's ribs. He pointed to the scar in his side.

'It's old,' said Clay. A couple of inches to the left and it would never have had the chance to get old. He had never understood it, this randomness.

The old man washed Clay's torso with the wet towel. He was very gentle and careful and Clay felt very grateful to this old man. Then the old man brought a bottle of water and a glass, some flat bread, Yemeni-style scrambled eggs. 'Drink,' he said. 'You must drink and eat.'

'*Shukran*,' Clay managed.

'God bless you,' the old man replied, handing him a bottle of painkillers.

Clay ate and drank a litre of water.

Hussein handed him a clean *thaub,* some thin cotton trousers and a black-and-white Palestinian *keffiyeh*. 'Do you need help?' he asked.

Clay shook his head no and walked to the bathroom and closed the door. A stranger looked out at him from the mirror, naked, underweight, hands propped on the edge of the basin, the glass cuts along his jaw just showing through a five-day beard, lower lip cut and swollen, swathes of blue under his eyes, deep black bruises along his ribcage. He stood in the tub and turned the tap and with the shower nozzle washed the caked excrement from his lower body. Then he dressed in the clean clothes and wrapped the *keffiyeh* around his head to cover the bandages. He could almost pass for a Yemeni.

Soon they were back in the big, new, white Pajero, heading East. Clay dozed, hanging in the shoulder harness, floating on a cushion of deadened pain. He was vaguely aware of the kilometres passing, slowing for a checkpoint, rolling through as Hussein flashed his ID, the soldiers standing aside, some saluting, the hiss of the road again. By the time he woke, they were well past Bir Ali and the sun was setting behind the mountains. Hussein looked over and reached into his jacket and handed him an envelope.

Inside was an Australian passport issued to a Declan W. Greene of Perth, Western Australia, W for Wyndham. Clay looked at the photograph, taken in Nicosia a year ago for his first Yemeni visa, his hair longer then, his face fuller. He flipped through the pages, examined a scattering of stamps from Australia, Indonesia, Canada, several Yemeni visas covering a span of three years, an entrance stamp to Oman dated two days ago, and a new valid entrance visa for Yemen. On the inside back cover someone had scribbled a series of numbers in pencil, ten in all, of varying length, and the word *dovetail*. A scrap of paper was folded into the back of the passport, details typed with a fading ribbon: mother Mary Charlotte Greene, née Blanchard, deceased; father Dominic Curtis Greene, deceased. Only child. No living relatives. In the pouch there was also a Visa bank card, a valid Western Australian driver's licence, an airline ticket from Muscat to Cairo departing in a month's time on Egypt Airlines issued to D. Greene, and a Yemen government pass card, issued to the same name, folded in a black wallet. Clay looked over at Hussein.

'Your new passport.'

A military transport truck flashed past in the opposite direction.

'Declan Wyndham Greene?'

'You, or who you used to be, have just been listed by the PSO and the CIA as an Ansar Al-Sharia operative, my friend.'

Clay swallowed hard. What had Rania said about the PSO and Al Qaeda working together? He had dismissed it as rubbish at the time, another Press inaccuracy.

'So you are Declan W. Greene now. How does it feel?' Hussein grinned and lit a smoke, steering wheel in one hand, lighter in the other.

Clay forced a laugh, looked out at the sea. Still heading East. After a while he turned and faced Hussein, studied the man's face, the eyes drawn and crimped, shadowed. 'Hussein,' he said.

Hussein turned his head.

'Enough bullshit.'

A resigned sigh, eyes back on the road.

'I want to know who the hell you are, where we are going, and what the fuck is going on. Pull over now, or it's going to hurt.'

'What is?'

Clay braced his right foot against the door, pulled back his right fist. 'When I break your jaw.'

Hussein looked disappointed. He slowed the car, pulled over to the shoulder and turned off the engine. Clay opened the door and stepped out onto the sand. They were very close to the sea, the beach just beyond a set of low dunes. He could hear the crash of the waves, the hiss of the water running up the beach.

Hussein walked to the back of the car, opened the tailgate and pulled aside a tarpaulin spread across the back cargo area. 'Have a look,' he said. 'Everything you need should be there.'

Five heavy-duty aluminium cases were wedged into the rear of the vehicle. Clay unclasped the nearest, flipped open the lid. In the dim interior light he could see the instruments peering out from their foam cradles. A pH-EC meter, factory new, with all the calibration fluids, the instruction manual still in its sealed plastic sheath. He opened each case in turn. It was a portable laboratory, complete with sampling equipment, a variety of sample containers, gloves, and surprisingly, a scintillometer, the best you could get. Over thirty thousand dollars' worth of equipment, he estimated.

Hussein handed him a camera – a brand new Olympus SLR. 'We are going back to Al Urush,' said Hussein. 'And we are going to find out what is killing those children.'

'That's what Al Shams wants.'

'Exactly.'

'What about my driver? Do you know if he was released?'

'That,' said Hussein, tossing his cigarette to the ground, 'I couldn't tell you. Now, can we get going?'

Clay took a step back and stood looking at the aluminium cases. How could anyone have conjured up this much equipment, of this quality, here, now? It was too good to be true. And yet here were the means to determine the truth, set out in these cases.

'OK, Hussein,' said Clay, slamming the tailgate closed. 'For *them*.'

Hussein reached into his pocket. 'I almost forgot,' he said, 'I did manage to retrieve this. It might be helpful at some point.'

Clay caught the yellow fieldbook with both hands. The cover was battered and stained. He pulled off the rubber band and flipped through the pages of notes, the data scrawled in his Hittite hand, sketches, descriptions, thoughts, the twisted fragments of dehydrated dreams. His UK passport was tucked into the back cover.

'And the most important thing.' Hussein sent Clay's hipflask spinning through the air.

Clay caught it and looked up at Hussein, decided not to ask.

Hussein lit another cigarette and exhaled a thick stream of smoke, leaned back against the side of the car. 'Oh and there's one more thing, Clay. The sheikh, the one you bribed, was found dead five days ago in Um'a'Lat. Shot in the head. You are wanted for his murder.'

Prophets of Chaos

It was dusk by the time they reached Al Mukalla. They checked into a small local hotel and were directed to a second-floor suite overlooking the sea. Dressed as a Yemeni, bearded, Clay didn't draw a glance from the hotel staff.

Hussein checked the windows, searched the bedrooms, and then placed a bottle of whisky, J&B, and a black Beretta 92 on the kitchen table.

'Don't leave the room. I'm going to the mosque to pray.'

Clay raised his brows, surprised.

'I won't be back 'til after dark.'

Clay jutted his chin towards the pistol. 'And that?'

Hussein looked at Clay through a wreath of cigarette smoke. '*Inshallah*, you won't need it.'

'And if I do?'

Hussein smiled. 'Then God help you.' He stepped into the hall, closed the door behind him.

Clay stood on the balcony and watched the sun set over the Indian Ocean. Haze cloaked the ragged seafront. Grey fingers rose up from the town as if from the grave, wood smoke from cooking fires, toxic vapours from heaps of burning garbage scattered along the roadside and smouldering in vacant lots. Low clouds scuttled in from the sea. A solitary minaret pierced the brume like a lighthouse on a dangerous shore. Its upper turret gleamed in the last of the sun, and he could see the loudspeaker from which the muezzin would soon broadcast to the faithful, Hussein apparently among them.

Clay walked into the kitchen and poured himself a whisky. The gun, ugly and mean, was there on the table where Hussein had left it. His hand shook as he poured and some of the alcohol splashed onto the table. He walked out to the balcony, leaned against the railing and drank, watching the sun disappear into the sea. After a while he went back inside and sat at the table and poured himself another drink and sat staring at the gun for a long time.

There was a knock at the door. The call to prayer had not gone out yet. Even if he had returned early, Hussein had taken a key. Clay got to his feet and slid the fingers of his right hand over the Braille of the Beretta's grip and pushed the weapon into the waistband of his trousers at the small of his back. He padded to the door and stood against the wall, tried to control his breathing. He would wait until whoever was there went away.

More banging, harder this time. Clay reached back and touched the grip. It was damp with sweat.

Jesus, he thought, just go away.

Again, banging at the door, this time with what sounded like an open palm, louder than before, more insistent. His heart hammered like a piston but he stayed where he was, the Beretta now drawn, safety off.

Then a voice from the other side of the door, in English: 'Open up for God's sake.' A woman's voice, a boy's.

Clay unlocked the door, pulled it open. A woman stood in the doorway, covered head to foot in a black *burqa*; even her eyes were shrouded. She inclined her head, nodded in the direction of the gun still hanging from Clay's hand.

'Sorry,' said Clay, pushing the pistol back into his trouser band.

She set down her bag, unfastened the cover-all and let the shroud float to the floor. Then she removed the veil. Rania. She smiled and threw her arms around his neck. '*Al hamdilluluah,*' she whispered. 'Thank God you are safe. I was so worried.'

He held her tight, closed his eyes. Something hard pressed into his hip bone. He stood back, looked down. 'What's that?'

Rania looked down at the protrusion, barely noticeable. 'It is nothing.'

Clay reached down to touch it but she stepped back. She looked deliberately into his eyes for a long time, never wavering her gaze. But it wasn't the stare-down look he expected, it was something altogether different, as if she were trying to unpeel his retina and look into whatever lay behind, nerve endings, ocular fluids. He did not look away.

She reached into a fold of her dress and withdrew a pistol. Clay recognised it – French, a PA-15, rare enough. An SAAF Mirage pilot he had met once in South-west Africa had had one, let him try it, said he got it from one of the French pilots who came down to train them on the Mirage. She held it there for an instant and then replaced it.

'Standard AFP issue?' he said, shocked, not sure why.

'Certainly not. Please do not tell anyone, Claymore. It makes me feel safe. I know it is silly. I have never even fired it.'

'I'll teach you.'

She smiled, just a flash. Beautiful. 'They said you had disappeared, vanished.'

'Who did?'

'Petro-Tex. They held a press conference in Sana'a.'

Clay held her at arm's length, looked her up and down. She looked tired. Dust covered her face. Her hair was a hive of tangled wire.

'How did you find me, Rania?' He had a pretty good idea.

She reached up, touched the sutures on his lip, ran her fingertips over the bruises under his eyes. Her touch sent neurons firing.

'What happened to you, Clay?'

'I made some new enemies.' He told her some of what had happened since he'd seen her last. 'And now I'm a terrorist, apparently, and a murderer.'

'What about the children, the people of the village?' she asked.

'Tomorrow you can see for yourself,' he said. 'I assume that's why you are here.'

She nodded yes.

'Did you get the story published, Rania? About Al Urush?'

She frowned. 'Yes, in the *Yemen Times*.'

'When, Rania? When did it appear?'

Rania looked down at the ground. 'I am sorry, Clay,' was all she said.

Clay's heart lurched, tumbled. 'When?'

'I wrote it the night you called. I went to Dhamar with the editor to meet you, as we had agreed. But because you missed our rendez-vous, he did not want to publish the piece. It took me three days to convince him.'

Clay dropped his hands to his sides, let the implications of this surge over him like a barrage. 'Three days?'

Rania stepped back. 'The editor insisted on checking the data with contacts in the Health department. In the end he agreed to publish a warning about suspected water contamination, advising people to look for alternative sources in the affected area. He would not add a statement about ongoing investigations, and he declined to name Petro-Tex as the possible source. I tried with AFP, too, Clay, but they turned it down, as I knew they would. I am sorry. I did my best.'

Clay nodded. 'Then Abdulkader is dead.'

'You do not know that.'

Abdulkader's severed hand was there at his feet, the fingers reaching up to him, signalling him come closer. The moon had waned away; his friend's time had run and he'd been unable to stop its course. 'Some things you know,' he said.

They stood for a while, close but not touching, looking at each other, saying nothing. There was nothing to say. After what felt like a long time she frowned and looked away. 'I feel so dirty,' she said, reaching for her bag. 'I am going to take a shower.'

Clay pointed to the far end of the suite. 'Over there.'

☾

Hussein returned while Rania was in the shower. 'I need a drink,' he said, slumping onto the couch. He was red-eyed and jumpy from qat. A burning cigarette hung from his mouth. It looked like he hadn't slept in days. Clay went to the kitchen and returned with the whisky and a pair of glasses. He set the glasses on the table and poured two measures.

'The South will announce secession tomorrow morning,' Hussein said, crushing out the cigarette in a stone ashtray. 'Troops are mobilising on both sides. Tomorrow Yemen will be at war with itself. Again.' Hussein leaned forward and picked up the glass, examining its contents intently. 'Cheers,' he said, and knocked back the whisky.

The last major civil war, between the royalists, led by Crown Prince Muhammad Al-badr and supported by the Saudis and Great Britain, and the rebels, led by Nasserite army officers backed by the Egyptians and the Russians, had lasted eight years. By the time it ended in 1970, five percent of Yemen's population lay dead and the country was near economic collapse.

The call to prayer filled the air, echoed through the open room, overlapping pleas from a half-dozen minarets: God is great, Muhammad is his prophet, there is no other God but God; and from the bathroom the sound of falling water.

Hussein glanced towards the bathroom, pulled a softpack of Marlboros from his jacket pocket and cantilevered out a cigarette.

Clay declined, palm over his heart, reached for his whisky. 'Remember what I told you about those, *broer*.'

Hussein edged a smile. 'Every day, one step closer.' He tapped the cigarette on the back of his hand, closed his lips around the filter, flicked a cheap plastic lighter and lit the tobacco. 'So,' he said, exhaling a stream of smoke towards the ceiling., 'She's arrived, then.'

Clay hung on this, the *then* arcing up towards him like ground fire, the tracer past before you'd even registered it, like a memory, an afterthought. 'You knew she was coming?'

Hussein drew on the cigarette, squinted, nodded through the smoke.

'Why the hell didn't you tell me?'

'I didn't expect her until later.'

'That's not an answer.'

'I thought you'd be pleased.'

'Fuck you, Hussein.' Clay pulled the pistol from his waistband and put it on the table. 'And you forgot this,' he said.

Hussein reached into his pocket and placed two fresh magazines on the table, pushed them towards Clay. 'Keep it.'

Clay stared down at the pistol and the magazines. 'How did you find me at that prison, or whatever it was?'

'Pour me some more of that whisky.' Hussein drank. 'Your detention was not legal, not even registered. The Oil Ministry acted outside its jurisdiction. There is a lot of that going on.'

'You didn't answer my question.' He was getting used to it.

Hussein looked into his glass, drew the last breath of smoke from his dying cigarette, filter viced between thumb and forefinger. 'I am with the government, like I said. I have connections.'

'The same government that wants Al Shams dead, that massacres its own people, that colludes with terrorists? That one?'

'The situation is complex.'

'I didn't expect you to tell me anyway.' He pulled out D.W. Greene's passport, flipped to the inside of the back cover. 'Tell me this then. What are these numbers?'

Hussein smiled. 'That is for later, when this is finished. Not now.'

Just like the Battalion. No one tells you a goddamned thing.

Hussein leaned forward and pressed his hand around Clay's forearm. 'Please, Clay. Be patient. As soon as we are done, I will explain. It is safer for you this way.'

'I don't need looking after.'

Hussein ignored this, finished his smoke, lit another. It was about then that Rania emerged from the bathroom. She'd put her hair up in some sort of chignon, wisps coiling like black lichen around her ears, feathering her jaw. Her dress breezed around her legs, her bare arms, the thin cotton the colours of an oasis: water and cloud and frond. She sat next to Clay and ran her finger across his lower lip. For a moment he thought she was about to kiss him, but she turned away and exchanged glances with Hussein.

'I am sorry, Clay,' she said.

He swallowed hard, fifteen years of death and disappointment in one brutal pill. 'It's not your fault, Rania,' he said. 'You tried.' Abdulkader was dead. And in the dulled, washed-out, bruised prison of his psyche, something flared – a flame of sadness perhaps, of guilt, or regret, burned for a moment, and was gone before he could grasp it.

Rania looked at Hussein, he at her. They sat a moment like that, staring into each other's eyes. 'Not that,' she said.

Clay looked at Hussein. 'What is that supposed to mean?'

'Ask her,' said Hussein.

Rania unfolded a copy of the *International Herald Tribune* and slid it across the table. It was dated 18th May, three days ago. The headline read:

AMIDST RUMORS OF WAR, YEMEN OIL CONSPIRACY

Clay felt his diaphragm hollow out. He picked up the paper, not quite believing the words:

As tensions rise in the Arabian Peninsula, Petro-Tex, the major player in Yemen's lucrative and burgeoning oil industry, announced today that one of its contract employees, Claymore Straker, a South African national, has disappeared. The company accused Mister Straker of bribing local officials, falsifying reports, theft, and gross professional negligence in connection with its planned expansion in the Masila region of Southern Yemen, and stated that it has started legal proceedings against him. The government of Yemen confirmed at a press conference today in Sana'a that Straker, who is believed to be a member of an Islamic extremist group operating in the hinterland, is wanted for questioning in connection with a number of murders recently perpetrated in Southern Yemen. The government believes that this latest spate of violence is linked to the emergence of a new Southern rebel movement, which seeks independence from the North.

Clay looked up at Rania and Hussein. They sat watching him, their faces grave, expectant, as if waiting for some reaction, a rebuttal. He looked down at the paper again, re-read the article, slowly this time, deliberately, marvelling at the power of words to distort, to subvert truth, to try and convict. He slammed the paper down onto the table. 'You wrote this?'

Rania sat implacable.

Hussein shrugged and got to his feet. 'They're scared.'

Clay could feel the fury boiling in his chest, black, pure. 'You think so?' He looked at Rania. 'Jesus Christ, Rania. You said you would help me.'

Hussein strode to the door, turned to face them. 'Be ready to leave at sunrise,' he said. 'Bring everything. We are not coming back here.'

'You're leaving?' said Rania.

'I have business in town. Don't leave the apartment. You're safe here. I'll see you in the morning, *inshallah.*' And then he was gone.

The Illusion of Commitment

Rania stepped out onto the balcony, stood with her back to the railing, dress billowing in the land breeze, the lights of the town flickering along the coast behind her. Clay followed, stopped at the threshold, stood there looking at her, trying to understand what she had done, trying to see through the anger collapsing in on him.

She moved towards him, put her hands on his chest and turned her face up to his. Her eyes were closed, her lips parted.

Clay caught his breath, took a step back.

She opened her eyes. 'Please, do not be upset.'

'Abdulkader is dead. And now you've just convicted me of murder.'

'I am a reporter, Clay. I report.' She stepped closer, reached out for him.

He pushed her away. 'No, Rania.'

'Two press releases. I reported them, that is all.'

Clay looked out over the sea. 'You know I didn't kill those people.'

'I cannot let my personal feelings …'

'Yeah, I know. You can't get involved. Well, don't worry, we're not involved, Rania. I'm a source, that's all. Your big mistake. I gave you information about the massacre, about the poisoning at Al Urush. But you didn't write about that.' He turned and pointed at the newspaper sitting on the tabletop. 'Instead you published *this*.'

'Please Clay, try to understand. I cannot write about Al Urush, not without facts to back it up.'

'Facts?'

'Verifiable truth.'

Clay could feel the frustration rising in his chest, out of control. 'What about Petro-Tex?' he shouted, regretting it before he'd even done it. 'Do you think they're waiting for the facts, Rania? Jesus Christ Almighty.' Clay lined up the table and let go a side kick. The table flipped over and crashed in a heap, legs in splinters.

Rania jumped back, covered her mouth with her hand, stood staring at the broken table.

Clay slumped against the window frame. He was shaking, suddenly cold, the fury gone. He looked down at the broken furniture. Shame flooded through him, bruise hot, straight from childhood, ridiculous.

She was close to him now. Her breast brushed his arm. Heat poured from her neck and shoulders. She smelled sweet, like before, citrus and wildflower. He closed his eyes, overcome. He wanted to tell her how good it was to see her, how much he had missed her, how he wanted to make her understand what he couldn't understand about himself, now that he had lost his job, now that he was broke, now that he was someone else. And a part of him wanted to grab her and shake her, throw her down, overpower her, possess her, force her to the flames and hold her there.

He turned away, terrified of himself, of what he knew he was capable of doing. He walked to the kitchen and poured himself a whisky. Outside, the sounds of night: the surge of the waves against the breakwater, a solitary vehicle clattering along the coast road, the silence of ten thousand slumbering souls. He drank. Felt the deadening work of the alcohol. Caged it all back inside.

After a while she came and sat across from him. The whisky was almost gone.

'I have done some research,' she said, putting a dossier on the table. She opened the folder, flipped through the pages. 'Petro-Tex seems to specialise in operations in unstable countries with minimal internal regulatory capacity,' she said, her voice calm and sure. 'Bottom feeders, you might call them. The company is registered in Cyprus, part of a conglomerate owned by Rex Medved, Russian oligarch, self-styled playboy philanthropist.'

Clay looked up at her face, the delicate upturned tip of her nose, the long dark eyelashes. 'I've met him.'

Rania raised her eyebrows, continued. 'The son of a wealthy Russian émigré and a British society woman, he was raised with the best of everything: Marlborough College, Cambridge, father's villas in France and Spain.'

'And a jet.'

'The parents died about ten years ago under suspicious circumstances. Medved and his sister inherited everything. Before Perestroika they reconnected with Russia, and then, as the USSR came crumbling down, they leveraged private money to buy up state-owned assets at fire-sale prices – steel, oil and gas, pipelines. Medved is very well connected, particularly in political circles. And to top it off, he acts as patron to several high-profile charities, and makes certain that the world knows it.'

'Do the right thing.'

She raised her eyebrows, a question.

'Something he said to me.'

She looked at him for a moment then continued, all business. 'But the allegations that follow him are persistent and nasty: systematic intimidation of opponents, extortion, bribery, several open cases where members of the press and local community groups who have opposed his ventures have disappeared or been found dead. None have been proven, of course. He is a very controversial figure, hailed by some as a champion of free enterprise, a golden boy of philanthropy, vilified by others as a dangerous, unscrupulous operator. His sister, Regina, actually runs the operation. She makes all the big decisions. By all accounts she is completely ruthless, driven, psychopathically cruel, and terminally ill. Apparently, they hate each other. She resents his fame, his looks, his health – he her power. A lovely family.'

Rania paused, looked up at him a moment as if to check he was listening, continued. 'Petro-Tex is only one of the companies in the Medved empire. Its recent history includes an infusion of capital from Russian and European investors to develop the Yemen oil discoveries, exploration licences in Iraq and Libya, and widespread interests in oil and gas assets across the most remote and pristine parts of Siberia. There is also a Western partner, another Cyprus-registered company called Hurricane Resources, Canadian-owned. There is a Norwegian connection, too – several of the senior people involved in running Petro-Tex are based in Norway, and there seems to be some channel for funds from the Oslo stock exchange, but I do not know how or from whom. Cyprus is a common thread.'

'That's how I started working with them,' said Clay. 'Cyprus is a tax haven. I set up there three years ago, met some of the Hurricane guys at a reception. The Chairman, a guy called Redmond Perry, was there visiting. He got me onto the Petro-Tex bid list.'

Rania pulled a glossy corporate prospectus from the dossier. 'Hurricane has an environmental and social policy statement, if you want to read it.'

'No thanks.' He'd seen it and dozens just like it, all the same, full of statements about working with stakeholders, conforming to local laws and standards, about 'aspirational targets' for improving environmental and social performance, targets that they might reach someday, but not now, and not tomorrow. All in language carefully crafted to provide the illusion of commitment without actually promising anything. It had been his job to make sure they never did.

'I have also heard from a good source that Petro-Tex is colluding with the Rebel leaders for exploration rights for a series of major leases throughout the Masila.'

Clay shifted in his seat. Hussein had said the same thing.

'That is only the start,' she said. 'I have reason to believe that Petro-Tex has also bought an insurance policy. Because securing the new leases depends on the rebels taking power, they have paid for the leases with weapons. Small arms, missiles, electronic equipment, even fighter jets. Everything the rebellion needs to succeed. A good example of Regina's touch.'

'Where are the weapons from?'

'According to my sources, it is all ex-Soviet equipment, Russian, Romanian, Bulgarian.'

'Zdravko,' Clay said.

'Who?'

He told her about his evening with Zdravko in the guesthouse, seeing him again in the Mövenpick with Medved. It all made sense. Zdravko was helping Medved secure the arms he needed. Perhaps he was even the supplier. 'And you can prove this?'

'My source is very reliable.'

'I won't even ask.'

'No.'

Clay finished off the last of the whisky, let it settle. 'How did you know I was here, Rania?'

'I waited until evening for you at Dhamar. When you did not arrive, I knew something must have happened. A few days later, Hussein came to my office in Sana'a. He said he had a message from you, that I should meet you here, that you needed my help. And so here I am.'

'I didn't send you a message, Rania. I was in a black hole some-where. Do you know who this guy is? He's with the PSO. And if he's not, it's something worse. What are you doing here Rania, really?'

'It is my job, Clay. This is a career-making opportunity.'

'What do you mean? What did he tell you?'

'That you would get me an interview with Al Shams.'

Clay stood and walked to the balcony and looked out at the lights of the harbour and the stained-glass opium surface of the bay. And then she was there behind him with her fingertips touching his shoulder but he didn't turn to face her, just stood and stared out at the dark horizon of the Indian Ocean.

٢٩

Missing Octaves

The next morning Hussein returned as promised. Soon they were trundling along a dusty road, the escarpment looming before them, this part of the world so familiar now to Clay in its mute scale, its naked desolation. Rania rode in the back seat, covered head to foot in black, silent, a desert away.

By the time they reached Al Urush, the sun was high. Hussein took the wadi track as far as it would take them, then they got out and walked. The sun was a physical weight on their bodies as they scrambled up the loose scree towards the cliff face. Hussein walked ahead, bent at the waist, his face turned to the ground as if leaning into a driving storm. Rania struggled to keep up, encased in the long black *burqa*. Clay led them up Mohamed's hewn-rock passageway to the ledge.

They looked down at what had become of the oasis. The pools were recognisable only by their shapes, the smallest furthest up the slope, almost perfectly round, the others tiling down successively longer and larger, like a pyramid of rounded river rocks stacked and then pushed over. The largest lay just below them.

It was if nature's palette had been tipped over into a negative of itself. What had been lush, green and dark was now white like scored bone. Even the hardiest halophytes, the salt-tolerant palms that had anchored the soil for decades, stood naked and brown, their once verdant crowns limp and dead. The pools sparkled in the sunlight, the black richness of before replaced by a clear acid sterility, each now noosed with a thick necklace of white crystals that glinted in the sunlight.

They climbed down to the first pool and stood gazing into the water. A child's plastic doll floated face-down near the far edge of the pool, its naked torso covered in small pink blisters. The barest hint of a breeze moaned in the rocks overhead.

Rania removed her hood and veil. Her face was flushed and red, her hair matted and soaked with sweat. She gazed at the miniature corpse. 'The water looks so clear,' she said.

He crunched the layer of salt at the edge of the pool with his boot, then dipped a finger into the water and let a drop fall onto his tongue. 'That's because it's dead.'

He opened the small aluminium case, took out the electrical conductivity meter, switched it on and checked the calibration. The digital display flickered as the instrument stabilised. Rania crouched nearby, watching.

'This water is over twenty thousand years old, according to the isotope studies,' he said. 'It fell as rain on the plateau when the Neanderthals were around, been making its way here ever since. The rocks filter and purify it. Normally, it's purer than Evian.' He paused as the numbers stabilised. 'But this is hyper-saline – saltier than the ocean.'

He checked the electrodes and the connections. The instrument was functioning properly, but the readings didn't make sense. Even without dilution, the formation water pumped out with the oil wasn't nearly this saline. Dilution with the normal flow from the spring should have made it less saline, not more. He opened the fieldbook, leafed through a couple of dozen pages packed with dense cuneiform script and scribbled down the reading.

A shriek echoed out from the canyon walls. He jumped up, looking for the source of the noise. Hussein spun around and then sprinted off in the direction of the Pajero. Up among the rocks, almost hidden, a small boy in a jacket and red headscarf stood watching them. Hussein was already picking his way up the rocky slope towards the child; he moved rapidly through the jumbled terrain. The boy seemed to fix his gaze momentarily on Rania, as if she were some rare animal not seen here for decades; then he turned and vanished among the boulders.

Clay opened the case and took out the scintillometer. He watched the readings jump then smooth and stabilise. He swallowed hard. A few days ago he had drunk from this very pool.

'Don't touch the water,' he said. Why hadn't he thought of this before? The symptoms, everything – it all made sense. 'It's radioactive.'

Rama snatched a breath. 'Is this possible?' she whispered.

Somehow, formation brine being disposed of up at the CPF was finding its way to the base of the escarpment. That he was now sure of – everything pointed to it. And according to the reading he had just taken, that formation brine was radioactive. How had Hussein known? Clay remembered reading a couple of papers about the phenomenon back at university – naturally occurring radioactive elements found in deep oilfield brines, radium, thorium, uranium. Evaporation at the CPF must be concentrating the radionuclides, creating a potent super-saline solution. He had just witnessed the result – withered crops, poisoned water, dead kids. And it had happened fast. How long had it been since he was here last? A few weeks. The front arrives and everything dies. He felt sick inside.

'I can't speciate,' he said, 'but you're looking at over two thousand Becquerels per litre here. That's at least a thousand times the drinking water standard in most countries. There could be alpha particles – they can't penetrate a sheet of paper, but get them inside and they cause massive damage. Probably beta and gamma, too. This is only a crude measurement. I need to get samples to a good lab.'

'My God,' she gasped.

'God has nothing to do with it. This is physics, Rania. Put this shit into the water, and it flows, moves. Put it into people's bodies, and they die.'

'Is this the little boy's village, the one you told me about?'

Clay nodded.

Rania was silent. She had replaced her veil and now stood like a reaper, the funereal black robes fluttering in the breeze. Here was her story.

They worked their way up to the second and the third pools, collecting samples and taking readings. When they reached the level of the fourth pool, Hussein appeared on the rocks below, breathing heavily.

'The boy?' Clay called down to him.

'Ill, like the others,' said Hussein. 'We must go. He says there are soldiers nearby. Hurry.'

'I need one more sample. I'll meet you at the car.'

Rania and Hussein started back to the vehicle. Hussein carried the small cooler with the samples. Clay measured salinity, pH and activity levels in the fourth pool and recorded the readings in the fieldbook, then he scrambled up to the top pool, turned for a moment to look back down the canyon at the wadi floor, blazing white in the sun. A column of road dust twisted skyward, moving closer – soldiers.

He crouched to set up the instruments. This was the smallest and most sublime of the pools, now like the others, a place of decay and silence. He remembered the children playing, the sounds of the women laughing and the deep resonance of the spring as it surged up from the ground, the thick drip from the rock face above, the rivulets trickling over the grooved limestone, the water scaling in octaves down the pools. He stopped and listened, but heard only the moan of the wind high up on the plateau.

The others were waiting for him in the idling vehicle. He ran down the slope and jumped into the front passenger seat. Hussein put the Pajero in gear and started back down towards the village.

'The spring has dried up,' Clay said breathlessly. 'The flow has stopped completely. No wonder the pools are so saline. There is no dilution at all.'

Rania leaned over from the back seat, put her hand on Clay's shoulder. The vehicle lurched and crashed over the uneven surface. Clay grabbed the handle above the passenger-side window, and held on. Hussein was pushing it hard.

Soon they were on a single-lane track paralleling the escarpment, heading east.

'We have to lie low,' Hussein shouted out, his voice oscillating with each rut and ridge. 'There are patrols criss-crossing the area. It's all about to boil over.'

٣٠

Such a Small Thing

They arrived at the farm an hour later. It sat in a lush depression a kilometre or so from the cliffs, one of many similar freeholds strung out along the plain, roughly parallel with the base of the escarpment. It was like entering a clumsy re-creation of Eden. Ordered rows of date palms shaded small plots of ground crops: alfalfa, tef, legumes. An orange grove, the trees heavy with fruit, spread up the slope towards the cliffs. And laced through it all, the *aflaj* spread like veins carrying the alkaline spring water to each plot and orchard.

Hussein stopped the vehicle under a clutch of palms outside a low brick farmhouse. The trees cast long evening shadows across the gravel courtyard. 'We stay here tonight,' he said without turning his head.

They unloaded the equipment and Hussein showed Clay and Rania through into a tiled kitchen area with a sink and counter along one wall and a large wooden table with a pair of rough timber benches. Windows on one side let on to a treed courtyard, and at the back were a pair of small bedrooms. Rania peeled off the dark shroud, sending a cloud of dust into the air. Her face was covered in sweat and her breathing was laboured.

'Are you alright?' Clay took her arm to steady her, reached out to help her with her case.

She twisted away from him, moving to place herself between him and the case so he could not reach the handle. 'I am perfectly fine,' she said: *sternly*, Clay thought. 'Thank you.' She smiled, as if to mollify him. 'It is the heat.'

'These are your rooms,' said Hussein. 'Rest. I have business to attend to. I'll be back soon.'

'Thank you,' she said. 'I think I will lie down for a moment.'

Hussein smiled at her, turned and strode out. Rania disappeared into her room and closed the door. Moments later Clay heard the Pajero roar to life and move away.

Clay busied himself with the samples. He laid everything out on the kitchen table, checked caps and labels, packed the bottles into one of the small coolers. He tore a page from the back of the field-book and wrote in block letters on the waterproof cotton-composite paper clear instructions for the laboratory – which compounds to test for, what methods to use. He slipped the page into the cooler, closed the lid and wrapped the box shut with winds of silver duct tape. In the fading light he cleaned and rinsed each piece of equipment, removing any traces of radioactive water or sediment that may have remained from Al Urush, then he washed out the sink with hot water and soap.

He was sitting at the kitchen table, notebook before him, a rough sketch of the geology at Al Urush taking shape, the likely movement of groundwater, when the bedroom door opened with a creak. He looked up. Rania appeared in the doorway, her hair a chaotic tangle, breasts straining against a tight olive-coloured singlet.

'I can't sleep,' she said, hoarse. She sat down next to him, eyeing the notebook.

He didn't answer, pretended to work on the sketch. The air was filled with her scent, wild grasses, sweat. After a while she reached over and put her hand on his forearm. He did not move away, just sat feeling the pulse in her wrist against his skin, this fleeting connection. Time slowed to breaths, beats, flutters. Darkness came. Clay lit the small kerosene lantern, adjusted the flame, watched it paint the inside of the farmhouse, Rania's hand still on his arm, pressed there as if the scar were yet a wound, she his attendant. He looked down at her hand, up to her eyes.

'What did this, Clay?' she whispered.

'A piece of metal about the size of your thumbnail. Cuban, actually.' He could have told her that it was part of a 122-millimetre rocket that had also severed the leg of the man next to him, but to what purpose?

She looked down at his arm, traced the scar with the palp of her fingertip as she had before, near the sea in Aden that day. 'Such a small thing to do such terrible damage.'

Never a truer sentence composed. It didn't take much. He reached up with his left hand, touched her hair. 'Be careful, Rania.'

She looked up at him, a question in her eyes.

'I might start thinking that you care.'

She seemed about to speak, about to explain something important, when the drone of a diesel engine broke the silence. It came to them as if over a distance, high-pitched, plaintive. It was getting louder now, coming closer, travelling quickly. He could hear the engine surge as the vehicle powered over bumps in the road. He stood, palmed the Beretta, walked to the window, looked through a gap in the shutters as headlights split and banded across the walls and ceiling of the room. A vehicle ground to a halt outside the house. 'Hussein,' he said. 'Someone's with him.'

A few moments later Hussein appeared at the door. The other man stood behind him, a Yemeni with dark skin and a white moustache. The man was short, even by local standards. He carried an AK47 slung over his right shoulder. Hussein closed the door and the two men approached the table.

In the dim lamplight, Clay could see the deep creases around Hussein's eyes, the tightly drawn mouth sucking on a cigarette. Clay offered him the hip flask. He took it without asking what it contained, drank deeply once, and then again, and handed it back. Hussein sat on one of the wooden benches, glanced at Rania, and adjusted the lantern until the room was bathed in a warm kerosene glow. The other man set his rifle on the table, sat next to Hussein. Then he reached into his pocket and produced two banana-shaped magazines and a box of 7.62-millimetre ammunition, unfolded the stock of the Bulgarian-made AK-47s and started to disassemble the weapon. Clay watched, mesmerised, as the man stripped, cleaned and oiled each component before placing it on the table. Eben had started carrying a '47 after killing that *terr* during Operation Vasbyt. Clay watched the man's deeply veined hands move over the instrument with absent-minded familiarity, and suddenly he was back in the bush, and these were Eben's hands, obsessively breaking down and reassembling the weapon, smiling up at him from his hole, talking, always talking, his face young, eyes bright, full of life's diamond adventure.

Rania's touch brought him back. He glanced over at her. Her look was a question. He nodded, raised the hip flask to his mouth, drained it.

Hussein burned through another Marlboro and erupted in a fit of coughing that seemed to rip from deep within his lungs. He spat, crushed the empty pack and threw it to the floor. Finally he spoke. His voice was strained, harsh from the chain-smoking. The Army had split in two, he said. Northern regiments stationed in the South were engaging Southern units stationed nearby, and Southern units barracked north of the border were attempting to fight their way south.

Northern jets had bombed Aden. Confusion reigned. Sana'a, the Northern capital, appeared secure. The new Southern republic had been immediately recognised by Saudi Arabia, but so far no other country had followed. There was talk of a major tank battle in the mountain passes along the new border.

'When the rich wage war, it is the poor who die,' murmured Rania.

Clay looked at her.

'Rimbaud,' she said.

'The war will change nothing,' said Hussein.

'Al Shams seemed to think it would,' said Clay.

Hussein was silent for a moment, as if considering these words carefully. 'Al Shams is an idealist. If the rebels succeed, they will simply divert the oil revenue to their own Swiss bank accounts.' He turned and spat on the ground.

'And Petro-Tex will be free to continue with business as usual,' said Rania. 'This story needs to be told. I can tell it. It can bring international pressure to bear on Petro-Tex and its partners. The war will heighten attention on Yemen. People will listen. I need to interview Al Shams.'

'You must go to him and tell him the science of Al Urush,' said the stranger in Arabic.

'And who are you?' asked Clay.

'This man can take us to Al Shams,' said Hussein.

The stranger laid the partially disassembled weapon on the table, looked across the table at Clay. 'You are the *nazrani* whose driver is called Abdulkader?' he said in Arabic.

Clay glanced over at Rania, nodded.

'He told me something for you.'

Rania gasped, reached for Clay's hand, squeezed hard.

Clay looked at her, unsure of what he'd just heard, the Arabic grammar twisting in his head. Past tense, present, subjunctive? 'Told?'

Rania nodded. 'Tells.'

Jesus Christ. Clay looked at the stranger.

'He says you should pray.'

٣١

Truth

Clay caught his breath. Rania's story in the *Yemen Times*, watered down, three days late, must have been enough. Al Shams' had given Clay the benefit of the doubt, had trusted him, and he'd kept Abdulkader alive. *Al hamdillulah.*

'I take you to Al Shams tomorrow,' said the stranger.

Rania leant forward, forearms crossed on the table, listening intently.

'No,' Clay said. 'Not yet.' He watched Rania deflate. 'We are missing too many pieces of the puzzle.' If Abdulkader was still alive, then he was going to make damn sure that next time he saw Al Shams, he had the information he needed. All of it.

The stranger pointed to the cooler of samples. 'You have already found the poison,' he said in Arabic.

'I need to get to the CPF. If that's the source, it's the only way to put it all together. That's what Al Shams wants. That's what we all need. The truth.'

The stranger picked up his weapon, slid the gas tube into the rifle, pushed the bolt carrier into the gas tube, fed in the coiled return spring, and pushed down the receiver cover. Then he opened a carton of shells and started feeding the rounds into one of the magazines, pressing each tapered brass missile in with his thumb, pushing against the loading spring. Clay counted thirty rounds. The stranger clipped the magazine into place.

'*Inshallah*,' said the stranger. 'But the CPF is heavily guarded. There are many soldiers, helicopters coming every day.'

'Helicopters?' said Rania.

'Many. We have seen them unloading large boxes. Many boxes.'

Rania glanced over at Clay. 'The weapons?'

'Is there a way in?' asked Clay

The stranger wiped his hands on the long front of his *thaub*. 'There is a small wadi that joins Wadi Urush below the facility. It is deep and narrow. There is an old Bedou well there. The fence there has been damaged in the rains.'

The Chief of Bawazir had said the same thing. Clay remembered seeing the tributary wadi on the air photos. It cut down through the plateau ten or more kilometres to the east of the CPF. If he could get to the head of the wadi without being detected, it might work.

Rania turned to face him. 'It will take too long, Clay. I need that interview, now.'

'I thought you needed proof, Rania. That's what you keep telling me. Well, we don't have it.'

She shot Clay a fierce glare and twisted on the bench so that she was facing the stranger, riding side-saddle. 'Can you take us to him?' she said in Arabic.

'Yes,' said the stranger.

Hussein searched his pockets and produced a fresh packet of cigarettes. 'I agree,' he said. 'This is the time.'

Clay stood and walked to the front window and peered through the shutters. The Pajero sat in the courtyard, moonlight glinting on its windscreen. He scanned the trees along the edge of the courtyard. A dog barked somewhere in the distance. He flipped down the louvers and walked back to the table.

'Don't worry, we're safe here,' said Hussein.

Clay stood at the end of the table, locked his gaze on Hussein. 'After everything I've been through, do you really think I'm going to lead you right to Al Shams?'

'What are you talking about?' said Rania.

'He's PSO for Christ's sake, Rania. They want Al Shams dead.'

The stranger was staring at him, hands out of sight below the table, the Kalashnikov there on the table, loaded and ready.

'That is ridiculous,' she said. 'If he was PSO, why would he be helping us to tell the truth about Al Shams?' It was the first time he had heard her acknowledge that Al Shams might have a legitimate cause.

Hussein exhaled a stream of smoke that swirled in the lamplight. 'Listen to her, Clay. Think. I've helped you every step of the way. Without me, you wouldn't even be here, any of you.'

And then it all became clear. All the questions that had been swirling around in his head for these days and weeks were answered in one remarkably simple equation.

'Exactly,' he began, addressing Rania, looking into her eyes. 'It's because of him we're here. He tracks me down after I escaped from that hell hole, after somehow rescuing my notebook and passport. He miraculously produces an entire lab so I can come here and test the water, then casually informs me that I'm a wanted terrorist. He knows you and I have been talking, knows what we've been talking about. We've been under surveillance, Rania. He followed me that day, all the way to Sana'a. Then he finds you and brings you here, saying that I asked you to come, promising you an interview. It was an outright lie. Don't you see, Rania? It's exactly what Al Shams needs: the science explained, data to back it up, a ground-breaking interview with a famous journalist. How could he resist? It's the perfect set-up. Al Shams has eluded them for years. This way, we lead them right to him. We've been played, both of us.'

Rania stared at Hussein.

Hussein ran his hand through his hair, fingers as tines, and took a deep breath. 'Your logic is flawed, Straker. Western, Euclidian logic. It doesn't apply here. There is more going on than you realise.'

'Tell us, then. Why are you doing this, Hussein? Why are you helping us?'

'I told you, back at the hotel.'

'Yes, the truth. How noble. How about the truth, then? What were you doing in the interrogation room that day, when I was being questioned?'

'Protecting you.'

'Protecting me?'

'Making sure that they didn't …' Hussein stumbled, looked at Rania. 'That they didn't get carried away.'

'More bullshit,' barked Clay. He was getting angry now, frustrated that Rania hadn't immediately seen what was now palpably obvious to him. 'That's all he's ever given me, Rania. Riddles, obfuscation. Never a straight answer about anything.' He made eye contact with the stranger and then turned back on Hussein. 'You say you're interested in the truth. How about starting right now, *broer*. Tell us the truth.'

Hussein pushed back the bench and stood, a cigarette burning down between his fingers. He looked tired. For a moment, Clay thought he was going to turn and walk back to the Pajero, but he wavered, looking at each of them in turn.

'What you need to understand,' he said, stubbing the cigarette out on the saucer he had deployed as an ashtray, now a cleared forest of filter stumps, 'is that if you're going to have any hope of leaving this country alive, Straker, you are going to have to do exactly as I tell you. And perhaps you should reflect that just two weeks ago you were not far from here bribing these very people you now claim to support, trying to keep them quiet.' He looked over at Rania. 'What you wrote in that story is substantially correct.'

Rania gasped. 'Clay, is this true?'

Clay shuffled his feet, looked down at his hands. Damn him.

'Claymore?' she was staring at him, arms crossed over her chest.

He swallowed. 'That was before.'

'Before what?'

'Before you.'

'Ask him, Rania,' said Hussein, pressing his advantage. 'Ask him how long he has been doing this.'

Rania was glaring at him now. He could feel her reproach crushing him like a dark sea. He took a deep breath. No. He was not going to allow himself to be side-tracked. 'Look, right now there's only one question. Are we going to let this guy dupe us into giving Al Shams away? What if I'm right? Can we take that chance? Can we destroy the only hope these people have of fighting this?'

Hussein was backing away from the table now, reaching behind his back. Before the stranger could react, Clay grabbed the AK from the table, whipped it around and trained it on Hussein. The barrel gleamed with fresh oil. He chambered a round and flicked off the safety. 'OK, Rania. You'll get your interview,' he said. 'And Al Shams will get a deal he can't refuse: a PSO operative for Abdulkader.'

You Will Burn

They tied Hussein to a chair with duct tape. Rania went to her room and closed the door. Clay and the stranger took turns watching Hussein through the night.

Half-asleep, the events of the last days turned in Clay's mind like some whorled galaxy, the fragments incongruous, nebular. The stranger seemed to have accepted Clay's assertion, and sat contentedly chewing his *qat*, his AK cradled in his lap. He was Al Shams' man, that was clear, and Clay was bringing his master a prize. For that he would be rewarded, if not while living, then in the eternity after.

Clay was jolted awake by the sound of voices. At first the muffled pulses of sound were woven into the tapestry of a nightmare, an accompaniment to doubt. But slowly the thread frayed out through the cinder-block filter of walls and doors, and he sat up, knowing that it was her voice, and hers alone, a hushed monologue from the far bedroom. Hussein was asleep in the chair, his head hung to one side. The stranger, too, was asleep, slumped against the wall, breathing deeply. Clay looked out into the dark void of the kitchen.

A faint light showed under Rania's bedroom door. He stepped across the tile. Her voice rose again, subsided. He could not make out words, just tones, changing pitch and cadence, now urgency, then silence. Was she dreaming like he had been, talking in her sleep? For a long time he stood outside her door, listening for a reprise, unsure of what to do. Ever since the confrontation with Hussein, he had wanted to talk to her, to explain his actions, but she had rebuffed his attempts at conversation and had retired early, claiming fatigue.

He put his ear to the door. Still nothing. He was about to go back to his room when he heard it again, the soft murmur of her voice. He knocked on the door.

'Rania,' he whispered. He tried the door but it was locked from the inside. The sound must have woken her because she abruptly stopped talking. There was a scrape, like a chair being pushed over tile, the light went out, then silence. And that was all.

They left before dawn under a cloudless star-lit sky and struck north. They crossed broad gravel washes devoid of vegetation, emerging occasionally onto higher ground where low scrub thorn acacia grew thick in the brown silt, dropping again into wide sunburned swales, the rounded boulders blushing in the low-angle morning light. The vehicle rattled and lurched over the cobble, suspension groaning, the seatbelt strap digging into his clavicle, the car shuddering so that it felt as if his teeth would shake free of their sockets.

Hussein was in the back seat, hands bound, hobbled about the ankles, the stranger beside him, looking distinctly unconcerned, as if they were on a sightseeing trip. Rania was in the front passenger seat, fully covered, black and silent, brooding.

By the time they reached the remains of the Queen's Highway, the sun was directly overhead. Frayed and covered over with drifts of sand, the hand-laid flint and cobble track had been built centuries ago for the spice caravans that once trudged this relic line along the base of the escarpment bound for Oman.

The stranger tapped Clay on the shoulder. 'Stop, please.'

Clay brought the vehicle to a halt under the sparse shade of a lone acacia rooted into the bank of a gravel wash just beyond the track. The escarpment shimmered white in the distance, floating on a river of haze.

The stranger opened his door and stepped down to the ground. From a green polyethylene bag he produced a woven prayer mat. He looked at Clay.

'Five minutes,' he said, stepping down from the vehicle and clambering up the bank and out of sight.

Clay turned off the engine, opened the car door and stepped out onto the baking ground. He took a long swig from his water bottle and looked out across the mirage. Abdulkader was out there, some-where amongst those cliffs and gorges.

The stranger returned, climbed into the car next to Hussein. 'You do not pray to Allah,' he said.

'I probably should,' said Clay.

'You will burn.'

He looked over at Rania, veiled beside him. 'I expect so, yes.'

☾

By dusk they were travelling east, skirting the base of the bluffs, bumping along a single-lane gravel track. They had not seen a soul since leaving the main road. Soon it would be dark. After a while the stranger directed Clay to turn north. They followed a small wadi that narrowed down into a steep canyon cut into the cliffs. The Pajero lurched and scraped over the cobbles. The track ascended and then vanished altogether. Soon they were entirely in shadow, the cliffs looming above. Clay stopped the car.

'Wait here tonight,' said the stranger, slinging his Kalashnikov.

'Where are you going?' asked Clay.

'Wait here.'

They watched the stranger move off down the wadi. Within a few minutes he had vanished into the landscape.

They set up a makeshift camp in a small clutch of acacia at the base of a spur in the bluff. Clay made a fire. They ate a meal of bread and boiled eggs, untying Hussein's hands briefly so he could eat. They rolled out blankets in a loose semi-circle around the fire. Clay found a patch of sand near the gnarled roots of the largest tree and lay on his back. Orange firelight trembled through the branches and then died away into glowing coals. The first stars appeared. Darkness enveloped them and it was as if they were alone in the universe, and even the planets they could not see were barren of life.

He opened his eyes. Stars, the dark-bladed phyllodes of an acacia. Yemen. Voices. Clay jumped to his feet, handgun drawn. From the darkness beyond, a voice called out in Arabic. Clay stood in the darkness, the Beretta clutched in his hand. Rania was awake, back in the shadows with Hussein.

Three men emerged into the dim orange glow of the coals, tribesmen, all armed. Clay slid the Beretta into his waistband, raised his hand in greeting, signalled them come closer, sit. He threw a handful of twigs on the fire. Flames leapt up into the night, illuminating the faces of the men who now squatted on their haunches before him, the leader, older, flanked by two heavily armed, fierce-looking mountain tribesmen.

The leader glared at Clay, his left eye socket a blind weeping distress, the result of some botched local surgery, his hennaed beard thin and grey in the roots. It was the old guy from the roadside, the one who'd hijacked them. For a long moment he said nothing, just stood staring intently at Clay, his half-gaze fixed on Clay's right eye as if by force of will he could pluck out what he had lost and graft it to himself, right the wrong.

'You have the truth, *nazrani*?' he said finally. A *nazrani*, a follower of Jesus of Nazareth – a prophet yes, but not the Son of God – conspicuously destined for hell.

Clay blinked slowly for yes. 'And something else.'

Clay offered them bread and water. The men spoke for a long time amongst themselves, Hussein clearly the focus of the discussion. Occasionally one of the tribesmen would glance over at Clay. He could make out enough of the clipped dialect to sense the direction of the conversation.

Then the old guy looked at Clay and said: 'Your company takes the oil, *nazrani*, but we get nothing.' The old man shifted his feet and put his Kalashnikov across his knees.

'I am not with Petro-Tex now.'

'You give money to the *mashayikh*.'

'A lot of bloody good it'll do him now,' Clay said under his breath, in Afrikaans.

Rania had moved to his side, her blanket wrapped around her shoulders. She was unveiled.

'You give money,' said one of the younger men in English, holding out his hand. He was tall and lanky with a ravaged gravel-pit complexion.

Clay looked over at Rania and back at the men. 'No money,' he said opening his arms palms-up.

The tall one with the ravaged skin pointed his rifle at Clay's chest. The muzzle was only inches from his solar plexus. 'Money,' he shouted again.

'Stand,' barked the old guy in Arabic.

Clay stood, opened his hands out at his sides.

'Gun,' said the old man, pointing to Clay's midsection.

Clay pulled the Beretta from his waistband and dropped it to the ground. 'We're trying to help,' said Clay

'We do not need your help, *molhed khawga*,' said the man with the scar. Godless foreigner. True on both accounts, thought Clay.

Another surge of Arabic, rapid, angry syllables. The old man raised his hand. For a moment it looked as if he was about to turn away and melt back into the night. But then he levelled his weapon at Clay. The other two men did the same. Three high-powered assault rifles aimed at his torso, point blank.

Hussein spoke an oath to the Prophet and God.

The old man looked towards Hussein, sitting hobbled and tied at the edge of the firelight. 'Who is this, *nazrani*?'

'He is PSO,' said Clay. 'We bring him for Al Shams.'

The men murmured amongst themselves. The tall one grew increasingly agitated. He pointed at Hussein, talking rapidly in Arabic, his voice rising.

'No,' said Rania in Arabic. *La*. She spoke quickly. Clay could not keep up. The men stopped, looked at this woman who dared speak.

'What is it, Rania?'

'This man's son was murdered by the PSO six months ago. He wants to take Hussein.'

The old man spat on the ground.

'No,' said Clay. 'He could be valuable to Al Shams.' He spoke quickly, knowing that Rania would have to translate. He needed time to think.

The old man barked a command. The younger tribesman grabbed Hussein by the arm and hauled him forward. Hussein said nothing.

'Please,' said Clay, moving towards Hussein. There had been enough killing.

The other man, the one who had not spoken, motioned to Clay with the muzzle of his weapon, jerking it up and down. His eyes were lambent and cold. Clay backed away. The Beretta was there on the ground, useless.

Clay planted his feet. 'This man is my responsibility,' he shouted, parade ground. 'I have an agreement with Al Shams. Take us to him, verify what I have said.'

The tribesmen stopped for a moment, surprised by his outburst. Clay's voice echoed from the canyon walls and died away. Then the old man signalled with a tilt of his head and Hussein was shuffled into the darkness at gunpoint.

'*Yallah*,' said the old man. Let's go.

Clay and Rania started down a darkened footpath into the wadi.

A few minutes later a single gunshot pierced the night.

٣٣

Killer Hypothesis

They walked through the night, trudging over the rocky, barren ground. By the stars, they were heading north, up-wadi, into the buried heart of the uplands. After some hours they reached a place in the wadi where the canyon narrowed and scaled near vertical above them. A chaos of smashed and broken rock choked the wadi floor. Here, within this settled avalanche, they were separated.

It happened suddenly, quietly. One moment they were walking along in starlight, Rania ahead with the old tribesman behind, Clay a way back, the young gunman behind him, and next she was moving off through the rock, almost invisible in the flowing black *burqa*, the old tribesman shunting her off onto a different track. As soon as he realised what was happening, Clay stopped and turned, tried to move back to the place where Rania and her minder had peeled off. He called her name, but she kept going. The muzzle of an AK47 stabbed him in the abdomen. In that silver-blue light that comes just before the moon sets, he saw the young tribesman narrow his eyes, tighten his grip on the weapon. Clay was much bigger, could easily have overpowered him. But there was no margin. Too slow and the bullet would rip through his lower intestines at the speed of sound, keep going for another three hundred metres. Clay stood, watching Rania disappear.

'*Yallah*,' the young tribesman said, pushing the weapon's muzzle harder into him.

Clay raised his hands, backed away, looked the man in the eyes and said in Afrikaans: 'You touch her, any part of her, my brother, and you and your friends will be in paradise sooner than planned.'

The gunman muttered something in Arabic that Clay could not make out, pointed along the track with his weapon. Clay walked. A few minutes later they reached a low stone hut built into the rocks. A door was opened and he was flung inside. The door slammed shut. He heard the sound of grating metal, a steel bar sliding across the planking. He stood in the darkness and listened for a while to the men talking outside, and then he sat on the floor and closed his eyes. Ten years ago he would have continued clawing at the walls, trying to find a way out. But now he would be patient. Al Shams needed him, needed Rania. He would wait.

He must be getting old.

☾

The morning broke clear and hot after a night of broken sleep. Clay rolled over on the dirt floor, shoulders stiff and aching, sat up back against the wall. He stood, walked to the hut's wood-plank door and peered out the gap between mud brick and door frame. The hamlet was set into a clough in the canyon wall where the overlying marls and siltstones sloughed onto the limestone beneath. A dozen buildings were set amongst the boulders as if they had grown from the rock itself. Except for the occasional wisp of smoke from a cooking fire threading up into the blue sky, the place was almost invisible, indistinguishable from its surroundings.

The door opened and the old man with the hennaed beard, the one who had ordered Hussein to his death, who'd led Rania away, motioned Clay to come out into the glare of day. A small boy stood at his side. He could have been no older than Mohamed. 'My grandson,' said the old man in Arabic.

Clay glared at the old man. Hussein may have been PSO, but he had not deserved such an end, walked off into the night bound hand and foot and brutally shot. And Rania. Jesus Christ Almighty. His stomach felt like bruised cartilage. 'Where is the woman?' he said.

'Safe.'

She had better be. He said nothing.

The old man led them along a narrow footpath that wound its way around massive limestone boulders and past low-slung stone dwellings, the ancient log roof joists sagging under sheets of black tiled slate and blocks of grey mudstone. With each step, puffs of white powder rose from the path until his boots and trousers were covered. As they moved through the village, a small crowd gathered, boys and young men, most armed, following them silently. After a few minutes, the old man stopped and motioned him come forward. Clay stood in a small clearing in the base of the wadi, surrounded by ancient twisted cedar and scrub camelthorn. In the centre of the clearing was a low stone well.

Clay looked down into the mouth of the well. He could not see the water. The young boy, the grandson, dropped a goatskin down the shaft. The rope zipped along a groove in the stone edge until the skin landed with a splash and filled. The boy hoisted the skin dripping to the surface with practised over-arm tugs. Thick droplets of water fell into the darkness below.

The old man called in Arabic and two young men appeared carrying the instrument cases and his backpack. They must have retrieved them from the Pajero last night, after they had all been marched away. 'Is our water safe, *nazrani*?' said the old man.

Clay spent the next hour testing and retesting the well water, half the village peering over his shoulder. He calibrated and checked the instruments, re-calibrated, asked the boy to haul up more water, tested again. He wanted to be sure.

After he was finished he was put back in the hut. It was late afternoon before he was summoned. Clay followed the old man to a stone building built into the side of the bluff at the community's highest point. From here, you could see all the way back down the wadi to the plain and the Indian Ocean sparkling far off in the haze under a crown of billowing white cumulus. They bent low and entered. His escort remained outside.

Inside, it was much cooler. At first, the darkness was complete. Slowly, Clay's eyes adjusted. Al Shams was sitting on a carpet thrown over the hard-packed earth floor, dressed in a loose white robe and headscarf. He was alone. He bid Clay sit, then nodded, his face contorting into a half-smile. It was almost hideous. 'You have brought a friend,' he said after a moment.

They looked up. Rania entered, face uncovered, a shawl thrown over her hair and tied under her chin. A gigajoule of energy shot through him. The tips of his fingers were tingling.

'Welcome, Mademoiselle,' said Al Shams, signalling with his arm for her to sit.

Rania sat, stared straight ahead.

'Tell me now, please, Mister Claymore. What is so terribly inflicting my people?'

Rania looked over at him, raised her eyebrows.

Clay pulled out his yellow fieldbook and placed it on the carpet before him. 'It's all in here,' he said, tapping the hard cover of the book with two fingers. 'But before I tell you anything, I want to see Abdulkader. And I want to know why your men murdered the PSO man we brought with us.'

Al Shams looked surprised. 'I was not told of any murder.'

'Come on. You know everything that goes on within a hundred miles of this place. Your men marched him away and shot him last night. His name was Hussein.'

Al Shams called out in Arabic and one of his men appeared in the doorway and approached. Al Shams whispered something in his ear, the man answered briefly the same way and departed. 'I can assure you, there has been no murder.'

'Your men are lying to you.'

Al Shams closed his eyes, zen-like, a Bodhisattva sitting upright, palms on knees. 'Please, Mister Claymore. Tell me about the village, my people.'

'Where is Abdulkader?'

'He is safe and well.'

'And mutilated.'

Al Shams closed his eyes, waited.

Clay took a deep breath, looked inside himself, forced his pulse lower. Something Koevoet, his platoon commander in Angola, had taught him. Stay in control, stay calm. Focus. Think. If you don't, you're halfway to dead. You can freak after.

His heart slowed. He looked at Rania. She was OK. He looked at Al Shams, still sitting there, calm, tranced almost. He decided to play, trust that Al Shams would hold to his side of the bargain. He hoped he would. Because the monster was awake now. He could feel it, close to the surface, raging to get out, clawing at the bars, sniffing blood, and it was taking everything he had to keep it there. It wouldn't take much to break the chains.

Clay opened the densely scribbled fieldbook, folded out a sketch map: dashed lines pencilled along suspected faults, red triangles for water samples that had tested positive for contamination, electrical conductivity readings and pH levels scratched in pencil, shaded areas of colour – yellow for the Cretaceous sandstone outcrops that would contain groundwater at depth, green for the carbonate caprock that built the towering cliffs and overhangs, brown for the desolate crumbling shales, remnants of an ancient sea bottom, parting easily on ferruginous layers to reveal the plasms of extinct bivalves, whorled nautilus, trilobites, brachiopods, proof of time. With a mechanical pencil Clay traced a solid line that bisected the pages.

'This is the escarpment,' he said, the anodyne of science starting to do its thing, as it had so many times before, calming, ordering, explaining.

He moved the pencil tip along a series of lines that cut towards the top of the page, like hairs growing from an arm. 'And these are the wadis that cut up into the plateau.' He indicated the position of the CPF, the blue dots for the *ghayls* at Al Urush and Bawazir, and in red, according to the old Russian geological maps, a series of major faults that intersected Wadi Urush several kilometres to the north.

'What I have is only a hypothesis,' he said. 'As far as I can tell, produced formation water is leaking from the CPF – a lot of it.' With the information he had obtained from Parnell's office he was now sure that was the source. Exactly how that much water was getting into the ground, and why, he did not know, but something was seriously wrong up there.

Al Shams breathed out a long sigh, nodded.

'Based on what I've seen at other facilities, the source must be a leak of some sort. My best guess is that the formation water is flowing through fractures in the rock.'

'But he needs more data to prove it categorically,' said Rania.

Al Shams frowned. 'Please continue, Mister Claymore.'

'Hydro-geologically, it's the worst possible scenario,' he said. 'That's what we saw at Al Urush: very rapid migration, low attenuation.' Clay paused, aware he was getting too technical. The calculations flashed in his head, a simple conservative approximation of linear groundwater flow velocity using the Darcy equation: $v = K_f \cdot \{dh/dx\}/n_e$ – water moving through rock with an equivalent fracture permeability of 10^{-5} metres per second, driven by a hydraulic gradient of about one in eight (very steep, based on the topography), with an effective fracture porosity of 1 percent, with no attenuation.

'I understand, Mister Claymore. It moves quickly through the fractures, and does not dilute or disperse.'

'Exactly. Contaminants are travelling about eleven metres a day. That's 3.9 kilometres a year. Based on what we've seen, I'd guess two or three times that fast in some of the major fractures.'

Al Shams cupped his hands to his mouth.

'And the risk of lateral off-trend movement, to the *ghayl* at Bawazir, for instance, or even here, is real. The readings I have taken confirm this – the areal extent of contamination is massive, much bigger than I would normally expect.'

'And what is the poison that this water carries?'

'My guess is that the attempts at evaporation at the CPF are concentrating the brine, making it significantly more toxic and raising concentrations of naturally occurring trace elements, including, most damagingly, radionuclides: almost certainly thorium 232, perhaps radium 228 and 226, even uranium 238.'

He still had no idea what was causing the drop in water levels he had seen at Bawazir and Al Urush, but the lack of dilution was undeniably exacerbating the problem.

'Your people are suffering from radiation poisoning,' Clay said. 'I'm sorry.'

Al Shams stared at him for a moment as if he did not understand and then dropped his head. He did not speak for a long time. When he spoke again his voice was tight, strangled. 'And here, are we safe?'

'Based on the readings I took this morning, you are seeing the earliest signs of impact, the most mobile elements at the leading edge of the plume, including radionuclides. The contamination might not reach you in the same concentrations as at Al Urush, but you must find another source of water, especially for the children and women. The fractures in the rock all along the escarpment are deep and long. Every day that Petro-Tex keeps doing what it's doing, the risk increases. When the main plume arrives, it hits hard and fast.'

Al Shams sat unmoving, staring at the sketch before him, silent. After a while he looked up at Clay, nodded, and called out. An assistant came to his side, the same man as before. Al Shams whispered into his ear and then he left. 'Now do you see, Mister Claymore, why I needed you here, doing this work? Many lives are at stake. What more do you need to tell the full story, to prove this hypothesis, to link this horror to Petro-Tex without doubt?'

Clay looked over at Rania. 'We need samples and readings from the CPF evaporation ponds, and from the wadi just below the CPF.' He indicated each place on the sketch map with the point of his pencil. 'Then we can establish chemical evolution from source to receptors, connecting Petro-Tex with the deaths in Al Urush. Definitive proof.'

'That is what we call them,' said Rania. 'Receptors. That is all they are, these people. Even the language conspires.'

Clay closed his eyes a moment, continued. 'It's over two hundred kilometres by road to the CPF. There will be road blocks.' He looked up at Rania. 'If I can get to the top of the tributary wadi just to the east of the CPF, I can get through the fence down by the old Bedou well, be into the CPF by nightfall, and get to Al Urush down the wadi on foot, be there by morning. All I need is two more days.'

Al Shams nodded.

'And then we will have a story to tell,' said Rania.

'Ah yes, Mademoiselle LaTour. I have seen your work. Very professional. Very balanced. But does our small struggle warrant the attention of such an important international news agency?'

'That is why I am here. A private interview is all I ask. The world needs to know what is happening here.' She said it in Arabic.

Al Shams sat gazing at Rania for a long time. 'You speak well, young lady. Most of my countrymen cannot speak God's own language so beautifully.' He was clearly impressed, and not only by the beauty of her speech.

Rania smiled. Clay knew that she was where she needed to be, where she should be.

Al Shams turned to Clay. 'If you would do this for us, Mister Claymore, collect this information, we would be grateful until the end of days. And to do this, you will need a dependable guide.' He waved his hand. A side door opened.

A scowling Yemeni stood in the gloom. He was pale and thin, in a dirty *thaub* and a loose headscarf. Al Shams waved him closer. The man shuffled forwards, head bowed, stood before them with hands crossed. He looked up, grey eyebrows crimped under the headscarf so that his eyes were almost completely obscured.

'Allah has been merciful,' he said in a rock-and-cobble baritone that made Clay jump.

Clay stood and faced the man, looked into his eyes, pulse racing now. He reached for the man's weathered hand, took it in his. And there it was, the white mark on the index finger where the ring had shielded his skin from the Arabian sun ever since his father's death.

Clay threw his arms around Abdulkader and held him like a brother, hiding his face in his friend's headscarf, relief scouring away days of guilt. Abdulkader stood rigid and unmoving, arms at his sides. Clay composed himself, pushed himself back and held Abdulkader at arm's length, pored over him. It was really him, crags and frowns and all. Rania smiled up at them with that big beautiful mouth.

'I'm sorry, Mister Clay,' Abdulkader said.

'What do you mean sorry? Jesus, no, Abdulkader, it's me who's sorry.'

Al Shams waved his arm in a slow arc over them. 'Mister Claymore, Abdulkader my friend, you will leave for the CPF in the morning. Please leave us now. Miss LaTour, you shall have your interview.'

Flirting with Extinction

That evening Clay was moved to a small stone building near the top of the settlement, not far from where he had met with Al Shams. Inside was a small table and two chairs, a hand-woven rug thrown over the packed dirt floor, and a wood-frame bed with a straw-filled mattress. A kerosene lamp hung from one of the ceiling beams. Two small wood shuttered openings at the front of the building looked out across the wadi and down to the coastal plain. A low back door led out onto a small courtyard ringed with stone walls. A pomegranate tree grew in one corner, well-tended, heavy with ripening fruit.

The guards were gone. Clay moved a chair into the courtyard and sat watching the sky fade as he picked small red seeds from fleshy yellow husk. It had been hours now since he had seen Rania or Abdulkader. After leaving Al Shams, the guards had taken Abdulkader away and escorted Clay here. It was made clear that he was not to leave the building.

He crunched a mouthful of the tart seeds, his fingertips red from the juice. The shock of finding the first traces of contamination so far off-trend, over a hundred kilometres from Wadi Urush, was still with him. Where would these people find water? Perhaps they could try to dig a well further up-wadi; the further north, the lower the probability of contamination. He must tell Al Shams the next time he saw him. He thought back to their conversation. What had Al Shams meant calling Abdulkader 'my friend'? He had done so without a trace of artifice, his tone completely genuine. Had Abdulkader succumbed to Stockholm Syndrome, falling in with the common cause? Clay's mind raced, the sky now sea blue, the first stars tentative above the darkening rock walls.

He rummaged in his backpack for the bottle of whisky, but it had been taken. The hip flask had been spared, though, and he unscrewed the cap and let the cheap duty-free blend flow into his throat. He took a deep breath, looked up at the stars. He was going to finish the job, collect the vital source data. Then Rania would write the story and perhaps something would change. And then what? Already labelled a terrorist, a wanted man, he would now be the prime suspect in Hussein's death as well. He could only assume that his new identity would not protect him – it would have been registered with the PSO when Hussein secured it. He took another swig of the whisky, but there was no deadening of the fear that grew within him like a cancer.

He walked to the door, opened it. There were no guards, just the wadi spreading dark and deep below. Now he knew why. An outsider in a country riven by war, without money, the nearest border a thousand kilometres away through some of the driest, most inhospitable and rugged terrain on the planet – there was nowhere to go.

The sky was dark now and a breath of hot wind flowed across the village. Clay raised his face to the stir of air and emptied the last of the whisky into his mouth, suddenly feeling very tired, aware of the crease of pain across the back of his head. It felt like days since he had slept. He ducked under the doorway, fashioned a pillow from the jacket Hussein had given him, stretched out on the mattress and closed his eyes.

He had just fallen into a furtive sleep when there was a knock at the door. He rose and swung open the crude planking. Rania stood in the dust looking up at him from behind the narrow opening of a drawn veil. 'Please, Claymore,' she whispered. 'I must speak with you.' There was urgency in her voice.

Clay stood aside and closed the door behind her. It was dark inside now, too dark to see her face. He grabbed the other chair and led her out into the back courtyard where the rising moon bathed the small enclosure in quicksilver light. She walked the perimeter of the courtyard, peering over the walls of hand-laid unmortared stone, and then sat facing him.

'Did they go through your bag?' she asked in a whisper.

'They took my bottle.'

'But you have a reserve. I can smell it.' She smiled, just a flick of her lip.

He pulled out the empty hip flask, pinged its side with his fingernail.

She looked down at her clasped hands. 'They took my case.' She looked up at him, took a breath, parted her lips as if to speak, then closed her mouth again and curled back into the chair. She was quiet for a long time.

After a while he leant in towards her and said: 'What is it, Rania?'

She hesitated a moment, seemed to collect herself. 'Is what Hussein said true? Did you bribe that sheikh, Clay? Did you mislead those poor, unfortunate people?' There was effort in her voice, as if she was forcing the words out, one at a time.

Clay stared hard into her eyes. After a while he said: 'Don't look so surprised, Rania.'

Rania opened her mouth, held back a gasp. 'Please, do not say that.'

'What did you expect?'

'Clay, I know ...'

He cut her short. 'No, you don't. So don't say it, Rania. Don't even think it.'

'I know enough.'

He pushed his hands hard into the chair frame. 'You think so?' he said. 'This,' he looked around the stone walled courtyard, 'this is nothing, just one project. I've been doing this for a long time. I don't even know how many people I've screwed over.' He slumped back in the chair and looked out into the night. 'It hasn't turned out like I wanted.' Not even close.

'What happened, Clay? Tell me.'

'I would rather not,' he lied.

She leaned over in the darkness and kissed him on the cheek. 'Please, *chéri*.'

He told her everything. Almost. He told her about the money they paid him and his need for it, about the falsified reports and bribes, here and in other places, desolate places where the law was no more than a veneer, a rumour, where anyone could be bought and anything could be done. And the more he told her the more he wanted to tell, to rid himself of it, and before she could answer or question or react he spoke of all of the other jobs, the other bribes, so many that he could no longer remember the faces or the amounts or even the reasons, and of all the ruined places, the bulldozed marshes and the dredged reefs, the displaced people, and of the parts that he tried never to think about, how he lied and deceived the poorest and most vulnerable, how he had been doing it for a long time, ever since the war killed the person he was and replaced him with someone he despised. He could not stop. It poured out like venom, black and ugly, and as he spoke he felt the inevitability of her reproach crush him like a hundred million years of rock, an epoch.

And even then he kept back the worst, the part that he had almost managed to convince himself had never really happened, the part that now only came to him at night, in the hallucinations of nightmare, the part that even the SADF had expunged from the record.

She listened in silence and pondered for a long time after he finished. She had pulled back her headscarf and let down her hair. She reached for his hand, took it in hers. 'The war did this to you.'

He breathed her in. That's exactly what the court-appointed doctor had told him in London, after he'd pronounced his diagnosis. A disease, he called it, like any other, like malaria or dengue. Something that infects you, that comes on when you least expect it, something you're just going to have to learn to live with. No one *wants* to get sick, he said. It's not your fault. God, how he wished it could be true.

'You are *good*, Claymore Straker.'

Clay said nothing. How to respond to this?

'And I am sorry for how I treated you in Sana'a.'

'I've never been treated better,' he said.

Her eyes fluttered, closed, opened. She directed their full glory at him. 'I never imagined, Clay. It was overwhelming. As if I was losing myself. That morning you left, I was so confused. I was frightened. I *am* frightened.' Rania pulled up her feet and curled into the chair, knees clasped to her chest, and sat looking out into the darkness for a long time, saying nothing.

When she finally spoke her tone was deliberate and soft, like that time out on the coast in Aden. 'Sometimes you do not have a choice, Clay. No matter how much you might wish you did. Sometimes it is simply not up to you.'

This was not what he had expected from her.

'And now it is too late,' she said, only a whisper.

He waited for her to continue, but she just sat, mute, staring into the night.

'What do you mean? Too late for what?'

'For everything. All the things I thought I would do.'

'It's never too late, Rania.' She was teaching him this.

She leaned in close. He could feel the warmth of her skin, the caress of her breath on his neck. 'Do you believe that, Clay?'

'Sometimes.'

She sat back in her chair, drew up her knees, wrapped her arms around herself, hid her face.

After a while he said: 'What happened with Al Shams, Rania? Your interview.'

She looked up at him. 'You were right.'

'He's not Al Qaeda.'

'Or Ansar Al-Sharia, or Islamic Jihad,' she said. 'No more than you are.'

Clay forced what he hoped would be a quick smile.

'Will you get the rest of the data you need?' she asked.

'I'm going to do my best, Rania.'

'You must, Clay. No matter what happens, you must get the proof, and make sure the story is told. It is the only way to protect these people and clear yourself. Promise me.'

She was right. He needed the remaining data as much as Al Shams did. Needed it for a lot of reasons. He reached out for her, found her hand. 'I'll get the data, Rania, if you write the story. We'll do this together.'

She reached under the fold of her robe and pulled out a sheaf of loose-leaf pages. 'I already have.' She thrust them towards him. 'Here.'

Clay took the pages, looked down at the tight disciplined script in the sombre light, scanned the first few paragraphs. 'Who killed the *mashayikh*?' he asked.

'Al Shams claimed responsibility. But I think he's covering for someone. It was an honour killing. Once they found he was taking bribes …' she hesitated. 'From you.'

'Jesus.'

'He likes you Clay. He knows you have helped him. He says he sees something in you.' She squeezed his hand. 'But he is determined, convinced of his cause. Be very careful.' She stood and took his hand. 'Come, there is not much time.'

She closed the door and the window shutters, turned down the lantern, lit the candle on the bedside table, and sat on the bed. He sat next to her and gazed at the small flame that flirted with its own extinction at the tip of the wick. She was crying now, silently, weeping thick salty tears into her hands. He put his arm around her shoulder and kissed her on the cheek and the ear and the neck. Her tears smelt of rain on the red soil of the *veldt* when he was a kid. It didn't matter, he told her. It was going to be alright. But he didn't say the things he should have said, about how glad he was that she was here with him now, and how he admired her courage and the way she refused to compromise her ideals. At least they had tried, he said. They had come here and they were going to do what they could.

After a while she wiped her face on her sleeve and stood before him. He looked up at her, the candlelight flickering across her face. Was it for the murdered, this offering of tears? Was it for the polluted waters that sickened her as if the poisons flowed through her own veins? She looked into his eyes for a long time and then without a word she reached into her robe and pulled out her pistol and laid it on the floor. He was about to speak when she touched her fingertip to his lips. 'They did not search me,' she whispered. Then she reached behind her back and let her dress fall to the ground. She stood naked before him.

'Please,' she whispered, 'I do not want to be alone tonight.'

He pulled her to him. They fell to the bed, mouths locked. She raised her arms above her head, palms open, up. He kissed the salty ridge of her cheekbone, pinning her hands with his own. She closed her eyes. He kissed her cheek and the tip of her nose and the curved cartilage of her ear. She sighed and arched her back. He wrestled off his shirt and threw it to the floor. Her legs enveloped him. The air around him was afire with swirling chemicals, and it was if they were alone in the universe, locked in some furious elemental communication, apart from the chaos of the world; for those few moments they spun in harmony, and when he came inside her it was as if something were being wrenched from within his core, drawn out like un-distilled poison.

Afterwards, he fell into a cloud of sleep. He awoke sometime later and watched her sleeping under the blanket in the half-moon's reflected light until he could no longer resist waking her. She pulled his mouth to hers and the touch and the smell of her inflamed him and he took her by the hips and turned her over and pulled her up onto her knees. She tilted her pelvis and buried her sighs in the pillow.

Later he awoke to the distant sound of gunfire. For a long time he lay holding her, listening to the whispers of the warm breeze that flowed down from the plateau across the plain to the ocean. Her head was resting on his clavicle, hair splayed across his chest. Her warmth filled the bed. He ran his hand over the soft curve of her hip. 'Are you awake?' he said.

Her eyelash flicked the skin of his chest.

'Another mistake, Rania?' he whispered.

She held him tight, kissed his chest.

When he woke again much later he knew she was gone. The depression beside him was still warm, still damp. Her story was on the floor by the bed where it had fallen, the pages scattered. Her handgun was gone. He stood and pulled on his trousers and T-shirt and grabbed the pages. Outside the remnants of a quarter-moon burned in the sky like an eclipsed sun. The village was in a coma of sleep, silent, lost in the rock from which it was built.

To his left, beyond one of the big boulders that stood like obelisks in the heart of the village, he saw something move, a flash in the moonlight, a person in the shadows. An instant later the figure slipped behind a boulder and vanished.

Clay moved barefoot in the direction of the obelisk, drawn forward. Reaching the house-sized rock he stopped and looked along the narrow footpath. The figure was moving steadily along the moon-white path, gliding phantom-like in a billowing robe. Clay watched the apparition approach Al Shams' building, slow and stop before the lone guard standing outside the door. The two figures stood for a moment, as if in conversation, and then the guard opened the door and led the figure into the building. At just that moment, a flash of movement drew Clay's gaze – two men moving among the rocks beyond and above the building. They glowed in the moonlight like painted targets, despite their dark clothing. The men moved in staggered surges, one then the other, closing on the building. Clay hugged the cold surface of the obelisk, pulse loping. Fifty metres from the building, the men split up. One disappeared among the rocks behind the building. The other man was on the path now, about fifty metres ahead of Clay. He stopped, looked both ways. He carried a short-barrelled submachine gun, H&K it looked like. Boots, black fatigues, flack vest, brain bucket with night vision goggles. Military-looking. Special Forces. The man set off at a sprint towards the building.

Clay broke cover and sprinted after the man, bare feet hammering the dust, closing the gap. The man was almost at the front door of the building now. He slowed. Clay was close, ten metres away, in full flight. Gunfire ripped open the night. Loud. Very close. An AK on auto, the buzz of an H&K. From inside the building, behind. Clay crouched in his run, ready to tackle. The man kicked in the door, darted inside. Clay reached the door just as more shots cracked out, flashes in the darkness. He could smell cordite, fear. Without stopping he surged inside, blind without the moon, the muzzle flashes dancing on his retina. His feet hit something and he crashed to the floor. More firing, very close, rounds cracking into the stone walls, splintering wood. He scrambled to his knees as his eyes adjusted. The back door was open, a wedge of moonlight thrown across the floor. A body lay just outside, one of Al Shams' men, the guard. Inside, the SF man Clay had chased and tripped over, leaking blood onto the floor. In the corner by the back door, shrouded in darkness, Al Shams, and a few metres away, crouching by the side wall, the robed figure. It was Rania. She was holding a pistol. It was aimed at Al Shams.

'No,' Clay shouted.

٣٥

Immiscible All

He had read the story earlier that night, Rania's head cradled in his shoulder, his hand on the soft silk of her side, feeling the slow rise and fall of her chest, the flicker of her eyelashes dancing in a dream. It was all there. Everything Clay now knew to be the truth about Al Shams, a man fighting for his people, for dignity and justice in the face of the seemingly unstoppable forces of unbridled greed and deep-seated corruption. Oil and water: one polluted the other. One brought life, the other nothing but suffering, violence, death, an unravelling of things. Western governments, desperate to secure geopolitical advantage in the Middle East, ever-protective of their increasingly fragile oil-dependent economies, were willing to countenance any injustice to keep the oil flowing. The emergence of the new radical Islamic movements was a clear threat.

Condemning legitimate unrest as terrorism, as in the case of Al Shams, was simply another cost of doing business with friendly regimes. Saleh had told the West what it wanted to hear, that he was fighting terrorism, keeping the oil flowing, all the while supressing dissent. Blood and money. The physical description of what had happened to Al Urush was technically accurate and heart-breaking. She wrote well, with controlled passion, part reportage, part manifesto. It was a call-to-arms for the oppressed, a cry to the people of free nations to wake from their television slumber and act. It was not only here, in the wilds of Yemen, in a tiny village of which no one had ever heard, the tragedy of a few dozen uneducated farmers. It was everywhere, every day. Truth and lies. Loyalty and deceit. Faith and nihilism. Apathy and action. Immiscible all.

Clay looked at her, uncomprehending.

Just then he heard footfall behind him, the pulses out of phase with the hammering of his heart. He only had time to turn his head slightly before he was caught on the jaw with a shuddering blow. He hit the ground hard but conscious, getting his elbows out in time to break the fall. He twisted onto his side and looked up. It was Hussein.

Clay's mind clattered through the possibilities, facts and suspicions coalescing in his mind. Rania and Hussein had been working together all along. It made sense. He cursed his own naïveté, the arrogance of this manufactured shell he had become: war-hardened cynic, preying on the venal, judging their bankrupt morals, above it all, beyond it. And all the time he had been dancing, the strings jerking his limbs now revealed as cables. All of this took a fraction of a second and coalesced into a surge of anger. He lunged for Hussein's leg, but Hussein kicked out with the other foot, catching him just below the chin, smashing his larynx. He rolled back, gasping for air.

Hussein raised his weapon, taking aim. Rania looked at him, no more than a flicker of the eyes. She raised her shoulders, a little breath, almost imperceptible under the dusty shroud.

A shot cracked out. The sound rang around the stone room. Rania spun back against the wall and slumped to the ground. Clay looked up. Hussein lowered his Beretta, glanced down at Clay, strode over to Rania, picked up her weapon, turned and ran out the back door.

۳٦

Our Tortured Country

The sound of gunfire close by echoed from the cliffs, the rattle of a submachine gun answered by the bark of an AK. Bullets smashed into the stonework above his head, shredded the palm-frond roof, filling the air with flying debris. Clay crawled to Rania. She was slumped against the stone wall, her face cast in thin starlight, eyes closed, unconscious but breathing. The front of her *burqa* was torn, wet with blood. He ripped open the *burqa*, exposing her pale shoulders. Hussein's bullet had entered just below her collarbone. Blood welled from the hole in her skin. He rolled her gently onto her side, pulled the *burqa* aside. That fine pale skin so brutally punctured. Such a small thing. The bullet had passed through her, exiting just above the clavicle. There was a lot of blood, but she'd been lucky. A few centimetres lower and it could have been a lot worse. If he could stop the bleeding, she had a chance.

Holding her carefully on her side, he pulled off his T-shirt, ripped two thick strips from the hem with his teeth, rolled the two strips into makeshift compresses, placed the first against the exit wound and rolled her onto her back. He straightened her out, placed the second compress onto the entrance wound and applied pressure. Then he looped what remained of his shirt over her arm and shoulder and tightened it down hard over the compresses. He had just finished tying the makeshift bandage in place when he was jerked to his feet by two tribesmen. Outside, shouts in the darkness, the close hammering of gunfire. He looked around the room. Al Shams was gone.

He turned to the gunmen, pointed to Rania. 'She needs my help,' he shouted in Arabic, straining against their holds.

They dragged him back a few steps. He twisted and swept out his right foot, taking out one tribesman's legs. The man toppled to the ground, but held fast to Clay's arm, trying to bring Clay down with him. Clay crouched, braced his legs, set himself as a fulcrum, closed his arm around the other man's hands and used the rotational momentum to whip the other tribesman over his shoulder and bring him crashing down hard on top of his kinsman. Grunts as the two bodies collided, took the full force of the accelerated mass. Clay reached down, grabbed one of the AKs, was about to move back to Rania when Al Shams appeared in the doorway. He was unarmed.

Al Shams looked at Clay, at the two men in a heap on the ground, at the dead SF soldier, at Rania. 'Leave him,' he commanded. 'She needs medical attention,' he said, stepping inside.

Clay dropped the AK, ran to Rania, crouched down beside her. A young man, Yemeni, clean-shaven, appeared in the doorway behind Al Shams. He was carrying a stretcher and a medical kit. His face was spattered with blood. The young man placed the stretcher on the ground beside her, crouched down beside Clay. With long, bloodstained hands, he reached for the makeshift bandage Clay had applied. Clay grabbed his wrist, stared him in the eyes.

'I have trained in Britain as a medical technician,' the young man said in clear, accented English. 'Please.'

Clay released his grip. The medic drew back the bandage and inspected Rania's wounds. His touch was sure and gentle. He glanced up at Clay. 'This will do for now,' he said. 'We must move her.'

Clay helped him shift Rania onto the stretcher. Together, they carried her through the village. The gunfire had stopped and quiet had descended again like a shroud. Children and old men lined the pathway, whispering as they passed. They took her to a small hut near the wadi floor, placed the stretcher between one set of two wooden trestles, another wounded man laid out similarly nearby, the place acting as some kind of makeshift dressing station. The medic hung a kerosene lamp from a hook in one of the ceiling beams, lit it, and set about cleaning and dressing Rania's wounds. He worked well, with practiced efficiency, ran an IV, hung the bottle from the ceiling. Then he turned and looked at Clay.

'She is stable for now,' he said. 'But there is a lot of bleeding. The brachial artery is damaged …' he trailed off. 'I have tried to clamp it, but I am not sure I have succeeded. I'm sorry.'

Clay looked at the man, over at Rania. 'Thank you,' he said.

'Watch her,' said the medic. 'Call me if there is any change.' His English was good, almost mid-Atlantic. 'I'll be back soon.' Then he turned and left the building.

Clay stood at Rania's bedside, the pages of her manuscript crushed tight in his blood-stained hand. The sound of her breathing filled his ears, shallow, erratic. Her eyes were closed. It was as if her mother's Mediterranean pigment had been drained from her skin, revealing the pale of her father's Nordic chromosomes. Clay had seen that look before. It wasn't good.

His mind lurched, pure turbulence. Why had she left him and gone to Al Shams just as the SF types had moved in? It couldn't be coincidence – things didn't just happen that way. Had she known they were coming? And Hussein. Alive. Was he working with Al Shams? Did they have some sort of arrangement? Had he shot Rania to protect him? Nothing made sense. Clay walked to the door, peered through a gap between the rough planks. Two guards stood outside. He went back to Rania, sat listening to her breathing, watching her chest rise and fall in the pulsing frailty of the kerosene light.

'Clay,' she said, her voice a thread.

He knelt on the ground beside her. 'I'm here, Rania.'

She opened her eyes, blinked in recognition, opened her cracked dry lips to speak, but fell back from the effort. He moved closer, his lips hovering just above hers.

'Stay still,' he said.

'I tried, Clay,' she said. He could barely hear her. 'I tried.' A breath escaped from her lips and her eyes closed.

Clay jumped to his feet, hammered at the door. 'Tell Al Shams I want to see him. Now,' he shouted in Arabic at the guards. 'She's awake. Bring the medic.'

One of the guards muttered something and shuffled away.

Soon after, the young medic appeared at the door. Al Shams was with him, carrying a large case. Clay recognised it. The medic checked Rania's IV, took her pulse. Al Shams stood beside Clay, looking down at Rania. His face was ashen, the lines in his brow like fissures in dolomite, his good eye sunk almost as deep as the dead one. After a moment Al Shams turned to face Clay and placed Rania's case on the ground. 'I am very sorry,' he said. 'Will she live?'

'She has lost a lot of blood,' said the medic.

Clay ran his hands across the back of his head, laced his fingers there. His jaw and throat still ached from Hussein's blows; he could feel the rough welts of the sutures in the back of his head. An image of Rania lying dead, cold, open-eyed, came unwanted into his head and made him gasp with shame. He thrust Rania's manuscript into Al Shams' hands. 'Read this,' he said. 'She wrote it yesterday.'

Al Shams looked down at the pages. After a while he looked up. 'Is this true?'

'She gave it to me last night. It's hers.'

Al Shams opened Rania's bag and pulled out a black case about the size of shoe box. 'What do you know about this?' he said.

Clay unfastened the clasps and flipped open the top. Clay had seen military-issue satellite com systems before. He looked up at Al Shams. 'She is a reporter,' he said. 'She needs to file her stories.'

Al Shams held up the paper. 'And more?'

Clay remembered the night at the farm, Rania's voice behind the bedroom door. 'What are you suggesting?'

Al Shams placed the sat-phone back into the case. I seek only answers, Mister Claymore, God willing.'

Clay looked at Al Shams, dread welling up in his chest. 'I don't care who you think she is or what she's done, we've got to save her.'

Al Shams pushed Rania's manuscript back at Clay. 'We are not animals, Mister Claymore. We are not terrorists. But we have limited resources.'

The medic stood, faced them. 'There's no more I can do for her,' he said. 'The bleeding is bad. She must get proper medical attention, or she will die.'

'There is a hospital in Al Mukalla,' said Clay. 'Three hours by road. I'll take her there myself.' Clay reached for Al Shams' shoulder. 'Please,' he said. 'Let me take her.'

Just then Hussein ducked under the low doorframe, followed by two armed fighters. Sweat covered his forehead and dark stains bloomed across the front of his shirt. He was breathing heavily. 'It is arranged,' he said to Al Shams, acknowledging Clay with a nod of the head.

'You bastard,' blurted Clay, closing on Hussein.

Hussein took a step back and levelled his handgun at Clay.

Al Shams held out his hand. 'There is no time for this. If you want her to live, you must hurry.'

Clay glared at Hussein. 'What's arranged?'

'She will be evacuated,' said Hussein. 'Back to France. A French Air Force Hercules with a surgeon on board is on its way from Djibouti right now.'

'How the hell did you arrange that?'

Hussein said nothing.

'Take her to Riyan Airport, Mister Claymore,' said Al Shams. 'Abdulkader and Hussein will go with you. Then go to the Petro-Tex facility and get the data you require. Once that is done, Hussein will return here with the information, Abdulkader will take you to the Omani border, and you will be rid of our tortured country.'

٣٧

Unburied Lies

They left the village in two vehicles, Clay and Abdulkader in the old Land Cruiser with Rania on a stretcher in the back, Hussein in the white Pajero. At the main road, Hussein peeled off towards Al Mukalla. They would meet afterwards at the farm. That was the plan. And then Clay would kill him.

The Riyan airport terminal building, built by the British in the 1960s and degraded by the Russians over the next couple of decades, sat at the apex of a horseshoe-shaped road lined with trees. Normally, traffic flowed in on one side, passed the drop-off area in front of the terminal, and moved back out along the opposite side of the horseshoe. But now both arms of the road were clogged with vehicles: pickups trying to cut across the direction of travel, a stranded fuel carrier, an assortment of military vehicles spanning five decades, Toyota Land Cruisers and beat up old Nissans, their drivers gesticulating from rolled-down windows or standing in irate clusters next to open doors, voices raised in frustration at the complete breakdown in order, fighting to be heard over the relentless landing and take-off of heavily loaded jets.

Clay and Abdulkader left the car at the main road and sweated their way on foot through the mire of tangled vehicles towards the terminal, Clay in back, *keffiyeh* wrapped around his face, only his eyes uncovered, Abdulkader in front, Rania quiet on the stretcher between them, the sample cooler at her feet.

'Lean,' said Abdulkader, as they walked towards the terminal.

'What?'

'You are too tall. Lean.'

Clay hunched his back, kept his face directed groundward.

'There are soldiers. Say nothing.'

They kept walking, Rania's weight swaying in their hands. At the terminal's main entrance, four draftees in oversized steel helmets and a middle-aged Yemeni army officer with a megaphone attempted to maintain order. A group of exasperated and hoarse expatriates stood on the pavement waving passports above their heads as if they were on a stock-exchange floor trying to dump shares in a collapsing market. The soldiers were checking documents and drip-feeding people into the terminal building in ones and twos.

They pushed to the front of the ragged queue, drawing stares from some, concern from a few, hostility from others. They were close now, third or fourth from the doors. Sweat flowed freely from the officer's greying temples and dripped from his chin. He had a fatherly face, until a few days ago a policeman or bank manager perhaps. The door opened again and another expat was allowed to pass, a tall overweight man in jeans and a T-shirt that said: 'Chernobyl – take your radiation like a man'.

A tall fair-complexioned officer in a perfectly pressed uniform with crisp boarded epaulettes and a blue shoulder lanyard emerged from the terminal building and stood blinking in the sunlight. There was a small French tricolour patch on his sleeve. He scanned the crowd, fixed on the stretcher, spoke briefly with the Yemeni officer. The two men moved forward and ushered Clay and Abdulkader towards the door. There was a collective groan from the mass. Someone yelled out from behind them: 'What's so special about them. I'm an American, for fuck's sake.' They kept moving, almost inside now.

'Wait,' called the officer in Arabic.

They stopped, just beyond the doors.

'You,' the officer barked. 'What is your name?'

Clay froze, hunched. He could feel the soldier's eyes piercing the back of his head.

'I am Abdulkader Mohammed Al Gharar of Marib,' said Abdulkader over his shoulder.

Clay stood still, gripped the stretcher handles. He'd carried men like this before, some alive still, some not, remembered how much heavier a dead man always seemed, as if life's regrets hardened to leaden ballast as soon as the spirit fled. In comparison, Rania seemed weightless, a six-year-old boy in his arms as he ran through the sun-struck confusion towards the helicopter. As if she wasn't there at all.

Clay heard the officer say: 'Show me your identification,' watched as Abdulkader gestured with his chin towards the breast pocket of his jacket, both hands still locked to the stretched handles.

There was a pause. Clay looked straight ahead, didn't move. 'Please,' he heard the French officer say in Arabic. 'She looks as though she needs immediate attention. We must hurry.'

'What's the hold-up?' he heard someone shout from outside, other voices raised in complaint, half a dozen languages.

'And this man?' said the Yemeni officer.

Abdulkader glanced at Clay, expressionless. 'He is my brother. He cannot speak. By the will of Allah he was born wrong.'

Silence. Just the milling of the expats outside the doorway, the rumble of aircraft, the confusion of the traffic clogging the airport entrance. Clay dared not turn around, just stood watching his friend, looking down at Rania. '*Mashallah*,' said the Yemeni officer finally. 'Go.'

They moved into the building, stopped just inside as the doors closed behind them. The French officer leaned over the stretcher and spoke into Rania's ear. Clay watched her lips move in reply, her eyes flutter open. The French officer reached into the pocket of her jacket, pulled out her passport. He flipped through the document and found the photo page and held it next to her face; his hazel eyes flicked back and forth between her and the likeness of her, comparing the real with the image of reality. He nodded, replaced the passport, stood.

'We must hurry,' he said. 'This way.'

The departure hall was a churning sea of heads. They plunged in and fought towards the far end of the hall. They pivoted the stretcher around, Clay leading now. He used his height and weight to drive through the crowd, pulling her along in his wake.

The big doors at the far end of the departure area had been rolled back, opening out onto a fringe of brown scrub grass and a line of swaying palms. Three Russian-built attack helicopters stood on the concrete apron amidst a jagged landscape of crates and boxes, airfreight containers, ammunition and spare parts. MiG-29 fighter-bombers lined the far ramp, six in all, crews swarming over them like fire ants. Just beyond the runway, set against a sparkling blue sea, a pair of SCUD missiles on mobile launchers hulked in the brown stubble. Two jet fighters in tight formation screamed low over the runway, afterburners flaring, and then turned out over the coast in steep climbing turns. The stench of burnt jet fuel wafted through the building. Across the tarmac a French Air Force Hercules stood at the edge of the apron with engines running, propellers turning, rear ramp open. The noise was deafening, the sound of war.

The officer waved them forward towards the edge of the apron. Two khaki flight-suited airmen took the stretcher. Clay looked down at Rania. Her eyes were open. She reached up and pulled him toward her. He put his ear to her mouth.

'Come with me,' she said above the drone of the turboprops. The pilots were powering up the Herc now, checking the turbines, getting ready to go. 'If I tell them, they will not leave you.' Her voice was a whisper, a thread. 'Come with me, *chéri*, please.'

He pulled back and looked at her.

'What happened, Rania, back in the village?'

Tears welled up in her eyes. 'I …' she breathed, stopped. 'Please, Clay. Come with me.' She reached out for him. Her hand was cold.

He looked away, across the runway to the sea.

'You will die here,' she said.

'I don't care what you did, Rania. Tell me.'

'They want Al Shams dead.'

'Who does?'

'Everyone. And they will kill you, too.' She closed her eyes.

'I can't leave, Rania.'

'I do not understand.'

He took a deep breath. 'That story I told you. The boy in Angola.'

She looked up at him, blinking away the tears.

'I lied. It was me. I shot him.'

Her eyes shone like the night, constellations swirling in her tears. It was too hard to look.

'The squad was behind me, still in the trees. I saw movement and I fired. As soon as I'd done it I knew.' And because he had taken the boy back to the helicopter and sent Eben ahead with the squad, his best friend had been hit and would spend the rest of his life in hospital. If Clay hadn't panicked, shot without confirming the target, if he hadn't tried to save the boy, hadn't succumbed to his guilt, it would have been him out there at the front of the squad. It should always have been him: him who'd taken the bullet, him lying there deaf and dumb in a fucking coma in some shit hospital for all these years.

Clay looked down at her, this woman he barely knew and yet who seemed to know him so well, and it was like coming out of a morphine sleep of years, feeling again. And in that moment it was so clear: now is all there is. The past is gone, locked away. The future doesn't exist. It's what we do now, the decisions we make right now that create the present, seal the past.

He reached into his pocket, slid the folded sheaf of papers into her hand. 'Tell the story,' he said.

She nodded, tried to reach up for him but she was too weak. He bent over and kissed her. He could feel her lips trembling, the smell of her mixed with the JP4, the roar of the turboprops.

The officer touched Clay on the shoulder. 'We must go.'

Rania slid something into his hand, the back of a cigarette pack. 'Find me,' she mouthed as the airmen started across the burning concrete. And then she was moving away from him towards the Hercules, looking back over her shoulder, carried by the French airmen, almost now to the ramp. She raised an arm and tried to wave, the airmen leaning into the blast from the propellers, her hair streaming horizontally. He waved back and then she disappeared into the dark mouth of the transport.

The Hercules taxied to the far end of the airfield and turned and stopped short of the threshold as a massive unmarked four-engine cargo plane thudded down onto the runway with a puff of smoke. The turboprops opened up with a roar and the Hercules started to move down the runway, slowly at first, gaining speed before rotating and clawing its way into the blue Arabian sky, wings flashing in the sun, a black trail of exhaust falling away to the ground. He stood and looked up at the sky as the point that held her diminished and then was gone.

Part IV

٣٨

Unanswered Questions

Clay and Abdulkader escaped the tumult of the airport and the din of aircraft engines and drove eastwards through a deserted landscape. Dust eddied back through the open windows like a fog of unanswered questions, covering the seats and Rania's discarded *burqa* in a thin layer of silt. When they reached the farm, he was going to wrench some answers out of Hussein, one way or another. Why had Hussein shot Rania? And then why had he organised her evacuation, and how had he done it so quickly? He was going to get answers, and then he was going to apply Sharia law.

Clay searched through the smoking battleground of his feelings, the strewn corpses of lost friends, the wrecks of terminally short relationships. What he felt for Rania was real, strong. He knew that now. And it was getting stronger, growing and kicking inside him, something he could not will away, could not kill. And now she was gone.

He opened his shirt front pocket and pulled out the scrap of paper that Rania had pressed into his hand at the airport, looked at the scrawled handwriting. The words were almost illegible, jagged, smudged with her blood. *Genève/Rimbaud/anges et hommes/Aden.* There was a number: 022 347 38 29, or was it 022 391 38 14? He couldn't tell the fours and nines or the sevens and ones apart. *Find me,* she had said.

An hour into the journey, Clay broke the sepulchre of silence that had descended upon them. 'Do we have enough fuel to get to the CPF and back?' His voice sounded thin and taut in his own ears.

'*Mafi mushkilla.*' No problem. 'Also five cans at the farm.'

The farm, where Hussein was waiting for them. 'Enough to get to Oman after that?' he said. The Omani border was about 850 kilometres from Ash Shihir following the coast road, most of it unpaved. The alternative was to drive north to Shibam, Abdulkder's birthplace, and follow Wadi Masila back to the coast and then to Oman, covering about 1200 kilometres through some of the roughest and most empty country on the planet. It was the edge of the world.

'Enough, *inshallah.*' Abdulkader trailed off into Koranic verse, eyes narrowed, body rocking forward over the steering wheel, the voice of God pulsing through him in low surging rhythms, invoking the certainty of the *al-Furqan*, that which distinguishes between truth and falsehood, and the other Sura that he had taught Clay: the *al-Nur*, the light; the *al-Bayan*, that which explains all things; and whoever intercedes in a good cause has a share in it, and whoever intercedes in an evil cause has a portion of it, and Allah is ever keeper over all things. And one of his signs is this: that He created mates for you from yourselves that you might find quiet of mind in them, and He put between you love and compassion. Surely there are signs in this for a people who reflect.

They reached the farm in the rising heat of day. Abdulkader sped along the farm road between the palm groves towards the house. Ahead in the courtyard, he could see Hussein's white Pajero parked under the big palm tree. There was another vehicle there, too, a big silver Toyota in the middle of the forecourt, doors open. Abdulkader slowed the vehicle and rolled it to a stop.

'What's wrong?'

Abdulkader reached for the binoculars and passed them to Clay. 'Look near the Toyota.'

Clay raised the glasses to his eyes and brought the car into focus. The windscreen was opaque, crazed. He scanned down to the open door and then to the ground. At first he thought the man was sleeping, escaping the worst of the day's heat. His legs were twisted beneath his body, his neck cocked at an angle so that the top of his skull was wedged into the ground. It wasn't until he saw the dark stain around the head that he realised the man was dead.

Abdulkader rolled the vehicle to the side of the road, turned off the engine and pulled out the Kalashnikov. 'Come,' he said.

Clay followed Abdulkader through the trees towards the farmhouse. They stopped and crouched behind a steel water tank at the edge of the forecourt and looked over to the house and the outbuildings. The house baked in the kiln of the midday sun. The front door was ajar and the curtains fluttered through open windows. The floor of the veranda flashed and shimmered in the sunlight. They waited and watched.

Abdulkader chambered a round and signalled him to follow. Just as they left the cover of the water tank, a dog darted out of the front door of the house and loped off into the trees. Its hindquarters were riven with mange, pink and raw. They crossed the forecourt at a run. Abdulkader stepped up onto the veranda. Something crunched under his sandals. The tile floor was covered in shattered glass. Long curved shards edged the window frames; the curtains were torn and holed.

'Stop,' whispered Abdulkader.

Clay froze in place, one foot on each step. A low moan came from around the corner of the building. Abdulkader stepped slowly along the veranda, avoiding the broken glass, his back to the wall. He stopped just short of the corner and looked back towards Clay and signalled quiet.

For what felt like a long time Clay stood immobile on the steps, trying to keep his breathing under control, looking up at his friend standing back to the wall with something or someone just around the corner. Sweat rolled down his sides and welled up in the backs of his knees. Another moan from around the corner, louder this time. In one movement, Abdulkader pivoted through 270 degrees and stepped forward into a crouch, swinging the AK up and around to bear down the length of the far wall. For a moment he remained frozen in position, rifle raised to his jaw. Then he lowered the weapon and signalled Clay to follow.

The man lay slumped back against the wall of the house in a spreading slick of blood, his hands locked across his abdomen. His white shirt was splattered crimson. He was conscious and looked up as they approached. A submachine gun, a Heckler & Koch MP5, blunt with a long curved clip, lay on the tile out of reach. Spent cartridge casings littered the veranda.

Abdulkader said something in Arabic. The man muttered in reply. Abdulkader picked up the man's weapon and slung it over his shoulder. The man looked around as if searching for something, eyes half-open. He looked weary. Clay had seen that look before. Abdulkader barked at him again, weapon levelled at his face. The man peered down the gun barrel and replied in an angry wheeze, blood frothing from his mouth. Abdulkader turned away and walked back along the veranda. Clay followed, cold.

Abdulkader signalled quiet and moved back towards the front door. He crouched and nudged the door open with the lightest touch. Hussein lay on his back in the middle of the tile floor, eyes fixed on the ceiling fan spinning lazily above him, his body resting in a pool of thick arterial blood.

The Weight of Sin

They buried Hussein's body that same day under the most prolific of the pomegranate trees behind the house. The sandy ground made easy digging, and working in turns they fashioned a good, deep grave, with clean, straight sides and a flat base, the Kalashnikov and the Beretta close by. The sun burned Clay's skin as he sweated in the grave.

Afterwards they stood over the product of their labour and Abdulkader spoke from the Koran, entrusting this brother to Allah all merciful. Then they dug another hole, far from the house this time, and buried Hussein's assassins together. Clay wrapped his headcloth over his mouth and nose and tried not to look at the faces or the eyes. Shifting the bodies was hard work, like manhandling sacks of grain, heavier than they appeared, the flies feasting on the corpses and the sweat of their minders. After the burial, Clay walked away into the trees and found a place where he was hidden; he sat on the ground and stared up at the sky.

By the time he returned to the house, Abdulkader had moved his Land Cruiser behind the buildings and loaded the extra cans of diesel from one of the sheds into Hussein's vehicle. The Pajero was newer, bigger and faster, a better bet for the difficult road to Oman. Clay drew a pail of water from the well and found some soap and a mop in the kitchen and tried to wash Hussein's blood from the floor. Blood and water formed a slick of emulsion that spread across the tiles and settled into the grouted troughs between, the liquids only partially miscible, rejecting each other. One after the other, he dumped pails of red water down the sink. Then he washed down the veranda, the two men's blood mixing freely in the pail.

After the washing they filled water bottles and collected what food they could find in the kitchen, some stale flatbread, figs. 'Let's go, my friend,' said Clay. 'Two days from now we should be on our way to Oman, God willing.

❨

An hour and a half later they reached Wadi Idim and the main road up the escarpment to the highlands beyond. The narrow ribbon of crumbling tarmac scaled a thousand vertical metres from the plain to the top of the plateau in a series of eight switchbacks. There were no outside railings, only a narrow gravel verge and a sheer drop to the wadi floor. The Pajero's diesel strained against the steepening grade, choking on an enriching fuel mixture. With altitude, the coastal plain soon disappeared under a shroud of haze and dust, and beyond, the Indian Ocean opened up before them until it filled the southern horizon.

At the top of the climb, Abdulkader pulled the car off the paved road and navigated a short stony track back towards the cliff edge. He rolled the vehicle to a halt. They got out and walked until they were only a few steps from the edge of the precipice. The coastline stretched away until the horizon dissolved into a vapour, land, sea and sky somehow atomised, boiled into constituent elements, earth's essential plasma disaggregating there at the farthest edges, as if the whole world could fray and gasify at the slightest impulse. There was God-like power here, a sun's rapid expansion and consumption of its satellites, time become decaying orbits and grains of sand.

Clay looked down at his boots, at the dark ironstone pebbles scattered in uniform confusion over the limestone upland. The smells of the desert came on the hot breeze, sun-baked rock, dust, minerals. Abdulkader stood beside him, hands clasped at midriff, swaying back and forth, eyes half-closed, as if distilling meaning from all of it: the rock and stone of the desert, the limitless ocean, the sun's fierce fusion.

They drove on in the direction of the production facility, still two hours away on the graded dirt road, across the polychrome plateau of fist-sized ironstones and shale plates the colour of bone.

Clay reached for his water bottle and took a swig and offered it to Abdulkader.

'What did he say to you, back at the farm, the one who was dying?'

Abdulkder took the bottle, put it to his mouth and tipped it back, then passed it to Clay and wiped his mouth with the back of his hand but did not respond.

'Who was he, Abdulkader?'

Abdulkader spat out of the side window and then turned his eyes back to the road ahead. 'Afghan. Ansar Al-Sharia.' And after a few more kilometres: 'He said Hussein was a traitor.'

'Betrayal,' said Clay after a while. 'It doesn't take much.'

Abdulkader kept driving, staring out through the windscreen. The vehicle rattled along the road, sending an oblique scar of dust into the sky. So stark was the land that he thought he could discern the curvature of the earth's surface moving closer. But as with so much here, this was an illusion – a sixty-mile horizon cannot reveal a discernible arc, even at the edge of the world.

☾

The checkpoint was so carefully hidden, nestled at the base of a blunt-layered upland, that they almost ran straight through it. Abdulkader pumped the brakes to keep the speeding vehicle from skidding out of control, wrestling it to a stop in a shower of gravel.

The road was barred by a length of steel pipe balanced on a crudely welded cradle, weighted on one end with a can of ironstone chips and held in place by a noose of rope. Larger stones had been arranged across the road to force traffic towards the barrier. The sloping nose plate of an armoured personnel carrier jutted out from behind a shelter of piled stone and corrugated tin sheeting.

A soldier appeared from beneath a canvas tent pitched among a cluster of boulders at the base of the mesa. He walked down towards them, rifle slung muzzle-down over his left shoulder. His boots were unlaced and he wore no socks. The tongues of his boots lolled like a dog's on a January day on the Highveldt. He was young, no more than fifteen or sixteen. Another solider emerged from the shelter, an officer with epaulettes and a sidearm strapped over desert camouflage fatigues. Abdulkader tensed and rolled down the window.

The officer placed his hands on the side of the vehicle, hunched forward and peered in at them. His eyes were moist, with dark irises, the whites shot through with angry red veins. Abdulkader handed him their documents. The officer leafed through Clay's passport, looked up, glared at him, and then unfolded Abdulkader's papers. The adolescent had unslung his weapon and now held it at high port as he circled towards the back of the Pajero. Clay could see him eyeing the tarpaulin that covered the extra cans of fuel.

The officer barked something in Arabic and signalled Abdulkader to get out of the vehicle. Abdulkader opened his door and stepped to the ground, walked to the rear of the Pajero. The two soldiers followed him. Clay sat motionless in his seat and scanned the outpost. There were no other soldiers visible.

Abdulkader was arguing with the officer. The pitch of their voices rose suddenly. Clay glanced down at the floor where the AK lay waiting under the seat and looked back at the three men. The officer was shouting at Abdulkader, pointing at the plastic sheeting in the back. Abdulkader opened the tailgate. In the side mirror, Clay watched the young soldier pull away the tarpaulin and unload one, two, and then the third and last jerry can and place them by the side of the road. The officer stood back, drew his pistol, and trained it on Abdulkader.

The young soldier slung his weapon and removed the spare tyre from the rear door and rolled it off to the side of the road. Then he pulled up the cover of the back cargo space and rummaged through the compartment, tossing the jack and emergency tool kit to the ground. Abdulkader watched and said nothing.

The officer shouted an instruction, waving his pistol at the open tailgate. The soldier clawed open the inside panel, pulling the plastic from its mounts. Something caught their attention. They both moved closer and peered into the newly exposed compartment. The officer reached in and pulled out a small package wrapped in clear plastic and grey tape. He unwrapped the tape and pulled what looked like a block of putty from its sheath. For a moment the officer seemed to puzzle over the strange material, unsure, sniffing it as if it were bread.

Then the officer jumped back into a crouch and raised his weapon. Abdulkader clasped his hands behind his head, two weapons trained on his torso. The officer was screaming now, waving the package in the air, his tone higher and more hysterical by the moment. Clay reached behind his back and wrapped his hand around the butt of Hussein's Beretta. The soldiers seemed to have forgotten about him, so intent were they on their find and Abdulkader. Both were now directly behind the vehicle, the younger one tearing out the rest of the material from the compartment, the officer standing next to him, pistol trained on Abdulkader.

Clay knew he was staring over the edge, only a few decimal points from annihilation. The soldiers were apoplectic, and it was going to get Abdulkader killed. No margin remained. He glanced in the mirror. Both soldiers were directly behind the vehicle, busy with their find. Abdulkader was on his knees in the middle of the road. Clay slunk down in the seat so that his head was below the backrest, pushed himself along to the driver's side and gripped the steering wheel.

The engine was running. The wheel was centred. He grabbed the gearshift and found the accelerator pedal with his right foot. Then in one movement he jammed the Pajero into reverse and hammered down on the accelerator as hard as he could. The vehicle lurched backwards and cut down the soldiers with a quick double thud. There was a sickening jump as first the back and then the front suspension buckled over the bodies. He locked the brakes and looked out. The two soldiers lay crumpled in the dust.

Abdulkader sprang up and slammed the tailgate shut and sprinted around to the passenger seat. 'Go,' he said.

Clay backed the vehicle away, swerved around the bodies, and pushed the accelerator to the floor. The Pajero slammed through the barrier and careened off down the road trailing a spume of grey dust.

Clay looked over at Abdulkader. If they weren't screwed before they sure as hell were now. There was no way those poor bastards could have survived.

'*Yallah*,' yelled Abdulkader above the noise of the engine and the pelting road. Go.

Clay looked over, searching Abdulkader's face. Go where, my friend? For me there is no eternal salvation, no penance I can make. I will not be absolved, for I have broken my promise to myself. And, as he drove, the weight of his sin bore down into him and a hurt welled inside his chest and up to his throat – and his vision blurred so that he had to hit the brakes hard and try to keep the vehicle straight, although he could no longer see the road. He opened the door and fell to the ground, retching bile from deep within out into the dust.

٤٠

Allah Knows

Nightfall was still a few hours away. They sped along the high plateau, west into the sun, not far now from the CPF. The cost of doing something good had just escalated. He wondered what Rania would think if she knew what he had just done, that he had killed, as she had seemed prepared to do only a day ago. He wondered if she was even alive. The very thought that she was not was impossible to bear. He weighted it, sank it deep.

After passing the turnoff to the Kamar-1 oil well, the road veered west. They continued through the stark landscape of stone-strewn flatlands and broad low-relief mesas, alone.

An hour past the turnoff, a shadow flashed over the car and darted away across the slope of a mesa. He tapped Abdulkader on the shoulder and pointed to the dragon-like thing warping dark along the desolate ground.

'Helicopter,' said Abdulkader.

Clay looked out and up. There it was, close enough, a bulb-nosed Russian-built Hind gunship tracking away from them, behind and off to the north. The machine's underside bristled with rockets. It was impossible to tell whose it was.

'It's turning away,' said Clay.

'*Inshallah.* Watch it.'

The helicopter was just a speck in the sky now. Perhaps it was just a patrol. He wondered if the soldiers from the checkpoint had somehow survived and managed to crawl back to their tent, call for help on the radio. He watched the black dot as it hovered in the distance for a moment and then slowly disappeared.

They continued towards the CPF, keeping away from the main road, skirting the track that ran along the edge of the mesa, glancing up at the sky. Less than an hour later they stopped in the long shadow of a tabletop *jebel* of purple shale capped with weathered brown sandstone. To their right, the shallow bight of the tributary wadi head opened up like a wound in the planet's crust.

They scrambled to the top of the ridge and laid on the back slope, looking out along the graded dirt road. About half a kilometre away, a small cinderblock shack baked in the heat. A new South Yemen flag flew from a pole stuck in the ground out front. Just beyond was a sand-coloured four-wheel-drive truck with a recoilless rifle mounted on a fixed stand in the bed. Two soldiers squatted on the ground in front of the building. Beyond the guard post, stretching away from the road, a haphazard mosaic of evaporation ponds, their surfaces blue and cloudless, tiles of Masila sky spread over the plateau. At the far edge of the scarp, the squarish metal-clad buildings, rounded vessels and cylindrical towers of the processing facility glinted in the sunlight.

'I'll start from here,' said Clay. 'I should be at the old Bedou well before sunset.'

Abdulkader pointed back from where they had just come. '*Inshallah*, I will drive to Wadi Azir. There, I will hide the Pajero.'

Wadi Azir was about 150 kilometres back, half-way between where they now stood and the checkpoint. It wouldn't be long before someone found the crushed bodies by the side of the road. By now the flies would be at them, covering over the eyes, moving like breath through gaping mouths, the final scream that electric motor whine of a hundred-thousand pairs of tiny wings. And then half the rebel army would be heading their way.

'You'd better hurry,' said Clay.

Abdulaker nodded. '*Inshallah*, I will walk down the wadi to Hussein's farm for the Land Cruiser.

Yes, bloody *inshallah*. Maybe there was still a chance that he could do this and get to safety. Get out through Oman, find Rania somehow. 'I'll meet you tomorrow morning at the Al Urush pools.'

'If God wills it,' Abdulkader murmured.

And for a moment, as he lay prone on the rocky edge of the ridge surveying the bare lifeless expanse of the Empty Quarter, he considered that perhaps, as Abdulkader so fervently believed, Allah was merciful and all-seeing, and perhaps his destiny was indeed predetermined and locked in place for His everlasting scrutiny, and maybe, just maybe, his life was solely in the hands of God. And for just those briefest few seconds he wished that it would be so, and that he could ask Allah's forgiveness for all he had done and his divine protection in what was to come. He looked up. But there was only the sky and the desert stretching away to the horizon with not a trace of any green or living thing.

They backed away from the edge of the ridge and scrambled back down the slope. Clay slung his pack and wound the headscarf around his head. 'Those soldiers,' he said. 'I hope they're alright.'

'If Allah wills it.'

Clay turned to Abdulkader, guilt welling up inside him. 'What was Hussein doing with all that plastic explosive, Abdulkader?'

Abdulkader shrugged.

Clay thought about it for a moment. 'Is it the CPF? Is that what this is about? Was Hussein planning to blow up the CPF, with our help?'

Abdulkader looked at him, expressionless. 'Allah knows.'

'Not good enough, Abdulkader. Allah bloody well knows, but so do you. Tell me.' He thought he knew this man, trusted him, but now doubt forced its way into his mind like an unwanted dream, dangerous and intimidating. He had been foolish, trusting. And then it dawned on him, a crushing reality. He was alone, and he was not going to make it out of here. This was where he was going to die.

The Arab looked into his eyes. 'There is no time for talk. You must finish this. It is the only way. Go with God, *hanif*.'

Abdulkader got into the Pajero and sped away, back in the direction of the checkpoint with the dead soldiers and the next wadi and the way to the coast, and left him standing under the sun, reluctant monotheist, alone.

A Mass Grave of Stars

The wadi cut down through the plateau of softer rocks, shales and marls, down to the hard limestone that formed the base of the first scarp. He followed the drainage down, losing elevation, moving steadily into the past. The wadi sides steepened and he looked up at the stratified, fractured face of time where a hundred millennia, the whole of human history, lay compressed into a single layer – a hand span's width of lithified sand grains, quartz and plagioclase from a beach on a lonely stretch of coastline that once basked under clear skies, the crystalline blue of the shallows teeming with freakish new life, all now extinct.

As he descended, the walking became more difficult. Where the canyon narrowed to a defile and water had eddied away the carbonate over millennia into a deep round bowl, he had to climb down, lowering the instrument case by rope, finding vug and fracture hand-holds, one move at a time, the rock burning, almost too hot to touch.

He moved on in the heat like some proto-hominid, barely upright, picking his way through the Palaeocene landscape of faulted surfaces bare in the sun, ruptured rock and bleached wadi gravel, blocks as big as houses sloughed from the cliffs above. High above, corrugated sheets of heat poured from the edges of the plateau like the silver distortions of turbine exhaust. He strained to hear the sounds that this turbulence told his ears to expect. But there was only the rock, deaf and mute, and the blind uncaring sky, and the sound of his own breathing. And then, on a shift of current, the grinding sound of internal combustion, the big diesel generators at the CPF, but just as suddenly it was gone, and it was if the sun had burned away the atmosphere, and nothing lived.

He reached the confluence with the tributary wadi as the sky began to darken above the top of the canyon walls. The old well was exactly as the chief of Bawazir had described, at the intersection of the two wadis, in the lee of a huge wedge of limestone splayed off from the spur and slumped back against the canyon wall to form a deep-vaulted cave. Over the years, sporadic flash floods had drifted sand and rock up against the wedge so that a ridged chine of sediment now blocked the entrance to the cave and crested over the lip of the well. In a few more decades the well would be covered over and buried forever.

He opened the fieldbook and drew a quick pencil sketch of the well's location and the key markers. Then he took a plastic bailer from the rucksack and lowered the device into the well, guiding the line down through one of the ancient grooves in the lip stone. He peered over into the well. An overpowering chemical odour knocked him back, nostrils stinging, eyes watering. The water level was within a couple of metres of surface – much too shallow. He stood back and pulled on the rope, retrieving the bailer. The water was foul, black, awash in oil. The readings confirmed it: the well was dead, poisoned.

Night came quickly and with it a measure of relief from the heat. He looked up at the strip of moonless sky cut from the dark shadows of the canyon walls. The sooner he got moving up the main wadi towards the CPF, the closer he would be to getting the last and most important samples, the ones that would lock down the truth, or at least part of the truth, and the nearer he would be to going … where? Home? Did that word even have a meaning? He looked up at the stars and the sheets of pale rock and down into the ancient well. He imagined the Bedouin here, long ago, looking up at this same sky, these same rocks. Like them, he was no more than an itinerant, his time short and without certainty.

He kept going.

Moving through the chaotic jumble of rock and stone had been difficult enough under the harsh illumination of the sun. But now the faint luminescence of starlight altered the topography utterly, so that even simple geometries became distorted and took on a looming ethereal aspect, the lithic architecture of planes and angles shot in a monochrome of black and grey, prisms of shadow and substance indistinguishable. He moved towards the glow of the facility's floodlights, studying the ground as he went. He would have to come back this way soon.

Soon he came to the facility's perimeter fence. The four-metre mesh and razor-wire line clattered its way from the edge of the plateau down to the wadi floor. He stopped, looked left and right. The steel posts had been drilled and cemented in place, anchored to rock bolts with heavy-gauge wire. The mesh was like chain-mail. There was no way though. He felt the energy drain from his body.

Clay set down the instrument case, dropped his pack, took a sip of water. He reached out, touched the thick wire meshing, looked up. There was no way over. He would have to go under, or through. He began tracing the line of the fence, step by step, examining every foot of mesh, every post, feeling his way in the dark. Soon he had reached the wadi flank. Here the rock was vertical, smooth, metres high. Perhaps the gap in the fence that the chief had described was further up, on the wadi sides. He looked up towards the plateau, still high above. That would mean scaling the rock. It could take hours, precious darkness slipping away. He turned back, retraced his steps along the wadi floor, checking the fence, considering options.

He was almost to the far cliff when his hand caught a fold in the mesh. He stopped, peered down to where the wire met the wadi bed. The mesh had been dug into the sediment and cemented in place. But here, a boulder the size of a small car had been driven into the fence on the up-wadi side. The posts had held, but the wire bowed out, like a trawler's net filled with a big catch. A flash flood had done this. He had seen something similar once in Oman, a wall of brown boulder-laden water flattening everything in its path, over as soon as it had begun. He moved to the far side of the boulder. Here the mesh had burst open. There was a gap.

He prised back the mesh and squeezed under the flap. His trouser leg caught on a barb, tore the canvas. He stopped, pulled himself free, kept moving towards the lights in the distance. Again he wondered about Rania. What had she been doing in Al Shams' building that night? She said she had tried. Tried to do what? Kill him? Had she known about the attack, perhaps heard about it from one of her sources? Had she tried to warn Al Shams? And, if so, why would Hussein have gunned her down? Had it been a mistake? He had seen so many men blown to pieces by their own airstrikes, villagers maimed in crossfire. Once the monster was released, no one was safe from its blind slashing fury. He pushed it away, focussed on the ground under his feet, the lights ahead.

It took the best part of an hour to navigate up the wadi floor to a point immediately below the CPF. He was about to start the climb up towards the edge of the plateau when his foot fell through a crust in the soil. He lurched forward and steadied himself against a boulder. His foot came away with a sucking sound, covered in mud.

He bent down and scrabbled at the loose sand with his hands. There was water within inches of the surface. He touched his finger to the water, let a drop fall onto his tongue. It was brine, saltier than the sea. He continued up-wadi, through a graveyard of dead, stunted bushes. Fifty metres along, he found the first pool, no more than a metre across, a mirror of stars. He kept walking. Soon there was water everywhere, rivulets of brine trickling from pool to glassy pool. He squelched along in the deepening water, boots soaked.

He heard it before he saw it. As he approached, the air thickened with aerosols of barium and chloride and a hundred other compounds unknown until the stench was unbearable. He wrapped the tail of his *keffiyeh* over his mouth and nose and sloshed ahead in the darkness towards the sound. He was knee-deep in it now, the water warm, malevolent. The steel pipe, standard twelve-inch drill casing, was warm to the touch. Industrial sewage spewed from its mouth in a continuous arc, thundering down into a deep wide pool.

For weeks he had imagined a leaking membrane or vessel, some accident of poor maintenance or bad design left unexamined, brine leaking unknown into the ground. Ignorance and stupidity, yes, wilful neglect, perhaps, but not this, this deliberate evil. His diaphragm contracted violently. He doubled over, spewing vomit into the cesspool around his legs. Unsteady, he staggered to the bank, the night sky oscillating crazily at his feet. Vertigo loomed as he scrambled up away from the fumes and collapsed onto dry ground.

After a while his head cleared and he pulled himself up, still woozy; he scrambled back down to the pipe, collected a sample, made the required measurements, stowed the instruments and started back along the wadi floor towards the CPF.

When the glow of the lights was directly above, he started up towards the plateau, scaling three terraced slopes of loose ironstone and shale tiles, each separated by a bench of flat-lying carbonate. The last slope was the longest and steepest. His feet ploughed into the loose rock, the tiles sliding away beneath his feet, and the sound they made, like the empty ring of a submerged bell, seemed to grow with each step, despite the din of the generators. Several times he stopped and looked along the crest line above and tried to slow his breathing and open his ears, but all he could hear was the punching of his heart and the uninterested grind of the diesels.

Finally, he reached the hardpan layer that formed the crust of the plateau. He hunched down behind the low wall of rock and peered out across the no-man's land of the plateau towards the arc lights of the facility. No war-time blackouts here. Neither side was about to destroy the prize for which men were being sacrificed. Had this been Hussein's target after all, a scorched-earth plan of last resort?

The main process compound stood bathed in light, surrounded by a three-metre chain-link fence topped with an angry barbed-wire lip. Just within the enclosure were the generator skids, separators and storage tanks, and, further along, the control building, workshops and the main entrance leading to the access road. Somewhere beyond the compound were the evaporation ponds – a series of football-field-sized depressions scraped into the ground. According to the chief, the new well had been drilled just outside the facility, near the head of the main wadi.

He scanned the facility from one end of the darkness to the other. Other than the night-orange glow of the flare that danced across the sand and warped the Euclidian geometries of the buildings, nothing moved. He slumped down on his haunches with his back to the hardpan layer and gathered his knees to his chest.

The night shift would be on now, if they hadn't changed their routine. Everyone else, managers, engineers, labourers, would be in the camp compound just beyond the main complex. Normally a night watchman was posted at the entrance to the camp. They would have added more guards now.

He looked up at the black sky, the stars, so many of them here. He breathed deep, held it a long time. His pulse slowed. He imagined her that night, waking and slipping from the bed as he slept, moving off into the night, alone, a weapon in her hand. What had she been thinking, what had driven her? Why had she given him that story? And why had she given herself that night, only to … to do what, short hours later? Attempt murder? Give warning? He shivered. Don't think about it, any of it. Just get it done. Then find her.

He picked up the instrument case and clambered up and over the limestone parapet, then set out in search of the well, the lights of the facility spectral and forbidding on the darkened plain ahead.

He moved over the extinct Cenozoic landscape like a ghost, sliding across the black tableland, keeping the glow of the CPF lights to his left, moving indiscernible over the open ground. He located the well easily enough. The wellhead was fitted to a stem valve connected into a three-inch steel pipeline that ran away over the ground in the direction of the facility. A totaliser was fitted between the stem valve and the pipe weld, and a small diameter sampling port was tapped into the main line. The configuration was unlike any oil well he had ever seen.

He crouched low over the sample port and cracked the valve. A steady stream of clear liquid poured to the ground, splattering his boots. He scooped a handful and brought it to his lips. It was sweet and pure. He dropped his mouth to the stream and gulped down the cool, delicious water. Then he pulled out his water bottle and filled it to overflowing.

He swung the pack off his shoulders and fished the torch from one of the outside pockets and grabbed his fleece jacket from the main pouch. He flipped open the totaliser's plastic cover, pulled the jacket over his head like a hood, and flicked on the light. The curved number plates ticked away as the water rushed through the pipe. He recorded a number, counted out a minute, read the dial again, subtracted the two values, multiplied by sixty, then by twenty-four. The figure he calculated was far too large. He must have made an error. He timed it out again. Same result. No mistake. They were pumping the aquifer for all it could give, changing the natural gradient, taking so much water that flow down to the base of the escarpment had stopped. That was why the spring had dried up at Al Urush. It also explained the falling water level in the *ghayl* at Bawazir. But what could they be doing with so much fresh water? There was only one possibility he could divine, but it was too perverse to contemplate.

He moved on towards the ponds. Directly ahead, the main evaporation pond loomed silent and dark like a mass grave of stars. He crouched and scanned the facility for activity. The big oil tanks screened most of the rest of the compound from view. He could see no one. He took a deep breath and set off at a run. With each stride he emerged further from the darkness, and as the noise from the generators increased he accelerated steadily, adjusting his direction to keep the big oil tanks between him and the buildings and walkways beyond.

He reached the outer berm of the main pond and flattened himself against the piled dirt slope, breathing hard. The outer berm was in partial shadow of the lights, and from where he lay he was completely hidden. He could hear the gush of the main discharge pipe just a few metres away inside the pond. An overpowering stench filled the air, an alchemist's blend of volatile aromatic hydrocarbons and the latent bitterness of barium, the smell of fossil water released from a hundred-million-year prison term vibrating with pent-up energy. He pushed his face into the crook of his elbow and forced back the urge to gag. It was the same smell as before, down in the wadi. They must be piping the water from the ponds, dumping it into the wadi.

And then, above the hum of the machines, he heard the distinct sound of voices. He froze and looked out into the darkness. Two orange embers, cigarette ends, burned in the distance. Two men were talking and laughing, sharing a joke in Arabic, walking along the well access road, camp workers perhaps, or soldiers. They were coming towards him.

There was only one way he could go. As quietly as he could, he slithered on his stomach to the top of the berm and slipped over the crest and down the interior slope into the pond enclosure. The berm was about two metres high on the outside, but inside the water level was lower, so there was room to lie on the slope without touching the impounded fluid. He crabbed his way along the slope, away from the men, and squeezed under the discharge pipe. The vapours here were even stronger, the smell a queasy mix of sulphur, chlorides and decaying solvents. He retched into his hand. The lights and shadows thrown from the compound and the swirl of stars reflecting on the slick surface of the pond disaggregated before him, like a nebula released from the laws of gravity. He put out one hand and dropped to his knees, vomiting uncontrollably. Between each bitter contraction he managed to scramble a few feet away from the pipe and up towards the lip of the berm. He collapsed just as he reached the clear air flowing over the crest.

He gasped and opened his eyes wide, gulping in the fresh night air, filling his lungs, purging toxins from his system. Gradually his vision widened as he reclaimed the dark periphery of consciousness. He was lying on his back with his head just below the lip of the berm. The voices were closer now, back from where he had come, probably just beyond the berm. His escape route was blocked. He grabbed the handle of the instrument case and scrambled along the inside slope of the berm towards the second discharge pipe, away from the voices. Every few metres he stopped and slithered to the top of the berm to breathe deeply of the clean air that flowed from the wadi. He had to get the sample now and find a way out. Soon the vapours from the pond would overcome him and he would slide down into the liquid and drown in a metre of toxic slurry that he had helped to produce.

He pulled the pack from his shoulders, opened the case and balanced it against some larger stones near the top of the berm. If the men decided to walk up to the crest they would have a clear view of him, prone on the slope, bathed in the orange light of the flare. He had to work quickly. He gulped in a lungful of clean air, twisted down the bank and scooped up a sample of the emulsion. Then he crawled back up to the crest, exhaling as he went. He worked the instruments, recorded the numbers in the fieldbook, capped and stowed the sample.

That was it. He replaced the instruments in their individual protective foam graves, took a deep breath of good air, and then slid back down to the starry surface, pushing the open case before him. He pressed the lid of the case under the surface of the emulsion and let the weight of the water drag the case down. The dark liquid flowed over the instruments and penetrated quickly into the foam, covering over the shining eyes of the dials as the case sank out of sight.

He scrambled back to the lip of the berm and sucked in air. Then he pushed his head up and blinked into the harsh manmade light. Just to his right, where the second discharge pipe pierced the fence, was a gate, and just behind, a small workshop building, the larger main works shed, the cubic control room capped with a satellite dish, and the main entrance. The wadi edge was less than fifty metres beyond.

The gate was open. He couldn't go back. The two men were still smoking and talking at the far end of the berm. If he stayed inside the pond any longer he was sure he would pass out from the fumes, this time for good.

He scuttled along the inside of the berm all the way to the second discharge pipe, immediately adjacent the gate, climbing up to breathe and oscillating back down towards the water each time to make a little more ground. Finally he reached the second pipe. Waste gushed from the outlet into the pond; a fine spray of atomised liquid and toxic aerosols swirled in the flare light, floating in the already thickened air. Even the smallest breath seared his lungs, lurched him into spiral of vertigo and nausea.

He clawed his way to the crest of the berm and peered over at the contorted fence and the open gate, and into the shifting ground of the compound. Lights burned from inside the control-room window and he could see someone moving about inside. Otherwise it was clear. He must go now.

He rose to a crouch, but toppled over as the blood rushed from his head. He fell to his knees and dropped his head to the ground, struggling to fight off the modulating whine that filled his ears. The sound abated and he raised his head, certain that he must have been seen, so exposed was his position in the full light of flare and flood-lights. But there was no one to see him. He lunged down the outer slope of the berm and through the gate and flattened himself against the wall of the small building just inside the fence. The door to the main works shed was directly across the gravel walkway, only a couple of metres away. Yellow light shone from a small window to the left of the door. He scanned the walkway and the buildings up ahead. Still no one. He was breathing so hard he thought his lungs would rupture, and his head felt as if it would collapse in on itself at any moment.

Someone shouted above the din of the generators. The voice came from the far side of the compound, back from where the Arabs had been smoking at the end of the berm. He sprinted across the walkway and moulded himself against the corrugated steel wall of the work shed and pushed open the door and peered inside.

A tracked vehicle sat on the smooth concrete floor covered by a heavy canvas tarpaulin. The bogeys and armour plating were painted in desert camouflage. Behind the vehicle, against the far wall, supply crates of various sizes and shapes were stacked almost to the ceiling. On the near side, to his left, drums of diesel fuel, more wooden crates, work benches, drill presses and grinders, a compressor, shelves of tools, but no one to use any of it. The big sliding doors were only partially closed, and through the gap he could see the main entrance way. The big chain link gates were wide open.

He ducked inside and moved across the shop floor, the armoured vehicle on his right. The wadi edge was only a sprint away. He walked towards the open door with steady strides, past the crates and the tools hanging from hooks in their silhouetted dead-man spots on the wallboard, clear of the vehicle's sloped front, until he was no more than a few paces away from the open door. He glanced at the stack of containers on his right – wood and formed metal, each stencilled with numbers and Cyrillic characters. Outside he could see open floodlit ground and the edge of darkness where the wadi would be. He was almost there. Just a few more metres to the safety of the wadi, then a couple of hours of hard walking down to the *ghayl* – meet Abdulkader, a two-day drive to the Omani border, and get the next flight out from Muscat. He could be in Geneva in six days.

Just Economics

Perhaps it was because he had allowed himself to believe, at just that moment, and for the first time, that he deserved this, that he deserved her. That kind of superstition had always plagued him, despite his professed determinism and his rationalist's training that dictated every event was purely causative, without inherent glory. Things happened because someone or something made them happen. You pulled the trigger and the bullet left the muzzle, and if your aim was good and its path was true, it hit the target, but more often than not its course was altered by wind, or humidity, or gravity, and the difference might only be a matter of millimetres, and it hit where it hit – in a kid's belly, a friend's brain, a lover's chest – and that was all there was to it. Or maybe Abdulkader was right. Perhaps Allah had willed it for some reason mysterious and wholly unknowable, and, if so, it was already done, already set. And there was always the possibility that he himself had caused it, through some symmetry between decisions made and the things he had decided he would not do. He would never know.

A man appeared in the door. He was squat and powerfully built. A small blunt-nosed submachine gun hung muzzle down from a strap over his shoulder, a *Ksyuka*. The man stood between Clay and the wadi beyond.

At first Zdravko appeared not to recognise him. The Bulgarian stood in the doorway, blinking in the harsh light. Clay bowed his head and backed away, mumbling in Arabic, hoping Zdravko would take him for just another bearded local worker. He knew now, instantly, what the crates contained, and why they were stored here.

'Stop,' Zdravko barked.

Clay froze, pushing his chin down into his chest.

'What the fuck you doing here, Abu?'

'Sorry, *effendi*,' he mumbled.

'Come here,' Zdravko shouted. 'This restricted area. Where is your badge?'

Clay fumbled with his pockets, pretending to look for his badge. Zdravko still hadn't recognized him. He had to do something now, or it would be too late. The Bulgarian reached for the weapon hanging at his side and started to swing the muzzle up level. Clay charged.

The collision drove the Bulgarian back hard into the steel door and sent the *Ksyuka* clattering across the smooth concrete floor. Zdravko groaned as his body slammed into the unyielding metal plate. The force of the impact drove the air from his lungs and whipped his skull back into one of the door's protruding steel ribs. Blood erupted from his head and sprayed over the door as if flung from a painter's sweeping hand. Zdravko slumped to the ground, back against the door.

Clay jumped up and moved towards the open doorway. He was almost clear of the doors when Zdravko shot out a foot, sending him crashing to the ground. He slammed down hard face first into the gravel just outside the doorway. Dazed, he rolled over and looked back. Zdravko was up and crabbing on hands and knees across the concrete floor towards the AK74. Clay twisted onto his side and reached for the handgun in his belt. Zdravko had reached his weapon and was swinging it around towards him. Clay pulled the trigger just as a sickening clatter erupted from the *Ksyuka*.

Blinding pain tore through his arm. At first it felt as if someone had taken a sledgehammer to his hand – a sudden crunching impact followed by a scorching wave of pain. He looked down at his left hand. The bullet had torn through the outer knuckles, severing the ring and baby fingers, leaving a bloom of ragged pulp. He could see no trace of the missing digits.

Zdravko lay motionless inside the building in a spreading pool of blood. Voices rose in the distance, from the camp and from somewhere back towards the ponds, shouts of alarm. He raised the Beretta and fired at the big floodlight that glared at him from directly above. His hand was shaking so violently that he missed altogether. He steadied his hand on his left forearm, the knuckles seeping blood, and fired two more shots. The third round found its target with a crash and spark, and a semblance of darkness was restored to this small piece of the desert.

He staggered to his feet, fighting to stay conscious, cradling his damaged hand in the crook of his other elbow, the Beretta still clasped in his right hand. He could see figures running around the camp compound, opening the gate, coming towards him now across the few hundred metres of open ground. They hadn't seen him yet, but there was no way to make it to the wadi now.

The control room was only a dozen paces ahead. He loped to the building and pushed open the door with his shoulder. A man sat at the control panel, one hand on a cradled telephone handset.

Clay closed the door behind him and levelled the pistol. 'Put it down,' he said, sliding down to his haunches with his back against the door.

The man removed his hand from the phone and swivelled in the chair to face him. Karila's television-blue eyes stared out from wide-stretched sockets. Outside, a confusion of voices moved closer. Clay raised the Beretta and pointed it at Karila's head. There was a loud rap at the door. Someone yelled in Arabic. Karila stood up and moved towards the door.

'Don't,' said Clay.

'Please,' said Karila, 'I'll make him go.'

Clay gave a brief nod. Blood flowed from his hand down over his forearm and dripped from the point of his elbow, soaking into his trousers. He felt faint, vaguely elated. Karila moved to the door and pulled it open slightly. Clay leant forward, ready to snap the door shut.

'I saw him,' Karila said.

Clay jabbed the Beretta hard into Karila's knee.

'He ran that way,' Karila blurted. 'Towards the tank farms.' Karila stepped back inside and Clay slumped against the door, slamming it shut. Outside he could hear the muffled footfall and excited voices of a dozen or more men as they ran past in the direction Karila had indicated.

'Now get back,' said Clay.

Karila retreated to the console. 'You're badly injured. You need a doctor.'

He waived the Beretta at Karila. 'You think so? Fuck you.'

'Please, let me help you, Clay.'

Clay laughed. It surprised him. 'It doesn't suit you, Karila.'

Confusion joined fear in Karila's eyes. 'What?'

'Compassion.' Clay pulled himself to his feet, cracked open the door a few inches and peered outside. The way was clear.

'Wait,' said Karila. He reached into a cabinet and pulled out a medical aid kit. 'Please take this.'

Clay slid off his backpack, dropped it to the floor, and kicked it toward Karila. 'In there,' he said. A swell of pain surged up through his arm and slammed into his brain. The periphery of his vision started to go dark, like curtains closing. He staggered and bent his head low, trying to swim back towards consciousness. Slowly he fought back the darkness. Clay leant his shoulder against the door, steadying himself. Blood dripped from his hand to the steel plate deck.

Karila put the white box into the pack.

'Throw it to me.'

Karila tossed the pack at his feet.

Clay raised the Beretta. 'Now move back.'

Karila retreated to the control panel, holding his hands up in front of his body as if they might somehow shield him from the bullets.

'Please,' he begged. 'I have children, a wife.' Face-down in the desk drawer.

'Everyone has someone,' Clay croaked.

'I saw the damage, I …' Karila stumbled. 'I'm sorry.'

'What happened at Bawazir, Nils? I saw Zdravko there.'

'I don't know. Please believe me, Clay,' Karila blubbered. 'We just wanted the chief arrested. He was making trouble, turning the villagers against us. It wasn't supposed to happen that way.'

Clay stood glaring at the man who only a few weeks ago had signed little Mohamed's death warrant. He raised the Beretta to Karila's face, his hand shaking, and said: 'Tell me one thing, before I … What are you doing with all that fresh water from the new well?'

Karila looked down at the floor and dropped his hands as if resigned to his fate. 'We're injecting it into the oil reservoir, to keep the pressure up.'

'So you can produce more oil.'

Karila nodded.

'Why not use the formation brine, Nils? Why not just put all that crap back where it came from? I saw the discharge pipe in the wadi, you lying bastard. You're killing these people.'

'Please, Clay. It wasn't my decision.'

Clay pushed his injured hand hard into his side. 'Do you know sharia law?'

Karila shook his head.

'Well, you better start studying.'

Karila mumbled something he could not understand. The words were garbled. Clay felt faint. He doubled over and steadied himself against the edge of the console. Karila took a step forward.

Clay raised the weapon. 'Don't,' he whispered. 'Now tell me.'

Karila backed away. 'We have no choice, Clay. Please believe me. Once the brine comes out of the ground and contacts air, its chemistry changes completely. Treating it so that it can be re-injected is too expensive. The groundwater is so pure it can go straight in. And we don't pay anything for it. It's just economics, Clay, that's all. Please understand.'

'Just economics. Beautiful.'

Clay raised the handgun and aimed at Karila's chest. 'And all those weapons you have stored here. That's just economics, too, isn't it?'

Karila fell to his knees, hands clasped before him as if in prayer. He was crying, heavy tears rolling down his face. 'Please, Clay,' he mumbled through his sobs, 'I'm just an engineer. I'm only doing my job.'

Clay tightened his finger on the trigger, felt it move. 'Does your job include killing people?'

'I don't make these decisions. Oh God, please, Clay.' Karila crumpled to the floor in a heap.

Clay stood looking down at his boss, his client, the Beretta shaking in his hand, the trigger partially depressed. Karila's words tore through his pain-shattered brain. He could feel himself shunting towards the far edge of clarity. 'No,' he said. 'We all do.'

Clay lowered the weapon, turned, pulled open the door with three bloodied fingers and staggered outside. He glanced over to the shed. Zdravko was gone. Without looking back he ran as fast as he could through the main entrance and towards the wadi and the safety of darkness.

Flailing in the Void

He covered the distance to the edge of the wadi so quickly that his eyes had not adjusted to the enveloping darkness by the time he launched himself into the void. He knew the cap-rock layer was only about a metre thick all along this part of the wadi and that the slope of loose shale fell away from its base at about a 45-degree angle. But as he fell through the cool night air, both time and space seemed to stretch out, and he hovered as if suspended on some current, so that the solid ground his feet expected did not come, and still did not come.

He hit the slope with a crunch. Such was his speed that he catapulted forward, somersaulting down the slope in a shower of clanking ironstone plates. After a few rotations his angular momentum slowed and he pushed his legs out hard, down into the loose rock to break the spin. On the second attempt his boots dug in, preventing the forward motion of his head, and his body snapped back to the slope. And then he was ploughing through the rock on his back with feet facing the wadi floor.

He slid to a stop and lay on his back breathing heavily, shaking from the cold or from shock or both. The mangled appendage clutched in his right hand was spiky and raw, a throbbing alien mass that he could not look at, and he was glad for the darkness. He lay very still and looked up into the stars, listening for any sound behind him. There was the whisper of a breeze flowing along the wadi floor, and then, over the efficient hum of the generators, farther away to the north, the distant crack-crack of AK47 fire.

Karila had seen him go. Soon they would be coming after him. He lurched to his feet and tried to focus on the terrain ahead, but a tide of nausea and dizziness flowed over him, and he fell back onto the shale. He sat on the slope and looked down into the depths of the wadi. His hand throbbed and the pain was a presence within him, indifferent and uncaring as the ocean.

He put his head between his knees and tried to regulate his breathing, calm himself. He pulled off his canvas vest and his T-shirt and then using his teeth and his good hand he covered the wound and tied the shirt down as hard as he could on the hand, grunting involuntarily as the knot pushed down onto the flesh and protrusions of bone. He sat hunched over, breathing hard, fighting back the pain and the fear that squeezed up from his diaphragm and into the back of his throat like vomit.

More gunfire crackled in the distance. If they followed him down, if they were coming right now, he would surely hear them scrabbling over the loose slates. He reached for the Beretta, as much for comfort as for any reasonable likelihood of defence. It was not in his belt. He searched his pockets and felt out across the stones like a blind man groping for a light switch, but he knew that it was gone, somewhere behind on the slope, irretrievable.

He pushed himself on, sliding towards the wadi floor, stumbling in the darkness. When he reached the old Bedouin well, the moon was gone and the steep sides of the canyon had collapsed the night sky into a narrow ribbon of time above him. He was shivering uncontrollably. His mouth felt as if it was full of sand and his throat ached. Dehydration and shock were taking over. He knew he needed to rest and drink and get warm soon. He sat on the ground by the lip of the well and breathed in the heady benzene vapours flowing up from the depths. And though the rock walls and the sand under his feet and the stars above and everything insensate stood deaf and uncaring, he cursed them all and then he cursed himself.

Then he remembered the wedge of rock and the ridge of sand and wadi stone – and the cave beneath. He felt his way along the chine of sand towards the wedge and then past the inner plane where the huge slab had cleaved away from the cliff. In the dim starlight he could see that the wedge had toppled inwards, pinning a smaller lozenge of rock beneath it, leaving two gaps, a smaller one below, the opening no larger than a television screen, and a larger one higher up which reached its apex halfway up the canyon wall. Like a wounded animal, he wriggled over the top of the chine and skulked down into the lower opening.

Inside, the darkness was complete. He shuffled on his flanks deeper into the shelter, pushing himself along with his legs and his good hand until he reached a spot where the ground felt soft and he could lean up against the rock. Then he pulled off his pack, placed it between his legs, pulled out Karila's medical kit, the jacket Hussein had given him, and the water bottle. He held the plastic cylinder between his knees and unscrewed the top. He drank deeply, gulping down more than half a litre, more than he had intended, his throat muscles contracting hungrily even as he willed himself to stop. He would need it even more later. When he finally tore the bottle away from his mouth, there was less than a quarter of a litre left, enough for two or three good gulps at most. He swirled the meagre remnants around in the bottle. Water everywhere.

Shivering from the cold, he replaced the lid and stood the bottle upright on the sand to one side and felt for the jacket. He found the collar and the arms and threaded in his good arm and reached behind him to gather the jacket around his shoulders. The other arm dangled uselessly. He was warmer immediately, and soon the shivering stopped. He took a deep breath and reached into the pack and pulled out the torch and turned it on. The light dazzled his night eyes as the beam split and then split again. The whole surface of his rocky crypt was encrusted in a thick vein of crystal gypsum so pure and translucent that the light penetrated deep into the mineral layer before refracting back out from a million crystal faces. He played the torch over the worthless jewels for a moment, and then opened the medical kit.

First he flipped open the lid of the codeine package and jerked out the formed foil panel of painkillers. In succession he punched four pills through the covering and pushed them into his mouth, swallowing each one hard to force them down his already dry throat. Next he untied the T-shirt, releasing the pressure on the wound. A torrent of pain flooded over him. He sunk his head to his knees as the turbulence roiled through him, brutal and strangely sinister, like a gale at night, until finally it ebbed away and smoothed into something more laminar.

He tore open a phial and poured saline over the wound, washing away sand and partially coagulated blood, the lumpy red liquid dripping from claws of bone. He repeated the procedure, cleaning away grit and more blood, thinner now, and what appeared to be fragments of shattered bone. Then he doused the whole offending thing in antiseptic, turning his face away, eyes shut hard as the chemical seared into his raw flesh. Tears filled his eyes and streamed down his face and he had to wipe them away before he could focus again to apply the sutures across the open edge of his hand. As quickly as he could, he ripped open a compress and folded it over the sutures. He held the compress in place against his chest and unravelled a bandage. He wound it around the compress, across his palm and over the remaining knuckles, alternating over and under the thumb, pulling the gauze in tighter with each turn.

He had started to tape the bandages in place when he heard the echo of voices. He flicked off the torch and waited, ears straining. A beam of light sliced past and for the briefest moment his crystal vault lit up like day. He was sure he had been seen. He sat blinded in the darkness with the sound of voices rising, echoing from the rock walls, cancelling, amplifying, until they were upon him, and he could see lights flashing all around outside his hide.

He stayed perfectly still.

Outside, soldiers with guns stood near the well, talking, shining their torches on the ground. They had seen his footprints. They seemed to be arguing. Torches flashed up-wadi, some down-wadi, some directly past him in the direction of the *jebel* where Abdulkader had left him so long ago now. Four men broke off from the group and started towards the entrance of his cave. They had seen him. He closed his eyes.

And she was out there somewhere, he hoped, he prayed, in a fine European hospital, at home even, curled up safe asleep, and he wondered if he would ever see her again.

The voices rose and then passed, moving up the tributary wadi, others receding back towards the facility. He opened his eyes. Darkness again. They were gone.

More than an hour had passed, by his reckoning, and the soldiers had not returned. He wondered how Abdulkader had fared, if he had reached the farm safely, managed to find enough fuel for the Land Cruiser, or if he too had been apprehended, shot, killed, or if he had simply abandoned him altogether. He pushed the doubts away and scrabbled to the opening and out into the starlight. Water and warmth and the bandaging of his hand had stabilised him. The bleeding had stopped. He moved steadily along the wadi floor, working with gravity, quickening his pace as he descended towards the coastal plain and the Indian Ocean, still so far out of sight. Soon the sun would rise again and pronounce its death sentence on the Masila, and there would be nowhere to hide.

He pressed on, threading through the rhombic jumble of massive dolomite blocks and tilted sheets of sandstone. Every few minutes he paused to listen, but hearing only the whispers of the rock, continued on. His pursuers must have tracked down this way, beams of light jerking across the jagged landscape, weapons levelled. Perhaps some of them were in Al Urush now, waiting for him. His mind raced through the possibilities, each darker and more sinister. But he could not go back, could not go up. The only way was down.

When he reached the last precipice the sky was lightening in the east. He stood at the edge of a flat dolostone sill wedged like a plank step between the sheer walls of the defile and looked down the featureless vertical face of the drop to the wadi floor below and then along the contour of the scree to the upper pool of the Al Urush *ghayl* in the distance. The dead palms were clearly visible against the canyon wall, but he could see no soldiers or Abdulkader – or any other soul.

The drop must have been twenty metres, more. He moved to his left, along the sill towards the far wall. He peered over the side, searching for a route that would take him to the wadi floor and on to the *ghayl*. At the far wall he looked back across the full width and height of the rock face towards the other side of the gorge. There was no way down.

He moved to the edge of the fall, put his good hand on the sheer wall of the canyon and looked back across the face. He studied each joint and crevasse in the improving light. The precipice was as smooth and accusatory as one-way glass, without fault, and with no flaw to seize. He stood for a long time gazing at the rock all around until each slab and face and all the wondrous diversity of it blended and blurred and there was no contrast or dissemblance to any of it.

He slumped to the ground and closed his eyes as the pain overwhelmed his will. For what felt like a long time he sat and cradled his injured hand and let the barbiturates of agony wash through him. *Yallah*, Abdulkader had said. Go. Find it. He opened his eyes and looked across the valley.

There, on the far wall, about a metre below the bench, was a small ledge. It was no more than a hand wide, less, jutting out along the canyon wall, a bedding plane in the limestone, only two or three metres long. Below it was another ledge and then another, each longer and wider than the next so that they formed a pyramid of steps building up from the wadi floor. It was the only way.

He slung off the pack and removed the fleece jacket, pulling his bandaged hand gingerly through the sleeve, and then rolled up the jacket and put it in the pack. Then he tightened the shoulder straps a notch and shouldered the pack over his vest and moved to the edge of the step. The ledge was just wide enough for one boot side-on. He stepped forward and placed one foot on the ledge. He twisted his torso to face the rock and glued his cheek against the wall. With the fingers of his good hand he hooked into a fracture just above his head. Then he swung his back foot around and forward. He edged along the narrow strip of rock, one step at a time. High above, a falcon's cry echoed off the canyon walls. The second ledge was now somewhere just below, although he could not see it. He would have to crouch down, use the first step as a handhold, and swing his legs over to the ledge below.

The first part of the manoeuvre was simple enough. He crouched, balancing his weight on his front foot, and lowered the trailing leg slowly down into the void, searching for the step with the toe of his boot. His palm was splayed flat on the ledge behind him. Then, in one movement, he pivoted off his right hand and swung the other leg over the side, twisting his torso towards the ledge and taking the full weight of his body onto both forearms laid flat across the ledge. His feet flailed in the void below, boots scrabbling against the sheer canyon wall as he searched for the step.

He pointed his toes and lowered his shoulders, probing further down the wall. The muscles in his upper arms burned with the effort. He lowered himself further, a few more inches, but still could not find the ledge. It had to be there, somewhere, just out of reach. He walked his forearms away from the wall, trying to keep weight off the bandaged hand, and gained a few more centimetres. He swung his legs back and forth, kicking at the wall. Nothing. Crumbs of loosened rock ticked and tapped down the cliff face to the wadi floor below. Now his forearms were right at the outer lip of the ledge. There was nowhere else to go. His shoulders screamed with the strain. He couldn't hold this. He would either have to pull himself back up to the sill, or let go and trust that the ledge was where it should be and that he would somehow be able to cling to it.

He started to slide into the void. Then the toe of his left boot touched something solid. He pushed his left arm out so that only his right hand was still on the ledge above. His left toe was now anchored on the lower ledge. He swung his right leg towards it and found the edge of the step so that he was glued almost diagonally to the rock face. He shuffled his right forearm ahead in small increments, righting himself, gradually shifting weight to his legs. He stood there for a long time, plastered against the wall, breathing heavily, his hands and feet tingling and his stomach hollow.

He moved along the second ledge. Then he stopped and looked down. Below were three more levels, each about two vertical metres apart and then, further down, a bench of talus sloped up against the canyon wall. It was still a long way down. After he had rested for a while he started to move along the narrow bedding plane. He was about halfway to the start of the third step when the thin layer of rock beneath him gave way and he fell flailing into the canyon below.

٤٤

The Killing Price

Abdulkader's craggy bearded face loomed above him. He was lying on his back, his chest and face covered in a film of sweat. The heat was stifling. His head ached from the inside out, as if his skull had been peeled back in a vice.

'*Al hamdullah*,' said Abdulkader. 'Thanks be to God most merciful.' Abdulkader put a water bottle to Clay's lips, tilted it. Clay tried to sit up but a barb of pain pinned him to the ground. He moved his legs, his shoulders. He must have hit his head in the fall.

'Your hand.'

Clay raised his bandaged hand. '*Howzit*, my *broer*. I'm sorry I doubted you.'

Abdulkader blinked once.

A gunshot rang out, echoed along the canyon walls. Abdulkader reached his arm behind Clay's back, helped him to his feet. Raised voices from below, in the direction of the village. More gunfire cracked in the distance, diffracted, faded away up-wadi.

'Soldiers?' Clay asked.

'We must hurry.'

Clay followed Abdulkader down-wadi, moving in the shadow of the eastern cliffs, the wadi floor below on their right, towards the firing. As they neared the pools, the noise intensified, the rattle of automatic rifle fire, the single pops of handguns. Below, a ragged skirmish line strung out across the wadi. Soldiers in green uniforms, a dozen perhaps, had fanned out from the village and were moving up-wadi. Beyond, two vehicles, Army transports, sat apparently unguarded in the village square. Clay could see two, three, four tribesmen among the boulders, firing at the soldiers, moving, retreating up-wadi. The tribesmen were hemmed in.

Abdulkader turned and handed him a Beretta and two magazines. 'We must fight our way out.' Abdulkader started to move down towards the tribesmen.

'No,' said Clay. 'This way.'

Clay led Abdulkader in the opposite direction, away from the firing, towards the eastern cliff. Soon they were skirting the base of the lower pool. Clay stopped at the ledge, the village far below, breathing hard, and looked down. The soldiers had pushed the tribesmen back and were now strung out across the wadi, east–west. As the wadi constricted, the tribesmen were being forced back into a narrowing funnel of crossfire. Puffs of smoke floated up and were caught in the breeze. Tracers zinged among the rocks. The noise was deafening. Abdulkader knelt beside him, raised his Kalashnikov and took aim at one of the soldiers below.

Clay touched him on the shoulder. 'No. Follow me.'

It took him a moment to find the entrance, stumbling around among the rocks, the firing intensifying below. Everything looked different going in than it had coming out that day, little Mohamed perched on his shoulders. Finally, Clay found the path. Running now, he descended into the rock, down the hewn steps. Abdulkader followed. As they moved deeper into the heart of the rock, the sounds of the battle diminished, muffled. It was cooler here, the walls shaded, close. Down they went, breathing hard, the sound of their footsteps primary now, gunfire fading into the background, then growing again, louder, and then the coastal plain came into view, a narrow vertical slice of it at first, opening up as they moved towards the base of the stairway.

Clay stopped and pushed himself against the wall, the Beretta in his right hand. He could smell the cordite, the blood, that old drug flooding his senses now, an ancient addiction, like nothing he had felt since. Everything was clear, pure, the colours vibrant, living, a heart beating inside every single thing. The base of the stairway was only a step away, the bluff footpath Mohamed had led him along just short days ago. He could reach out and touch it.

The firing was very close now, just off to the right, magnetic. He could hear the voices, shouts of command, the air hot and close like a lover's breath. Abdulkader brought his rifle to the ready, checked the magazine. Clay checked the Beretta, fingered the trigger. Abdulkader looked skywards, mouthing something Clay could not make out.

'Ready?' Abdulkader whispered.

Clay looked into his eyes. They were clear, bright. Clay nodded.

Abdulkader stepped out onto the path, wheeled right. Clay followed him in a crouch, Beretta levelled, adrenaline pumping, the rush coming. Two soldiers turned to face them, close. They stood side-by-side, weapons facing up-wadi. The closest one was young, just a kid. His face opened into a question, bathed in the soft warmth of the morning light. Abdulkader's AK roared. The first round tore into the kid's side, shearing through his chest. The second round decapitated the man standing next to him. Both bodies toppled to the ground. A third soldier, ten metres beyond the first pair, spun to his right and started to bring his rifle around for a shot. Clay took aim, centred the Beretta's barrel on the man's torso, the biggest target. A kind of calm flooded through him, a certainty, everything he'd been taught, the things he'd honed with years of practice taking over. He pulled the trigger three times just as the soldier made to fire. The nine-millimetre slugs hit in rapid succession, a tight grouping that blew open the man's chest cavity, splintering ribs, shredding his aorta, severing the carotid artery, tearing through the left ventricle. The kid, that's all he was, probably had a moment, a few seconds maybe, just after, to register a last thought, to perhaps see the shower of blood erupting from his body, to take a last glimpse of the too-blue sky. Other soldiers, five of them further along the line turned, open-mouthed, surprise and terror frozen in their faces. They had been caught in enfilade. At the far end of the line, a man in a black jacket jumped from the path just as Abdulkader opened up on full automatic. Clay emptied his magazine into the line's exposed flank. Three seconds later, five more soldiers lay sprawled in the dust, broken and bleeding.

Clay stood staring down at the waste, the Beretta smoking in his hand. Abdulkader was already moving along the line, stepping over the twisted corpses, treading in their blood, tracking it across the sand. Clay took a few steps, stood looking down at the lifeless face of the man he'd killed, the question still frozen in the dark-brown eyes. He was very young. Moments ago he was alive. Now he was not. It didn't seem possible, had never seemed proper or right or even mathematically feasible, time's unassailable dominion over life, its ability to rob you of everything. Clay crouched, hung his head, closed his eyes, felt death's touch, cloaked, merry, grateful.

An AK opened up somewhere nearby. Rounds snapped over his head like electricity, raising the hairs on his neck, the back of his hand. He looked down-wadi. The remaining soldiers were breaking cover and running back to the village, the tribesmen in pursuit. From here they looked tiny, insignificant, like toys. Clay watched one uniformed man stumble, pull himself up, hobble a few steps, then crumple to the ground. The firing was ragged now, dying away. He peered down into the forest of boulders. A glimpse of movement, a flash of black. He waited, breathed deep, everything honed, heightened. There, again, fifty metres down-wadi, a lone figure shuffling between two slabs of limestone, a *Ksyuka* swinging from his neck. There was no mistaking that build, the fair hair. Clay jammed a fresh magazine into the Beretta's grip, jumped to his feet and set off in a running crouch.

The man was moving slowly, seemingly unaware that he was being pursued. Clay closed on him quickly, caught him in a small clearing, an amphitheatre of tall boulders.

Clay levelled the Beretta. 'Stop,' he shouted.

The man froze, hands at his sides.

'Turn around. Slow.'

Zdravko looked dazed. There was a deep gash on his forehead.

His shirt was bunched up around his midsection, a bloody bandage around his torso.

'Drop the weapon,' said Clay.

Zdravko raised his hands. He tried to smile. 'My friend. Look what you do to me.'

Clay raised his left hand. 'Yeah, look, *broer*. Drop it.'

Zdravko lifted the strap over his neck and dropped the *Ksyuka* to the ground.

'Brother, yes. I know when we meet.' He rapped a closed fist on his chest.

'Afghanistan. Marines.'

Brothers, then, as he'd suspected. Members of the same fucked-up family. 'Step back,' Clay said.

Zdravko backed away.

Clay picked up the *Ksyuka*, squared up, took a deep breath. He kept his voice low, sought as much control as he could find. 'I'm going to ask you a few questions, *brother*. And if you don't tell me what I want to know, I'm going to kill you. Right here, right now. Do you understand?'

Zdravko's eyes flickered. He wasn't smiling anymore.

'Who killed Champard?'

Zdravko looked away, down at the ground, back up. 'Al Shams kill him.'

'We both know that's bullshit.'

Zdravko's lip curled. 'Fuck you, Straker.'

'You don't think I'm serious, do you?'

Zdravko stared him in the eyes.

Clay slung the *Ksyuka*, pointed the Beretta at Zdravko's face. Zdravko's eyes widened. Clay could see him composing himself. 'I don't have time to piss around, Zdravko. Who killed Champard? I know it wasn't you. Who was it?'

'Ask your terrorist friend, Straker.'

Clay stepped closer, pushed Zdravko to the ground. 'Why is Mansour for Import faking invoices?'

Zdravko struggled to his feet, defiant.

Clay's stomach lurched. The pain that had somehow vanished during the battle came roaring back. His whole body was aflame.

Abdulkader called his name. His voice seemed far off, thin, diffuse after the din of the shooting, the cries of dying men.

Clay took a deep breath. 'I won't ask again.'

Zdravko spat. 'Fuck you, son of a whore.'

Clay lowered the weapon and fired once. The pistol jerked in his hand. Zdravko fell to the ground, his knee a blossom of red pulp. He grabbed his smashed limb, screamed in pain. Clay crouched, put the gun to Zdravko's head. 'It was me, up in the rocks that day at Bawazir,' he whispered. 'I know what you did. I photographed it all.'

Zdravko looked up at him, realisation in his eyes.

'And if you don't tell me what I want to know, I'm going to do to you exactly what you did to that chief.'

Zdravko lay clutching his knee, panting.

'Last chance, asshole.'

Zdravko looked down at his knee, his face contorted in pain. 'It wasn't me,' he cried. 'I pay someone. They do it.'

'I know, Zdravko. Who paid you?'

Zdravko's eyes fluttered, closed. He was going into shock.

Abdulkader was standing behind Clay now, rifle slung muzzle down, staring down at Zdravko's knee. 'We must go,' he said. 'Now.'

Clay looked up. Abdulkader gazed down at him, stone.

Clay shook Zdravko awake. 'Mansour for Import?'

'I pay them.'

'Who are they? Tell me.'

Zdravko looked down at his knee and closed his eyes, shook his head. 'Look what you do to me,' he hissed through clenched teeth.

'Worse coming.'

'And I save you, motherfucker. Tell them kill only Champard. No one else. You live because of me.' Zdravko pounded his chest. 'You owe me, motherfucker.'

There it was. Rania had been right.

'You dead, Straker. I fucking kill you.'

'We'll leave that to Allah.' Clay pushed the Beretta's muzzle into Zdravko's temple. 'Last chance. Who did it?'

Zdravko's eyes widened. 'Ansar Al-Sharia. They did. Mansour is cover.'

Clay blinked twice. Holy Jesus. 'Who paid you?'

'The company,' Zdravko blurted.

'Who?'

'Parnell.'

Clay's guts somersaulted. He glanced up at Abdulkader. 'Why, Zdravko? Why did they do it?'

Zdravko's eyelids fluttered and closed. Clay grabbed him by the shoulders, shook hard. 'Why, damn you, why?'

Zdravko's eyes opened, just a sliver. 'I don't know,' he whispered. Then he was gone.

A man appeared behind them, face swathed against the dust. He stopped for a moment then approached, white *thaub* flowing, unarmed. There was no mistaking the misshapen head, the dark intelligent eyes. He stopped a few paces away and looked at Clay. It was over. The wadi was quiet again, dead again. The violence echoed in Clay's head. He turned and looked out over the plain as the vehicles disappeared into the distance trailing wefts of dust.

Al Shams came and stood by his side. 'Did you find what you were looking for, Mister Claymore?'

'Some of it.'

Another tribesman appeared, walked towards them. It was the old cyclops with the hennaed beard. As he walked, he changed the magazine on his weapon, stuffed the empty banana clip into the pocket of his jacket. He nodded to Clay. 'Two dead,' he said in Arabic.

Al Shams hung his head, muttered a prayer. 'We must leave, quickly. They will send helicopters.' He turned and surveyed the scene, looked at Clay, that single window dark, full of stars. 'The price is high, Mister Claymore.'

'Always too high.'
'God is great.'
'It seems he is,' said Clay.

'Yes, I know. Once I found they were missing, I made enquiries. I have spoken to the Ambassador himself.'

'And?'

'He told me not to pursue the matter.' The Consul frowned. 'Apparently your case has been taken over by a special department. It is beyond my security level. I have received instructions from the Ambassador to keep you here. A team is on the way here from France to interrogate you.'

'Interrogate?'

'It is most irregular. I can only assume ...'

'That I am the accused.'

The Consul nodded. 'You are a wanted terrorist.'

Clay paused, gave himself four seconds, breathed. 'I came to you. You've seen the evidence. You know I'm not a terrorist.'

The Consul raised his hands to his head, exhaled. His lip twitched. 'I telephoned Paris this morning. I spoke to a senior colleague, someone I trust. He called me back a few moments ago.' The Consul paused, glanced over his shoulder again.

Clay waited, watched another bead of sweat track down the Consul's neck. The Consul held out the duffel bag, placed it in Clay's lap. 'You are in danger, Monsieur Straker.'

Clay opened the bag. Inside, a pair of shoes, a navy-blue suit, white-collared shirt, an airline ticket, an unmarked envelope. He looked up at the Consul.

'You were gone before I got here,' said the Consul in a whisper. 'The hospital staff didn't see you leave.'

Clay opened the ticket docket. Air France, first class to Paris.

'They don't know about Declan Greene. I didn't tell them.'

Clay nodded, looked into the Consul's eyes. 'How long have I got?'

'About an hour.'

٥٢

Very Soon Dead

As soon as the Consul was gone, Clay got out of bed and disconnected the IV. He stripped off his hospital gown, pulled on the boxer shorts and the navy-blue trousers, hopping barefoot on the concrete floor. He sat in the chair, pulled a pair of socks from the duffel bag, slipped them on his feet. Boots next. Clay fumbled one-handed with the laces, a seemingly simple task rendered impossibly slow. Finally he stood, half-dressed. He figured at least ten minutes had gone since the Consul's departure. He grabbed the white shirt from the bag. It was freshly ironed – hotel laundry folded and pinned. He pulled out the baubled pins with his lips, spat them to the floor, ripped the cardboard support from the collar with his teeth, shook out the shirt, started to thread his damaged arm into a sleeve. His arm jammed painfully into the constriction. The bandage was too wide. The harder he pushed the more it hurt. He grabbed one side of the cuff in his teeth, the other in his right hand and ripped the sleeve lengthways. In the hospital quiet the tear sounded like a scream, a dry rupture in the fabric of the night. But his arm was through. Clay buttoned the shirt, slipped on the jacket – a little tight around the shoulders but otherwise not bad – and slid the airline ticket, the unmarked envelope and the money into his inside breast pocket. Outside, the lights of Oman strobed in the swaying palms, flashed across the wind-swept sea.

The Consul's surprise late-night visit played itself out again in his mind. There were clearly some pretty important people who had no intention of letting the truth about what had happened in

Yemen come out. People with influence inside the French government. People with enough power to co-opt an Ambassador, dispatch a 'special team' from Paris. And, if they wanted the evidence gone, it was pretty likely they wanted the witnesses gone, too. The Consul had taken a career-ending gamble in warning him, had given him a way out and just enough time. The guy was smart, gutsy. With the money Clay had now, Hussein's money, with his new identity apparently still safe, he could disappear for good, leave it all behind.

Clay looked down at his bandaged arm. The possibilities flashed through his mind, options cascading, scenarios playing out. Why would the French government, so publically committed to justice in the case of Thierry Champard, choose to sequester the very evidence needed to achieve that goal? And why had the Consul felt compelled to disobey his own ambassador and provide Clay with means of escape? Something was terribly, fundamentally wrong. He knew this viscerally, as a truth, as you know right and wrong from the earliest age, and keep knowing it, even when it is blasted down into the deepest recesses of your being.

There was only one course he could take. As Rania had said all that time ago outside the hotel in Aden, he was locked in now, committed.

Clay stood, grabbed the empty duffel bag, walked quickly to the doorway. He was going to find out who was coming for him, and why. And he was going to do it on his terms.

The corridor was empty, the lights dimmed for night. He paced down the hall, found Afia's office. The door was unlocked, the office dark, empty. Clay closed the door behind him, switched on the light, walked into the storeroom, scanned the shelves. Almost immediately he found what he was looking for. A box of sterilised green hospital scrubs. He found the biggest coveralls he could find, and threaded them over his suit. A bit short in the arms and the legs, but it would do. He grabbed a second pair of coveralls from the box and draped them over his shoulder. Nearby he found another box containing surgical masks and elasticized caps, selected one of each, stuffed them into the oversized coverall pocket. In the corner, a pail, a mop with a sturdy wooden handle. He found a full bottle of commercial strength bleach, placed it in the pail, put the mop under his arm, carried the pail into the office, set them on the floor beside the door. From the glass cabinet he took two large syringes in their sterile packaging, four big compresses, bandages, a tube of the antiseptic that Afia was using on his wound, a couple of rolls of medical tape, a box of painkillers, and dumped them into the duffel bag. It took him longer to find the anaesthetic, two big phials of fentanyl, a hundred times more potent than morphine, fast-acting. Those, too, went into the bag.

Clay closed the cabinet, grabbed the chair from Afia's desk and placed it at the office door. He cracked open the door, checked the corridor. Deserted, still. Then he wedged the door open with the mop end, turned out the light, sat in the chair. He had a clear line of sight to his room.

Clay estimated that about fifteen minutes had passed since the Consul's departure. Whoever was coming for him could be here at any moment. He opened the bleach, poured the contents into the bucket, gagged on the chlorine vapours as the heavy liquid glugged in the darkness. Quickly he covered the pail with the extra scrubs to keep the vapours down. Soon the air cleared. He took a few deep breaths, grabbed one of the syringes, tore open the packet with his teeth. He placed a phial of fentanyl between his knees, pushed the needle into the cap, pinched the plunger casing between his fingers and pulled up the plunger with his teeth, drawing in the liquid. In a few minutes he had two charged syringes ready to go. Big doses. With the plastic caps covering the needles, he gently lowered the syringes into the outside pocket of his coveralls. Then he pulled the cap over his head and strapped on the surgical mask. He was ready.

Time passed. An orderly pushed a trolley down the corridor past Afia's office, his back to Clay. The trolley wheels squeaked as he turned and disappeared into the north wing. Clay shifted in the chair, the pain in his arm awakening now, stirring. And with the pain came doubts, battalions of them, regiments. The Consul had given him a head start. Now that was gone. An hour, the Consul had said, but how could he have been sure? It could be a lot more. The flight for Paris left at 5:00. Afia would be back on shift at four. He didn't want to mix her up in this. That gave him another two and a half hours at most. He'd have to leave for the airport by 3:30 at the latest, and hope he could find a taxi.

The hospital was quiet, as if all the patients had died in their sleep and now lay cold and open-mouthed in their beds, the staff yet to find them, yet to realise. Whoever was coming for him, this would be the time.

Clay reached into the breast pocket of his suit, withdrew the envelope the Consul had given him. Inside were two folded newspaper clippings. He slipped one from the envelope, and unfolded it. There it was, in the dim wedge of corridor light, in an article dated 14th June, yesterday: Finnish engineer Nils Karila, 39, shot dead in Yemen by South African national Claymore Straker, a member of an Ansar Al-Sharia terrorist cell. Straker, a suspect in the murders of at least twelve other soldiers and oil workers, was killed by government forces as he was trying to flee across the Omani border, along with several other terrorists.

Clay looked up, scanned the corridor. Jesus Christ. They must have shot Nils for helping him escape. He remembered the photograph in Karila's office, the kids in the snow, their smiling faces, and swallowed down a gasp. He thought of Abdulkader, of the body of the dead soldier lying in the back of the Land Cruiser as they fled to the border, its head thudding on the floor with each bump in the road, miles and miles of it, him unable to stop it, to help the boy rest, until the sound of it had coalesced with his own dreams, the beating of his heart. It was with him now still, that ragged whunk of soft bone and hair on car-rug and particle board, the bloody headless torso lying in the sand, Clay's passport in the torn chest pocket. Jesus, he breathed.

He replaced the clipping in the envelope and waited.

The same orderly squeaked past with his trolley, coming back towards Clay this time, past his room. Clay pushed the door to with his foot, the mop head compressing until the gap was less than an inch. The orderly passed by without a glance. Clay released the pressure and the door cracked open a bit more. Fifty minutes now, maybe a bit more since the Consul's visit. The pain in his arm was back, insistent, demanding. He was about to reach down and grab a box of painkillers from the duffel bag when a lone figure appeared at the end of the corridor.

Clay filled the deepest part of his lungs, exhaled slowly. The man was powerfully built, medium height. He wore a dark leather jacket, jeans, black military-style boots. Everything about the guy – the number-two cut, the gaunt over-trained face – said military. French intelligence? SF? Whoever he was, he was striding down the corridor now, his gait long, confident. He stopped outside Clay's room, reached to the small of his back, tugged down the hem of his jacket, glanced both ways, turned the handle and disappeared inside.

Clay jumped to his feet, jammed the mop handle under his left arm, flicked the scrubs off the top of the bucket and picked the bucket up by the handle. He stepped out into the corridor. Afia's office door clicked shut behind him. In a moment he was at his door. His heart was racing. The pain in his arm was gone, obliterated by adrenaline. He breathed deep and opened the door.

The man was standing beside the bed, looking down at the twisted empty bed sheets, the disconnected IV line hanging from his hand. He turned and faced Clay. His expression betrayed nothing. He just stood there looking at Clay.

'What are you doing here?' Clay muttered in Arabic, deepening his voice.

The man let the IV line drop, took a step away from the bed. His hands were by his sides. He said nothing.

Clay lowered his head, shuffled forward a few paces. Three metres separated them, less. 'No visitors now,' Clay said, in Arabic again.

The man looked over to the window, the door to the balcony, back at Clay. He pointed at the bed. 'Where he is?' the man said in English. His voice was cigarette rough, heavily accented.

Clay hunched his shoulders. 'No visitors now,' he said in English, shuffled a few steps closer. 'You go.'

The man raised his forearm, glanced at his watch. 'Where this man?' he said, pointing at the bed again. *Vhere zees man?* Not French. The accent was Slavic, Russian perhaps.

Clay paused, looked back at the door, faced the man. 'Toilet,' he said in Arabic.

The man seemed to understand. He started towards Clay, towards the door. Clay bent as if to put the bucket on the floor, reached his bandaged arm under it, cradled it close to his body, watched the man's boots step closer. A pace away now.

Clay burst from his crouch, flinging the contents of the bucket into the man's face. The man threw up his arms, too late to prevent the concentrated bleach from reaching his face and eyes. He screamed in pain, stumbled back, tearing at his eyes. Clay grabbed the mop handle in his right hand and drove its butt-end hard into the man's throat. The man gasped and collapsed to his knees, fumbling behind his back. Clay lined him up and let go a withering kick to the head, toppling him to the ground. Still conscious, blinded, gasping for breath, the man squirmed on the floor, pulled out a silenced handgun.

Clay jumped left just before the man fired. The bullet smashed into the concrete wall behind him. The man adjusted left on sound, fired again, missing Clay by an inch, no more. Clay moved right as the man fired again, further left this time, missing completely. The round clattered into the metal frame of the bed. Clay circled right, getting closer. The man heard him, swivelled on his back, tracking the sound. He fired blind again, four quick shots that smashed into the wall at close range. Shattered masonry filled the air. Clay whipped out another kick that caught the man's arm, sent the handgun flying from his hand and spinning across the bleach-slick floor. The man dove after the gun, arms sweeping desperately across the floor, searching. But he'd misjudged the direction. The handgun lay two metres away to his left.

Clay stepped past him, picked up the gun, pointed it at the man. A Russian Makarov PMM nine millimetre. Eight round magazine. One round left.

Outside in the hall, commotion. A door opening and closing, voices, footsteps.

Clay pulled off his mask, the cap, threw them to the ground. 'On your knees,' said Clay in English.

The man was in pain. Tears streamed from his eyes. The skin of his face was seared bright pink. The man pushed himself up, sat on the floor.

'Who sent you?' hissed Clay.

The man said nothing. His face was twitching.

'Tell me what I want to know and I'll get you help. Save your eyes.'

The man struggled to his knees.

'Who are you?'

No answer.

'Who are you?'

The man pushed his knuckles into his eye sockets. 'Not important,' he breathed.

Shouting now from the corridor, lights coming up.

Clay pushed the silencer into the man's head, made him feel it. 'Important to me. Tell me or I'll give you something they can't fix.'

'Fuck you. You dead man. You and your bitch.'

Clay started. 'What did you say?'

'We know you here, asshole. We find her very soon. Both. Dead.'

Clay staggered back, stared down at the blinded stranger swaying on his knees. He stood a moment, not quite comprehending what he'd heard. He dropped the Makarov into his pocket, reached into the other, grabbed one of the syringes, pulled off the cap, and plunged the needle into the man's neck.

٥٣

Angels and Men

30th June, Geneva, Switzerland

Clay flung open the double doors and stood looking out over Lake Geneva from his room at the Hotel Métropole. The sky was clear, the air crisp. Ice-capped mountains burned like white phosphorous in the distance. A ferry slid across the glassy early-morning surface of the lake.

He'd left the hospital through the gardens after climbing from the balcony, the would-be assassin unconscious on the floor. He'd hailed a taxi in the street and arrived at the airport just in time to make the Air France flight. By the time he arrived in Paris, half-smashed on airline booze, he'd almost convinced himself that Rania was still alive. We find her soon, the assassin had said. Who else could he have meant? It had to be her.

He'd gone straight from arrivals to the ticket desk, bought an ongoing ticket to Geneva, arriving late the same evening. At immigration, a lone bearded Aussie had attracted no attention, just another tourist in the queue, passport stamped and on his way.

But now Clay sat on the bed, looked out over the lake, and tried to think clearly. Sober, hungover, he put his head in his hand and crushed the weak part of himself that had dared to hope. He knew the damage had been too extensive. He'd seen it too many times. The medic had said that the brachial artery had been hit. He'd tried to clamp it, he'd said, frowning, unsure. With a wound like that, she would have had little chance, despite the evac, despite the medical attention she would have received on the plane. And, yet, she'd seemed almost stable when he'd last seen her in the Mukhalla airport, the world tearing itself apart all around them. Had the news reports of her death been a ruse designed to protect her? Koevoet had told him stories of South African DCC agents whose covers had been blown and had been provided with similar stories, new lives.

Find me, she'd said.

He'd been here for more than two weeks now, trying to do just that. He'd tried every possible combination of telephone numbers from the note on Rania's cigarette package, transposing fours and nines, ones and sevens, zeros and nines, everything that could remotely be misconstrued as something else. He'd made hundreds of telephone calls. And with every perplexed, muttered negative, in French, in German, in Italian, he'd felt her slipping away. And with every day that went by, more lethal radiation was pumped into the groundwater in the Masila. More dead kids. More miscarriages. Lives ruined. Fortunes made.

He'd tried to decode Rania's words, spent days in Geneva's solemn public library researching the history of Aden, scouring maps of Geneva, lists of street names, reading Rimbaud. *Anges et hommes.* Angels and men. The pure and the totally fucked-up. He'd finally found the words in a poem, written not by the eighteen-year-old genius, but by a love-struck absinthe-soaked Verlaine in 1884:

Nous avons tous trop souffert, anges et hommes,
De ce conflit entre le Pire et le Mieux …

We have all suffered too much, angels and men, of this conflict between the worst and the best. What the hell that was supposed to mean, he had no idea.

Clay stood staring out of the window, poured himself a tumbler of vodka and downed it in one go. He was about to leave the room when the phone rang.

'Yes?'

'Monsieur Greene?'

'Who is this?'

'Your friend from Muscat.' The Consul from the French embassy. He had DWG's details, passport number. With his diplomatic access it wouldn't have been difficult to track Clay down.

Clay shuddered, let the line hang, heard every mile there in the silence.

'Someone has tried to contact you, or rather who you were, through the Embassy, Monsieur Greene. I thought you would want to know. They said it was important.'

'Go on.'

The Consul coughed, shuffled some papers. 'The man said to tell you to contact the Canadian company, that someone there has information for you. About RM, if that means anything. He didn't leave a name, or a number.'

'That was it?'

'I wrote it down word for word.'

Clay pulled in air, filled his lungs, held it awhile. Jesus Christ. So much for disappearing. 'What did you tell him?'

'I told him that Claymore Straker was dead.'

'Thanks. For everything.'

'Goodbye, Monsieur Greene. Be careful.'

The Gare Cornavin was the busiest place in the city. Crowds streamed by, train times and destinations clicked over machine-gun quick on the big overhead boards, people stood on platforms with newspapers and steaming cups of coffee. Clay found a big bank of public phones and picked the stall at the far end. He checked his watch, wedged the receiver between his shoulder and jaw, pushed in the pay-card. The Canadian company. It would be late in Calgary, but you never knew. People like Raymond Perry gave their lives to work, night and day, chasing God only knew what, wealth, status, position, power, recognition, all the shit he had once vaguely believed in. He dialled the number. Everything was getting a bit easier now, the everyday tasks that had, at first, frustrated and infuriated him, relearning the most trivial of lifetime habits.

Clay looked around the station, the thousands of anonymous faces hurrying past. The phone rang, twice, three times. Clay let it go on ringing, imagining the thing calling out into a dark empty space, computer screen-saver light weeping over plush office furniture.

'Hello?'

'Mister Perry?'

'Do you know what time it is?'

'It's Clay Straker.'

'Just a moment.' The line went quiet. And then: 'Give me your number. I'll call you back.'

A few minutes later the payphone rang. Clay picked it up.

'You're supposed to be dead.'

'I am dead.'

'Indeed.'

'How did you find me?'

'That's not important.'

'What do you want?'

'I give you my word that I had no idea what was going on out there.'

Clay said nothing, doubted it.

'You did me a big favour, son. Now I'm going to do one for you.'

Clay held the receiver to his ear, tried to slow his breathing.

'It wasn't Parnell who gave the orders for Champard's murder. Or any of the other killings.'

Clay swallowed. 'How do you know?'

Perry chuckled. 'Since your call I have made it my mission to know. Listen, son. Champard never gave that letter to Parnell. He sent it straight to Medved. He must have thought it would have more impact, going straight to the top.'

It made sense. Champard would have known what Parnell's reaction would be. Medved's carefully crafted image of the caring CEO, champion of social justice, his well-publicised philanthropy, would have made him a more likely choice.

'Medved brought in a contractor to solve the problem, a Bulgarian mercenary.'

Clay took a breath. Jesus Christ. 'Zdravko Todorov.'

'That's right, son. Parnell is an unprincipled crook, but he's not a murderer.'

'Who can you trust these days, eh, Mister Perry?'

The line was quiet for a moment. 'Look, son. You were right. Medved was screwing us, selling us all the big lie about Petro-Tex. He was pulling millions out of the operation, funnelling it to his own accounts. Nobody fucks with me, son. So listen. In three weeks, Medved will try to launch a substantial private offering in London. He needs money, and lots of it, to develop those new fields. I have documents in my hands right now that prove everything I've just told you. More. If you're interested, I'll be in London on the 7th of July. You can reach me through my office.'

Clay walked back to the hotel in a daze, an oblique drizzle falling now, wet green leaves swirling in the streets. It always went to the top. Saleh, Medved, Perry – these were the people who ran the world. Was it a surprise? It shouldn't have been. These were the '*they*', the people who held the controls to the whole machine, yanked the levers and flipped the switches that sent the soldiers into the helicopters, got all those people at the train station scurrying in their thousands of directions, to their millions of tasks.

It all made sense. He reached into his pocket and pulled out the envelope the Consul had given him in Oman, slid out the larger of the folded newspaper clippings, reread it for the sixth time. Rex Medved in the news again, hailed by the French Minister of Foreign Affairs as a heroic example of the West's steadfast commitment to moderate secular governments in the Middle East. Despite personal threats, despite having members of his staff murdered in Yemen (Thierry Champard was mentioned by name), despite a war raging, his company continued to operate, continued to generate wealth for the people of Yemen. The story hinted of deep links between Medved and the Minister, shared business interests, campaign contributions. There was a photo of Medved shaking the Minister's hand in front of the Palais du Luxembourg in Paris.

If it ever got out that Medved was responsible for Champard's death, his own employee, a French citizen, his credibility and influence inside the French government would be destroyed. The Minister himself might be implicated, their cosy relationship exposed. Once the news of Claymore Straker's appearance in Muscat had filtered back through official channels to the Minister, he must have informed Medved and then used his influence to secure the documents from the Consul's office. And it was Medved's man who'd come to the hospital that night. They were tying up loose ends, ensuring that Champard's death and everything else that had happened in Yemen remained firmly tied to the so-called terrorists. And if Rania was still alive, if that was possible, they'd want her silenced, too.

Clay ran all the way back to the hotel through the darkening streets, along the lakeside, past couples walking hand-in-hand, the city lights shining white and red on the wet pavement, the cars hissing past, the summer rain in his eyes, his heart pounding.

He was sliding the key into the lock of his hotel room door when he heard the phone ringing inside. He closed the door behind him, ran to the desk, picked up the receiver.

'Yes?'

'*Bonsoir, monsieur.*' A woman's voice, soft, broken with age.

'*Oui, madame?*' he said in halting French.

The line was quiet a moment. He could hear the woman breathing on the other end. '*Rimbaud,*' she said.

Clay stood, pushed the receiver to his ear, heart palpitating. '*Anges et hommes,*' he said.

The line went quiet. He heard shuffling in the background, a scraping sound.

'Meet me at the Café Grand Quai, Rue Général Guissant, the day after tomorrow at five o'clock in the evening,' she said in English. 'Sit at the third table from the entrance, next to the window.'

'Wait,' said Clay. 'How will I …'

The line went dead.

The Conflict Within

Clay checked out of the Métropole that same night, slipped out the back way into the night. He knew that his continued, relative anonymity depended entirely on the French Consul's nerve, his goodwill. He needed to keep moving.

A few streets away he hailed a taxi, and asked the driver to take him to a local pension, somewhere quiet. He found a small, family-run guesthouse on the outskirts of the city and signed in under an assumed name, paying cash up-front. That night, unable to sleep, he sat at the little desk under the eaves and started to rebuild his field notebook from memory, one page at a time. Each measurement, each set of numbers he'd recorded, the location of the sampling points, concentrations, units. Each came to him as a picture, a photograph almost, the numbers stamped in his memory so that he could see the corner of the page where they had originally been recorded, the red glow of the digits in the instrument's window, explanatory sketches there as clearly in his mind as if he were looking at them now on the page. By morning he had reconstructed half of his Masila work, all of the Al Urush field measurements, the conceptual models, the preliminary groundwater flow calculations. Finally, at about ten, he managed to sleep for a couple of fitful hours.

By 16:30 the next afternoon, Clay arrived at the Café Grand Quai. The café hummed, sparkled in the low-angle light. Cups and saucers clinked, waiters moved with steaming trays among the well-dressed patrons. The windows were open, the lake calm beyond the car-filled street. The third table along the window was empty. Clay sat, looked around the café. He ordered a beer, waited.

Five o'clock came and went. Clay scanned the café, the crowd growing now, groups of suited businessmen standing at the bar with after-work beers, couples holding hands across tables, laughing, leaning in to kiss. A group of women in summer dresses and heels floated past him, and sat in the corner window booth, three tables along from Clay. Perfume drifted in their wake, the mingled scents of expensive brands, heady, overpowering. By a quarter to six, the place was packed out, loud. Clay ordered another beer, looked out over the lake. The women in the corner booth had ordered champagne, and sat sipping from tall elegant flutes. The pretty blonde at the end of the table glanced at him, held his gaze a moment, smiled. She had big eyes, slender, pale forearms. Clay nodded and looked away.

Clay finished his beer, glanced at his watch. Gone six. He took out a twenty-franc note, put it on the table, stood to leave.

A woman in a black head scarf stood before him. 'Please,' she said, 'sit.' She sat, pulled back her scarf to reveal grey hair gathered back into a neat bun. She was diminutive, frail almost. He guessed mid-sixties, clear grey eyes; soft, powdered skin.

'Will you take tea?' she asked.

Clay waved a waiter over. The woman ordered tea. Clay pointed at his empty beer glass.

The woman waited until the waiter was out of earshot. '*Ce roc affreux*,' she said. That terrible rock.

'Aden,' he replied, the last word of Rania's note.

She smiled, reached across the table, put her hand on his arm for a moment as if she knew him, had been expecting him. Her tea came, his beer.

'Thank you for coming, Monsieur Straker.'

Clay swallowed. 'How did you find me?'

'You found me,' she said. 'We spoke last week on the telephone.'

One of the calls he'd made. 'Rania?'

She nodded, frowned into her tea. 'I was with her in the hospital in Marseilles when she …' the woman choked back a gasp, reached for a handkerchief, and covered her eyes. 'When she passed away.'

Clay's heart lurched, stumbled. Nausea overcame him. He felt himself sinking away, darkness encroaching. It was why he'd come. Despite everything, he had wanted to believe. He had been stupid.

He fought his way back. After a while he said: 'I am sorry for what happened.'

'Yes. It is very sad.'

'You knew her well?'

'Yes.'

Clay looked at her.

The woman sipped her tea. 'She looked so much like her mother, but she always reminded me of Yves, her father. He, too, was very idealistic, naïve almost.'

'She told me her father died when she was young.' He was back on the hotel balcony in Sana'a now, so close to her, the aurora of a million night fires flickering beneath them.

The woman looked into his eyes a long time. 'She was always a very serious girl, like her father. They were very close. After Yves was killed, she and her mother left Algeria and moved to France. She was twelve, I think, at the time. A very impressionable age for a young girl.' The woman sipped her tea, dabbed her soft unweathered lips with a cloth napkin. 'Twelve, yes. I remember, because I spent the summer with them in Algiers that year. It was the last time I saw them all together.'

Clay watched her disappear into the dark jaws of the Hercules again, her hair blowing in the engines' wash, her arm raised, replayed that very moment when he lost sight of her for the last time, the brutality of that instant, then the ramp closing, the turbines powering up. He swallowed. 'How was her father killed?'

The woman put her hands together as if in prayer and raised them to her mouth. After a while she looked up at him. 'Yves was a very principled man. Though he did not support the Marxist government of the time, he was very vocal in his support for a secular Algeria. He was assassinated by the Algerian Islamic Movement. Not long after, of course, the whole country descended into civil war.'

He could see Rania now, sitting in the car beside him in the darkness, the lights of the hotel glowing beyond the palms, the veil drawn up over her eyes, everything about her hidden away.

The woman was peering at him intently. 'Rania was raised as a Muslim – her mother was very pious.'

Was. They had shared something else, too.

The woman continued: 'I never approved; of course, it wasn't my place to comment. But you could see the conflict within her. From her father, she got that hunger for change and all things modern, from her mother, a bedrock of tradition ingrained since childhood. The poor girl was caught between two cultures, one side of herself always battling with the other.'

Clay looked out across the lake to the mountains. All of these souls, these individuals, each with fires inside, loves, fears, hopes and conflicts unknowable, all of them gone now, and him still here somehow, able to consider what had been lost. And all of it as unknowable as the universe, the birth of stars.

'Maybe that was why she wrote so well,' he said, choking on it.

The woman looked into his eyes. 'I can see why she was so attracted to you, Monsieur Claymore. I am pleased that you came.'

'What did she tell you?' It hurt thinking of it.

'From Yemen, just before the …' She stopped, looked down, took a sip of tea. 'Before the accident. She said she was going to finish something important and come home, that she had had enough.' The woman looked off over the lake. 'In the hospital, she seemed a different person, as if she had finally found some peace. She had never spoken to me of a man before.' The woman pulled a handkerchief from the end of her sleeve, crumpled it to her eyes. 'I'm sorry. You must excuse me. She loved you.'

Clay looked out across the lake to the mountains, scribed the silhouette, each crag and valley.

The woman reached into her handbag and withdrew an envelope, handed it to Clay. 'In the hospital, just before …' she stumbled, recovered. 'She told me you would come, that I was to give you this. She said you would understand.'

Clay opened the envelope. Inside were three battered, handwritten pages. It was Rania's story, the one she had given him that night in Al Shams' village.

Clay reached across the table, took the woman's hand, held it for a long time.

After a time the woman said: 'If you want to know the truth about what happened in Yemen …' She paused, scribbled something on a small notepad. She handed him the paper, looked him in the eyes.

Clay glanced at the paper, looked up.

'It's not far from here. Two hours by train.' Then she put a fifty-franc note on the table, stood, rearranged her scarf about her face, and was gone.

∞

All That Hateful Beauty

The train pulled into the station. It was the end of the line. Outside, the white spires of the Dents du Midi towered into a flawless summer sky. He left the station and walked up the main street, a warm breeze bringing the smells of cut grass, pine, wood smoke. He set out past the Auberge des Arcs, all dark wood and geranium window boxes, shutters flung open and pinned back, flags fluttering in the breeze, a postcard. The sun was hot, the sky deep blue, cloudless. Mountain ice sparkled high above. He breathed deep, working his legs as the pitch steepened, sweating already, endorphins kicking in.

After crossing a narrow one-lane bridge over a steep ravine, he followed a footpath that led up through a dense copse of pine, the air dark and cool, and emerged onto a wildflower meadow, the village already far below, a cluster of toy houses, and the valley opening up between soaring peaks of rock and ice. For two hours he climbed, moving though sunlit glades and cool wet ravines, stopping frequently to rest and drink.

He was pretty sure he wasn't being followed. He had taken several trains, backtracked, watched carefully. He'd had no formal training in surveillance or counter-surveillance of any kind. Just a bush soldier, once, so long ago now. A dull, blunt instrument. Point and shoot. All of them. Ignorant. Stupid. Careless. Scared. Cruel.

And this address, this place where the truth, apparently, lay. What form would the truth take, if indeed such a thing even existed? Was he being set up, lured into a trap? He had no reason to distrust the woman – despite the fact that she'd never told him who she was.

That she knew Rania, seemed to know a lot about her, had to be, was, enough. And still, doubt spread like acid in his veins.

Finally he emerged, soaked to the skin and breathing hard, onto a narrow single-lane road that contoured the mountainside. He followed the road for about a kilometre through steeply pitched fields and dense stands of pine. Ahead, a chalet emerged from the hillside. Such was the gradient here that its cedar shake roof was set into the slope, while the front peak towered three storeys above the ground, overlooking the valley below. Split wood was stacked ground to eaves along the side wall. A thin line of smoke wisped from the chimney.

Clay continued past the chalet, checked the number on the post box at the top of the drive as he passed. Number 12. The number the woman had written down for him, the address. Clay passed by, kept to the road. It continued for another half-kilometre, entered a tall stand of densely planted pine. Within, it was dark and cool. He came to a switchback in the road, followed it up and around. As soon as he'd cleared the switchback, he left the road and clambered down into the forest, moved downslope until he had a perfect view back along the road to the chalet. Hidden behind a fallen trunk, he settled in to watch.

A few cars trundled past. A tractor. After a long while a farmer, on foot, driving three dairy cows down the road, gallon-jug bells clanging at their necks. No one entered or left the chalet.

Clay waited a full two hours before leaving the woods, satisfied he wasn't being followed. He covered the ground quickly, peg-legged down the gravel drive, calves and quads aching, stiff. A woman's black bicycle leant against the wall, the tyres flat, the chain rusted, a frayed wicker pannier hanging from the handlebars. Weeds ran rampant over what once was a vegetable garden. A lone sunflower, stunted, malnourished, poked its face through the tangle. The building itself, close up, was old, with heavy wooden beams, big stable doors on the ground level, and above, a balcony, shuttered windows, boxes of long-dead geraniums, stems withered and brown. The view across the valley was spectacular, a Technicolor backdrop. He breathed deep, climbed the stairway to the balcony, and knocked on the oak-plank door, his left arm thrust deep into his jacket pocket.

The truth. That's what he was here for. Something to fight the growing void within him, the gaping incompleteness that swallowed every beam of light, every warmth. He waited but no one came. He knocked again, looked out across the valley, at the glaciers shining in the sunlight, at all that hateful beauty. A couple walked by on the road above, hand-in-hand, their laughter dancing on the breeze. After a while he turned away, started down the stairs.

He was halfway down when he heard the door open. He turned and stepped back up to the balcony. A woman stood in the doorway, still in shadow, hand above her eyes to shield the sun. She was young, thin, her hair short with a blunt fringe, jet-black. She wore a long black skirt and a grey woollen sweater with the sleeves pushed up to the elbows.

'*Bonjour, monsieur?*'

She stepped forward into the light. Her incredible eyes shone out at him without recognition. He stumbled backwards, hung on to the railing, blinked hard, questioning what he saw.

Her eyes narrowed. She stepped out onto the balcony, reached up and touched his beard. '*Clay?*'

٥٦

Everything That Had Led Him Here

He held tight to the rail. 'Rania?'

She threw her arms around his neck and kissed him hard, almost knocking him off his feet. '*Mon dieu, c'est toi,*' she gasped between kisses. '*C'est vraiment toi.*' She pulled him inside and closed the door, engulfing him with a flood of kisses.

'You …' he took a deep breath, looked into her eyes. 'Thank God.'

She touched her shoulder. '*Al hamdillulah.*' The skin of her forearms had come up in gooseflesh.

He held her for a long time, there inside the doorway, the late-afternoon sun streaming particle-lit through the open windows, the blond pinewood floors and walls glowing, her face buried in his chest, just feeling her, convincing himself, not wanting to let go.

After a while she whispered: 'They said you were dead.' Her voice was thin, breathless, rougher than he remembered. 'There was a story in the newspaper with your photo. It said you died trying to escape from Yemen. It said you killed seven oil workers.'

Shame burned through him. He looked away.

She led him through to the chalet's main room, a big window looking out across the valley, heavy pine beams overhead, a wood-burning stove, old lived-in furniture, a writing desk. She put her hand to her mouth and coughed. The sound came from deep within her lungs, rasping phlegm. 'When I heard you were here, in Switzerland, I did not believe it.'

He was quiet for a long time, looking out at the mountains as if they, too, had just somehow rematerialised. A solitary cloud scuttled past the highest glacier.

'The woman I met? Was she one of your people? DGSE?'

She shook her head, looked down at her hands. 'They are not my people any longer, Clay.'

Clay turned and faced her. A frisson ran up the back of his spine. 'What happened that night, Rania? At the village.' He had been waiting a long time to ask that question.

A spasm of coughing shuddered through her body. She looked up at him, her face pale, pained. 'I had only been in the service two years. All I did was pass along information to my contact.' She hung her head. 'It was the first time I had been asked to do anything, how do I say, *direct*. I was instructed to find Al Shams. We knew that he wanted desperately to tell his story. But he needed you to be able to tell it.' She stopped, looked down at the floor. 'Before the interview I activated a short-range directional transmitter and hid it on the roof of his building. I had already called in the operation the night before. But then after you ...' she paused, putting her hands to her cheeks. 'After we were together, it was all so clear. I knew he was not what they thought he was. I could never have lived with it. I had to warn him.'

He understood. We have a choice. All of us.

He put his hand on her shoulder, turned her so she was facing him, held her close. She felt frail, bone thin.

Rania looked up at him. 'It was supposed to be retribution, Clay. For the murder of Thierry Champard. Justice. And a warning. We had intelligence that Al Qaeda was planning to hit a target in France. We had to act. It was not until yesterday that I read the story about Parnell in the newspaper.'

'Parnell?'

'He was picked up by Interpol on his way through Amsterdam and taken into custody two days ago. The French government is pressing charges of conspiracy to commit murder. Petro-Tex has denounced him. They said they had unearthed evidence that proved that Parnell had hired an assassin to kill Champard. Apparently, Parnell and Champard had been working together to embezzle large sums of money from Petro-Tex. When Champard got cold feet and threatened to confess, Parnell had him killed. Not a difficult thing to arrange, in Yemen.'

'Don't I know it.'

'Rex Medved himself has been on the news today saying that Parnell acted on his own, without the knowledge of senior management, and against company policy. Petro-Tex is cooperating fully with the investigation.'

Clay tried to breathe, felt the air rasping through his constricting windpipe. 'It wasn't Parnell, Rania. It was Medved.'

Rania gasped. 'Are you sure?'

'Medved had Champard killed because he threatened to reveal what was going on up at the CPF. I have proof. Or will have soon. That's why they've blamed Parnell. They're worried the truth will get out. So they decided to pre-empt whatever might be revealed, set a smokescreen.'

Rania face hardened.

'Medved tried to have me killed, a few weeks ago in Oman.'

Rania gasped.

'He's looking for you, too, Rania. They're trying to wrap this whole thing up. They want anyone who knew what really happened to disappear.'

She stood for a moment looking past him, out across the valley or out into the future, perhaps, saying nothing. Then she took his hand and led him to the kitchen. A wood fire flickered in a big steel stove. She moved a cast-iron kettle a few inches onto the hotter part of the stovetop. In a moment it was wisping steam. He watched her reach two earthenware mugs from a wooden cupboard and pour tea leaves from a jar into a strainer.

'I convinced Hurricane to pull out of the Petro-Tex joint venture,' he said.

'That is good.'

'It's as far as I've got.'

She took the kettle from the fire and poured two cups of tea, handed him one. 'And Hussein?'

'Murdered. The day you left.'

She frowned. 'I am sorry.'

Clay looked into her eyes, surprised.

'If he had wanted to kill me, he would have,' she whispered. 'He contacted DGSE – arranged for my evacuation. Hussein would have to have gone through PSO channels to do it. That was probably what cost him his life. In saving me, he ruined his cover inside PSO.'

'Jesus.'

'And Abdulkader, your friend?'

Clay swallowed. 'He was killed. Saving me.'

Rania's face contorted. Tears flooded her eyes, sharpening the fiery corona.

'Hurricane pulling out will have been a big blow, Rania. But Petro-Tex is hanging on. They're looking for new money. Without it, they can't expand, and if they don't expand, the existing wells will water out and the whole operation dies.' He put his mug on the table, stepped towards her, reached into his pocket, pulled out the crumpled handwritten pages of her story, put them on the table. 'We can finish this,' he said.

He searched her face. 'I can get everything we need, Rania: eye-witness statements, photographs, reports, sample data, field meas-urements. We can blow this thing to pieces, Rania. If this gets out, Medved is destroyed, politically and financially. We can crush the bastard, Rania.'

She looked down at the pages. 'Ten thousand Ogoni were massa-cred by government troops in Nigeria just a few weeks ago, Clay, and it barely made the news. People are fatigued. There is too much injustice, a deluge. It's not news anymore.' Tears pooled in her eyes, overflowed.

'This matters, Rania. You know it does.'

'It is not a question of whether something *matters*, Clay. Lots of things matter. It's whether you can actually do anything about it. It is like building a sandcastle on the beach when I was a little girl. I would work all day and make something beautiful. Then the tide washed it all away.'

It sounded too familiar. It sounded like him. He swallowed hard, could see the hardened disillusionment in her. 'That is exactly what they want you to think, Rania.'

'*They*?' she said.

'All of them. Petro-Tex, Medved, the morons that sent us to Angola, your lot. The people who control the system. The people who have been using us our whole lives, making us do their dirty work.' He checked himself a moment, paused. 'You have to finish that story.'

'Do you not understand, Clay? I wanted to. Believe me. I have spent hours and days drafting and redrafting it until my head split.' She slumped down onto one of the kitchen chairs. 'But you were dead.' She wiped the tears from her face with her hands, left then right, blinked away the beads from her eyelashes. She buried her face in her arms, breath rasping through her lungs.

Clay felt his chest tighten. He sat beside her and put his arm around her and held her for a long time, feeling the tremors running through her body.

She gripped his arm and looked up at him. Her eyes were like prisms, tears refracting the alpine light. 'That person you saw with the gun, it was not me, Clay. It never was.' She grabbed a newspaper from the stack next to the fireplace and put it on the table, an old copy of the IHT. 'This is me, Clay. This.'

He looked down at the paper, another of her by-lines.

'I had convinced myself that I was doing something noble, something righteous, but it was all a lie.'

'Your father.'

She nodded. 'And then losing you …' she bent double, her lungs rebelling, her body shuddering in a series of wrenching coughs. When it was over, she looked up, tears in her eyes, pushed the fringe from her eyes. He could see the price she had paid in every part of her face. She looked into his eyes. '*Mon dieu*, Clay. It was like dying.' She wrapped her arms around him and pushed her face into his chest.

That's exactly what it was like.

And then, without warning, Abdulkader was there, real, close, his shattered body pumping blood out onto the hot dry sand, his eyes looking out across the shimmering plain towards that place the living will never know. A shiver ran through him. He closed his eyes, tried to blink Abdulkader away. 'I'm here, Rania.' His voice sounded far away, as if he was listening to himself in another room.

She wiped the back of her hand across her eyes. '*Allah akhbar.*'

Clay swallowed hard. 'Maybe He is.' He kissed her. The smell and the feel of her calmed him. He reached up and touched her cheek, a phantom. By the time he realised what he had done it was too late.

She gasped. '*Mon dieu*, Clay. Your … your *hand.*'

He stopped and pulled away, and held it up for her to see.

She stared at it for a moment and then took what was left of his forearm in her hands and kissed every part of the stump. 'I am so sorry,' she said.

But he did not want her pity, or her remorse, for now he could see the abrupt physics of it all, of everything that had led him here.

OV

Entropy

Clay woke with a start. Moonlight reflected from the glaciers and threw long shadows across the bed and lit the walls of the bedroom. He pulled up the duvet against the cold, breathed the mountain air flowing in from the open window. It was getting warmer now, summer's zenith in the air, the smells of ripening fruit, cedar, rain on the way. She murmured something and snuggled close, snaked her arm across his chest, the warmth of her plastered against his side, the smell of him all over her, of her on him. He could see the scar clearly now, an angry welt arcing down from just below her collarbone towards her side, the larger one on her back where the shoulder blade had been reconstructed.

Hussein's aim had been good. Two inches lower and he would have ripped out her heart. As it was, she had almost died of secondary lung infection. He pulled her close, kissed the scar. She looked so vulnerable, lying there naked beside him. Desire coursed through him, a deep chemical swoon. He was morning hard, aching for her. But he breathed deep, found control. He didn't want to wake her.

Clay slipped from under the covers. In the semi-dark he pulled on trousers, a shirt and a fleece-lined jacket, and crept to the kitchen. He got the stove fire going and soon had a pile of glowing coals. He filled the kettle, poured out tea leaves and made a quick breakfast.

It had been six days now since he'd found her. Still weak, Rania slept long daylight hours. When she could, she worked on the story, threading in the technical detail Clay provided. While she slept,

Clay walked alone in the mountains, high up to the alpine slopes, returning to the chalet after dark, always watching, alert for any sign of danger. He was healing. He watched Rania grow stronger. Soon she was able to accompany him, short distances at first, longer each day. They spoke of the future, the imminent and yet seemingly distant danger they faced, Medved's people out there looking for them both, hunting them. And yet up here in the mountains they seemed immune, insulated somehow from all of it. On the radio he heard of the changes in South Africa, of reprisals and reconciliation. Petro-Tex's growing success in Yemen was in the news, too. Despite the war and the controversy swirling around its operations, production was set to increase. If the reports could be believed, the new oil discoveries were world-class. Rex Medved announced the launch of a major new charity helping underprivileged children in the developing world. Yemen would be the operation's flagship.

Clay was about to open the front door when he heard footsteps behind him. She was standing in her nightgown, arms wrapped around herself.

'Where are you going, Claymore?'

'I didn't want to wake you.'

She stood looking at him.

'I need to make some calls, get some cash.'

She frowned, that little negative smile he found so enchanting. 'Someone might recognise you, Clay.'

He stroked his beard. 'Looking like this? My own mother wouldn't recognise me, *Allah* keep her soul.'

She bit her lip. 'I am sorry,' she said. 'I did not know.'

Entropy. It was all about the inevitable disaggregation of things, of people. You couldn't escape it. Clay grabbed the door handle.

'Please do not leave, Clay. It is safe here.'

He turned, looked at her. 'We can't hide forever, Rania. Al Shams is still out there, still fighting. We have to help him.' He reached up, stroked her cheek with his fingers. 'Don't worry. I won't be long. Back tonight.'

Soon he was descending the ridge trail, the lights of the town flickering below in the valley, the first grey light touching the ice on the peaks, his breath clouding in the air.

Three hours later he was in Geneva. He went straight to the Standard Bank building on *Rue des Alpes*. Two weeks ago he'd set up an account there, arranged a sizeable transfer from the Cayman Islands branch. Now he walked through the dark granite foyer, aware of the closed circuit cameras following him. He filled out a withdrawal slip at the counter, presented it to a teller behind an old-style wood and glass wicket. The man looked down at the slip, over his spectacles at Clay, and then picked up the phone. He spoke into the handset, listened. After a moment he replaced the handset.

'*Un moment, s'il vous plaît*,' he said, and disappeared into a back room.

Clay kept his eyes lowered, away from the cameras, nerves jangling. A minute passed, two.

Finally, the clerk reappeared. He counted out Clay's cash, and then slid a sealed envelope under the glass, along with a yellow chit. '*Signature*,' said the clerk.

Clay picked up the envelope. It was unstamped, bore the logo and address of Standard Bank, Cayman Islands. He signed the chit, stashed the envelope and the cash in his jacket pocket and made for the street. Soon he was walking down the *Rue des Alpes*, heading towards the lake. He found a payphone outside the Swissair office, slotted in a card, punched in the Consul's number, let it ring.

The Consul answered second ring.

'Declan Greene here.'

Silence, and then: 'It is good that you called.'

'They have blamed Parnell,' said Clay.

'Yes.'

'It wasn't him.'

Dead air filled the line. After a moment: 'I don't want to know.'

Clay said nothing.

'The young lady's cover has been compromised.'

Rania. 'Jesus. By whom?'

'I don't know. But she is in grave danger.'

'Thank you for telling me. I know ...'

The Consul cut him off. 'I have done what I could. Please do not call me again.' The line went dead.

Clay reattached the receiver, stared out into the street, fear welling up inside him like a cold ocean current, heavy, dense. He needed to move fast. The Gare Cornavin was two kilometres away. He made it there in eight minutes, checked the train timetable for Champéry. The next train wasn't for another eighteen minutes. He walked over to the big bank of public telephones outside the station café.

The line clicked open. '*Ja?*'

'Koevoet, is that you, *broer?*' Crowbar.

'Who the *fok* wants to know?' The answer in Afrikaans.

'It's Straker, *broer*, from *Valk* 5.' Crowbar had been his platoon commander in Angola, had stayed in right until the end, spent the last four years in SA Military Intelligence, the DCC – Directorate of Covert Collection – stationed in Europe. They had kept in touch, spent some time together when Clay was studying engineering in London after fleeing South Africa.

'*Ja, ja*, fucking *soutpiele*.' Salt dick – English South African.

'*Fokken boere,*' said Clay. Farmer. Their usual routine.

Crowbar laughed. It sounded like a rusty hinge. '*Howzit, broet?*'

'I'm coming to London,' Clay said in Afrikaans. 'I need a Glock. Clean.'

Pause. 'No problem.'

'And I may need a quiet place to stay for a while.'

'Done. You know where to find me. Come by when you get here.'

☾

Clay watched from the window as the little train ratcheted its way up the slope. The clouds had lifted and he could see up the valley, tried to spy the edge of the woods where he and Rania had walked the day before, up past the Auberge des Cols with its big sloping roof and little patch of grass where you could sit on wooden benches and drink local beer and look down across the valley – over the stone footbridge and then up along the ridge and into the trees, cool and dark here, moving over the moss-quiet carpet, fingers laced, breathing hard as the pitch steepened through dappled sunlight up to where the trees thinned and stunted. After about an hour they had stopped at a steep rushing stream, taken off their boots, sat on a rock and let the water run glacier cold over their feet. They sat for a while watching the water foaming around their ankles, the turbulence writ on the surface in eddies and dips, the ever-changing liquid topography splattering a dance of sunlight over their faces, over everything. They had continued on, breaking out into a moraine and cloud-strewn high valley, the limestone and slate here like the sky, a monochrome of grey, so different from the explosion of Hadramawt colour. They had unpacked lunch and sat close, catching glimpses of the valley through the shifting clouds, saying little, like that time in Aden so long ago now, a different lifetime, looking out over the Indian Ocean. Back home, they'd lit a fire, shared a cup of tea. At night, they'd made love, alone in the little bedroom overlooking the valley and the towering peaks, and it was as if being someone else had unchained her somehow. His feet tingled, thinking of her ardour.

He reached Champéry by late afternoon. By the time he returned to the chalet it was dark. The windows glowed kerosene yellow. Smoke curled from the chimney. He climbed the steps and knocked on the door.

She stood in the foyer in her slippers and wool sweater, a cup of tea in her hands.

He pulled out the envelope. 'It's the rest of the story,' he said. 'The missing piece.' He closed the door, took her in his arms, kissed her lips, her cheekbones, her neck. 'We have to leave,' he said. 'Now.'

Saint Fucking Mandela

By early evening they were back in Geneva. They rented a car, a little white Peugeot 306, and drove through the night, catching the morning ferry from Calais. No sign of being followed. The ferry was busy. They sat in the cafeteria on the main deck and had breakfast. The Channel was calm, ridges of stratocumulus running in skirmish lines across an otherwise clear blue sky. He told her about Medved's capital-raising, about his conversation with Perry.

Rania moved aside her plate, spread a copy of the *Independent* across the table, pointing to an article on page ten. 'It says here that Aden is under siege. It's almost over, Clay. The rebels have lost.' She read on. After she had finished she looked up. There was fear in her eyes.

'What is it, Rania?'

'It says here that Vance Parnell was found dead last night in his cell in Amsterdam. The authorities have determined that it was suicide.'

'Parnell, suicide?' So filled with remorse over what he'd done that he killed himself? No chance of that. Parnell was a survivor. 'Medved got to him.'

Rania frowned.

'Now Petro-Tex will blame Parnell for everything.'

She sipped her coffee, looked at him across its steaming rim. 'LeClerc agreed to meet me in London. He doesn't know it's me, but I gave him enough to get him interested.'

Clay sent her a silent question.

'My editor, before I died.'

Clay nodded. 'Good. We don't have long. The story has to come out as soon as Medved launches. That's in three days.'

'Then we are going to need all of the documentary evidence, as much as we can get, and quickly. LeClerc is a stickler that way. He is not going to agree to publish anything unless we can satisfy him that it is the truth. He will want to go through all the background information in detail.'

'It's coming, Rania. I've redone my field notes. We'll meet Perry tomorrow or the day after. He has material from inside the joint venture. I'll contact my Cypriot accountant when we get to London, get him to courier us the originals of the stuff from Yemen, including the photographs from Bawazir. We should have it all in the next couple of days.'

'Do you trust your accountant, Clay?'

'I called him from Oman. That was weeks ago. If he was going to tell someone, he would have done it by now.'

Rania frowned.

'We don't have a choice, Rania. Look what they did to Parnell. They're desperate now, cornered. They know we're out there. They know we have at least some of the information we need to sink them. If we don't end this soon, we're dead. Both of us. It's only a matter of time.'

(

They reached London later that afternoon, checked in at the Churchill Hotel in Marble Arch as Mr and Mrs Greene, paid cash. Clay called Perry's office in Calgary while Rania was in the shower. They were expecting his call. The Chairman of Hurricane Resources was already in London. He would be expecting Clay at the Excelsior Hotel, Mayfair, Room 2108, tonight at seven-thirty pm.

Clay put down the phone and watched Rania emerge from the bathroom, a white towel wrapped across her breasts, another flipped high on her head. She walked over to where he was sitting, leant over and kissed him on the forehead. He reached up, pulled away the towel, let it fall to the floor, drew her to him. Her skin was still damp.

'Well?' she said.

'We're going to meet Perry in two hours.'

'Then we do not have long, Clay,' she whispered into his hair.

'Exactly,' he said, scooping her up and carrying her to the bed.

☾

They arrived at the hotel an hour early, at Rania's insistence. While Rania watched the lobby, Clay climbed the stairs to Perry's floor and posted himself at the end of the corridor, 2108 in plain sight. Three-quarters of an hour ticked past at one-fifth speed, and Clay wondered how a lifetime without her would have felt. At 19:15, as agreed, Rania called up to Perry's room, asked him to meet them in the lobby. A few minutes later Clay watched Perry leave his room, alone, and get into the lift. Clay waited ten minutes, and satisfied there was no one else in the room, took the stairs back down to the lobby.

Redmond Perry had aged since Clay had seen him last. His big, athlete's frame had lost some of its bulk. His neck looked thinner, the shoulders less broad. Intelligent hazel eyes glared out from under the eaves of bushy grey brows. He looked long-haul tired.

'Not here,' he said, looking around the lobby. 'Please.' They agreed to go up to his suite. In the lift no one spoke. Clay stood behind Perry as he unlocked the door, then pushed him inside.

'Stay here,' he said to Rania and closed the door and left her in the hallway.

'What are you doing?' asked Perry, as Clay pushed him through the suite like a dozer blade, one hand on the back of Perry's collar.

'Just making sure. A lot of people want us dead.'

The place was empty.

Clay went and opened the door for Rania, showed her to the suite's living room, where Perry was pouring himself a drink.

'I could use one of those myself,' he said.

Perry nodded and poured another whisky. Clay and Rania sat next to each other on the sofa. Perry sat in the armchair facing them; he smiled at Rania, a quick weary effort, then placed a thick A4 envelope on the table.

'It's all in there,' he said. His voice was deep, experienced, a lifetime of authority there. Shaky, too. 'Financials, memoranda and emails linking Medved directly with the events in Yemen. He had personal oversight of everything. Also, four invitations to Medved's capital-raising launch tomorrow. You didn't get any of it from me.'

Clay stashed the envelope in his pack.

'Why not go to the Press and tell the story yourself, Mister Perry?' said Rania. 'Better yet, let me interview you.'

Perry looked at her a moment. 'Invisibility, young lady. That's what industry wants. That's what company directors want. We just want to be left alone to go about our business. The lower our profile, the better. Profit prefers anonymity. That's the condition, Straker. Do you understand, son?'

Clay nodded. 'All in the background.'

'Just how we like it.' Perry drained his glass, placed it on the table, stood. 'Now, if you will excuse me, I have a dinner engagement. Good luck.'

They left the hotel, returned to Marble Arch on foot, lost in the lamp-lit crowds. Clay left Rania at the Churchill, and took the tube to Kilburn. He didn't say where he was going, and she didn't ask.

Crowbar's flat was on the top floor of a run-down, nondescript building off the high street. Clay climbed the stairs and rapped on the door. Crowbar let him in. The flat was as Clay remembered it: a couple of rooms, a shabby couch, cramped kitchen with a sink overflowing with unwashed dishes, empty tinnies lining the countertops like soldiers on parade.

He pushed away some newspapers and sat on the couch. 'Place is looking good, *broer*.'

'Beer?' asked Crowbar, holding out a tin.

Clay waved it away. 'I don't have long.'

Crowbar cracked the beer, tipped it to his mouth. He had put on weight. His platinum hair was thinning. He looked more like a middle-aged accountant in a shit job than the fiercest bush fighter Clay had ever known. When the beer was gone, Crowbar tossed the tin towards the kitchen sink. It bounced off the counter and rattled to the floor. '*God verdoem*, Straker. You were a pussy back then, and you're still a *fokken* pussy.' He grabbed another beer and thrust it into Clay's hands. 'Now have a beer with me.'

Clay took the beer and opened it. Crowbar opened another.

'*Valk 5*,' said Crowbar, raising the tin. 'We killed a *fok* of a lot more of them than they killed of us.'

'*Valk 5*.'

They finished their beers in silence.

Crowbar opened another beer and took three big gulps and filled his refrigerator ribcage with air. 'Seen what's happening at home?'

It hadn't been home for a long time. Clay nodded.

'Fucking ANC,' said Crowbar. 'Can you *fokken* believe it, *broet*? Saint fucking Mandela, *ja*?'

'*Ja, broer.*' That's what you did with Koevoet. You agreed.

'Fifteen years I fought for my country. And now, *vrek*, fucking gone. Flushed away like *kak*.'

Three years or fifteen, it didn't change anything. They had been duped, all of them, lied to, sacrificed for a bankrupt ideal. At least he had seen it, eventually, rebelled, got out. He held the air in his lungs, closed his eyes, breathed out long and steady the way he'd practised so many times. 'Did we really do those things, Koevoet?'

'I don't know what you are talking about, Straker.'

'You know exactly.'

Crowbar ran his hand over his scalp. '*Goddamn*, Straker,' he whispered. 'We all agreed a long time ago. Leave it. Forget it.'

Clay stood, fought back a wave of nausea. 'When this is over, I'm going back.'

'You think they'll let you go home now? Saint Mandela give your poor white *rooineck* arse a pardon?'

'I'm serious, Koevoet. The government has set up a truth and reconciliation commission. They want people to come forward.'

'The government, *ja*. Bunch of *fokken* terrorists. That is not a government.'

'I'm going back, and I'm going to tell the truth.'

Koevoet stood and stared at Clay for a long time, said nothing. When he finally spoke, it was in a hoarse whisper. 'You swore, Straker, we all did, that it would stay out there, in the bush. You think anyone cares? Something that happened ten years ago? A little *fokken* village in the middle of *fokken* nowhere? No one gives a shit, Straker. No one. It's done. Gone. Nothing you can do is going to change that. The only thing you'll do is fuck yourself. Yourself and me and the rest of us.'

Koevoet was close to him now. He jabbed his meaty forefinger into Clay's chest. 'You made an *oath*, Straker. An oath to your brothers. That's something you can't break. Ever.'

Clay stood, stared back hard into his commander's sky-blue eyes. A flicker of the old battle light was there now, strobing through.

Crowbar put his hand on Clay's shoulder. 'Look, *broet*. I know what you're looking for. You want some kind of absolution. I can understand that. We all do. But that's not where you're going to find it, believe me.'

'I've made up my mind. Sorry, Koevoet.'

Crowbar reached behind his back and produced a matt black handgun. 'G21,' he said. 'Forty-five. Stop a rhino with this, *broet*.' It looked new.

Crowbar jammed a magazine into the grip, worked the mechanism. Like silk. It was a beautiful weapon.

Clay stood. Said nothing.

'If you open it up again, Straker, I promise you it won't end well.'

'The truth has to be told. You can't just make fifty people go away.'

'It *fokken* has been told, Straker. What we all told them, what went into the official records, *that* was the truth. Fifty,' he spat. 'You think we were the only ones? *Fok*, it could've been a *thousand*.'

Clay looked down at the Glock, back up at Crowbar. His calves quivered, flight triggers firing. 'What are you going to do, Koevoet?'

Crowbar stood staring at him, hands clenched at his sides, the weapon pointing to the floor. 'You do this, Straker, our friendship is over.' Crowbar raised the weapon, palmed the barrel, handed it to Clay grip first.

Clay weighed the gun in his hand, checked the safety, pushed the Glock into the waistband of his trousers. '*Danke*, Koevoet. I'll remember that.' He peeled off eight fifty-pound notes, and put them on the listing coffee table.

Crowbar grabbed the money and stuffed it into Clay's shirtfront pocket. 'Keep it. From what I hear, you're going to need it.'

'Maybe.'

'There's a price on your carcass, *broet*. A hundred thousand pounds. A lot of people are looking for you.'

Clay paused, took a breath.

'And that friend of yours, Moulinbecq. They know she's here in London. Whoever is angry at you has friends in customs. They picked her name up coming into the country. Looks like the lag is about a day,' he said in Afrikaans, tossing an extra mag onto the couch.

Clay's heart rate stratosphered. 'Medved.'

Crowbar nodded. 'If you need to disappear, come here,' he said, handing Clay a key. 'We'll get you to a place I have in Cornwall. Very quiet. On the sea. Good direct access to the continent.'

Clay reached down, grabbed the extra mag from the couch. They shook hands. Outside, the clouds had closed in and the rain had started to fall. He ran to the station, and as he sat on the Tube watching the people flash by, the darkness of the tunnels, the faces reflected like ghosts on the window glass; he wondered again about those fifty people, so many of them children, and what they might have been.

A Place You Can Go

The next day, the day of Medved's launch, Clay and Rania walked into the lobby of the Mansion House Hotel in Hammersmith. It had rained all morning and the air was fresh with the smell of wet summer pavement. Rania made for a table in the lobby café, where a man in a dark suit was sitting alone reading a broadsheet. Clay followed, scanning the café, the patrons.

Rania tended a gloved hand. 'Thank you for meeting me.'

The man opposite took it, searching her face.

She wore dark sunglasses and a silk headscarf that completely covered her hair.

'This is my friend, Monsieur Greene.'

Clay shook the man's hand. He had a firm grip, businesslike, had that distinguished just-greying look, tanned and fit.

Rania reached for Clay's hand. '*Chéri*, this is Monsieur LeClerc, chief editor of Agence France Presse.'

They sat. Clay called over the waiter, ordered coffee, tea for Rania.

LeClerc ordered espresso, checked his watch. 'Please, Madame. I do not have long. You have information for me?'

Rania reached into her bag and pulled out a manila folder, opened it, withdrew a sheaf of four typewritten pages and handed it to LeClerc. He took them, started reading. His eyes flashed back and forth. He flipped over the first page, the second, raised his eyes up to Rania, went back to reading. Finally he put the papers down on the table and looked hard at Rania. 'I know this writing,' he said. 'Where did you get this?'

Rania reached up and untied her scarf, took off her glasses, thickrimmed librarian's frames. She had dyed her hair a dull shade of fair, wore a fawn blazer and skirt that flattened her curves. She looked like a university sociology lecturer, or a bookkeeper in a factory that made kitchenware, like someone else.

LeClerc blinked, looked left and then right, leaned forward, staring into her face. 'Rania? *Mon Dieu.*'

A long conversation ensued in French, rapid, hushed. LeClerc reached across the table and took both of Rania's hands. His face was flushed. '*Oui*,' he kept saying. '*Oui, je comprends. Certainement.*'

Rania nodded to Clay. He reached into his pack and pulled out two file boxes. Inside, copies of everything. The report he'd delivered to Ali that day in Yemen, signed by Parnell and Karila, both now dead. The photos of the massacre. Perry's dossier. Champard's letter, Clay's painstakingly recreated field notes. He handed them to LeClerc. 'It's all in here. The whole story.'

LeClerc nodded, opened the top of the first box, pulled out the envelope containing the photos, folded back the flap. His eyes widened as he flicked through the prints. '*Mon Dieu*,' he whispered, replacing the photos.

Clay slid a ticket across the table. 'Your invitation,' he said.

Leclerc nodded, stood, emptied the last of his coffee, folded the story lengthwise and slid it into the inside breast pocket of his jacket. 'By the way,' he said. 'I thought you would want to know. Northern troops captured Aden early this morning. The war is over.' He smiled at Rania, nodded to Clay. 'Monsieur Greene, a great pleasure.' And then he was gone, through the mid-afternoon crowd and out into the rainy London streets.

Clay and Rania jumped into a black cab, went straight back to the Churchill. Medved's event was due to start at nine pm. All they had to do now was wait. Clay shook out his jacket, hung it over the back of a chair. Rania sat in front of the mirror and started brushing out her hair. She held the brush in her left hand, used the right to catch and fold the thick, soft mass.

'Is there somewhere you can go?' he said. 'Somewhere safe?'

She put down the brush, turned to face him. 'What do you mean?'

'It's done. LeClerc has the story. In a few hours, the whole rotten *opfok* will come crashing down. I want you to leave now. It's safer.'

'What about you?'

'I asked if there was somewhere you could go, Rania.'

She bit her lip, started braiding her hair. 'The chalet.'

'It's not safe, Rania. Medved has friends in the French government, inside the DGSE too, most likely. Your cover has been blown.'

'The DGSE did not set me up there, Clay. I took my own precautions. They are still paying rent for Lise Moulinbecq's flat in Marseilles. No one knows about the chalet.'

'Medved knows about your change of name. Crowbar says there's a day's lag on the information Medved gets from customs. They know you're here in London. They probably figure we're together. Go via Spain or Italy. Germany, even. You can be home before they even find out you've left.'

Rania frowned, didn't answer.

'It's going to get hot here, Rania. I want you to leave. Tonight.'

She stood, unmoving, glaring at him.

'Are you going to answer me?'

'It wasn't a question, Clay. It was an order.'

'Please, Rania.'

'What do you mean *it's going to get hot?*' she snapped. 'What kind of silly language is that? What are you going to do, Clay?'

'I'm going to stay here and finish it. I'll join you after.'

She shook her head. 'No, Clay. No.'

'Jesus Christ, Rania. You've done your bit. There's a travel office in the hotel lobby. You can book a flight and be out of here tonight.'

Rania stood, folded her arms across her chest, glared at him. 'Done my bit? Is that what you call it? Listen to yourself, Clay. I am not your wife. I do not take orders from you.'

Clay took a step back. Would it change anything if you were my wife? He didn't say it.

She closed the distance between them, reached up and touched his face. 'Please, Clay. I know you are trying to protect me. And I love you for it, *chéri*. But I want to stay with you.' She put her arms around him, buried her face in his chest, held him tight.

Clay stood rigid. Didn't raise his arms. He wanted to but he didn't.

She looked up at him. Her smile was as big as the Rhub Al Khali, the Empty Quarter, as sun struck.

'We're going to do this together,' she said.

٦٠

The Things He Would Never Do

They arrived shortly after eight. Clay and Rania fell in behind a group of businessmen in dark, rain-spattered suits. The men had wet hair, carried glistening umbrellas. At the main doors, a pair of heavily-built security guards checked invitations, searched bags and briefcases.

The ballroom was filling up fast. Clay and Rania slipped into the back row of seats, close to the door, and sat watching the people file in, men in suits mostly, and find seats. Clay could see LeClerc talking to someone in the front row. Technicians scurried around the raised podium, the lectern, the huge backlit screen. Clay looked at Rania, unrecognisable in her librarian's guise, took her hand. She squeezed hard.

The lights dimmed. A hush fell over the assembled. Music filled the ballroom, catchy soft rock with a rousing guitar hook, a U2 rip-off. The screen exploded into life, a kaleidoscope of images: cars streaming by, planes soaring, bullet trains slicing through the countryside, cities lit up at night, and then oil rigs, tankers sailing on clear blue seas, refineries, oil workers in blue coveralls and white hard hats walking towards the audience in slow motion, smiles everywhere, high-fives, then the ancient mud skyscrapers of Marib, camels moving through sun-painted dunes, smiling Yemeni tribesmen, and, then, landscape rushing past, a helicopter's view, and Clay was looking down from the air at that same desert he loved, swooping down into those virid green valleys and rocketing back up above the lip of the canyon, the audience letting out an involuntary gasp, the music building to a crescendo, pounding now, the barren beauty of the Hadramawt flashing below, the colours impossible, primary.

The ballroom doors were closed and the two security men took station just inside.

'Ladies and gentlemen,' announced a booming voice. 'The Chairman and President of Petro-Tex International, Mister Rex Medved.'

The crowd broke into applause and Rex strode up to the podium, spotlights following. He stood on the platform, let the applause wash over him for a moment, looked bashfully at the floor, then raised his hands for quiet, that same demeanour Clay had seen in the office in Aden. Medved was smiling now, pointing to people he recognised in the crowd, acknowledging them with a mouthed 'hi' or a nod, connecting, accessible, a man you could like, a man you could trust.

'Thank you so much to everyone for coming this evening, despite the, ah …' he smiled, paused, wiped imaginary raindrops from his shoulders, '… atypical English summer weather.' A ripple of laughter moved through the audience. 'And thank you to our very talented, if not somewhat, well, over-enthusiastic marketing people for that introduction.' More laughter. He nodded to the sidelines, put his hands together. Polite clapping from the audience.

'Ladies and gentlemen, I am here today to invite you to join in a unique investment opportunity in one of the world's last true frontiers.' Scenes of Yemen flashed across the screen. 'Over the past few months, Petro-Tex engineers have confirmed and detailed the discovery of one of the largest reserves of light, high-quality crude oil on the planet. Here, in the South of Yemen.' Images of Yemen were replaced now by charts and graphs, production curves. Medved went on to provide reserve estimates, expected revenues, profit projections, investment requirements, and details of the private offering now available.

Finally, he walked to the podium and signalled to the technicians. The lights came up, and he stood, hands clasped before him, head bowed. He looked up at the audience. 'If anyone has any questions, there are investment packs available at the back to take with you before you leave, and of course, we would be pleased to address any specific queries you may have now.'

For a moment there was silence, as if the audience was contemplating the gold rush laid before their feet. A man raised his hand, stood. Medved pointed to him. 'Sir.' A skirted attendant with auburn hair and long shapely legs rushed to hand him a microphone.

The man fiddled with the device, blew into it. 'Charles Barclay, Diamond Equity. Thank you for that quite excellent presentation, Mister Medved. Can you please confirm that the EBIT estimates in your, I believe it was, fifth slide from last, are indeed 50 percent?' The man handed back the microphone, sat down.

Medved stepped forward, smiled. 'Glad you asked me that, Charles. Wasn't quite sure that everyone had picked up on that. Indeed, this is a conservative estimate. We expect major investors can have their money back in the first six months. Where else can one achieve comparable returns?' A murmur ran through the audience. Another man stood, heavy set, dark suit, grey hair, and took the microphone. Another question about finance, reserve estimates, production. More Medved back, charming, honest, compelling. Nodding from the audience, note-taking.

Then LeClerc stood. Rania was squeezing Clay's hand so hard he thought she would grind his knuckles into paste. A cameraman stood, too, switched on his lights, brought them to bear. The girl handed him the microphone. LeClerc turned and faced the audience, reached into his pocket and withdrew the papers that Rania had given him. 'Ladies and gentlemen, I have here a story that, come tomorrow morning, will run in newspapers across the globe.'

It was Rania's story, and Clay's. And it was Hussein's story, too, and Abdulkader's, and Al Shams'. Perhaps, mostly, Clay thought as he watched LeClerc, it was Mohamed's story, a story he would never get to tell himself, just one of all the other things he would never do.

The letter from the Cayman Islands Bank, delivered to him in Geneva, had pulled together the final strands. Written in an elegant longhand on rough tablet paper, it read:

My friend,

By the everlasting power of God, you are well. Our guest, too, is much better, and has been extremely cooperative. Fear is powerful. Our guest brokered delivery of almost thirty million dollars' worth of arms to the rebels, including the SCUD missiles that fell on Sana'a, indiscriminately killing women and children. His client and partner was Rex Medved. But the rebel movement is collapsing quickly, and many of the weapons have been left undelivered and unpaid-for. Medved has blamed our guest, and now the suppliers, a Russian syndicate, have made our guest the target of their anger. They are searching for him here, and in an irony only Allah could conceive, we are now his protectors. All the details of Medved's treachery, his manipulation through our guest of Ansar Al-Sharia and the rebels, the atrocities he ordered and paid for, are contained in the attached, our guest's own account.

That very thing that brought us together, my friend, continues to operate and spread its poison, as you have explained it to us. We have had to abandon our ancient homes. But we remain steadfast, certain that by Allah's will we will find justice.

My friend, I remain deeply shocked that so much sadness has been caused by something that Allah saw fit to bury out of harm's way.

There is purpose in all that He does.

Your good friend's family are well, thanks God, and he is in paradise, most surely.

I conclude by reminding you of your promise, however I am sure this is no longer necessary. Your reckoning has come and you have understood, and for the rest of your days Allah will watch over you and guide you.

There had been no signature.

Now LeClerc raised the sheaf of papers in his hand. 'I am chief editor of Agence France Presse. This story, backed by official documents, eyewitness testimony, and scientific data, reveals the extent to which, under Mister Medved's direct leadership, Petro-Tex in Yemen has been systematically poisoning and killing the people of the Marib region through unregulated discharge of toxic and radio-active waste, with full knowledge of the consequences.'

A shiver spread through the crowd, a deep murmur. Medved, immobilised at first, shocked, stood open-mouthed. Then he waved to the back. The two security men who had been standing by the main ballroom doors started towards LeClerc.

Clay stood and moved quickly towards the doors, intercepting the security men before they had taken five steps.

'Let the man speak, gents,' he said with a smile.

The first one, not as tall as Clay, but built like a rugby forward, tried to push past. Clay grabbed his wrist, spun to the side and slammed his forearm hard into the back of the man's elbow. His stump was strong now, calloused, a weapon. The man grunted in pain as the joint hyperextended, and dropped to his knees. Clay faced up to his colleague, smiled. The other man stopped, backed away, put his finger to his earpiece, spoke into his collar.

LeClerc continued. 'The story will reveal definitive proof that Petro-Tex, under the direct control of Mister Medved, has engaged in murder, extortion and bribery to keep this tragedy quiet and to secure the oil leases, the development of which you are being asked to finance.'

The room broke into pandemonium. Everyone was speaking at once. Bankers and would-be investors stood, clustered in small groups. A few were moving towards the stage now to confront Medved. Some crowded around LeClerc so that Clay lost sight of him altogether. But many more were heading for the exits. The ones closest to the back were first, slipping out quietly in the commotion. Soon the centre aisle was choked with guests heading for the doors, anxious to disassociate themselves as quickly as possible from the stain spreading across the hall.

Clay pushed through the crowd and circled back to find Rania. As he did, he saw Medved unclip his lapel mike and slip away behind the screen.

Clay hurried towards the podium, rounded the screen. Medved was gone. Double doors, hidden from the audience by the screen, clicked into place. Rania appeared, took his hand.

'What happened?' she said.

'Stay here,' he said.

Rania tightened her grip on his hand. 'Where are you going?'

Clay stood, said nothing.

Rania narrowed her eyes. 'It is done, Clay. We have done it. As soon as the story hits the papers, Medved is finished. Leave it now, please *chéri*.'

He looked at her a moment, fought back the tide. 'I want you to turn around now, Rania. Go straight to the airport. Go home. I'll join you when I can.'

Her face crumpled, tears sheening already in her eyes. 'Is this what you meant when you said finishing it? Killing Medved? Is that where you are going?'

'Please, Rania. Now.'

She went rigid. 'No. I will not. The killing has to end, Clay. Medved is ruined. The French will try him for murder. He will be dragged into a political scandal as deep and nasty as France has seen for decades. He will lose his leases in Yemen. There is no way Saleh will let Petro-Tex continue operating. Not after they aided the rebels. It is over, Clay.' She tugged at his arm, tried to pull him towards the milling crowd. 'Please, Clay. It is time to start something new.'

He looked hard into her eyes. He knew she was right. He should let it go, take her away. They could go to Africa. Buy a little sailboat, head south, disappear. Away from everything, the people, the crowds, the bullshit, the diseased economic machine which fed on the poor and the young. An image exploded in his head, a lonely blue sea, a hazy coastline at the edge of perception.

He *knew* she was right. Medved was finished. Soon his enemies would close in, looking for revenge now that he was weakest. He pulled her close and kissed her on the lips, held her there, the seconds skidding away.

But the pull was strong, too strong. That part of him awakened in the dust and blood of Ovamboland all those years ago burned strong in him still. He took her by the shoulders, pushed her away, reached his hand into the deep right pocket of his jacket, and wrapped his fingers around the Glock's grip. Then he smiled at her and started towards the door.

٦١

The Right Thing

Within hours, the story was flashing around the world. The fallout was swift and severe. The French Foreign Minister immediately distanced himself from Medved, but by morning the Assemblée Nationale had announced a full enquiry into Medved's activities and his links to the Minister.

Later that day, French police issued a warrant for Medved's arrest on murder charges. The newly reunited Yemen Arab Republic, however, remained silent on the issue, and Petro-Tex continued to operate in the country. Overnight, Rex Medved had disappeared, and his sister Regina had left the country.

Clay opened the hotel-room window and looked out across the silver-green expanse of Hyde Park. The rain had stopped and low clouds scurried across a windswept summer sky. Rania padded up behind him on bare feet, reached her arms around his chest, and leaned her head against his back. Since returning to the hotel the night before, she hadn't mentioned what had happened after Medved had fled the podium. But he knew she was upset. All day she'd been quiet, distant. This was the first time she'd seen him like this.

'Why, Clay?'

'You know why.' He'd left her there, burst through the door at the back of the ballroom just in time to see Medved disappear at the end of the service corridor. He'd followed, sprinting towards the far doors, Glock in hand. But by the time he'd emerged into the back alley, Medved's chauffeured Mercedes was tearing away in the rain, turning out into the main road.

She didn't reply, just stood holding him. He could feel her warmth across his back. After a while she whispered: 'Surely what we have done is enough.'

'I'm going back to South Africa,' he said. He could hear her breathing, the slow rasp in her chest still there, an echo. 'Come with me.'

No reply. There still, warm, moulded to him.

'Sorry,' he said. 'I meant, want to come?'

Her arms tightened around him. 'I have always wanted to see Africa,' she said.

Clay turned to face her. She was naked. He put his arms around her waist, pulled her close, kissed her.

Forty minutes later he was standing in the British Airways office in the hotel lobby. He had just finished booking two return first-class tickets to Cape Town, leaving Heathrow tomorrow morning, and was waiting for the sales clerk to print out the tickets when three men strode into the lobby. They made straight for the front desk. From where he stood, Clay could not see their faces. They walked quickly, with intent. Two of the men were big, thick-necked, tough-looking. The third was leaner, but tall, very well dressed. They stopped at the front desk, called to a clerk. There was a discussion. Clay saw one of the men flash some cash. The tall well-dressed man turned, scanned the lobby, turned his face towards the BA office. It was Medved.

Clay turned away, lowered himself into the chair, faced the sales clerk who was tapping something into her keyboard. Ice crystallised in his bones. He glanced back over his shoulder. Medved and his men were heading to the lifts. Clay's heart lurched, valves slamming as a massive slug of adrenaline flooded his bloodstream. 'House phone?' he blurted out.

The clerk pointed to the next desk. Clay grabbed the handset, punched in the room number, waited. Medved was almost at the lift now, maybe twenty metres away. The phone rang once, twice, again. 'Pick up,' Clay breathed.

They were at the lifts now. One of Medved's men pressed the call button. They waited.

Rania answered.

'Rania it's me. Don't talk. Just listen. Get out of the room. Now. Medved's here. He's on the way up. Take the back stairs.'

'Clay, I …'

'Go now. You only have seconds. Back stairs. Not the ones near the lifts. Get to the airport. Go home. I'll see you there.'

The lift arrived, the doors opened. An older couple shuffled out. Medved and his men pushed in, turned, stood facing out. Clay slammed down the phone, stood, sprinted into the lobby. The lift doors started to close.

'Medved,' Clay shouted. His voice echoed from the walls, bounced from the granite tile flooring. Just as the lift doors closed he saw Medved's eyes open wide. He was staring right at him. The doors closed.

Clay sprinted across the foyer to the stairway doors, flung them open, took the stairs four at a time. Twelve flights of twelve, three seconds per flight. The lift slightly faster here, about four seconds per floor. With a ten second head start, they'd have twenty-two seconds on the 6th floor before he even reached it. If Rania had delayed even a minute leaving the room, they'd catch her in the hallway.

Clay burst through the fire door out onto the sixth floor. The corridor was empty. A string of ceiling lights disappeared down an adit of red carpet and colourless walls. The lifts were there, three sets of doors, closed. This side of the hotel faced the park. Clay and Rania's room was on the adjacent side, towards the back of the building. A rectangular footprint with a central courtyard, twenty-five rooms across the park front, twelve along each outer flank, twenty-five along the back. Stairwells and lift shafts set on the inside, fourteen rooms inner front, ten along each flank, twenty-two inner back, a hundred and thirty rooms per floor. It was a big hotel. Even knowing the room number, it would take Medved and his men time to find the room. Clay turned away from the lifts, dashed to the end of the hall, turned right and sprinted along the corridor towards 6119. He reached it in seconds. The door was closed. Either Medved was already inside, or they were on the other side of the floor, searching for the room. He put his ear to the door, listened. Nothing. Back down the hall, the lift gong sounded. Lift doors scraped apart. Clay shoved the key card into the slot, pushed the door open a couple of inches, wedged his boot into the gap, grabbed the Glock, and pushed open the door.

Curtains fluttered in open windows. Rania's makeup lay scattered across the bathroom counter. The closet was open, her clothes hanging there, her book on the bedside table, the unmade bed. The room was empty.

She'd gone.

Clay turned, ran for the door. Had the clerk given Medved's men the wrong room number? Had they stopped the lift on the way up, sent one of their number back down the stairwell to intercept him? He wasn't going to wait to find out. He jammed the Glock into his belt, grabbed the door handle, pulled.

The fist was large, the knuckles well-calloused, broadened by frequent impact. The body to which it was attached was big, thick with muscle. The blow shattered Clay's nose. He felt it go, the bone collapsing inwards, spreading. Clay toppled back at the knees, collapsed to the floor. Before he could move the man jammed his boot down hard onto Clay's throat, and applied weight. Clay reached for the Glock, but as he did his hand was kicked aside by a second assailant, the weapon snatched away. He looked up. Medved's face stared down at him from behind the gaping silenced muzzle of an H&K 9mm.

'So, Straker,' said Medved. 'You live. My information was correct.'

Clay said nothing. He had no doubt they would kill him, was surprised they hadn't yet. It could only mean they wanted something. And every second he kept them here gave Rania more time. She was trained. She'd disappear quickly enough.

Medved looked down at Clay's stump. A smile creased his face. 'I see you lost something along the way. How very unfortunate for you.'

'It was a good deal,' he rasped through a constricted windpipe.

Medved frowned, brought the handgun's muzzle closer to Clay's forehead. 'Where is your lady friend?'

She'd slipped out in time. Good. Clay gave them a blank stare. There were only two of them. The big man stood to Clay's right, his left boot and more than half his weight on Clay's throat. Medved was to Clay's left, bent at the waist, the H&K in his right hand, pointed at Clay's head. The third one might be outside, standing guard. Or after Rania. Clay lay still, evaluated options. There weren't many.

Medved glared down at him. 'Answer me, Straker, or you die.'

'You killed a friend of mine. Did you know that?'

Medved looked left and right, back at Clay. Then he laughed. 'Only one?' He moved his face closer to Clay's. 'Where is she?'

On her way to Heathrow by now. He imagined her on the Tube, or in a black taxi speeding down the M4. Without his government contacts, now surely silenced, there was no way Medved would be able to find her.

'It's over, Medved. The world knows the truth now. A bit different from that image you worked so hard on. Your sister will be very angry with you.' Medved – it was all about Medved. Get him talking about himself.

Medved's eyes flashed. He nodded to the big man who leaned in harder on Clay's neck. 'You greatly over-estimate the public's interest, my naïve ex-employee. They don't care about this. They care about their jobs, their pitiful mortgages, their pathetic little holidays and amusements. And governments? I keep the oil flowing. I generate the economic activity that keeps them in power. I'm their very best friend, *Clay*. Attentions spans are short. This will pass. Don't you worry. And as for my sister ...' Medved's eyes fluttered, wandered a moment.

Clay moved his right hand slowly across his torso, keeping his shoulder still. 'Do the right thing. Isn't that what you said, *Rex*?'

'Say it enough, people will believe it.'

'You're quoting Goebbels, asshole.'

'Paraphrasing, actually. No matter. He was right.'

'Thierry Champard believed you. And you killed him for it.'

'Unfortunate that you weren't with him.'

'I hate to be the one to tell you this,' said Clay, arching his back a couple of inches above the floor, slowly drawing up his legs, pointing his toes, transferring weight to the balls of his feet. 'Only God decides who lives and dies.'

Medved looked down at him along the handgun's elongated barrel, up at the big man, then laughed. 'Found religion have you, Straker? Become an idealist?' Medved spat in his face, a dry spray. 'You really are pathetic. About to have your face blown off, and you still don't understand, do you? I feel sorry for you in some ways, Straker. There is so much you won't be around to see.'

Clay watched Medved's hand tightening around the handgun's grip, readying himself for the recoil. Clay tensed, transferring more weight. 'You let those people die. Just so you wouldn't have to spend a few hundred thousand on a proper disposal system. That's all it would have taken. Greed like that, you're right, I don't get it. But of course you don't make the decisions, do you?'

Hate exploded in Medved's face. He jammed the silencer's muzzle into Clay's forehead, and pushed hard. Clay felt the steel cutting into his skin.

'A few hundred thousand?' Medved snarled. 'I don't give a shit about the money, Straker. I spend that much on dinner.'

Clay looked up at him, said nothing. He didn't have to.

'You still don't understand, do you? All that oil down there, and those fucking ragheads living on top of it? We …,' he stumbled, stopped, restarted: '*I* wanted the *land*, Straker. Poisoning the water was the quickest way to get rid of them.'

Medved pulled the handgun's muzzle back a couple of inches, aimed it at Clay's face, and tightened his finger down on the trigger. 'I want you to know that we will find her, Straker. Make that your last thought.'

Clay grabbed Medved's wrist a tenth of a second before he squeezed the trigger. A nine-millimetre round slammed into the floor, millimetres from Clay's head. Less than half a second later Clay's left boot caught the big man's right ankle in a vicious scissor kick. The big man toppled to the floor, back and away from Clay. Clay brought his stump up hard into Medved's throat, kept his right hand viced around Medved's gun hand, twisted inwards so that Medved fell into him, protecting him from the big man. Medved grabbed for the gun with his left, but Clay brought his knee up hard into Medved's torso. Medved grunted in pain. Two gunshots banged out, loud, unsilenced, milliseconds apart. Not Medved's gun. The big man's? The air was full of flying debris, splintered wood, the smell of cordite, burnt carpet. Clay levered his left leg up, turned Medved, pinned his right wrist to the floor, jammed down hard. The big man was up, facing them, reaching inside his jacket. The hotel room door was behind him, lock smashed, casement splintered. He pulled out his weapon. Clay slammed his forehead into Medved's face, felt his grip on the gun loosen. The big man raised his handgun, took aim at Clay. He hesitated. Didn't want to hit his boss. The door crashed open. The big man managed a quarter turn towards the door before the crown of his head disappeared in a flash of bone and blood. His body crumpled to the floor.

Medved's face was a mess. Blood poured from his collapsed nose, filled his eyes. Clay jammed the point of his knee hard into Medved's chest, heard the air escape from his lungs. He slammed Medved's wrist into the floor. His hand fell open and the gun dropped to the carpet.

Clay sprung, grabbed the gun, and looked up. Crowbar was standing in the doorway, a Glock .45 in his hand.

Medved scrambled to his knees. 'Get away from me, you fucking lunatic,' he shouted, blinking blood from his eyes.

Clay stood, looked at Medved, back at Crowbar. He looked down at the H&K in his hand. So many times he had been here, in this blood-soaked temple. And each time he had killed he had made the world poorer. The SWAPO kids – for that's what they had been, children, boys – had not deserved to die. Those soldiers in Yemen, too, Jesus Christ, what a total fucking *waste*. Medved was babbling now, waving his hands, his words roiling dyslexic through Clay's head, indecipherable. Time slowed. The big man's blood wicked into the carpet, spread around Clay's boots. Clay breathed deep, raised the gun to Medved's head.

'What are you doing?' blurted Medved.

'The right thing.'

Clay pulled the trigger. Medved slumped back onto the floor, a neat round hole between his eyes, the back of his head splattered over the carpet, the side of the bed. Clay dropped the gun to the floor and stared at Crowbar.

Crowbar stepped over the bodies, picked up the handgun, and started wiping it with the bedsheet. 'Time to go,' he said.

Half a minute later they were walking down the alley behind the hotel. Clay's steps were even, calm like the beating of his heart. When they got to the corner, he glanced back towards the hotel. Police sirens wailed in the distance. It had stopped raining and low clouds scuttled across a clearing sky. The air was cool and sea clean. Pedestrians streamed along the crowded pavements. Crowbar nodded to him, turned north, disappeared into the crowd. Clay turned away from the hotel and walked through the morning traffic towards Leicester Square, south to the Thames. After a while he stopped on the embankment and stood looking out at the river, the reflections of the city dancing on the metal-plate water, the traffic flowing on Southwark Bridge. For a moment, he was alone. And then he turned away and disappeared into the churning anonymity of the city.

Acknowledgements

I've been lucky in my life. And all of that good fortune has, in some way, contributed to this book. To my mother and father, for instilling a love of words and stories, my wife Heidi for saving me all those years ago and for her unflinching support as hours and days have slipped by, me hammering away on the keyboard or musing over a notebook while she kept everything going. To my sons Zachary and Declan who are already so much more than I'll ever be. I would also like to acknowledge and thank all the people who have helped bring this book to being: Claire and D for reading an ancient and much-changed version of the manuscript; my dad for his helpful ideas; Eve Seymour for her fabulous reviews, support and introductions; my agent Broo Doherty for taking me on in the first place and sticking by me; Gary Pulsifer for giving me my first chance; and Karen Sullivan, my publisher, for having the guts to start her own business and publish this book. And, of course, to all of those who chose to devote a few hours of their valuable time to sit down and read this story. I hope you enjoyed it.

EXCLUSIVE EXTRACT

Claymore Straker returns in
Paul E. Hardisty's
THE EVOLUTION OF FEAR
Published by Orenda Books in 2016

No Easy Way

Claymore Straker stood face to wind and watched the storm come in off the Irish Sea. Rain clouds scuttled overhead, low and fast, moving inland over the gorse and the stunted, wind-bent trees. The first drops touched his face, the cold fingertips of a ten-hour corpse. Two months he had been here now, anchored into the cliffside, staring out at the slate grey sea, watching the depressions deepen. Winter was coming, and he was a fugitive.

It seemed half a lifetime since he had walked into Crowbar's flat in London, the blood still wet on his hand. After the killing they'd separated, found their way through rain-swept London streets back to the Kilburn apartment. His old platoon commander, Koevoet – 'Crowbar' in Afrikaans – had sent him to the bathroom with a pair of scissors and a razor, given him a change of clothes. Ten minutes later they were speeding down the A4, heading west in Crowbar's old Ford. After eight hours on the back roads, they had arrived here, on the North coast of Cornwall, ten miles from the nearest village, the closest farmhouse six miles across the gorse.

Stay put, Koevoet had told him. There's enough food to last a year. No electricity, no phone. Kerosene lamps, coal for the fire, gas for cooking. Keep clear of the villages and farmhouses. The smaller the place, the more they notice. I'll be back soon to check on you. Then he'd clunked a Glock G21 onto the table, along with three spare mags, a box of .45-calibre ammunition and a silencer, and walked out into the night.

Clay Straker turned away from the storm and followed the low stone wall back towards the cottage, staring down at the bands and folds of the cliffside. The cottage was almost invisible, notched into the top of the bluff, made from the same stuff, slate and mudstone, fragments of extinctions past. At the gate, he stopped and looked back over his shoulder, out across the grey solitude of the sea.

And he was back there, in that damp ballroom in London amidst the shambles of Medved's capital raising, bankers and moneymen scurrying for the exits, the stench of bad publicity starting to rise like graveyard fog. He could hear Rania's voice still. 'We have done it, Clay,' she'd said. 'As soon as the story hits the papers, Rex Medved is finished. Leave it now, please *chéri*.' She'd pleaded with him. Africa, she'd said. Time to start something new, together.

And he'd tried. Tried as hard as he'd ever tried at anything in his life. But the pull was too strong. A black hole of lust. He'd even been given a second chance – how often do you get one of those in the real world? He'd followed Medved out of the ballroom's back exit, left her standing there among the financiers and speculators, chased him down the corridor to the alleyway behind the hotel. He'd had the gun out. He'd been ready. No, not ready. *Ravenous*. Ten days in the Highveldt without food, baying at the smell of blood. But by the time he'd reached the alleyway, Medved was gone, just the tail lights of his chauffer-driven Mercedes disappearing around the corner. And then that impossible second chance.

He remembered the last time he'd seen her, the next day, curled up naked on the hotel room bed. Africa, they'd decided. Together. He'd been down in the lobby booking the tickets to Cape Town when Rex Medved and his men had arrived. He'd warned Rania, made it up to the room just after she'd fled. But before he could follow, Medved's men had surprised him. Clay could still see the boardroom arrogance in Medved's eyes as he pointed the gun at Clay's head – the complete absence of fear, the invulnerability of money – could hear the bastard's voice, scorn dripping like toxic waste from each word, delivering a sermon to the lowly: know your place, be content with your pathetic jobs and mindless amusements. And, above all, leave the business of running the world to the people who know. People like *me*. Then

Medved had looked him straight in the eyes and told him exactly what he was going to do to Rania once he found her. Moments later, thanks to Koevoet, it was Clay holding the gun, Medved counting out the seconds. He didn't have long to wait. Half a minute later Clay put a .45-calibre bullet through Rex Medved's forehead.

And in that time suspended before his end, watching Clay's finger squeezing down on the trigger, Clay wondered, had he known fear?

Clay shivered, pulled up his collar against the squall, walked the ten steps to the little work shed buttressed into the side of the cottage, and opened the oak-plank door. He pulled the tarpaulin away and wheeled the old Norton out onto the wet gravel. He checked the fuel, clicked the transmission into neutral, turned the ignition, flipped out the starting pedal and gave it a crank. The engine roared, spat blue smoke, cleaned up, and settled into a low growl. He gave the throttle a couple of revs, pulled on the old helmet he'd found stuffed inside a dusty box on the bottom shelf of the workbench, and mounted the bike.

Eight and a half weeks now he'd stayed put, without a word from Koevoet – his only contact with the world the little radio he'd found in the cottage. Fifty-nine days now, 1422 hours not knowing where she was, not knowing if she'd made it safely to Switzerland, if she was alive or dead, burning away the very fibre of him, the sinew. And if she was there, Allah protect her, what would she be thinking now, hearing the same stories Clay had been tracking in the news, the brutal murder of Rex Medved, celebrity mega-millionaire Russian businessman and philanthropist, the appeals from his family for information leading to the arrest of his killer, the million-pound reward announced just this morning by his sister, Regina Medved, at a press conference held in the Byzantium foyer of her Moscow penthouse apartment.

A million pounds. Enough to change a life: pay debts, buy freedom, solve problems. It changed everything, for both of them, raised risk to the sixth power.

It was time to go, time to get back to Rania, find her and disappear for good. Keep that promise he'd made to her, to himself. Maybe change the trajectory, find some of those things he'd always wanted, atone for the wrongs. So many wrongs.

Clay set off down the gravel track, the wind at his back, the rain coming now in gusty sheets that flayed across the open bluff lands, the gorse shivering with each whip of the lash. Riding one-handed was more difficult than he had anticipated, despite hours of practice sitting on the bike in the shed. Managing the throttle and steering with his right hand was fine, but working the clutch was altogether more difficult. He found the best way was to curl his elbow under the handlebar and hook his stump up onto the lever, pulling inwards with his bicep to release the clutch while applying counter pressure with his right hand. Engaging the clutch was then a matter of easing the handle back out, keeping the front wheel straight by releasing pressure on the right. On his first change up to second, his stump slipped on the wet handle, the clutch popped and the bike stalled with a hollow double clunk.

He cinched the cuff of his jacket down over the stump for better grip, restarted the engine, tried again. He lurched along the pathway, the engine surging and lugging, learning to ride all over again. Again he stalled out, cursed, kicked the engine to life once more. Gradually he found the right balance, leaning in with his left shoulder on each change to get better purchase on the clutch lever. Soon, he was shifting smoothly, the engine repeating the scaled harmonics of engagement to redline, hum to whine, a pause for breath, the next acceleration. The track wound along the draw, the vegetation here thick, green and wet, before emerging onto the uplands between parallel hedgerows tall as a man. Three and half miles on, the track intersected a narrow single-lane road, the tarmac weathered and sunk deep into the ground, a grass-edged rut in the landscape. Clay turned west and opened the throttle, felt the bike accelerate, the dark hedgerows flying past, road spray hissing from the wheels. He passed the first farmhouse, a distant light across the fen, and joined the B road for Launceston.

Soon he was trundling along with the evening traffic, a light rain falling, the lights of the cars swimming across the wet pavement. He stopped at a newsagent, picked up a £50 phone card, paid cash. A few miles down the road he pulled into the parking lot of a Tesco supermarket on the edge of town, and levered the bike up onto its stand. The place was busy with after-work shoppers, the lot almost full. Outside the main entrance to the supermarket was a bank of public telephones. He pulled off his helmet, searching the eaves of the building. A single

CCTV camera watched the main entrance. Another was perched atop a lamppost at the far end of the lot. Clay placed the helmet on the seat, pulled up his hood, wandered to the opposite end of the car park and circled back towards the phones, avoiding the cameras.

Clay closed the phone-box door, brushed the rain from his jacket, cradled the receiver between his shoulder and ear, and composed the number. The line clicked, fuzzed, rang. Clay imagined the telephone on the little pinewood table next to the kitchen window, her walking from the lounge, looking out across the valley, the Dents du Midi towering in the distance, in cloud perhaps now, early snow falling at altitude. She was safe there, he told himself, veiled by a new name, a new identity, a place to live free from questions and intrusions. She had managed to convince him that her old employers, French intelligence, the DGSE – surely compromised by Medved through his close connections inside the French government – didn't know about her Swiss hideaway. He hoped it was so. The ring tone pulsed for the fourth time, fifth. Clay looked down at his boots, the rain falling across the pavement, the shoppers scurrying past with fists clenched over straining plastic.

'*Allo?*' A woman's voice. Not Rania.

'Is Rania there?'

'Who is calling, please?' A strong French accent, an older voice.

He decided to take a chance. 'It's Clay, *madame.*' He doubted that they would be monitoring her calls, that the police had made any sort of connection between them, yet.

'*Monsieur* Clay?' she gasped.

Clay knew the voice now. It was the old lady who'd led him to Rania after the violence in Yemen. The violence that had brought him here. *Madame Debret.*

'She is not here, I am afraid.'

'Where is she?'

Silence. Caution. Good.

'Do you remember the Café Grand Quai in Geneva?' he asked. Where they had met, where she had directed him to Rania, helped him to find her.

'*Oui.*'

'You held my hand. Told me about her father.'

A deep breath. "I am worried, *Monsieur* Clay. I told her that she should not leave, but she insisted."

'Where has she gone?'

'*Chypre.*'

He wasn't sure he's heard right. 'Cyprus?'

'*Lefkosia*, yes. Her editor has given her this assignment. He contacted her one week ago. At first she did not want to go. But he was insisting very much, calling her many times.'

'LeClerc?'

'She did not say his name. Only that he was with Agence France-Presse.' It had to be LeClerc, the man Clay had met in London, the one who'd finally published Rania's story, the one who in doing so had helped to blow the casket lid off Medved's corrupt and deadly oil-production activities in Yemen. Pretty quickly after, the Medveds lost all financing for their Petro-Tex venture in Yemen and were forced to sell the company at a loss.

'When did she leave?'

'You have just missed her. She left the day before yesterday. You might see the first story she has written in the *journaux* today.'

Damn. 'Did she say when she'd be back?'

'No more than a week.'

'Forwarding address?'

'None.'

'Telephone number? Mobile?'

'I am sorry.'

'Thank you, *madame*.' He was about to hang up when he heard her call out.

'*Monsieur* Clay, please. Wait. She left a message for you, if you called.' Noise down the line, scraping, a drawer being opened and closed. 'I have it here. She wrote it for me.'

Clay waited, said nothing.

'It says: "*Ecoutons la confession d'un compagnon d'enfer.*"'

Clay understood only one word: *enfer*. Hell.

'It is Rimbaud, I believe,' she said. 'Listen to the confession of hell's companion.'

A tumour of ice materialised in Clay's chest. He knew this, from the boy poet's *A Season in Hell*, the chapter entitled: 'The Infernal Husband'. He curled his lip, hung up the phone, stared out into the half-light of day. She'd chosen carefully, knowing he'd read this prose-poem over and over while he was in Geneva searching for her, this lament, taken by its power: *I am lost. I am impure, a slave of the infernal husband. A widow.*

Why this? Something was wrong. Clay pulled in a half-breath, let it flow back out as vapour, looked long both ways along the store-front pavement, out into the car park, through the big front windows into the fluorescent glow of the supermarket, the patchwork of vivid primary colours, his insides roiling in a Southern Ocean gale. Near one of the checkout counters was an in-store newsagent selling copies of the major British broadsheets and tabloids. There would be CCTV coverage inside the store, and no way to avoid it. He pulled up the collar of his jacket and pulled the grey hood of his jumper over his head, tugged it out to cover his profile, shoved his forearms deep into his pockets and strode into the store.

Less than five minutes later he was back in the phone box, a copy of the *Independent* under his left arm. Thirty-first October 1994: British soldiers freed by Bosnian Serb authorities after six days in captivity, a Tory sleaze enquiry, the England football coach accused of financial wrongdoing. He scanned the back pages. On page nine: a short article on the theft of cultural and religious artefacts in Northern Cyprus since 1974 and, more notably, in the last few months. Centuries-old illuminations, mosaics and sculpture, stolen from abandoned Greek Orthodox churches in the occupied North, were making their way to private buyers in Europe and Russia. The article claimed that the ring was highly organised, well-funded, and violent. The thing seemed to straddle both sides of the border, and the recent sharp upturn in thefts coincided with a dramatic surge in unsolved murders on the island. Outraged Greek Cypriots were calling on the UN and Turkey to take action to stop the plunder. The article was syndicated by Agence France-Presse, written by Lise Moulinbeqc, Rania's new identity, courtesy of her ex-employers the DGSE, Direction Genérale Securité Exterieure, French Intelligence.

Clay read the piece twice more, savouring Rania's use of her second language, her ability to meld technical precision with passion. A pang swept through him, spreading from his chest and surging down his legs, lingering in his knees, in the wrist he'd lost. Jesus. He stamped his feet on the concrete pavement, stuffed the paper into his backpack, combed his hand through his wet hair. The island of love. Definitely.

Clay picked up the phone and dialled his Cayman Islands banker. It was the first time he'd made contact since the killing. Clay gave the password, his account number. There was an urgent message for him, the banker said. It had arrived only three days ago. Clay jotted down the name, the telephone number, the South African prefix, Johannesburg area code. He put down the phone, checked his watch, and dialled. A receptionist directed his call. He was put through to the clinic's director.

'This is Declan Greene.' Clay's new identity, an unintentional gift of the Yemeni secret police, complete with offshore bank accounts, an Australian passport and an apartment in Perth. 'I had a message to call.'

The doctor paused, as if searching his memory. "Yes, thank you for calling, Mr Greene. We were expecting to hear from you sooner.'

'I've been busy, Doctor.' Doing nothing. *Waiting.*

'I am very sorry to disturb you like this, but you see …' The doctor stopped, cleared his throat. 'There is no easy way to say this, I am afraid, Mr Greene.'

The line crackled, empty. 'Then you'd better just tell me.'

'Yes, of course. We traced you through the payment you made to the clinic earlier this year, Mr Greene, and since there are no living direct relatives, you were the only person we could contact.'

Clay's throat tightened.

'I'm very sorry to inform you that Eben Barstow died four days ago.'

Clay's legs quivered, weak. Eben, the best friend he'd ever had, wounded in action in Angola all those years ago, a bullet to the head. Clay had carried him to the helicopter and he had survived, if you could call it that, physically functioning but otherwise dead. How many times had he tried to ask Eben's parents to let him die? Now it was done. Relief surged through him, a decade of regret. It took him a moment to catch his breath, to fully process this information. 'Did you say no living relatives?'

'That's right.'

'What about his parents?'

'They died the same day.'

Jesus. 'The *same day?*'

'Yes. Tragic. But there is something you should know, Mr Greene. The circumstances of Mr Barstow's death, were, how can I put this, unusual.'

Just say it, for Christ's sake. So many times he had anticipated this moment, such had been the inevitability of it, but now that it was here he couldn't quite believe that Eben was gone, that the tiny shard of hope he had carried with him all those years, wrapped up in a teardrop, a pearl, hidden away somewhere so secure that he'd forgotten it was ever there, had turned out to be the folly he always knew it was.

'Mr Greene, are you there?'

'Tell me.'

'He was shot, Mr Greene.'

Clay thought he had misheard. He was hot. Died of fever.

'Someone broke into the hospital at night, went to his room, and shot him three times. Twice in the chest, and once in the head.'

Clay's blood stopped pumping. Jesus Christ.

'And whoever it was, they also broke into our records department. It seems they were after information about Eben, about our accounts.'

'What did they get?'

'Everything, I'm afraid, Mr Greene. The police said it was a very professional job. The perpetrators were in and out without being seen by any of our staff, or waking any of the other patients.'

Jesus. 'And Eben's parents?'

'They died in a car accident. As I said, a tragedy.'

Clay's mind blanked, raced. All three of them, on the same day?

'Mr Greene, are you there?'

'Yes.' No, not really.

Outside, the rain was coming down again, hammering against the thin steel of the supermarket's cantilevered roof. He pushed the receiver onto his ear.

'There is a sizeable credit on Mr Barstow's account,' came the voice, faint against the din, 'which you paid in advance, if you recall. What would you have us do with it, Mr Greene?'

'Are there any others?'

'Pardon me, Mr Greene? Others?'

'Any others like Eben.'

'Sorry, I don't follow.'

'Vets.' Fucked-up unfortunates. The half-digested shit of a forgotten war, a failed system. Him.

'Yes, of course. There are three others.'

'Give it to whoever needs it most.'

Silence there, so far away, in a place he used to call home. And then, 'That is very generous, Mister Greene.'

Clay said nothing, waited a moment, was about to hang up.

The doctor's voice again, urgent. 'Mr Greene, before you go. There is something else.'

'I'm listening.'

'You must understand. We are all very shocked, here.'

Clay waited for the doctor to continue.

'When we found him …' The doctor paused, cleared his throat. 'You can imagine. It was a horrible sight.'

Yes, he could imagine. All too well. Did so on a nightly basis.

'The killer, or killers, left a message. We have no idea who it was intended for, or what it means.'

'Tell me.'

The doctor paused, then continued, his voice wavering. 'It was written on the wall, in Mr Barstow's blood. It said: "*She's next*".'

Clay stood staring down at the wet concrete, the implications of this moving through him now like a slow dose of poison. 'Are you sure, Doctor? Absolutely sure that's what it said?'

'No question at all, Mr Greene. The words were very clear, well spelled out, as if they had taken their time. They used a brush.'

'Did you say *brush*?'

'A paintbrush, yes. They left it in the room.'